This edition first published 2017 by Fahrenheit Press

ISBN 978-1-912526-01-7

10 9 8 7 6 5 4 3 2 1

www.Fahrenheit-Press.com

F 4 E

Briefly Maiden

By

Jacqueline Chadwick

Fahrenheit Press

For Jimmy and Muriel Pirie

"The RCMP stands to be embarrassed if the NSOR-D continues to have only limited functionality."

Melissa Martineau,

National Sex Offender Registry Database Manager 2006

PROLOGUE - THE HARVEST

Those of Bryce's ilk were only too familiar with the run-down apartment block situated at the curve of Pine Nut Circle – a no-thru-road cul-de-sac built in the mid-eighties by a town council who, in their infinite do-gooding naïveté, had worked under the mistaken belief that affordable housing for low-income families would be a boon to Cedar River and its residents.

Now, in the year 2002, the block was in a sorry state. Soon after a turn of the century that had promised much yet delivered only worsening unemployment and a resulting escalation of socio-economic problems within the cul-de-sac's growing populace of drug-and-booze-addled denizens, Bryce saw that the damp stucco was peeling from the exterior walls. Discarded hypodermic needles and used condoms littered the scratchy yard home to trash cans resigned to watching over the strewn rubbish they should contain.

The building's name was the biggest joke of it all. Mamisîw House. Mamisîw – an aboriginal word relating to putting one's trust in something – had no doubt been adopted by some well-meaning (probably caucasian) middle-aged housewife whose work as a councillor was more of a hobby than a civic duty and had been indelibly etched onto what would quickly become the town's paradigmatic symbol of all things untrustworthy.

The building was currently dangling by a bureaucratic

thread and, when the final snip was imminent, Bryce hoped to use the might of his growing influence upon council members to sway them in favour of bulldozing the site. He'd also caught himself dreaming of using his might to charge his growing throng of acolytes with the task of bludgeoning the skulls of its stinking inhabitants prior to the arrival of the heavy machinery.

The shared stairwell leading to all four floors of the block reeked of piss and poverty. On the third floor, Bryce found apartment 3B and banged his balled fist upon its peeling door three times. The door rattled back against him each time and he noticed that the doorframe itself was irreparably damaged and loose, probably due to multiple forced entries by local law enforcement.

Patience being an attribute he merely feigned in his rise up the ladder of promotion, Bryce bent to the metal letter box and flipped open its cold lid. "Josie Devlin! I'm going to give you five seconds. If you don't open this door, I'll…"

The sound of feet shuffling along a strip of linoleum satisfied Bryce enough to quell his threat and prevent drawing unnecessary attention to himself. The door opened and he saw the side of Josie's battered face, the eye she viewed him with still puffed and blackened, the white an angry scarlet.

Josie made to speak but her words were sucked from her with the inward draught as Bryce pushed the door open and stepped into her dank hallway.

"What's that fucking smell?"

"Can't smell nothing," said Josie as she pushed the door closed and passed him, leading him through to the messy living room.

The small window was clouded with condensation. The room was cold and Bryce noticed that the fireplace was out of commission, sporting a large yellow gas company sticker offering a warning of mortal danger to anyone foolish enough to seek warmth on a cold day.

The room was sparsely furnished but proudly sported a

large, silver television set in a bulky unit full of video cassettes and at least one DVD as well as a wicker basket of pink plastic flowers. Had the television been purchased legally, Bryce guessed that it would have set Josie back the equivalent of three months' rent. A three-seater sofa along the opposite wall had wooden arms and was upholstered in orange and brown balding velvet. Sprawled across the sofa was the near comatose form of a young man with ruined veins and a bottom lip rusted with herpes. He had the sparkling white Nikes of a welfare recipient.

Bryce stepped over to the sofa and raised his foot. He slammed it down heavily into the skinny youth's ribs. Although the kick woke him, the young man seemed dazed and slow to respond. It took a sharp slap to his face for the teen to become conscious enough to recognize the man standing above him.

"Get the fuck outta here," growled Bryce.

The man's eyes widened. He dived off the sofa, snatched up a purple tracksuit jacket and lurched for the exit in such a hasty panic that he slammed Josie against the living room door jamb as he used her body to propel himself faster from the apartment.

Josie righted herself and cringed lazily as her companion slammed the front door behind him, rattling its loose frame. She scratched at her inner thigh and, as the dry, white skin of her leg blanched pink under the pressure of her fingers, Bryce was reminded of the plucked surface of a raw chicken. He watched as she crossed to the now empty couch.

"What you want from me?" Josie sat heavily onto the sofa and reached down to the floor, shaking a cigarette free of an almost empty pack at her feet. "I went to the hospital like you told me, nothing broken just conchoo…bruises." Josie lit her cigarette and threw her disposable lighter onto the carpet.

"Put that out," said Bryce.

Josie looked at him. Realizing he was referring to her cigarette, she curled her split top lip. "What d'you care?" She pulled deeply on her cigarette then exhaled a long trail of smoke. Smiling, she gently rubbed the swell of the pregnant belly that had pushed the waistband of her obscenely short denim skirt downwards so that it was nothing more than a sardonic grin of blue across her pelvis.

"You're in a lot of trouble, Josie. You know that, don't you. One more strike and you'll be locked up. They'll let you squeeze that thing out in prison and while you're still screaming from the pain they'll take it from you and they'll place it in a foster home. You? You they'll cart off to a cell where your ripped-up cunt can fester."

Josie shrugged. "So? Don't want it anyway."

"*So*, you need me to help you right now, Josie."

Josie spat a laugh. She smoked and looked Bryce up and down from behind her bruised eyes. "I know the kind of help guys like you mean." Josie pulled her right leg up revealing a line of fading hickeys on her inner thigh. She placed her dirty, bare foot on the cushion next to her, revealing that she wasn't wearing underwear. "Oh yeah, I know what kind of help you're here for."

Bryce's lips tightened as he looked at her exposed vulva, furred with long pubes. A white waxy residue lay in thick lines within the folds. She reached down with grimy fingernails and spread herself open revealing a vagina that had been punished to the point that its bright cerise colour took him by surprise. Seeing that she had garnered a reaction, Josie laughed and flapped her grotesquely furred tongue back and forth. "This what you came here for? Huh?"

In a flash he was upon her. He snatched a thick chunk of her peroxide yellow hair and squeezed and twisted it all the way to its oily black roots. Josie yelped and froze, her eyes wide, her body petrified.

"You're a fucking disgrace, Devlin. You make me sick. I can smell that greasy gash of yours from here and I wouldn't touch it with a fucking stick." Pushing her head back into the musty sofa, Bryce brought his face close to hers. "You listen to me, you festering sack of fucking smeg. I own you now. And that kid you're cooking is mine too. You understand me?"

Josie didn't answer. Bryce twisted her hair tighter inside his grasp and felt the pinging release of taut hairs as they pulled themselves free of her flaky scalp. "You understand me?"

"No," she whimpered.

Bryce's teeth ground tight, squeaking against each other as he fought to maintain control. He spat in her face, his bubbled saliva sat thick upon her cheek. Josie eyed him and he saw reflected in her gaze the awesome effect of his power over her.

"No…I mean…you want my kid?"

Josie's lips trembled and he knew then that he had her. He'd broken her. "You're going to clean yourself up bitch. You're gonna quit the smokes and the booze and whatever else you stuff into yourself?" He rammed her head backwards into the mildewed cushion again, exposing her throat and pulling her eyelids upwards, his saliva began a glacial journey towards her ear. "Including all the random fucking dick you let slam you."

"But what 'bout my money? What 'bout Banger?"

"That piece of shit biker pimp of yours? Well let's just say, the next time the Nanoose chapter of the Demon's Fang come rolling into town, I'll be waiting."

"But he's its dad."

Bryce pulled the almost burnt away cigarette from between Josie's fingers, flicked free the tower of ash that had formed at the top of it and brought the glowing ember to her eye. "Like you'd fucking know whose spunk gotcha." Josie tried to close her eyes but Bryce's grip pulled tight the skin of her shallow forehead, leaving no wiggle room. "You're not listening, Josie. What did I say?"

"I don't know," she whined. "I don't know what you mean."

A tear fell from her eye and beat the saliva in its race to

her ear. Bryce wondered whether Josie was crying or if the tear was a physiological reaction to the heat of the cigarette near her eyeball. "I own you now. And I own that kid. While it's in you, you clean up. You clean this shit hole up. You quit the game and you quit the junk and I'll take care of rent and food and doctor visits."

"Then what?"

"Then nothing. Then you can go back to your shitty fucking life."

"And you take it? The baby?"

"No. I'm not its fucking dad! It's just *mine*. And any other ones you pop out too. Same deal. Got me?"

Josie nodded as best she could. "'kay. Whatever. Okay."

Bryce released her and stepped away. Josie lowered her leg and pulled her mini skirt as far down over her tightly closed thighs as it would go. Her sudden need to regain a dignity long since squandered amused Bryce but also made him want to slap her ugly face.

"Here," he said, dropping a heavy black object into her lap.

Josie tossed the item from her thighs as if it were hot. "What the hell? Is that a gun?"

"Why would I give a turd like you a gun? It's a taser. Use it if any cretins come sniffing for another dabble in that fetid snatch of yours."

Josie ran her finger along the taser's casing. "I don't know how it works."

"I'll drop the charger by after work and show you how to use it." Bryce pointed to the pack of cigarettes. "Give them to me," Josie reached for the cigarettes and tossed them to him, "and when I come back, I want every piece of crap you've got – booze, drugs, smokes, needles, even weed – all of it in one bag. And I'll be checking the place too so don't be trying to fuck with me. You don't leave this apartment unless I say you can. Wash. Clean up. Understand?"

Josie nodded but Bryce wondered if she was even capable of comprehending his adamance. He had a few months to teach her.

As he turned to leave, Josie addressed Bryce by his professional title. He turned and looked at her, his head cocked to one side. "From now on, you don't use my name, not ever. You don't tell anyone about me. Got it?"

"Tell me what you want with the kid," Josie asked with renewed cockiness.

"What I want with that kid is my business and you don't get to ask."

"So what do I call you then, if I can't use your name? You my new baby-daddy?"

"Baby-daddy? What? You black now?" Bryce smiled. He crumpled the cigarette pack in his fist, "Apu. You call me Apu."

Josie scrunched her face up and blurted another laugh, "Apu? What kinda name is that? What? You one of those East Indians now, are ya?"

Dropping the crumpled pack of smokes, Bryce crossed the room. He'd decided that Josie Devlin needed a good slapping after all, so he picked up where her Saturday night john had left off.

But Bryce was real careful not to go near the belly.

PART ONE
WEDNESDAY 29th NOVEMBER

CHAPTER 1 - THE MANIACAL GNOME

Ali Dalglish looked at the twenty-five-foot-high gnome with the disproportionately large thumb and took an extra long drag on her cigarette.

The Nanoose service station was an e-coli outbreak waiting to happen. Ali had left the woman who had become her unofficial partner in crime fighting, her sidekick and neighbour, Marlene McKean, in the gas station shop to pick from the selection of burritos, wraps and sticky meatballs squished onto skewers.

The gnome was symbolic of the burgeoning weirdness that intensifies as one travels north on the Inland Island Highway of Vancouver Island. As a freshly landed immigrant from the UK some eight years ago, Ali and her then husband, David, along with their two children had waved a pin over a map of Canada and plonked it anywhere that didn't suffer the harshest of snowed-in winters to find a place to live in their new country.

Now Ali and her children were settled in the quixotic hamlet of Mochetsin on the southernmost tip of the island, just outside BC's capital city, Victoria. However, prior to that, their pin-prick naïveté had found them desperately trying – and failing – to settle in a city called Cedar River, located three quarters of the way up the east coast of the island.

Having spent most of her working life in some of Britain's most populated cities, it always struck Ali as comical that islanders describe places such as Cedar River and even Victoria as cities. The entire population of Vancouver Island was less than one million, yet nine times as many people live in London alone.

Ali remembered the last time she'd looked at the giant gnome with the maniacal grin. She had pulled up at the same service station, followed by David in the rented cube van full of their belongings, as they had made their overdue escape from Cedar River. Back then, feeling drained and having barely survived the bleakest five years of her life in the loveless place, Ali had seen the gnome in an entirely different light. Three years ago it had seemed kinder, welcoming her to the marginally more civilized south. Yet now its massive thumbs up was less a gesture of greeting and more of a taunt – as if by heading north again (something Ali had vowed never to do) she was heading into a horrible, twisted game that the gnome seemed excited about.

Of course, it was true, Ali wasn't losing her mind, *again*, she wasn't imagining the threat, she had been hailed north under the assumption that she would immerse herself fully in all things horrible and twisted because as a criminal psychologist and a forensic pathologist, Ali Dalglish is only ever summoned as a player of the darkest of games.

"You know he's the biggest in the world, right?"

Ali turned to see Marlene trotting towards her, armed against the early winter sting of wind chill with three pashminas, all in autumnal hues wrapped around her neck.

"What did you get?" asked Ali, spying Marlene's bulging plastic bag of goods.

"Well, I didn't like the look of any of the hot food – not once I noticed a black hair pasted onto one of the sweet and sour meatball kebobs – so I got us a couple of apples and some chips, some candy and a can of pop each. Not much change, I'm afraid." Marlene rummaged in her coat pocket, her cheeks quivering with the effort she had to exert to bypass the old tissues and delve amongst the crumpled receipts ever-present in any of her pockets and handbags.

"It's okay, Marlene, we can tally up when we get to the hotel."

"Ali, hon, The Ocean Lookout cannot be described as a hotel – it's a skanky *motel* on a stretch of beach that smells like a tub of ferret innards at low tide. Believe me, an establishment that has a billboard out front advertising that they have new mattresses is a hospitality nightmare." Marlene sniffed, her little nose red with cold, "I wish you'd agreed for us to stay with my brother and his wife instead."

"Actually, I took the liberty of upgrading our digs."

"At whose expense? Shaw's, I hope." Marlene planted her hands on her hips as she referenced Superintendent Doug Shaw, the head of the Vancouver Island Integrated Major Incident Squad – more commonly referred to by its acronym: VIIMIS. It seemed to Ali that Marlene's dislike for the man grew each time she met him. Her distaste was somewhat justified – Marlene had initially encountered Shaw across Ali's dining room table as he'd conducted an interview during which he'd treated Ali more like a criminal than a victim following the slaughter of her beloved dog, Oscar the Newfoundland.

Ali herself had gone through her own stages of frustration bordering on hatred for Shaw, particularly when she'd had to sidestep the man and his team to rescue her daughter, Sandy, from the clutches of the psychotic Carter Burrows. But since that time, Ali had adopted a forced respect for the man and although he still managed to rub her up the wrong way, she couldn't help but feel gratitude towards him. Not only had he swallowed his pride and called her in to work alongside the team on two previous occasions, he had also been instrumental in her successful petitioning of the Canadian government who had finally allowed Ali's extensive British qualifications to be converted.

Although Ali had been required to re-sit certain exams and to jump through bureaucratic hoops, after fourteen months she'd finally been granted her Canadian licences and was once again permitted to do the job she had been born to do – one she had a certain talent for – finding monsters and bringing them to justice.

Yes, sometimes her methods were unconventional but in Ali's experience, the very best investigators always blurred the lines and ignored procedure when it mattered including her actual investigative partner, Inspector Rey Cuzzocrea, the real driving force behind Ali's inclusion in the VIIMIS team and the reason for her swift return to expert status, five thousand miles from home.

"So," asked Marlene, "where are we staying then?"

"The Artisan Lodge," said Ali.

Marlene smiled and straightened. "Ooh, fancy. Now I'm glad you refused to stay with Wayne and Colleen."

Ali checked the time and trampled on her finished cigarette. "We'd better get a move on, Cuzzocrea's meeting us at half three."

Ali clicked her Porsche key fob and held the passenger door open for Marlene. Ali helped her friend into the bucket seat and ensured her coat was tucked up since Marlene somehow always managed to get an item of clothing snagged in the car door. "Try not to spill Cheetos all over the place this time."

"Well try to drive like a normal person then, Ali Schumacher," Marlene replied. "You know, next time we come on one of your superwoman missions, I should drive."

Ali snorted. "That's a laugh, at the snail's-pace you drive? The investigation would be over and the case would be tried and concluded by the time you made it through the Malahat Pass."

Once in the car Ali felt her throaty engine rumble to life and heard the gaseous release as Marlene opened her can of Pepsi and took a deep swallow before thumping her fist upon her chest and letting out a manly burp – a ubiquitous part of Marlene McKean's digestive routine.

"Pardon me. You know we have the world's largest burl too? A big knot of wood from a tree trunk up in Pearson's Creek. I can take you up there to see it once you solve the case."

"Who says I'll solve the case? I don't even know anything about it yet," said Ali as she turned the car to face the northbound on-ramp.

"Ali, hon, you always get your man, we both know that."

Ali smiled and looked up at the gnome once more. "I don't give a shit if it's the biggest one in the world or not, I hate that fucking gnome."

Marlene tutted her disapproval of Ali's profanity but shrugged with acceptance. Ali's habit of peppering her vocabulary with the most offensive words possible was an inextricable part of her candour and something she vehemently refused to temper or dilute regardless of the situation or the company.

CHAPTER 2 - THE NEW TOY

The room is warm, as always. It is pink. It is blue. Pretty hearts and triangles and butterflies dot the softly lit walls.

There are always things to play with because this room is where children come to play and of all the rooms she's ever played in, this is probably her favourite.

It is the kind of room that most children could only dream about. There's a huge plasma-screen TV, a canopy bed and all the dress-up clothes you could ever dream of. There's even a fridge filled with treats – candy and chocolate and lots of fizzy drinks. There's lemonade and berry fizz and lemon and lime but they're special pops because you can only buy these ones in the liquor store even though they taste yummy.

But the very best thing about this room is that you can help yourself to as much of everything in it as you want because in this room there is never a limit to the fun.

Today though the room is even funner because there's a new toy to play with.

The new toy is big and bouncy and it has a funny belly – all hairy and fluffy. The new toy makes sounds too, when you do things to it. The new toy makes the best noises ever, especially when you push its belly – push it as hard as you can over and over, deeper and deeper and then the new toy screams. The new toy screams like a girl and that's real funny.

This room has had its fair share of toys – the ones that

make noises and the ones that stay quiet too. And it is pink and it is blue because, for the owner of this room those colours are significant, symbolic even. Both pink and blue in equal measure because the owner of the room does not discriminate between boys and girls. Pink and blue in equal measure.

And while the little girly scream dies away the plasma screen shows how pink and blue – girls and boys – are equally welcome in this room.

Pulling now, pulling from the bellybutton, pulling harder…stuck on something, then a new noise happens. It's not a nice noise. It's an unkind noise, it's cruel and it's threatening and it's not about the love that was once promised and justified in this room over and over and over again as the butterflies had fluttered and the hearts had opened and little triangles had snuggled within bigger ones.

So it is time to play. To really get to grips with this new toy. To find out exactly what noises it can make. Better still, it'll be even better to find out what it takes to stop the noises all together.

There's a special part of this big, fat, cuddly, sweaty toy. It's the toy's favourite part of himself too. It's a part of the toy that she is very, very familiar with. She pulls that bit out. Pulls it hard and stretches it as far as she can and then, when it's pulled out really long and when pleasure tickles at the edges of her fear and her loathing, she spears the bottom of it, forcing the knife all the way through the jelly flesh until it pops out at the other side and says, 'peekaboo!' and that makes her giggle just a little.

The new scream is fantastic, it's the very best scream ever, the best she ever heard, then there's sobbing, sorrys, begging.

"Poor, poor thing. It's okay. It's nearly done. It'll only hurt for a minute," she says.

Then she begins to saw. Pulling and pushing the serrated edge of her knife back and forth, back and forth until that special part finally springs loose but there is something stubborn holding it on still, like a tube of some sort so she has to hack at it, hacking and pulling, hacking and pulling and then it pops right off.

Now she can keep this favourite bit of the toy. She'll keep it for later because there are a lot of things she still has to play with and a lot more pretty rooms to play in.

CHAPTER 3 - DELIGHTFUL PROSPECTS

Marlene whistled her appreciation as she stepped through the foyer of the Artisan Lodge Hotel to the grand lounge area beyond. Each huge pillar that, as a serried team, supported the vaulted ceiling was the polished trunk of a Douglas fir. Comfy leather armchairs and sofas sat in cosy clusters around coffee tables fashioned from driftwood. Each of the six seating clusters was lit with burlap shaded lamps, their heavy bases elaborate wooden carvings depicting the varied indigenous species abundant in the region: orcas and bears, cougars and eagles.

At either end of the magnificent space, twin stonework fireplaces on the north and south walls challenged each other as to which one could produce the heartiest flame. The stone walls the fires roared in flanked the glazed eastern elevation of the lounge which looked out over the frigid and whirlpooled waters of the Inside Passage to Quadra Island beyond where houses were hidden within the dense forest and only trails of chimney smoke and the odd wink of a lamp lit to stave off the gloom of the late November afternoon hinted at the presence of man.

Ali waited for her credit card to be processed and she watched with affection as Marlene set about claiming her territory within the otherwise deserted lounge. After twice changing her mind about which seating cluster best suited her, Marlene was finally happy to settle in a soft, wingback armchair close to the southern fireplace.

Ali asked that their bags be taken to their rooms and ordered three coffees, two with a shot of brandy.

"Nice?" Ali asked as she dropped her laptop case and handbag onto the overstuffed couch facing the ocean.

Marlene, ankles crossed atop the coffee table and arms crossed over her ample breasts, grinned. "Very nice indeed. I could get used to this."

"You know, there's a great spa too if you happen to find yourself at a loose end one day. I'm going for a fag, there's coffee on its way."

"Coffee?" said Marlene with a hint of disappointment in her voice.

"Special coffees," Ali said with a wink as she headed for the front doors, already opening her packet of Peter Jackson's and finding her lighter in her coat pocket.

Outside, Ali checked the time and found herself reflecting upon her new circumstances. The past two years had been a whirlwind and she now found herself living a life more in tune with her soul, one where she was once again respected as a professional, an expert. Although the change was welcome it had brought with it a new insidious fear – a fear that, without her consciously noticing it happening (as was the case with mental illness), her mind would succumb to the cerebral rot she had worked hard to eradicate. And if that did happen, now that her life was actually fulfilling and pleasurable again, she feared that there would be no surviving it this time and it may finally torture her to death.

Pushing away what was quickly becoming a sweat-inducing fear, Ali reminded herself that she had unshackled herself from her former life where she had defined herself as a wife and a mother for so long that she had carelessly forgotten how to define herself as an individual. She had accidentally allowed herself to disappear into her role as one in servitude to others – as a mere part of a whole. The habit of thinking of herself in that way was hard to quash regardless that it had been David who had allowed their marriage to be put asunder by Miss Clickety-Clack-Dirty-

Crack (the nickname Ali joyfully used in reference to her ex-husband's lover).

Although it was petty and childish, Ali revelled in the fact that both of her children despised their dad's girlfriend. Sandy and Kenny were always forthcoming with stories about the couple's arguments or Clickety-Clack's failed attempts at cooking or at bonding with the children, who were closer to her age than she was to their father's.

But lately those stories had lost their lustre and were threatening to reignite Ali's depression too, as if sparking a strange sense of grief for a relationship that had had her gasping for breath at the time. Her son, Kenny, had confided in Ali recently that 'Dad seems really sad' which had Ali almost feeling sorry for David, but within the next breath she had thankfully managed to regress into the smug resentment that had gotten her through the tricky transition to her new forty-*something* single woman status.

Ali crushed her cigarette underfoot and hid the crumpled butt inside a nearby hedge so as not to cheapen the environment. The Artisan Lodge Hotel struck the perfect balance between luxury and the rustic nature of Canada, somehow pruning and manicuring the bucolic essence of the country and packaging it in a way that would satisfy the hunting parties and kayaking groups who descended upon the island in droves seeking to find the version of Canada they had been drip fed through movies featuring its majestic landscape and polished politeness.

But Cedar River's true nature was not unlike the crumpled butt of Ali's spent cigarette. Beneath an aesthetically pleasing surface, secreted in its core, laid its dark and ignoble truth. It was a town stripped of hope and connection, void of the anchoring quality of true community. Cedar River was a petri-dish for deviance to fester in.

Ali's skin prickled as she felt Cuzzocrea's nearing presence. It was a phenomenon she'd observed since their very first encounter. Akin to that of identical twins who feel the other's heartbreak or injury, as if her soul was somehow entwined with his.

Ali batted her nonsense away. "Stupid fucking bitch, he's your partner, that's all. Pull yourself together." Ali chided herself for once more defining herself in terms of her relationship, or lack thereof, with a man.

Ali stepped around to the front of the hotel because, regardless of definitions and imaginings, nothing thrilled her more than the sight of Cuzzocrea walking towards her – nothing, that is, except for the delightful prospect of hunting a killer.

CHAPTER 4 - NEUROPLASTICITY

Cuzzocrea opened his trunk and donned his VIIMIS windcheater before gathering his case files and another VIIMIS windcheater – this one new and sealed in transparent plastic.

A BC flag snapped rhythmically atop its pole at the far right of the hotel, the lanyard rings tintinnabulating eerily against the mast. The wind was picking up and Cuzzocrea took it as an ominous sign. He had knowledge of two hidden things, yet to be solved: the first was in the expandable files he carried, therein lay the breadcrumbs of a trail that would undoubtedly lead to a new evil; the second was that somewhere inside the Artisan Lodge Hotel was the woman who had taken residence inside his brain – the ever-present, inescapable and inarguably formidable Ali Dalglish.

As such, Cuzzocrea's emotions were a solution of dread and excitement, a mixture which now permeated all his VIIMIS cases and made him wonder about neuroplasticity. It was a subject he had discussed at length with Ali since she claimed to have repaired (or, rather, to be in the process of repairing) her own damaged brain by applying forced neuroplasticity. She was manipulating changes in her neural pathways and synapses culminating in a positive renewal of neurological associations. He wondered, therefore, that as his affections towards Ali intensified and since their interactions revolved around grim and disturbing major crimes, would he begin to relish their occurrence? Would he even begin to subconsciously wish for more evil to manifest?

If his reaction to Superintendent Shaw's decision to call in Ali Dalglish late last night was anything to go by (the news had caused his heart to palpitate and his core temperature to rise despite the sub-zero conditions in the field) then that particular metamorphosis had indeed already occurred.

As he locked his Prius, Cuzzocrea was determined to remain composed and to behave counterintuitively upon meeting Ali again – he must defy his desires in the face of her and remain professional.

But as he walked the gravel pathway which led to the hotel from the carpark, Cuzzocrea's resolve was tested when his eyes met Ali's as she sheltered beneath the glass canopy of the hotel's frontage. His heart thrummed again as he saw her serious expression unselfconsciously brighten at the sight of him.

There she was, waiting for him. It was a sight he never felt less than honoured to witness, ever since the very first day he had encountered her in the foyer of the RCMP building in Glandford, before he was even aware of her most beguiling feature: her unique mind.

As he neared her he felt a sting of fear which whipped at him from the tail of his joy. It was a swirl of doubt that threw up all of the coincidences that had thus far conspired to place her in his life – the what-ifs and the what-if-nots making him unnaturally aware of the intricately played minutiae of their respective fates that had somehow brought them together from almost opposite sides of the globe, the ravelled lines, fragile as eggshells, that may crumble into dust under the foot of gratitude or assumed entitlement.

And just as Cuzzocrea was telling himself to pull himself together, that she was simply his partner, Ali Dalglish opened her arms to him and as he slipped his hand inside her jacket and around her waist, feeling her tiptoe up to him, he gladly accepted her embrace and drank of her intoxicating scent.

Cuzzocrea used the presentation of Ali's new VIIMIS

windcheater as an excuse to pull from the welcome hug and maintain a modicum of professionalism. Ali appeared to be genuinely pleased at the sight of the jacket and Cuzzocrea even thought he heard her suppress a charming, childlike giggle. As he watched her inspect the acronym emblazoned on the back of the garment, Cuzzocrea suspected that the windcheater was symbolic to her in some arcane way. For an instant he was able to forget the reason they had been brought together once more and, for the first time since he'd been faced with the gruesome image, Cuzzocrea even forgot about the severed penis.

CHAPTER 5 - SAPA

James Bartholomew returned from lunch and shuffled his chair under his desk, eager to access his desktop but his pursuit was thwarted as, from the corner of his eye, he saw Fern approaching him, her face seemingly on fire. He smiled as she sidled her way through the open door in the partition wall separating the main office from his own.

"Oh, Fern." James laughed as he watched his heavily pregnant assistant narrowing her eyes to protect them from the smoke exuded by the abundant candles on the cake. "You guys! You shouldn't have."

Fern was joined in the small office by the rest of *The North-Island Echo* team as she led them in a comically off-key rendition of 'Happy Birthday'. James rocked back in his chair and it creaked in revolt of his near three-hundred-pound weight. He mimicked a conductor as he chortled at their ear-sickening tune and was still enthusiastically applauding their combined effort as Fern placed the chocolate cake on his paper-strewn desk.

"Make a wish, make a wish!" said Fern, sucking chocolate frosting off her thumb.

"Jeez, that looks like more than twenty-one candles to me! Who's been lying to ya?" James's team laughed. "Hope you've got a fire extinguisher handy, Neil," he said to the office junior whose job it was to ensure that health and safety protocols were upheld at all times.

Neil had perfect timing when he raised a red extinguisher

above the crowd of heads in response and everyone, especially James, laughed and clapped.

"Blow them out, James, before they set off the sprinklers," said Fern.

James closed his eyes and was momentarily and uncharacteristically solemn as he made a wish, then darkened all of the flames with one powerful breath.

All of the staff silently empathized in unison, each of them under the belief that they knew exactly what James's wish had been. Considering his wife's sudden demise as a result of stage-four bone cancer, the granting of his wish would have been a miracle since the general consensus was that Ellen Bartholomew was unlikely to last out the year.

Fern led a delayed and somewhat forced applause as James stood and stepped around his desk to shake hands with each and every one of his staff members, thanking them with deep sincerity for their kindness.

Familiar with James's tendency to chat and knowing that he was far too polite to call a halt to such merriment, once the last thank you had been given, Fern ushered all of the employees out of his office with orders to get back to work since the print deadline would soon be upon them.

When the office was once again quiet James took his seat and Fern retrieved the smoking cake, planting a gentle kiss on the bald top of her boss's head. "I'll bring a slice in and I'll wrap one for Ellen."

"Thank you, Fern." James watched her leave and then called to her just as she crossed the threshold. "How's our wee one coming along?"

"Won't be long now, he's a bully, played ping-pong with my kidneys all night," said Fern, rubbing her swollen belly.

James leaned back again, he laughed heartily, his cheeks reddening and a glister of tears causing his eyes to sparkle. "Ah, Fern. Well, I can't wait to meet the little sucker – nothing like it, children, they make the world go round."

"Sure do," said Fern holding onto the doorknob. "Open or closed?"

"Closed please, Ferny. I have some things to be getting on with before home time."

Fern nodded and pulled the door closed behind her. James looked out at the office and smiled. He wondered what they'd all think if they knew what his wish had been. He wondered if they'd still bring him cake.

James allowed his smile to remain until all of the staff had finally returned to their work and the focus was no longer upon him. Only then did he return to his computer screen and log into his external email account. He clicked on the new message, the subject field read: SAPA.

James gritted his teeth. He'd given strict instructions that the name should not be used – or the email address, for that matter – unless it was with regards to circumstance of the utmost importance.

When he read the content of the email, his face drained of its previous cheery blush:

Sapa

Quispe is dead. Murdered.

Meet ASAP

Sinchi Roca

He realized that the email and the pseudonym had not been used carelessly because this matter was indeed of the uppermost importance.

CHAPTER 6 - DISARMED

In the Artisan Lodge's lounge, Marlene heaved herself out of the chair and hugged Cuzzocrea. Over recent months Ali had noticed that Marlene's reaction to the inspector had metamorphosed from the previous cooing, girly, near-salivating appreciation of his good looks to one more maternal and overly-protective in nature. This change had coincided with Cuzzocrea divulging to them both over dinner one night that his mother had passed away when he was five years old.

Ali guessed that Marlene – a woman who had lost her only daughter to cancer – was only too eager to fill her maternal void with a surrogate child. As she watched Marlene place her palm on Cuzzocrea's cheek and look into his eyes with concern, Ali's suspicions were confirmed.

"You're not eating."

"I assure you I am," Cuzzocrea said.

"Nope. You feel thin," said Marlene, squeezing the tops of both of his arms.

"Oh, put him down, Marlene. He's a big boy." Ali sat on the edge of the sofa and added two sugar cubes to her laced coffee. "Yours is the one without brandy," she said to Cuzzocrea who took a seat next to Ali on the couch.

"You ladies hitting the sauce already?"

"Just a little nip to stave off the cold. Annie Chaud swears that's how she has survived ninety-seven winters without so much as a runny nose." Marlene unfurled her pashminas. "Here comes the hot flash – only the third one today. God bless ovaries."

"How was the drive?" Cuzzocrea asked Ali.

"Dull. I hate the new highway. I'd much rather take the Old Island Highway along the coast."

"Not in this weather, too dangerous," said Marlene, failing to suppress a belch as she swallowed her coffee.

"Your car?" Cuzzocrea asked.

Ali noticed the delicate wrinkles that framed his eyes, laughter lines on a man she'd never seen laugh. "Yes, but now I'm regretting it because the receptionist here told me that a snowstorm's coming. My car is shit in the snow."

Cuzzocrea nodded. "Snow is forecast for the day after tomorrow but you know Cedar River, if you don't like the weather, wait ten minutes and it'll probably change." Cuzzocrea smiled as Ali and Marlene unenthusiastically joined him in the last part of the well-known local saying.

"You know, it might be worth us hiring a four-wheel-drive, Marlene," Ali suggested.

"I don't mind driving," said Cuzzocrea. "We'll be together the whole time, not like we'll be separating."

"But Marlene will have to get out and about."

Cuzzocrea smiled at Marlene as he sat back into the couch. "Yeah, remind again, what is your role exactly, Marlene?"

Marlene straightened. "I'll have you know, Reymondo, I am a vital component in any of the investigations Ali is involved with."

"Officially, she's my assistant. Unofficially, she just happens to be something I can't bear to live without, like mascara or toothpaste."

"I'm her Watson, you see. Sherlock is just a silly-hat-wearing eccentric without his Watson." Marlene turned to Ali. "No offence, hon."

"I'm sure I don't need to remind you both that Marlene cannot be privy to any investigative materials or…"

"Yeah, yeah, don't you worry about all that. As far as you,

Shaw and Strap-a-dick-to-me Walsh are concerned, Marlene checks my messages and, I don't know, picks up my dry cleaning."

"Strap-a-dick-to-me Walsh?" Cuzzocrea raised his eyebrows.

Ali shrugged. Since Superintendent Shaw had taken a personal interest in Ali's fight to be permitted to work in her professional field and as an expert consultant on VIIMIS's most testing cases, Trina Walsh – the team's head of forensics – had taken an obvious dislike to her.

This didn't surprise Ali in the least. Many years ago, during her rise in the world of criminal investigation, she had noticed a strange irony – her biggest battles on her way through the glass ceiling were fought against female colleagues. Trina was just another one of the many unfortunate and disappointing examples of the women Ali had encountered professionally who, whilst fancying themselves strong feminists, were actually the foot soldiers for a misogynistic hierarchy. Compelled unwittingly by their own insecurities and under the mistaken impression – as a result of years of negative social conditioning – that there may not be room at the top for more than one human with a pair of tits.

For women like Trina Walsh, it was a case of 'misters before sisters'; whether she was equipped to comprehend or even recognize that herself was beyond Ali. Hence Ali's nickname for her: Strap-a-dick-to-me Walsh. Of course a certain amount of friction was to be expected since they both specialized in similar fields and therefore unavoidably undermined each other on occasion. However, the real kindling in Walsh's bitter fire of resentment towards Ali was far more basic – Trina Walsh was in love with Superintendent Shaw (according to Detective Munro, another investigator on the VIIMIS team, the two of them had been having an extra-marital affair for years). Not to mention, Trina's sizeable ass was way bigger than Ali's and this, Ali knew, was a bone of contention for any woman lacking self-esteem or crippled by a negative body image who therefore feeds an animalistic need to feel that she is desired by the opposite sex.

"I bet she's going to be an absolute frigging nightmare on this case," said Ali.

"Why's that?" asked Marlene.

"She lives here, in Cedar River. It's her territory."

Marlene clucked. "Well, maybe she won't get any stolen moments with Shaw this time around then."

"Actually her husband's a heli-logger so he's away most of the year anyway," Cuzzocrea added.

"Yet another intrinsic problem with this little cesspit of a town – absentee husbands and their desperately lonely wives sniffing around for a bit of husband-stealing to pass the days."

Cuzzocrea looked a question.

"Never mind. So. You going to run me through the case files?" Ali said, standing. "We'll go to my room. We wouldn't want Marlene catching sight of our classified material, would we?"

Cuzzocrea stood, gathered his files and bent to kiss Marlene on the cheek.

"You two behave yourselves up there, no funny business."

"Marlene!" said Ali, looking daggers at her friend.

"I see the way you look at each other. You don't miss much at my age, you know, missy."

Ali shepherded Cuzzocrea to the elevators and pressed the up button.

"Nice hotel. I'm assuming you're on a lot more money than I am," said Cuzzocrea.

Ali shrugged. "Maybe. Or maybe I'm just a snob with a credit card. Anyhow, I suggest you don't concern yourself with my income – that's how David started, next thing I knew I was piss-poor and chained to the kitchen sink."

"I'm not David," said Cuzzocrea, following Ali into the elevator.

Ali cringed internally, with anyone else she would leap into defensiveness, justifying her stance but as always with Cuzzocrea, she found herself disarmed, her internal fort a barren ruin.

"I apologize."

The elevator doors closed, Cuzzocrea looked expectantly at Ali.

"What?" Ali snapped, her defensiveness called to arms. Maybe her apology, albeit brief, hadn't been sincere enough for him.

"Are we going to set up our incident room in here or are you going to press the button for your floor?"

"Shit, yes." Ali pressed five, blushing at her misapprehension.

CHAPTER 7 - MAIDEN WATCHES

Maiden watches through the window. It's not dangerous, there's no way he would see her. Nobody would.

Wednesday is Tommy's home-alone class, upstairs in the Community Centre's annexe and so from the ground-floor foyer she can safely watch through the window, past the bus stop and across the street to *The North-Island Echo* newspaper offices while she waits.

It's a horrible day. Bleak, grey and the wind can't decide whether it wants to blow or suck. Most of the people at the bus stop are kids from Maple Ridge High School, her school. She should be worried about them seeing her since she's skipped classes all week but then she remembers: nobody sees her.

They're bringing him a cake; it must be the fat fucker's birthday. His minions are all smiling and loving him. One of them holds up a fire extinguisher and they're all laughing.

It's not a surprise to her. Everyone loves him because that's how he likes it. He makes everyone love him. That's what he needs. Love. All about the love, baby.

Maiden checks her watch. It's four o'clock. Tommy'll be done soon. She should really go up to find him but she knows he can look after himself. Kids like them have to. It's why her little brother is in a home-alone programme to start with because when *they* – teachers, Child Protective Services, cops – know you're always on your own they send your mum to parent-craft sessions and the kids have to go to home-alone classes and all three of you have to go to family therapy in the little office above HSBC on the high street.

They'd once arranged a spot for their mum – or as *they* like to call her, *the mother* – in a sober living place too but since they couldn't track down *the father*, it didn't happen. They said they could make arrangements for *the children* but she told them there was no way they were taking her kids and she got her lawyer – her court-appointed duty council lawyer – to fight for her kids to stay with her. Perhaps they thought that showed promise – *the mother* cares about *the children.* But Maiden knows better. It only showed that Mum needed them, but for what, they'd probably never guess.

After the candles are dark on his cake and his work minions have dispersed, he turns to his computer. From this angle she can see his double chin. Maiden hates that double chin. It was even worse a couple of years ago when he'd been on that diet and it had gotten wrinkly and dangly like a turkey's wattle or an empty scrotum sack.

His name is James Bartholomew. But he has another name. A name only his closest, most loyal minions are privileged enough to know. Maiden doubts anyone in *The Echo* offices knows it.

That name is Sapa.

Maiden has a gift. She can always tell when someone is angry – even if they're pretending not to be. She always knows when somebody is displeased or if they're going to get mean, she can see the mean and the angry coming, she knows it even before the men themselves do. She once looked up why she's so good at that too, because she wondered, hoped, that she might have magical powers or that maybe she was a psychic like the woman who runs the bookshop on Quadra Island. But Maiden is not magic, or psychic. It's common. Common for kids like her and Tommy.

Now Sapa looks mean. She's seen him mean before. He looks angry. She's seen him angry before. He looks shocked. Maiden has never seen him look shocked before. She decides it's a good look for him – makes him appear to be almost human. It's a look she likes and maybe it's one she'll see more of.

Maiden narrows her eyes. She watches for a while as Sapa's dumpy, cylindrical fingers punch at his keyboard. Then she thinks maybe she will fetch Tommy after all because even though they can look after themselves, they'll always need each other.

Besides, Maiden misses Tommy when he's not right beside her.

CHAPTER 8 - DEAD MAN'S PLATEAU

"This is your file of duplicates, I know how you like to pin things up. Although you'll need to put your 'do not disturb' sign on if you do," said Cuzzocrea as he opened an expandable file.

Ali set about clearing the usual crap one finds in a hotel room from the top of the long dressing table.

"Seriously, who writes letters these days? You'd think hotels would save on the cost of a pile of personalized stationary in every room and charge a little less."

"Old people. They still write letters," said Cuzzocrea, laying out documents and photographs on one of the two queen-sized beds in the disappointingly generic room. "You mind if I turn this off?" he asked, referring to the flat-screen TV in the armoire alongside the dressing table. A loop of visuals promoted the Artisan Lodge's services and amenities, accompanied by the hotel's version of Muzak: pan pipes and eagle calls.

"God no, please do."

With the television silenced, Ali immediately focused. "Okay, hit me with it."

Cuzzocrea nodded. "At a little after six a.m. yesterday morning, local RCMP units responded to a call from Richard Grotsky. Whilst on a hike up to the Eden Falls, having passed the Hydro station on the north trail, Mr. Grotsky spotted something in the waters below, snagged on some low hanging bushes which overhang the pools at the foot of the falls.

"Mr. Grotsky, unsure what he was looking at, proceeded across the bridge and looked at the object from directly above, the clearer vantage point of Dead Man's Plateau. It became apparent to him then that the object snagged in the bushes was a DB."

"Okay," Ali said, taking a series of photographs from Cuzzocrea. Each photograph depicted the view of the body in the water from the various angles described in the witness statement. Ali studied them and retrieved her tub of thumb tacks from her handbag and set about pinning the photos on the wall above the dresser. "Do we have an ID?"

"Yes. One Tristan McMenemy. He was in the system, his tattoos flagged as distinguishing features on our ViCLAS database."

"ViCLAS?" asked Ali.

"Violent crimes case files. McMenemy was charged with aggravated assault four years ago after a bar brawl in Vancouver following a Canucks game. During the altercation, McMenemy broke a man's jaw. He was given a two-year suspended sentence, fined eighteen-hundred bucks and served one hundred and ten hours of community service."

"Any link? Revenge attack maybe?"

"If it was, we're looking at major overkill. Here." Cuzzocrea handed Ali a picture of McMenemy's body having been removed from the water and laid out on a sheet of tarpaulin.

"Hmm, sharp force injuries," said Ali, assessing the photograph. "Not incised, not chop. He was stabbed. How many times?"

"Twenty-six. Eighteen wounds to the abdomen and eight to the back."

"Cause of death?"

"Not confirmed, Trina hasn't performed the autopsy yet."

"And the removal of the penis – no way of knowing

whether it was pre- or post-mortem. Come to think of it, he was found in the water, tricky to know if any of the wounds were pre or post without a full autopsy."

"Trina thinks the penis may have been removed pre-mortem but as he lay dying. She indicated his blood loss at that point would have been so severe, he may barely have noticed."

Ali pinned up the photographs of the dead man. "Trina's full of shit. I can assure you, if he was alive at the time then he would have certainly noticed his dick being hacked off in the manner that it was."

"That's what I tended to think but you try telling Trina that."

"Glad to," said Ali. "The penis? I take it you haven't found it?"

"Nope."

Ali nodded. "Let's assume it's a trophy, that the killer took it – to keep or to dispose of separately. Either way we can assume that this was a sexually motivated crime. Unlikely, therefore, that it's a revenge attack linked to his previous assault charge."

"I concur." Cuzzocrea handed Ali a set of four photographs of the plateau from which the witness had called the RCMP. "Dead Man's Plateau. Aptly named in consideration of the circumstances. During the day it's a tourist destination, but after dark it's not only a popular suicide spot, it's also a meeting place for homosexual males."

"Cottaging," said Ali matter-of-factly.

"Sorry?"

"Cottaging. It's the word used to describe the activity prevalent amongst a subculture of homosexual males – particularly closeted homosexuals – which involves them meeting strangers in a variety of predetermined rural locations for the sole purpose of partaking in anonymous, often dangerous, sexual acts."

"Wow. And I thought cottaging was when you meet up with some buddies for the holidays at a cabin on the lake."

"Sounds about the same to me. Trying to tell me something, Inspector?" said Ali with a wink before reverting to her serious demeanour. "Perhaps a homophobia-driven hate crime?"

"Maybe but there was no trace of blood on the plateau."

"Yet we seem to be working under the assumption that he was killed in the locale? Not moved from another site and disposed of here?"

"There's no vehicle access for a minimum of two kilometres in either direction. There are two vehicle parking areas which allow access to the fall trails. The southernmost one leads to a downward sloping trail and access to the upper pools, Dead Man's Plateau is accessed via a set of steep, wooden, switchback stairs. The other parking area is at the entrance to a gradually upward sloping trail and although there are no stairs on that side, the terrain is, in many ways, trickier to navigate, particularly at this time of year. Once you have covered the dirt trail itself, you then have to cross the Hydro station. There is another carpark but that leads to the new suspension bridge, not the pools and not Dead Man's Plateau."

"Yep, I've read about the Rotary Club's shiny new bridge but I've only ever walked the old trails with the kids. You're right, he was most likely killed there unless our perp possesses supernatural strength and carried the body all the way from a car. I take it there was no evidence to suggest that he was dragged?"

"None."

"Defensive wounds? On the victim's hands or arms?"

"Yes." Cuzzocrea shuffled through the paperwork on the bed and found the photographs he was looking for. "Here."

Ali studied the pictures, turning them and titling her head. She pinned them up on the wall. "So, defensive wounds prove he was alive for at least part of the assailant's attack. How heavy was McMenemy?"

"Approximately one hundred and forty-two pounds."

"Do you have photographs of the surrounding area?

Specifically waters which flow towards the falls? Because I suspect our perp would have found it very difficult to lift McMenemy's body and throw it over the railings separating Dead Man's Plateau from the precipice at the other side."

Cuzzocrea handed Ali a series of photographs, one at a time. "I agree. My thinking is that he was killed upstream, near the pool of water, here." Cuzzocrea pointed to a pool of water surrounded by huge, smooth boulders. "This pool opens up to the fast-flowing waters which lead directly to the falls."

Ali nodded. "So he was stabbed up here maybe? On the rocks. That would explain why there was no blood found at the scene. The perpetrator then pushes the vic into the deeps of the pool and lets the current do the rest of the job."

"It's a theory."

Ali stood back, examining the wall. She folded her arms and chewed the inside of her cheek, thinking.

Cuzzocrea stepped next to her. "Well? What do you think?"

"I have to see the body to be sure but I think I can back up that theory of ours."

"How so?"

"Well, I have to analyse the angle of entry to be sure – since Trina Walsh seems incapable of using trajectory rods – but, judging from these photographs and what I can decipher in terms of the differences between the posterior wounds as opposed to those on his anterior region…I think he was killed by someone a lot smaller than him."

Cuzzocrea took out his cell phone. "I'll call the hospital."

"The hospital?" asked Ali.

"See if anyone can let us in to the morgue."

Ali frowned as she watched Cuzzocrea put the phone to his ear. "I'd like to speak to Anthony Douglas, please." Once he was put on hold, Cuzzocrea explained, "There's no ME's office here. The nearest one is in Nanoose so Shaw arranged for the body to be held in the local hospital's morgue for the time being."

Ali shook her head. "Fucking backward place. What city doesn't have a medical examiner's office?"

"It was only reclassified as a city a few years ago, up until then it was a town with a health centre and no hospital at all. Suppose it'll take them a few more years to catch up yet." Cuzzocrea shrugged and stepped away to talk to what Ali assumed to be the hospital's administrator.

She watched Cuzzocrea pace the room as he talked. Marlene was right, he had lost weight. However, Ali noticed, his buttocks were just as marvellous as they had always been.

CHAPTER 9 - A ONE OFF

Cuzzocrea's stomach wasn't easily upset. He was no stranger to gruesome scenes of death but now he had to turn his face away and force himself to admire the migraine-inducing, flickering fluorescent light above him. He suppressed the urge to make a run for the nearest sink which was just as well in consideration of his environment – he dreaded to think about what might have been swilled away down the drain of a morgue sink.

He had had a feeling that his time in the morgue with Ali could verge on the abhorrent when she'd insisted, in the carpark outside the Artisan Lodge Hotel, that he help her with her lab gear, consisting of three large cases (one silver, one black and one grey with yellow clasps), which she swapped from her car and deposited into the trunk of his Prius.

Watching Ali tenaciously at work never failed to mesmerize him and was fast becoming his favourite pastime, however, seeing her as she was in the morgue – a first for him – dressed in scrubs beneath a long dark apron, head covered with an inappropriately cheerful bandana featuring kittens at play over a white hair net and wielding a handful of multicoloured fibreglass rods, he was seriously considering taking up a more cheerful hobby like slaying lambs or dung sculpting.

"Okay. You got him?" said Ali, pulling a long probe from her bundle, this one pink.

"Yes, Ali, I've got him."

Cuzzocrea's face was mere inches from the bloated head of Tristan McMenemy. Now that she'd inserted a variety of coloured trajectory rods into the wounds in McMenemy's abdomen, making the dead body look like a porcupinesque piñata, Ali was about to do the same on his back.

For her to do so, she had instructed Cuzzocrea to roll the body onto its right side and hold it in that position, ensuring she not only had access to the wounds on his back but that the protuberant probes placed in his stomach would remain in situ, undisturbed.

"Just hurry up, will you?" said Cuzzocrea.

"Looking a little green around the gills there, my friend." Ali laughed.

Cuzzocrea scowled at her and then, as a whiff of something rank exuded from the dead man's mouth, he quickly turned back to admire the overhead light once again.

"Just a few more minutes," she said.

Cuzzocrea didn't need to watch Ali to know when each rod was inserted into a fissure of flesh; the accompanying squelching sound and inward sucking noise was akin to the work of a truly masterful Foley artist and painted a vivid image in his mind, turning his stomach all the more.

Finally, all eight rods had been placed and Cuzzocrea turned to see Ali standing back, admiring her work, hands on hips.

"Well?" he pressed, desperate for the ordeal to be over.

"Stay there, I need pictures."

"You're joking, right?" Cuzzocrea huffed. His muscles were trembling as a result of holding the body at such an unnatural angle. It seemed all McMenemy wanted to do was flop either forward or backward and rest in peace.

Cuzzocrea watched as Ali removed one pair of surgical gloves and snapped a fresh pair expertly over her hands. She retrieved an expensive-looking camera from one of her cases, checking the rear screen and the focus. Ali took several pictures of McMenemy's back from a variety of angles, then repeated the same in front of him before, much to Cuzzocrea's chagrin, she angled the lens towards him.

"Ali…" he warned, "…don't you…"

Ali snapped the photograph, "Just for me. I promise I won't show this to anyone on the team." She giggled mischievously.

Cuzzocrea began to straighten and the dead body moved.

"Wait! Wait! I want one from above."

"From above?"

"Yes, it'll demonstrate my point more clearly. It's imperative."

"It's imperative that you hurry up before I puke."

Ali looked around the morgue, thinking, "One sec."

Cuzzocrea sighed impatiently as Ali started rummaging in drawers, a storage closet and under the row of biers, one of which housed the shrouded body of what he assumed to be a child. Ali called to a morgue technician who was filling in a form near the child's corpse and asked him a question. The technician pointed to a wall of closets. Ali began searching them.

"Aha!" she exclaimed and crossed to Cuzzocrea. She carried two large, black wedges.

"You're kidding me," said Cuzzocrea.

Ali stuffed each wedge firmly under either side of the corpse, front and back. "Okay, you can let go now."

"What the hell?" Cuzzocrea let go of McMenemy's now securely scotched dead body and stepped back. "Why didn't you do that in the first place?"

"And where's the fun in that? Only joking, honestly I didn't know if they'd have them. Here, help me up, will you?" Ali slid a metal stool over to the edge of the table where the corpse was balanced. She stood on it and held a hand out to Cuzzocrea.

"What are you doing now?" he asked.

"Getting a picture from above, what does it look like I'm doing?"

"My God. Do you ever conform to norms?"

"Fuck norms," Ali replied as she steadied herself with Cuzzocrea's hand and stepped onto the autopsy table, straddling the body for the benefit of her bird's-eye view. Ali snapped several pictures and stepped back down to the ground. "Okay, Cuzzocrea, tell me what you see."

"I don't do forensics."

"Well start. Come on! It's fun."

Cuzzocrea reluctantly acquiesced and circled the body, studying the projecting rods. "Okay. So, the stab wounds to the back go downwards, towards his butt. The ones on the stomach though, they go upwards, except for one, which seems to go straight in."

"Exactly."

"Which means?" Cuzzocrea asked.

"What if the stab wounds to the back were the first?"

"So he was approached from behind and above. Someone taller than him."

"No. Someone *higher* than him."

"Right. So McMenemy was down low, lower than the killer when he was attacked from behind?"

"Yes. The killer came from above him and stabbed down, holding the knife in his or her hand with the blade pointing downwards, towards his or her own elbow."

"Yes."

"Then, feeling the stabs – all eight in rapid succession – you can tell that from the small distance between each wound. Short, shallow, almost timid. Fast, angry. Clustered. Of course, only the autopsy will show us which of the wounds led to death and his internal injuries should indicate which, if any, were inflicted post-mortem. I'm theorizing that the sharp force injuries to his back happened first simply because those injuries look to be mostly a cluster of hesitation wounds. But, like I say, we'll know a lot more after the autopsy."

"Okay. So he's stabbed in the back first. He feels the knife, knows he's being stabbed, he turns…" added Cuzzocrea.

"Yes, but not from his low position because if he was stabbed in the stomach with the killer looming above him still, the angles of entry on his torso would have mimicked the angle of trajectory of the wounds on his back."

"So McMenemy *stands* and turns."

"Yes."

"He is then stabbed in the stomach and chest?"

"Not yet. First he instinctively grabs the blade of the knife – evidenced by the deep lacerations to his hands across each finger, along the underside of the second knuckle but not the thumb."

"Ah," said Cuzzocrea, "so he grabbed the blade with both hands but the killer pulled it out of his grip?"

"McMenemy got the blade but then pulled it with such force that he accidentally stabbed himself."

"What?"

"Okay, so I reach out, I'm McMenemy," Ali stood in front of Cuzzocrea, face to face with him and mimicked the action of grabbing an imaginary knife between them, clutching her hands together, "I pull with force enough to get the knife from you but with so much force that the motion continues and I stab myself here…"

Ali pointed to a yellow rod positioned in a wound below McMenemy's navel. "This is a relatively shallow wound and it's the only wound on the stomach perpendicular to his spine. Its long axis runs between the twelve and six o'clock positions. He pulled the knife, the force pushes it into his stomach, low down too, he pulls it back out as soon as he feels it penetrate him. He's shocked…"

"Then what? The defensive wounds?"

"Yep. The killer grabs the knife, pulls it from McMenemy's hands, causing the lacerations we see on his hands. Then, this time holding the handle in his or her palm with the blade pointing outward, towards McMenemy, the perp proceeds to stab him eighteen times in an upward motion."

"Surely he wouldn't have remained standing throughout

an assault like that."

"Probably not. All the wounds on the front were made in an upward stabbing motion – except for the one I suggest was self-inflicted near his umbilicus – so if he did fall back, which he most probably did, the killer likely stooped or crouched above him and continued the attack."

"So what's the verdict?"

"He was killed on the rocks, eight stab wounds to the back whilst in a crouched position, he stands, he turns, grabs the knife, stabs himself. The killer pulls the knife blade back through his hands and then stabs him multiple times before sawing his dick off and pushing him into the water. I think our killer is small. McMenemy was only five feet eight inches himself, not a tall man but tall in comparison to someone petite, someone like me, for instance."

"A woman?"

"I think so, yes," said Ali. "And she knew him."

"The overkill?"

"Yes, and the intimidation which turned to anger, wrath even."

"Explain," said Cuzzocrea, folding his arms.

"When the assailant stabbed him from behind she was scared, timid – the wounds are typical of hesitation wounds. I'd guess it was an entirely new sensation to her, not only the act of stabbing another human but of taking power over him, McMenemy."

"And the anger?"

"A confusion of anger and pleasure once she was face to face with him. Once the killer could see McMenemy's reaction as she was stabbing him, she began to stab deeper. In fact, to the hilt as evidenced by the contusions around some of the wounds. Those are marks likely made by the handle of the knife. It was personal."

"Premeditation? She'd have to have taken the knife with her. Not likely they'd be a couple enjoying a picnic in late November."

Ali nodded. "I think she knew him. I think he had

victimized her in some way and that the victimization was sexual in nature – hence the messy removal of his penis. The knife she used was single bladed with a serrated edge. A bread knife, perhaps?"

"We should check out his acquaintances. Girlfriends? Ex-girlfriends, maybe a wife?" Cuzzocrea suggested.

"All of the above, yes," said Ali, "She's probably shaken up by it, she may be suffering from symptoms of PTSD as a result. This wasn't the work of an expert, practiced killer. It was a disorganized crime of passion, an act of vengeance, perhaps."

"So, I'm thinking a short woman, slight build, timid, shaken up and she was likely to have been involved in a sexual relationship with McMenemy."

"Spot on, Cuzzocrea," Ali said. "And the good news? We're not looking for a serial killer. This is a one off so, once we find her, it should be a clear-cut case."

"Nice." Cuzzocrea exhaled.

"Now, can you help me get Mr. McMenemy back into his drawer, please?"

After an attempt at whinging in protest, Cuzzocrea agreed. As always, he was utterly disarmed by Ali Dalglish.

CHAPTER 10 - A PINK HEART AND FETID LIPS

Although the slice of cake had been enough to fill him at the time, James Bartholomew was a man with an insatiable appetite, so he purchased a few of his favourite nibbles to enjoy with a nice bottle of red and a good book. He found that eating fine food always soothed his rattled nerves and since replying to his brother's email and agreeing to meet, Cheese Heaven seemed the best location to twin his dual tasks of allaying misplaced panic and gathering the necessary bits and bobs of his late-night supper.

"Now this one is the perfect balance between sharp and velvety smooth, it's crumbly and melts on the tongue. Not unlike a fine Cheshire, if you're familiar?"

"I am indeed and I shall therefore partake. Add it to the bag please, Susan."

Susan Kerluck, the owner of Cheese Heaven, smiled and picked up the waxen, white round of cheese and took it to her slicer. James offered a nod thick with his usual altruistic ardour to a fellow patron on her way out of the store, a woman who he couldn't help but notice had reddened when she'd heard the total price of her selection of nibbles.

James's immutable kindness and selfless concern for others was what set him apart and exalted him in the eyes of the people of Cedar River. As such, James enjoyed his status as honorary father of the city and never tired of setting a good example. For instance, he went to great lengths to support all the small businesses on the high street and encouraged others to do the same, choosing to shop locally in lieu of the nearby big-chain supermarkets.

It was the reason he was happily swallowing Susan's shovel of bullshit – the woman was quite the greedy minx – and was cutting the wedge of cheese as big as she dared without even so much as a mention of how much James wished to spend. Her conscience hadn't even flinched when she'd pushed her latest brand of balsamic vinegar of Modena on him when he'd arrived. James had noticed the price sticker as she'd placed it in the brown paper tote: twenty dollars! He could buy ten similar bottles of the stuff for the same price in Dollarama *if* he were a loathsome pauper more intent upon squirrelling away his meagre funds at the expense of the sole proprietors of the city.

Still, Cheese Heaven's ambience suited him. The deli counter and the range of luxury preserves and reductions transported him away from Cedar River's mass of concrete and stuccoed buildings to a more elegant, European-feeling place of culture and refinement.

Additionally, past the small charcuterie counter was a small eatery where each table glowed with the tangerine light cast by its own paraffin candle. It was a charming spot from which James often watched the harried comings and goings of office workers or labourers white with drywall dust and, of course, the schoolchildren being transported by well-meaning mothers who tirelessly shuttled their offspring from school to hockey practice and endless recitals and private tutoring sessions. It was also a private spot, thanks in part to Susan's extortionate prices and because the average Riverite possessed a defunct palate incapable of savouring the varied nuances of the establishment's fine epicurean fare.

"Anything else for you, James?" Susan said, avarice darkling her eyes as she snipped a square of tape from the dispenser and secured the parchment-wrapped triangle of overpriced cheddar.

"Ooh, your soup, the chicken noodle? I'm afraid it's all Ellen can keep down these days."

Susan donned a facet of deep sympathy. "I'll do you an extra large."

I bet you will, thought James. "Thanking you kindly, and I'll take a double espresso at the far table – actually, make it two, Steven should be here any minute."

"I've not seen your brother in a while, how is Steven?"

"We shall soon see." James stepped away from Susan and between the circular tables to the one positioned farthest from her counter. He slipped his heavy overcoat from his shoulders and draped it over the back of his chair. He sat and stretched his spine straight, rolling his neck; tension was beginning to curdle his thick flesh. He was in need of a massage. Perhaps he should make arrangements, he could do with some special time.

The old-fashioned brass bell above the door tinkled merrily as his younger brother, Steven, swept into the store with a serious, almost panicked expression. James felt the flesh on either side of his spine bunch and cramp further.

Susan's welcome was cut rudely short as Steven hurried past her, bumping his shin on a chair as he headed to James's corner table.

James may have been smiling, but anyone who may have seen his eyes dart quickly towards Susan at the counter, a glance so quickly devious it was almost imperceptible, would have seen the essence of something in polar contradiction to his outward jollity.

James was still smiling as he addressed his brother. "Sit and calm yourself. You're making a scene and you'll set tongues a-wagging."

Steven took the chair opposite his brother, his back to the window. He blinked in rapid succession, a child facing a vicious interlocutor.

"And put that away," snapped James from behind his grin. He was referring to the pink enamelled heart pendant on a delicate silver chain around his brother's neck.

Steven frowned and felt for the necklace, his fingers found it. He played with it affectionately before tucking it behind the neck of his t-shirt. "It's okay, I tell people that it was Mum's and then they don't ask again."

"Interesting," James said. "Smile. Now."

Steven followed the command as Susan approached with two small espresso cups and placed them on the table. "Gentlemen," she said.

"Bless you." James nodded and then watched her with hawk-like intensity as she returned to her counter. He became more at ease when the door's bell heralded the arrival of two new customers whose presence diverted attention further from the brothers.

Steven leaned in conspiratorially. "Quispe's been murdered."

James's true nature flashed across his face momentarily. "*Tristan*. *Tristan* has been murdered."

"But I thought…we should use *our* names…so that…"

James hushed his brother. "Steven, Steven, Steven. How I wish you had been an abortion. Those names are very, very private. Not to be bandied about with abandon. You know that."

"I'm sorry." Steven rubbed his knuckles nervously. "What if…"

"What if…what if…" James mocked Steven and then sipped his drink, eyeing his brother coldly, the rim of the cup barely hiding his disdain. He took a blue cotton handkerchief from his inside jacket pocket and dabbed his pursed lips. "This matter does not now and will never concern us."

"But don't you think we should have a meeting? I'm sure they're all nervous. First Yupan, sorry, *Glen*, now Tristan."

James sucked his teeth. "Glen was incarcerated, *brother dear*, a very different fate to that of Tristan's, don't you think? Drink – your – coffee – goddammit! or, so help me, I'll pour it down that pathetic gullet of yours."

Steven's hands trembled as he lifted the small mug to his lips. "I hate espresso," he said sheepishly.

James smiled. "I know."

Steven sipped and winced at the bitter taste upon his tongue. He studied his drink. "I think we should speak to Apu."

James slammed his espresso cup to the table with such force that it shattered. He jumped out of and away from his chair, wiping the droplets of coffee from his trousers. "Clumsy me! I'm very sorry, Susan."

Susan and her two customers were looking over at the Bartholomew brothers, alerted by the crash of porcelain. "Don't you fret, James. Would you like another?"

"Honestly, I should really be getting back to Ellen. Could you ready my bill? I *am* sorry about the mess."

"Oh, don't you worry about that," said Susan, eagerly totting up James's bill before turning the debit machine and placing it on the section of counter nearest to him. "Machine's ready when you are."

"Thanking you kindly," said James as he slipped his arms into his overcoat and shrugged it up to his shoulders. "Well, Steven, I wish I could stay longer but I must get home."

Steven nodded and tried to smile, his wide eyes trained upon his brother.

James stepped around the table and bent down to speak into Steven's ear. "If I ever hear that sacred name cross those fetid lips of yours again, I will kill you myself. Don't make me question your inclusion, Steven."

Steven remained seated and didn't even move when a rivulet of black coffee reached his side of the table and rushed over the edge to dribble into his crotch. Steven didn't dare move until he heard the chime of the teller drawer and the rip of the receipt and finally, the blissful tinkle of the brass bell above the door as James left the store.

Only then did Steven exhale and sweep the wetness from his jeans. He looked over his shoulder, out into the dark street as he heard his brother's booming voice shout a happy greeting to a passerby.

He watched his brother disappear from sight before he reached for his collar and flicked the pink heart pendant free of it. He twirled it affectionately in his fingers.

CHAPTER 11 - BAT SHIT

It felt like a lifetime ago that Ali yearned daily for peace and quiet and would become trapped in deep reveries of finding herself completely alone and locked away from humankind. During those years of hellish mental inquietude, when her depression had gripped her so tight she could barely breathe, absolute solitude had seemed to her like an elusive, utopian state, one where she could be allowed to rest and recuperate and perhaps restrain her bulging brain matter. She craved nothingness so desperately that the desire for it had driven her to attempt, on several occasions, to achieve the ultimate solitude. Eternal nothingness.

However, now that she was beginning to redress the balance of her mind and found herself existing in relative equilibrium, being alone had lost its allure. As such, she had begun to dread solitude as if therein lay a hidden gateway, a door to her old hell, the hinges lubricated by the potential unmasking of her own disguised fragility; that, during times when she was alone and her surroundings were peaceful enough to allow for true introspective thinking, that sinister entryway could open up again and allow free passage to a bevy of baying devils otherwise battened down by her determined will – tougher than teak – which protected her from her ultimate fear: the prospect of losing her mind. The prospect of utter madness.

Ali finally tracked Marlene down – arms outstretched with a serene smile on her face and her heavy breasts bobbing as if they were as light as helium balloons – in the hotel's jacuzzi.

"What was the point of me buying you a cell phone if you never have it with you, McKean?"

On hearing Ali's voice, Marlene opened one eye and held up a finger, "No cell phones in the spa area. There's a sign on the desk."

Ali put her hands on her hips, "Nice afternoon?"

Marlene sighed happily and closed her eye again. "Mmm. First I had a hot stone massage…" she suddenly sat upright and looked at Ali, "…actually, first I arranged for a hire car to be dropped off here by a local Hertz company and *then* I had a hot stone massage." Marlene pushed off the side of the hot tub and floated across to rest upon the edge nearest to Ali, leaning her elbows on the lip of the bubbling pool, "You know what a hot stone massage is?"

"I've never had one," said Ali as she slipped off her boots and socks and rolled her trousers up to her knees.

"Well," continued Marlene as Ali sat next to her and dipped her tired feet into the warm water, "They heat up some stones – I'm talking actual stones, like you can pick up off any beach – and then they put them on you, in a line, down your spine."

"Huh. Was it nice?"

"Not really. The massage afterwards was but that only lasted about five minutes, for the other twenty-five minutes of the session I was face down with hot bloody rocks on my back. I could do that! Pick up some rocks from the beach, stick them in my stove and charge you seventy-nine bucks. I'll tell you this, if I went home to Peter and did it to him, he'd have me locked up in a looney bin faster than a rabbit can chew a carrot."

Ali smiled. "It's all gimmicky shit. Some of it actually *is* shit, too. I saw one treatment on the brochure, the guano facial? You know what guano is?"

"It rings a bell."

"It's bat shit."

"What?"

"Yep. Bat shit."

Marlene pondered the idea. "Is it good for wrinkles?"

"No! It's like any shit, maybe good for bomb-making or as a fertilizer but that's it. Actually, it can be deadly if you breathe it in. Toxic. Biological waste. We excrete stuff for a reason. If it was good for us – or for bats – you think we'd shit it out?"

"Ha! Now then, I think bats nest in my attic. I bet that facial was pricey too. I could make a fortune back in Mochetsin, charge the locals for hot stone massages and bat poop facials, maybe convert Peter's tool shed into a spa. So, anyhoo, tell me about our dead guy, Hon."

Ali kicked her feet lazily through the water. "This may be a short and sweet one. Looks like a crime of passion, possibly at the hands of a disgruntled lover."

"Hey, we might have time to go and see that burl after all. So, you done for the night?"

"Yep. Briefing in the morning. Actually, I think I might grab my suit and join you."

"You do that, girl. Then we'll have a nice dinner, maybe rent a movie then have an early night. What d'you say?"

Before Ali could respond, her phone signalled the arrival of a message – a message from Cuzzocrea.

"An inspector calls?" asked Marlene with a giggle as she pushed herself back to the opposite side of the jacuzzi again.

Ali pulled back from the water and stood, gathering her boots and socks in her arms. "Go ahead and eat without me." Ali frowned. "Looks like I might have gotten it wrong."

"Well that's a first," said Marlene, waving to Ali as she left through the door to the spa changing area.

"Guano," Marlene said to the empty room.

CHAPTER 12 - LOONIES, TOONIES AND BITS

First Tommy's home-alone class runs over and then, as Maiden and he wait to cross the street, a crappy old Corolla swings around the corner, too close to the curb and sloshes into the puddled rain, sending it upwards over them both, high enough to soak Tommy all the way to his waist.

Back in the Community Centre, Maiden dries Tommy's clothes under the electrical hand dryer in the disabled toilet on the ground floor. She begins to worry. Tommy is already getting a cold; his little nostrils have sported a bright green crust of dried snot ever since their trek back from Eden Falls on Monday night.

With one arm still inside a trouser leg, Maiden feels blindly inside the little zipped pouch in the lining of her bag and scoops coins into her palm. She takes out the change and is heartened to see a couple of loonies and one toonie amongst the spattering of quarters, dimes and fives. She wonders if she'll have enough to stretch to a bottle of cold and flu stuff as well as the bread they need for tonight and for Tommy's lunch tomorrow. She doesn't think so but maybe she can afford a packet of lozenges.

As they leave the bathroom a grumpy custodian wearing yellow ear protectors is polishing the corridor's already shiny floor with a noisy machine but, over the monotone hum, Maiden hears the excited giggles and shrill conversation of a group of girls all trying to look like one Kardashian or another. The girls are about her age and are each drinking from expensive-looking, brightly-coloured bottles – the type of bottles that have a water filter built into the lid. They seem to be on a break from the hip-hop class in full swing in the main hall. Maiden feels the thudding bass of the music from within against her chest.

As she and Tommy pass them, the girls point and don't attempt to hide their giggled and cruel amusement. Maiden thinks maybe it is because Tommy's jeans have stiffened as they've dried and he keeps pulling at his crotch as he walks with equally stiffened legs, complaining that his jeans are rubbing against his skin. Maiden shoots a look back over her shoulder at the obvious ringleader of the group and communicates a silent threat. It works and the Kardashian wannabe blushes and pushes the double doors of the hall open, returning to the relative safety of the booming hip-hop session.

The dark of the moonless night descends and the high street becomes darker still. They round the corner and cross paths with the man she had earlier watched snuff out the flames of his birthday candles, James Bartholomew. Illuminated by the light cast from within the posh cheese shop on the corner, he sweeps past them, seemingly sheltered from the persistent precipitation as if shielded by an invisible force field. His overcoat flaps out behind him like the cape of a comic book villain and Maiden wonders, if James Bartholomew had been standing at the crossing forty-five minutes earlier, would the same rusty car have splashed dirty water up his legs or would his aura have repelled the puddle too?

"Kristen! Bundle up now, it's going to be a frigid night." James Bartholomew's voice booms loudly to them.

Maiden pulls Tommy back by his shoulders and hugs him to her under the shallow, yellow awning of the shop. As she watches the giant pass them she can smell warmth emanating from him – body heat and dryer sheets and coffee. A fat glob of freezing water drops from the vinyl awning above them and splats violently against Tommy's forehead, making him jump from her arms. Maiden takes her Kleenex from up her sleeve and dabs the wetness dry, then folds the tissue and pinches it around her brother's nose. Tommy winces and almost steps into the path of a harried old lady.

"Blow, through your nose," Maiden says.

The old lady pauses and stares at Maiden. Maiden wonders what the hell is up with people tonight.

Stuffing the tissue into her pocket, Maiden wonders if it is worth nipping back to the Community Centre to steal some bathroom tissue for later but, since they have a long walk ahead of them all the way past Home Depot and across the highway to Walmart, she decides she would rather wait and grab some from the store's toilets instead. It is best to make a move since they'll have to turn around after Walmart and walk all the way back home. Of course, she can buy bread somewhere else but Wednesday is a great night for picking up some half-price, pink-sticker bakery deals and may therefore leave enough over for something to remedy her little brother's cold. She just hopes the walk doesn't make him sicker and, as they step up to the crossing, Maiden holds Tommy back from the puddled gutter so they don't get soaked all over again.

A bell tinkles somewhere and the noise is so sweet that Maiden turns to see where it has come from. But the reason for the kind jingle is anything but sweet or kind. Sinchi Roca is standing in the doorway to the cheese shop, zipping what looks like a warm and waterproof jacket up around his chin of stubble.

Maiden hates that she knows his stubble scratches and always leaves a rash.

His eyes barely came to rest on hers but the moment shared is long enough for her to see recognition in his eyes and a sly nod in place of his brother's garrulous charlatanry.

Maiden watches Sinchi Roca head south on the high street and feels the tug of her brother's little hand in hers as the crossing began its impatient countdown from ten. Maiden hardly notices stepping through the puddle, so intent is she on him – her next one. She has to will her eager eyes to peel their focus from him and to concentrate on keeping Tommy safe as they cross.

Once on the other side of the street, Maiden glances back again and watches as the man meanders through the crowd of pedestrians on their way home to cosy houses and sleek apartments, too busy to know that they have bumped shoulders with a truly sick man, one capable of evils they're lucky never to have to comprehend.

Maiden smiles down at her brother as he readjusts his crotch again and sniffs deeply. And she wishes so much that they too could experience the bliss of such ignorance, and they too could rush home out of the rain to warmth and dryness, to a safe place with bread in the cupboard and fancy cups with water filters on them. A real home where clothes smell of dryer sheets and coffee, where a little boy's sickness is allayed and soothed and where Maiden doesn't have to hide her bag of severed bits.

CHAPTER 13 - CANDIES AND COOLERS

Hollyrood Estates was the epitome of the middle-class suburban subdivision. Perfectly manicured front lawns dotted with circular cut-outs containing barely established Japanese maples and shaped boxwood separated by large, grey boulders and weedless black mulch.

Each house was slightly different to the next yet all sported HardiePlank siding in varied yet complementary hues of greens and greys, blues and even black with the odd burgundy or yellow house thrown in for added diversity. Pathways were lit and soffits glowed. Every house, no doubt, possessed at least one expensive vehicle yet all were secreted in integral double garages big enough in themselves, perhaps, to comfortably house entire families.

Hollyrood Estates was a tangible example of dominance mimicry at play and Ali guessed that each homeowner must have mortgaged their way up the ladder of materialism and taken the leap onto the hedonic treadmill under the naive and mistaken belief that by merely possessing the same objects as those who appeared to be happy and successful (*rich people*), they would somehow attain the same level of happiness and success. Ali counted twenty-six homes from her position on the street, each worthy of a *House Beautiful* cover shoot, and knew it defied statistical probability that every owner had the financial means to actually buy their house.

Ali wriggled her arms into her Tyvek coverall and zipped

it up, ensuring every strand of her hair was safely netted inside the elasticated hood. "The Beverly Hills of Cedar River," she said.

"Legoland," said Cuzzocrea, perched on the edge of his open trunk, stretching the ankles of his suit over his boots.

"Tell me, where do people find the money for homes like this in a town with no industry? The pulp mill shut the year I arrived here. As far as I can tell, the only available jobs are for waitresses, shop workers or strippers."

Cuzzocrea stood and zipped up his suit. "Most of the guys who were laid off when the mill closed found work on the oil sands in Fort McMurray or Port Alberni, at the pulp mill there."

"Hence, all the lonely housewives," said Ali, tucking her coverall sleeves into her gloves.

"Yep. But the money doesn't seem to run out. Everyone I know here has a couple of cars, an RV, a boat and goes to Puerto Vallarta at least twice a year."

"Their bubble will burst. Once the recession finally hits this place, these lawns will be peppered with foreclosure signs."

Cuzzocrea nodded. "It hit. About five years later than for the rest of the world, but it hit. Target already closed down. It was only open for a year. Here you go." Cuzzocrea handed Ali a pair of bootees ready to don once they'd crossed the threshold of the house before them.

Ali looked up at the home. "This might cause a drop in house prices."

"A good murder usually does, especially somewhere like this where there's no anonymity. We already had a press enquiry from the Editor-in-Chief of *The Echo*." Cuzzocrea slammed his trunk shut.

Ali held the yellow crime scene tape up for him to duck under as he nodded towards the uniformed RCMP officer who stood sentry at the home's boundary and who was responsible for keeping the log which Ali and Cuzzocrea signed, marking down the exact time of their arrival at the house. Cuzzocrea and Ali approached the front door. Once they had donned their bootees, Cuzzocrea stood aside to allow Ali to enter before him.

"This isn't a date, Cuzzocrea. After you," she said, adamantly.

Another uniformed officer, this time guarding the foot of a curved staircase, was about to direct Ali and Cuzzocrea to the crime scene but was too late to do so since they had both ascended the stairs automatically, following the tell-tale sign of an active crime scene investigation: the overly bright light emanating from one of the upstairs rooms.

"You know I'm not going to let you forget this, if you were wrong about McMenemy being a one off," said Cuzzocrea over his shoulder.

"Whatever."

"It's only fair."

"Look, Cuzzocrea," said Ali as she followed him along the landing towards the lights, "technically I was merely premature and, as we women have been conditioned to say to men guilty of the same: it's okay, it can happen to anyone, *honey*."

Cuzzocrea was, Ali thought, about to laugh but the hint of amusement on his face was immediately eradicated as he turned into the doorway of the crime scene proper. Following him in, Ali was less interested in the body on the floor than with the patterns adorning the walls.

"Stay back! I haven't cleared this scene yet!"

Trina Walsh's voice rang out in its signature seagull-peal way – a tone that always reminded Ali of her mother's shrill and frequent admonishments and triggered long suppressed synapses, placing Trina Walsh at the receiving end of a neurological association that had Ali's fists balling and her inner troll squirming.

Deliberately ignoring Trina, Ali stepped carefully past Cuzzocrea, placing herself between him and Walsh. Superintendent Shaw, who was leaning against a large dresser to their left, began:

"Danny Gilbert. Twenty-eight. His body was discovered by his father, Peter Gilbert, upon his return from work at approximately five-fifteen this evening."

"Doug?" said Trina Walsh to Superintendent Shaw.

"Yes Trina?"

"I'd like to clear the scene please."

Ali sighed. "Get over yourself, Walsh. We're all familiar with crime scene etiquette. Nobody's going to piss on your chips."

"Excuse me?"

Trina was affronted which only served to delight Ali. "The symbols. On the walls…" said Ali pointing to the triangles, hearts and butterflies painted in glittery pastels around the pink and blue walls.

"What does that even mean? *Piss on my chips*?" said Trina, in a voice that surpassed even her ability to peal.

Ali looked the woman in the eye for the first time since entering the room. "I'm more qualified to be in this room than you are, Trina, so see if you can tuck that ego of yours away and gather your evidence while Cuzzocrea and I do our job."

Trina's eyes widened, her head snapped around to Superintendent Shaw. "Doug? A word? Outside, please."

Doug Shaw huffed and followed Trina out of the bedroom, throwing Ali a playful scowl as he passed her.

"Symbols?" asked Cuzzocrea.

"Look at the patterns, the shapes themselves," said Ali.

Cuzzocrea scanned the walls, carefully analysing the shapes. Ali's point quickly dawned on him. "Oh shit."

Ali nodded and turned. She pulled open the doors to the closet behind them both. "Kids clothes but no regular, daily clothes. Costumes. Dress-up clothes."

Cuzzocrea opened a small drinks fridge next to the dresser and held it open for Ali to see its contents. "Candies and coolers."

Ali looked at the body of Danny Gilbert, taking in the multiple stab wounds to his torso and a yawning hole gaped up at her where the man's penis had once been. Ali and Cuzzocrea shared a look.

"You thinking what I'm thinking?" asked Cuzzocrea.

Ali's lips thinned as she crouched down alongside Danny Gilbert. She carefully reached under his right arm and rocked his weight away from her just enough to look at the skin on the underside of his shoulder. "Fuck," she murmured to herself.

"Damn it," said Cuzzocrea, standing from where he had crouched behind Ali to look at the dead man's shoulder with her.

Ali sucked at her teeth. "Let's let Strap-a-dick-to-me have her crime scene, we'll talk to Shaw, share our suspicions and what we discovered earlier regarding McMenemy."

"Yep," agreed Cuzzocrea, "but first, I'll find Munro, he's probably taking the father's statement. Ensure that we're not jumping to any conclusions here."

"Right," Ali said.

Cuzzocrea left. Ali studied the room. Her stomach clenched as her eyes came to rest upon a large plasma screen on top of the dresser alongside which was a DVD player and a small HD camcorder. Ali swallowed. Dead bodies, she could take. Vicious, violent injury. Mutilations, decapitations, blunt force trauma and even crime scenes where body bags were less use than shovels and hoses but now, standing in this aesthetically charming room, Ali felt sick.

Ali had already crossed to the door before she noticed Trina Walsh standing there, glaring at her. Ali stepped up to her. "All yours. Oh, and don't forget to snap a few of that tattoo behind his shoulder for me."

Trina fumed as Ali threw her a cheeky wink and stepped out to speak to Superintendent Shaw, who was leaning over the bannister rail.

"Well? What do you see?" asked Shaw.

"Not good. It's going to be a grim case," said Ali, peeling off her surgical gloves.

"Go on."

"Mind if I just consult with Cuzzocrea first?"

Shaw smiled. "You mean, do I mind if you sneak off for a ciggie outside? Five minutes and then I want you both back here so you can bring me up to speed, understood?"

"If you think that's wise," said Ali.

"Why wouldn't it be wise?"

"Maybe back at wherever you've set up the squad room? I'd be uncomfortable sharing my thoughts in the same house as his father."

"Fair enough, we're at the local station at the top end of Dogwood, you're in Rey's car anyway, right?"

Ali nodded.

"Oh, and…" Shaw lowered his voice to a whisper, "…if you could, please try to get along with Trina, my life would be one thousand percent easier if you two stopped butting heads."

"Takes two to tango. Did you suggest the same to her?" asked Ali.

"She says you're not a team player – actually, she said you're not a *girl's girl*, whatever that means," Shaw said with a baffled shrug.

"Well, I haven't thought of myself as a *girl* since I was eleven and my first period stained my knickers, so she could be right," Ali replied before heading out for a hit of nicotine which she hoped would untwist the coil of dread now knotting up her insides.

CHAPTER 14 - ELLEN

The rhythmic flow of the ventilator punctuated by the soft click of the automated stop valve would be, to anyone else, a sound synonymous with peace. But to James Bartholomew it was the sound of an ancient grandfather clock ticking down the seconds, programmed to cease upon the final moment, the death of the withered soul of Ellen Bartholomew.

Once considered a formidable woman – a bit of a battle-ax – now her once-intimidating, stout form lay diminutively under the thin spread of blankets, giving her skeletal frame the look of vacuum-sealed meat. James remembered how the former school principal could command the thrall of an entire room full of attention-deficient teenagers without uttering more than a few syllables.

A shaft of light, a warm triangle of gold, was snuffed as quickly as it had appeared across the foot of the bed as Lana, Ellen's carer, stepped out of the en-suite bathroom clutching a bundle of damp towels and cloths. She dropped the bundle onto a larger one comprised of sheets and Ellen's blue nightie before she noticed that James had entered the room.

Lana tipped her head sideways in a show of empathy, "James. Welcome home."

"Good evening, Lana. How's our girl?"

Ellen grunted from her place on the bed. Four bony, spear-like fingers reached for Lana, mere inches from the mattress, but it was a display of what must surely have been an exhausting feat of strength on Ellen's part.

Lana smiled. "Funny how she always knows you're here. We have had a very good day. We washed, didn't we, Ellen? We changed all of our sheets." Lana crossed to Ellen and took her skeletal hand. "And the hospice team were here at two with Doctor Woods and they changed all of the important ins and outs for us. She's had all of her meds for today so she should sleep soundly tonight."

Lana was in her mid-fifties and was a motherly, barrel-bodied former critical care nurse who now dedicated her expertise to in-home palliative hospice care as part of the province's Quality Dying Initiative.

Ellen had initially made firm arrangements to complete her final transition in Strathcona House, the hospice on Witty Lane, near the SPCA Centre, but when her disease had progressed in a more aggressive fashion than previously expected and the transformation had begun, James had persuaded Ellen that it would be more dignified for her to pass privately. So shocking was her appearance now that James's confidence in his decision was renewed every night that he returned and saw her afresh.

Lana stepped around the bed, gathering the bundle of laundry into her arms as she did. She whispered close to James's ear, "If anything changes, we're all on standby. Don't hesitate to call me and I'll ready the team." She laid her gentle palm on his upper arm. "It won't be long now."

James patted Lana's hand. "Thanking you kindly, Lana. There's a tub of your favourite soup downstairs. I took the liberty of picking some up for you as I passed Cheese Heaven on my way home tonight."

"James, you shouldn't have. You're a very kind man. I'll be back at dawn."

James listened as Lana pulled the bedroom door closed with an apologetic click and headed downstairs. He heard the ticking twist of the washer's knob and saw the solitary lamp dim as the machine hummed into life and the sound of hot water flooding its drum. Moments later Lana's car reversed from his driveway.

James took the armchair positioned next to the ventilator, his eyes trained on the shadows beneath the bed. The chair was positioned so that Lana could easily administer the pain-relieving, time consuming massages to the bones of Ellen's fragile spine. Lana claimed that the rubbing and caressing made all the difference to the 'poor dears' suffering from Ellen's rare type of bone cancer. James not only marvelled at the selfless patience Lana had to sit for hours at a time rubbing and smoothing Ellen's calcifications but also at how the woman could even bring herself to touch the jagged outcroppings that pressed angrily against his wife's crêpe-like skin.

James readied himself, bolstering his courage and finally allowed his eyes to move up the sheets, all the way to the top where pointy, misshapen shoulders met a twisted, crooked collar bone in the centre of which, where once a charming 'v' had cupped a throat, were the spiky, crystalline stalagmites of a hedgehogesque growth that pushed rudely against his wife's already ghostly white skin.

He wondered if the spikes would snap and break against his palm if he were to press down on top of them or if they would remain resolute, concrete in consistency and burst her thin skin to pierce his own flesh.

And the face. Oh, God. The horror of that face.

While James could never have honestly described Ellen as beautiful, he did once use the word 'striking'. Little did he know that his choice of adjective was a prophetic hint at his wife's future because the face before him now was indeed *striking.*

Her chordoma had manifested itself in an asymmetrical deformity of her jaw. The result was something he had previously imagined to be the stuff reserved for gory movies or rubber Halloween masks. While the left side of Ellen's jaw had crumbled and disintegrated in response to the dark and hungry monster that is cancer, the right side of her mandible had bloomed forth, fattened with mound after mound of hard, mushroom-shaped growths as if the disease itself felt guilty for its own work and had attempted to compensate for its destruction.

And, in a further attempt at an apology, it had added more mass to her forehead so that now the grotesquely protuberant skull jutted out so far from her spattering of wispy hair that its sheer weight was beginning to tip over the socket of her left eye – the cancer seemed intent upon snuffing the eye from existence yet it was too cruel to snuff out the woman herself.

James's face twisted into the grimace of distaste that was his only sincere reaction in response to the sight of his elephant-skulled spouse. He clenched his fist over his mouth and trembled. As if his terror at the sight of her were not as much as any man could bear, now he could see she was looking at him. There she was, watching him baulk behind his hand.

Her eyes were barely solid things anymore; it was as if her pale irises floated in small bowls of milk. The effect was all the more pronounced as he watched the milky pools glisten further and shine with disappointment. James stood and turned from her, uttering the only kindness he could muster:

"Sleep well, my love."

As he left the room, James Bartholomew tried to ignore the guttural sob he heard force itself past vocal chords raped by a thickly concertinaed tracheostomy tube and he wondered what kind of cruel god would wish this hell upon him.

CHAPTER 15 - BORROWED WARMTH

The best thing about living in a Mamisîw House is that when Mum forgets or doesn't have the money to pay the gas company, there's still some heat on a cold night. With Tommy's mattress on the floor running lengthways along the wall between their house and the neighbour's, he can benefit from the warmth being belted out of next door's baseboard heaters.

Tommy's head is in his sister's lap and she strokes his hair between his hacking coughs and sniffles. Simba and Nala, adolescent lions by this point in the movie, have found each other after years of separation and are tumbling over each other in a display of love and playful fighting.

The Lion King is Tommy's favourite movie but the tape has been scratched after years of repeated play and so the Simba/Nala reunion is always the start of the movie for them. Earlier scenes are simply unwatchable and will skip, freeze or randomly pixelate but at least Maiden is spared having to answer questions about Simba's dad dying. Tommy has placed Mufasa upon a paternal pedestal ever since he was old enough to be devastated by the fatal stampede and Simba's heartbreak at being blamed for his father's death.

Tonight Maiden hopes that Tommy will fall asleep early. Her whole body is sore and she still has to wash her clothes. She'll have to show up at school tomorrow. She can't risk the school counsellor, Mrs. Mooney – or *Colleen*, as she prefers to be called (like it makes her more approachable) – sticking her nose in where it isn't needed and calling Child Protective Services again.

Tommy coughs and something feels like it is rattling beneath his ribs. Maiden rubs his back and feels her eyelids begin to close. The wall behind her is toasty warm and every now and then she can hear yelps of pleasure and giggles picking their way through the drywall. The Devereuxs are a new family in the apartment block. They seem happy. Nice. They won't stay long. The nice families never stay long.

She's noticed that the Devereuxs have put up their Christmas decorations, or at least the mum has while the kids have been at school. Maiden and Tommy had peeked in at the sparkly fairy lights through the front window of 3C as they'd arrived home after their trek back from Walmart.

Maiden wonders how nice it must be to spend a cold, rainy evening next door. A mum, a dad, three kids and a puppy. The baseboards banging out so much warmth you won't need your coat on top of your comforter for extra warmth *and* that coat will be dry because you've probably gotten back from Walmart in a car anyhow.

She wonders what the Devereuxs have eaten for supper. Probably something healthy. Mum has taken to calling Mrs. Devereux 'Granola' on account of her being a health nut, running every morning and always wearing sneakers. The thought makes Maiden feel a whole lot better because there's no way Tommy would swap his peanut butter and jam sandwiches for a plate of broccoli or stupid kale.

She wonders what Peter Gilbert will be eating tonight. She guesses maybe it won't be broccoli, kale *or* peanut butter and jam. She guesses Peter Gilbert might not eat anything at all. Not after getting home and seeing his fat, retard son dead in the playroom.

A scream jolts Maiden from her half-sleep and makes her heart jump to the left inside her chest. But the scream isn't anything to worry about; it is a happy scream from one of the kids next door.

Maiden slips herself carefully out from under Tommy's honey-coloured hair, her thigh immediately missing the warmth of his fevered cheek. She creeps out of the room, leaving *The Lion King* playing at a low volume, and makes her way along the short hallway. Her backpack is lying against the front door where she dropped it when they arrived home. She tiptoes back along the cracked linoleum runner, checking on Mum in the living room on her way to the kitchen.

The backpack is wet and so is everything in it so she lays a bathroom towel out across the kitchen table and places the contents of her bag on top of it, opening the books in the middle and laying them face down so the pages might dry. She finds her silver iPod and checks that it hasn't gotten too wet. It is her most precious belonging and it was given to her by the man whose blood she will now have to rub out of her best jeans and her Coca-Cola hoodie.

Before Maiden fills the sink, she pops her head through Tommy's open bedroom door – she thinks she can hear him gently snoring. She takes the Ziploc bag to her closet, baffled that there seems to be more blood in it now than there was back in the playroom earlier. Maiden chews the lid of her black sharpie as she writes the name 'Cápac' on the white strip reserved for labelling the bag's contents or for noting what date a nice mum like Mrs. Devereux might have deposited a chicken breast in her freezer.

Maiden runs her fingers over the rigid blue closure to make sure the bag is securely sealed then tucks Danny Gilbert's dick in amongst the old dolls and stuffies she keeps on the shelf next to her underwear box. The scruffiest of all the teddy bears, the one with a missing eye, is wearing a necklace of elbow macaroni painted with pink nail varnish. Maiden remembers the day she made it: it was the day Apu picked her up from kindergarten and took her to meet his friends for the first time.

CHAPTER 16 - THE SQUAD ROOM

While Ali searched for and saved all the images they would need to brief Superintendent Shaw, Cuzzocrea was on his knees hooking up various wires and cables to her laptop for it to communicate with the interactive whiteboard at the front of the large, neglected office space that was their makeshift squad room.

"Doesn't this sort of shit work without wires these days?" she said.

"Huh?"

"Like with Bluetooth or Wi-Fi or something?"

Cuzzocrea's silence was enough to let Ali know her questions weren't helping ease his frustration with the antiquated system.

A mist of the night's rain was still netted atop Cuzzocrea's dark hair. A vein pumped healthily in his temple as a trickle of the moisture traced its crooked course and headed for his cheek. Before she knew what she was doing Ali reached out and stopped it in its path with her index finger. The feeling of Cuzzocrea's soft skin, still kissed with the memory of a summer long gone, moved through her like poison, sparking a flurry of palpitations, then finished its journey by pulsing thickly, deeply. Privately.

Cuzzocrea stilled. Cables in hand, he lifted his eyes to hers. Ali pulled her finger away.

"Sorry," she said, suddenly feeling like she'd been caught peeking through a keyhole. She was saved from her awkwardness by the unmistakable ding that signalled the arrival of an elevator down the corridor outside the office.

"Cool, they're here. I need a pee." said Ali, hearing the chatter of Shaw and the rest of the VIIMIS team on their approach to the room. Ali passed Shaw as she headed to find the ladies room.

"You okay?" asked Shaw, carrying a large, flat box of Tim Horton's doughnuts.

"Yes, I'm just going to the ladies."

Once Ali had recovered from the embarrassment that had mottled her décolletage, she returned to the squad room with a stern look upon her face, determined not to allow herself to be distracted again. Shaw was standing at the front of the space with his shirt sleeves rolled to his elbows, running through the facts of the case.

Munro picked through the box of doughnuts until he found a sufficiently chocolatey one then sat heavily in a nearby chair to listen and consume. Ali smiled a silent hello to him and then to Eden Harrington – the team's Special Victims officer – as she passed her. Paul Abbott, the officer in charge of missing persons, moved his legs aside so Ali could step past him and take a seat in the chair Cuzzocrea had set next to his own. In his typical unassuming style, Cuzzocrea had positioned himself, and therefore Ali, at the rear of the gathered team.

"Munro already confirmed the father's alibi, multiple witnesses said he was in his store all day since the early hours of this morning.

"We have uni's doing house to house and canvassing the area. So far, no eyewitnesses to anyone leaving or arriving at the house however it is the kind of area where people are out most of the day. We'll keep on it and see what turns up, you never know. No sign of forced entry so our perp was either there by invitation or had access to the house. The father, Peter Gilbert, claims that only he and his son had keys."

"Wife? Mother?" asked Cuzzocrea.

Shaw shook his head. "The mother took off years ago. Peter and Danny have lived alone together ever since. Danny Gilbert, our deceased, attends a local learning disabled centre, his father indicated his son had an IQ equivalent to that of a young child's."

"What did the father say about the room? Whose is it? Danny's?" asked Cuzzocrea.

Munro cleared his throat and dislodged a piece of doughnut from a rear molar with his tongue before answering. "Nope. A guest bedroom."

"Do they have many young children in their extended family?" Ali asked Munro.

"No. No extended family at all. The only other relative was the deceased's paternal grandfather who passed away two years ago. Neither of them have any interaction with the mother's side of the family."

Ali wanted to take notes. Realizing she'd left her notebook and pen in her handbag, she left Cuzzocrea to retrieve her bag and pulled out what she needed from it. Returning to him she wrote: *think we have enough to support our theory yet?* Cuzzocrea read the message and shook his head, then shrugged. Ali was eager to switch gears, to brief Shaw on their shared belief but trusted Cuzzocrea's wariness.

"So, we need to find the mother," Shaw said. "They were never divorced so we can work on the assumption that she still goes by the name Sarah Gilbert. Paul, I want you on that. Peter Gilbert told us he last had an address for her up in Gold River. I believe Munro made a note of it, check with him."

"Sir." Corporal Abbott relocated himself immediately and took a desk along the rear wall of the squad room. Ali liked Abbott, he was fervently enthusiastic and, his shyness notwithstanding, was as valuable a member of the VIIMIS team as any of them.

"You thinking the mother off'd the kid, Supe?" asked Munro.

Shaw shrugged. "It's a line. She left him when he was just a little guy, who knows, maybe she had issues regarding his disabilities. Worth looking into. We also need to consider motive. Who had anything to gain by killing Danny?"

"The father's probably wealthy," said Munro as he scrunched up a paper napkin and rolled it between his palms. "Owns his own business and those houses on that subdivision don't come cheap."

"Siblings? Anyone stand to inherit money if Danny's out of the way?" Cuzzocrea suggested.

"Nope, unless Peter has fathered illegitimate children we don't yet know about. Anything like that's bound to come out of the closet as the investigation continues. I know Cedar Riverites, they're only too eager to break the boredom with gossip."

Ali nudged Cuzzocrea. He nodded and raised a hand to snare Shaw's attention. "Sir, may I suggest looking into the father, Peter Gilbert, in other areas too?"

"Specifically any computers at the home," Ali added.

Shaw grimaced. "You know how tricky that stuff is. I can't imagine we'd be issued a warrant for search and seizure of a grieving father's property following the brutal murder of his only son. We'd need something. Something big first and then we'd have to bring in a tech. Why? Is this linked to whatever you two are working on?"

"Yes, sir."

The elevator dinged from the corridor and Trina Walsh brought a blast of the outdoors in on her dripping wet VIIMIS windcheater which she removed and shook noisily before discarding it on a nearby desk and perching herself atop another one, closer to Shaw. She sniffed loudly.

"Trina. All finished there?" asked Shaw.

Trina ran her wrist under her wet nose. "My team's finishing up. The body was transferred to the morgue at Cedar River General."

"Good." Shaw turned his attention back to Cuzzocrea and Ali. "So, where are you guys on this? I know you spotted something back there. Ali, what are you seeing?"

"I don't think a warrant will be as tricky as you think when you take a look at the contents of the HD camera that was in the room," Ali said.

"You touched the camera?" Trina Walsh interrupted.

Ali didn't look at her but shook her head. "We will inevitably have to but no, I didn't. I can imagine what's on there."

"I'm lost," said Trina smugly. "We're using our imaginations here, are we?"

Ali stood and stepped up to the laptop. She typed in her password on the lock screen and spoke to Cuzzocrea who had stepped up behind her, "Will this just come up on the whiteboard?"

Cuzzocrea leaned across Ali and typed in a series of shortcut commands. The interactive whiteboard illuminated in response. Shaw turned to it and crossed his arms, studying Ali's slide show of symbols and items of jewellery.

"The symbols on the walls of the bedroom where Danny Gilbert was killed aren't random patterns or pretty decorations," Ali said. "They're code. They're the symbols used by paedophiles to communicate their specific preferences to each other." Ali paused on an image of a pink heart within a heart, the larger of the two open at its lowest point. "This is the GLogo and it stands for 'girl lover'. This one," Ali brought up an image of a blue triangle within a larger blue triangle, "is BLogo, 'boy lover'." Ali showed a series of similar images of the hearts and triangles but the symbols were less precise than before, as if drawn in crayon by children. "Now, when either are written like this, when they're displayed in this infantile manner as more of a squiggle, it represents a paedophile whose predilection is biased in favour of very young boys or girls, even infants and toddlers.

"Here's the other symbol in the room." Ali paused on an image of a four-winged butterfly. The upper, larger wing to the left was coloured blue and the wing on the right, pink.

The lower two wings were smaller and sported the same colours in reverse. "This is the CLogo, used by paedophiles who tout themselves as lovers of all children, regardless of their gender. The room itself was a symbol of the same: four walls, two blue, two pink. The room was furnished and designed and stocked to host minors with the goal of interacting with them sexually."

Shaw blew his cheeks out. "You're saying this is a paedo case?"

"That's exactly what I'm, *we're*, saying."

"There's something else, sir," said Cuzzocrea. "When Ali and I examined Tristan McMenemy's body earlier today…"

"Woah!" said Trina Walsh, slipping herself off the desk upon which she was perched. "You and Ali what? You examined McMenemy?"

"Yes," said Cuzzocrea.

"Doug?" Trina turned to Superintendent Shaw. "That's a violation of – "

Shaw held a calming hand up towards a furious Trina, silencing her. He nodded for Cuzzocrea to continue.

"Two things: first, McMenemy had a tattoo, seemingly innocuous, a simple word, capitalized, so perhaps a name? *Quispe.* Second, the angle of entry, the trajectory of the knife wounds led Ali to conclude that his assailant was small, much smaller than him."

"Jesus! What? Did you do a trajectory rod exam on him?" Trina squealed.

"Oh, so you do know what that is? Have to say, I was beginning to wonder," Ali said, raising her eyebrows at Trina.

"Guys! Guys! Come on!" Shaw snapped, the little patience he possessed was wearing thin. "Enough already. We're a team, we're working together. Understood?"

Trina pursed her lips at Ali and returned to sitting on the table. She nodded a vague agreement towards Shaw.

"I said, understood?" Shaw reiterated, his mounting anger focused entirely on Trina Walsh.

"Yes, sir," she reluctantly acquiesced.

Ali cleared her throat. "At first I thought, a small woman, perhaps a scorned lover."

"And now?" pressed Shaw.

"Now, seeing these symbols in the room where Gilbert was killed in the same manner as McMenemy, I'm wondering, it could still be a woman or a very small man, maybe an angry parent? But, I'm inclined to wonder whether this could be the work of a vengeful victim. A child."

Silence fell upon the squad room. Shaw's face was stern. "Trina, get to the morgue, please. I want you to re-examine both bodies with Ali and Rey's theory in mind. I want as close to an exact weight and height prediction of the assailant as you can get – any fingerprints at the scene today? Footprints? Anything that could help us to identify the type of killer we're looking for?"

"We had one partial patent, in blood, on the bedroom's inner door handle. There were multiple sets of prints on the carpet and on the laminate flooring outside the room. Those were tagged, photographed and covered by the time you guys got there but I can take another look at them." Trina gathered her belongings and headed towards the door of the squad room. Ali didn't watch her as she passed but imagined the woman was probably glaring at her. As usual.

"Wait! Trina? One more thing," said Shaw before turning to Cuzzocrea once more, "the tattoo. What's the significance there?"

"Nothing yet except that Danny Gilbert sports similar ink in the same place on his body. His reads: *Cápac.* Capital 'c' and the first 'a' is acute, having a diacritical accent," Cuzzocrea explained.

"French? Spanish? Latin, perhaps?" Shaw asked.

"We're working on it," said Cuzzocrea.

"Sir," said Ali, "we need to run McMenemy and Gilbert *and* the father through the National Sex Offender Registry, see if they have – "

"Ha!" Trina blurted from the doorway before sniggering

and leaving.

Ali looked at Cuzzocrea with a shrug. “Am I missing something?”

Cuzzocrea looked to Shaw who studied his shoes for a moment before answering, “Ali, I think maybe Eden should familiarize you with a couple of things before we continue.” Shaw nodded towards Eden Harrington.

“Sir,” said Eden, and smiled apologetically at Ali.

“Let’s grab a coffee, shall we?” Shaw suggested, rubbing his thinning hair.

Ali frowned and wondered what exactly had just happened to alter the dynamic in the room.

CHAPTER 17 - LEGIS-FUCKING-LATION

It was a rare occasion or set of circumstances, Cuzzocrea knew, that possessed gravitas enough to render Ali Dalglish speechless. He'd seen the woman don the archetypically British 'stiff upper lip' in the face of situations that would reduce a lesser being to a quivering wreck. He'd once seen her emotionally sidestep the revelation that her husband was embroiled in an affair with a woman half Ali's age and watched as she maintained absolute composure and her phenotypical stolid stoicism during the rescue of her daughter, Sandy, from the grasp of a lethal psychopath.

Now he looked at Ali, her face a tessellation of incredulity and frustration, her hands dug into her small waist. He could see her mouth trying in vain to verbalize a response to Eden's depressing summary of British Columbia's defunct Sex Offender Information Registration Act – better known as SOIRA. Cuzzocrea also knew Ali well enough to sense the nearing onslaught of the shit she was about to ladle upon them, the VIIMIS team, as a result.

Finally, with her eyes darkening, a furrow deep between her eyebrows and a vein in her forehead thrumming with latent power, she spoke:

"So, let me get this straight…you have a sex offender registry…"

Eden nodded and interjected, "The NSOR database – National Sex Offender Registry."

"…but," Ali spat as she threw her voice to address all of

the team present in the room, "it's basically fucking useless?"

Shaw huffed and stood up from a chair next to the little table in the corner of the squad room, which was laden with tea- and coffee-making equipment. "Thanks to legislative restrictions, yes. Not our fault. We've petitioned parliament time and time again, even provided them with a concise list of problems and fixes ranging from missing fields on the software – date fields that make it impossible for us to track when an offender's annual check-in date comes up – to Form 52, which is often overlooked or used as a bargaining tool by defence council."

"Form 52?" asked Ali.

Eden explained, "Following a successful trial, when someone is proven guilty of a sex offence, they are only added to the registry if the prosecutor requests a Form 52 from the judge at the time. The judge can also refuse the request."

Ali shook her head in disbelief. "Okay, so is that the only problem with registration?"

Shaw snorted. "Ali, it'd be quicker if we ran through everything that *works* with the registry and then we'd only have positive points if we lived on Prince Edward Island – never mind, I digress."

Eden replied to Ali's question instead: "Prisoners already incarcerated for sex crimes aren't automatically added. They are only required to report when they are released but the CSC – the Correctional Service of Canada – refuse to tell registry staff when offenders are set free."

"But surely the database negates the need for one-on-one communication between the CSC and NSOR," said Ali.

"We wish," replied Eden. "Offender release dates are available on two other databases – the Canadian Police Information Centre, the main computer that contains everyone's criminal record, and an internal system known as InfoPol, but the legislation that created the registry strictly prohibits 'data watching'. Basically, the RCMP cannot connect the database to any other police computer or operating system. The only way an officer can legally track release dates or renewal dates is by writing them down him or herself on paper and filing the information in a rolodex or another place not related to the registry."

"You are fucking kidding me, aren't you, Eden? I mean, you are sweet and you seem kind but you must be one twisted bitch because you are, surely to God, fucking with me." Ali's voice had reached a pitch that even Cuzzocrea had hitherto never witnessed.

Eden smiled and shrugged. "I wish I was, Ali. Seriously, it gets worse. For instance, say there's a guy hanging around a pre-school. The teachers and the mums are rightly concerned and so they put a call in to the RCMP. The officers arrive and they just know this guy's on the prowl, that his motivation is deviantly sexual – those officers can't look the guy up on the National Sex Offender Registry to see if he's a predator or if he has previous convictions because frontline officers aren't allowed to access the database themselves. They have to put in a formal request to the registry staff but there is legislation in place to restrict information held on the NSOR system with regards to investigative work. In summary, it is forbidden to use the registry in the course of an investigation; it is only to be used to *solve* a sex crime that has already been committed and cannot be used to prevent a crime from happening. An in-house study found that most Mounties, with this fact in mind, don't even put in requests to the registry staff."

"Wait, wait, are you saying that it's illegal for us to use the National Sex Offender Registry as an investigative tool?" Ali asked.

"Yes. But the biggest beef anyone has with it is that it can't be linked to RIGEL – our geographic profiling tool – or ViCLAS – the violent crime database of solved and unsolved cases."

Once again, Ali was bereft of words. Cuzzocrea saw in her eyes a sense of helplessness he had never before witnessed in the woman whose driving force seemed to be helping those who would be otherwise vulnerable to the predators around them.

"There are a multitude of problems besides those Eden is pointing out. Don't even get us started on the requirement for an offender to let us know if they are vacationing abroad – in Thailand, for example – or even moving house," said Cuzzocrea, handing Ali a mug of hot tea. "Basically, Ali, with regards to the investigation of a case linked to paedophilia, we are adrift and in constant danger of breaking the law ourselves. More so than on any other type of investigation. SOIRA turned out to be an act pitted with legislative restrictions that work *for* the child predator instead of against him."

"So the the architects of this legislation are, what? Are they all paedos? I mean, what's the political motivation here? Why hasn't this shit been rectified already?"

Silence emanated from all around.

"How do we work around this?" Ali pressed on, undeterred, "I'll tell you now, I'm not turning my back on this case. It clearly points to vigilante justice being meted out. The fucking paedos are the ones we're effectively being tasked with protecting by investigating the murders of McMenemy and Gilbert. You guys must have circumvented this shit before, surely. Eden, you must know, you're Special Victims, for Christ sake."

Eden cast a wary look at her superior. Superintendent Shaw stepped up to her and, by placing his hand on her shoulder, relieved Eden of the responsibility of providing an answer to Ali's question. Shaw looked at the ceiling above them in a manner that inspired paranoia and Ali couldn't help but shadow his glance, searching the white styrofoam tiles of the suspended ceiling herself.

"Where are you staying, Ali? The Ocean Lookout, right?" Shaw asked.

"No. I upgraded myself to the Artisan Lodge Hotel in an attempt to avoid a dose of impetigo."

Shaw nodded. "They have a bar?"

"They have a lounge. Probably a bar. I don't know, I just checked in this afternoon." Ali was more confused than ever.

"Let's head over there. We can assess our situation more clearly off site." Shaw looked at his watch. "It's late but we might need to pull an all-nighter on this one. Sorry guys. Eden, Paul, you're with me. Munro, you smoke so you can take your own car. I'll let Trina know where we are but I know she's got her own all-nighter ahead of her. Rey? You and Ali always come together, correct?"

"Sir." Cuzzocrea nodded.

Ali elbowed Cuzzocrea in the ribs, unable to resist an acknowledgement of Shaw's accidental double entendre.

"Okay, we'll meet at the Artisan Lodge. Let's go," Shaw said, clapping his hands and donning his windcheater.

Ali had a slight smile as Cuzzocrea glanced at her. "You have a dirty mind, Ali Dalglish."

"Yep. Listen, could you grab that laptop for me? I have to nip for a fag, like right now otherwise I swear, I could rip someone's gullet out with my bare hands."

"Sure. I'll meet you at the car."

Cuzzocrea watched Ali leave as she caught up with Munro, linking her arm with his as they bypassed the elevator and chose instead to bang open the doorway to the stairwell. Cuzzocrea wondered how a woman so ornery and whose very manner of communication was invidious managed to get on so well with everyone around her – Trina Walsh being the only exception to the rule. Cuzzocrea wondered if it was because Ali was a leading criminal psychologist. Was she so in tune with the workings of the human psyche that she could manipulate and control it to become a different version of herself for everyone she encountered, a version that somehow met their approval? If so, was she aware of that? Was she, with that in mind, playing him? In fact, he was starting to suspect he wasn't the only man on the team who had found himself at the mercy of her peculiar brand of theurgy. What was worse, Cuzzocrea felt the stirrings of something he had thus far in life remained immune to: jealousy.

CHAPTER 18 - NOT SO PASSIVE AGGRESSIVE

The interior of Cuzzocrea's Prius was pristine; its cream-coloured seats were indicative of his childless private life. The car had finally warmed and the windows were sufficiently de-misted enough to allow Ali a clear view of the many apartment blocks standing sentry, overlooking the Old Island Highway and beyond it, the choppy waters of the Inside Passage.

Almost every balcony was profuse with tacky multi-coloured lights, flashing candy canes and garish Christmas-themed inflatables. A self-proclaimed hater of the Christmas season, Ali found the spectacle a vomitus display of the fake joy expected of people during the abundantly materialistic 'holiday', as the Canadians called it. In Britain, a *holiday* was a two-week trip abroad to sleep on a beach and decompress from your shitty nine-to-five life.

"I hate sodding Christmas," Ali said as she checked an incoming text on her phone. It was from her ex-husband, David.

"Really? That surprises me," said Cuzzocrea, askance sarcasm in his eyes. "I thought you were all about the ho ho ho of life."

Ali typed a reply to the text as she spoke: "Apparently I needed to know that the kids are asleep. Like David should get a fucking medal every time he watches the kids – *our* kids. For what? Not letting them die? I mean, they're not babies. Sandy's twenty and Kenny's six-bloody-teen!" Ali dumped her phone into her lap. "Fucking men!"

"Hey."

"Not you. You know that. Just...*men*," she growled. "You know what Shaw asked me tonight? 'Who's looking after the kids?' I'm pretty sure he's got kids but I bet he'd be weirded out if someone asked him that. But a woman? Well a woman is clearly neglectful of her offspring to be spending time doing exactly the same job as any father happens to be doing."

"Sexism, Ali. It goes two ways, you know. You bunch all men together and stir them in one big pot of hate," said Cuzzocrea.

"Whatever. I'm fighting back against years – *centuries* – of suppression, inequality and forced servitude. Not to mention the collective propaganda we're subject to in the media, the subliminal messaging, the objectification, the de-humanization. The pressure on us to want to look like a fucking Victoria's Secret model whilst bearing children and being perfect mothers, lovers, cooks, cleaners, unofficial therapists, successful career women, social fucking butterflies and hostesses to an arrogant, unappreciative shit of a husband's colleagues and friends."

"Can we go back to you hating Christmas, please? You're far nicer when you're bitching about materialism. Hey, we could even get back onto the subject of paedophilia. Then we can really get down and party."

Ali shrugged and leaned forward to look up at the bloated sky, thick with a grey blanket of clouds. "Snow's starting. Shit. I hope Marlene picked up something that can handle these roads in a storm."

"She didn't send you a picture of it?" asked Cuzzocrea.

"The car she got? No. Did she send it to you?"

"Oh, yes. You are in for a big surprise. Literally."

"I dread to think," said Ali as Cuzzocrea pulled right and continued down a dimly lit street between two industrial-looking Quonset structures. One was an auto repair company, the other claimed to house the world's leader in custom boat and yacht interiors. Ali doubted if the world leaders of anything would be happy to be housed in a corrugated hut that looked like a WWII missile silo on the outskirts of a place like Cedar River.

As the road neared the ocean, it became a steep escarpment before Cuzzocrea followed the signs to turn right and passed through the rustic but somehow vaguely ostentatious gates of the Artisan Lodge Hotel and, finally, into an empty stall in the parking lot two spaces from Shaw's black SUV.

Fat slithers of snow now spiralled diagonally downward. Outside the car, the air felt denser than it did in the rain or sunshine, as if a spell of heavy silence piggy-backed each flake.

"Passive aggressive snow," Ali said as she retrieved her many belongings – the impedimenta that came hand in hand with her dual areas of expertise.

"How can snow be passive aggressive?" asked Cuzzocrea, as he helped to carry Ali's accoutrements.

"It is, look at it. All fluffy and light, pretty and peaceful but you wait and see, in a couple of hours it will have blanketed everything, it'll bring roads to a standstill and ground planes. It's like it comes down giggling, whispering sweet poetry and then fucks you up the arse."

"Wait, don't tell me," said Cuzzocrea, closing the trunk of his car and following Ali along the pathway to the front of the hotel, "you hate snow too."

"God, Cuzzocrea," Ali slipped into an exaggerated vocal fry, "you make me sound like a total hater."

"Well, I've yet to hear you wax lyrical about anything you actually like."

Ali stopped and allowed him to catch up to her, a snowflake landed on her nose and, with her hands full, she tried in vain to blow it off. "I like you."

Cuzzocrea transferred one of Ali's pathologist cases to his other hand and blotted the snowflake on Ali's nose with the cuff of his sleeve. "Thanks. I like you too."

Cuzzocrea set off again, quickly followed by Ali. "And I do wax lyrical about you, actually," Ali said. "The kids are sick of hearing about you, as a matter of fact."

Cuzzocrea hid his pleasure as he stepped through the front doors into the hotel's foyer.

Ali saw that the team had already gathered around one of the open fireplaces. With the lounge to themselves, they had rearranged a nest of furniture so that they could confer over the coffee table. Ali saw a tray of hot drinks had already arrived.

"Is this usual? For Shaw to pull the team away, off-site, to discuss something?"

"Most unusual. He's usually a circumspect stickler for procedure."

"How exciting," said Ali as Cuzzocrea stood back to allow her the lead on their way to join the team. "I wonder what he has up his sleeve."

"Well, we're about to find out."

Shaw began by instructing everyone present to keep their voices down throughout lest confidential, potentially classified information regarding the case should find its way to the ears of the hotel's night staff. Ali thought he was being overly cautious since, it seemed to her, the smattering of staff on duty were apparently only too happy to avoid any contact with their group of late-night guests.

"Now, Ali, you were asking if we ever worked around the various legislative limitations we were discussing back at the station," said Shaw.

"I was." She put her half empty cup of hot chocolate down on the wooden coffee table between them.

Shaw continued: "The official answer is, no. Absolutely not and any officer on this team found to be conducting themselves in a manner contrary to that or in contradiction to legislative rules and laws will suffer severe consequences as a result of his or her actions."

"And the unofficial answer?" asked Ali.

Shaw leaned in and spoke in a conspiratorial fashion.

"Unofficially, a few years back we did find ways and means to further an investigation of this nature but the methods, should we choose to implement them again, cannot be part of our official, documented work. It's the sort of stuff that plays into the hands of defence lawyers and can see a case thrown out and the guilty walk free after months, sometimes years, of hard graft."

Ali shrugged. "I'm game. Who gives a shit if it brings down a few scumbags?"

"All well and good until one or all of us is facing a dishonourable discharge and jail time," said Shaw.

Ali, who frequently and unapologetically allowed the line between lawful and unlawful to blur in the pursuit of her quarry, found Shaw's manner to be almost laughably overly dramatic. Even under the most mundane circumstances Ali had witnessed his penchant for drama to verge on hyperbolic attention seeking. He reminded her of the man she had once been foolish enough to marry, yet his drama-queen excitability was a trait in Shaw that Ali found strangely endearing and made his otherwise stalwart self far more human, relatable, even.

"Superintendent, we are talking about potentially uncovering a paedophile ring here. If, as Cuzzocrea and I suspect, McMenemy and Gilbert are the tip of a depraved iceberg, we could theoretically spare the suffering of scores, if not hundreds of innocents."

As she knew it would, Ali's comment spoke to Shaw's desire for action. "Okay, we proceed. With caution," he said, raising a finger of warning, "under the agreement that what is discussed here tonight is never discussed openly again. In fact, our way forward cannot involve the entire team. Maybe just Ali and Rey doing the grunt work with Eden doing what she can behind the scenes to take what they find and somehow manipulate it into our official investigation so we can safely act upon leads and document the trail if necessity demands it. Agreed?"

Shaw looked at each member of the team individually. Ali

found it hard not to laugh at his performance and she suspected that, in a strange way, he was enjoying the prospect of leading his herd ever so slightly astray. Perhaps he was a rule obeyer with a secret desire for naughtiness, and Ali imagined he may have dabbled in other timid ways to be marginally rebellious. Perhaps he didn't quite come to a complete halt at stop signs. Maybe he 'borrowed' stationary for his own personal use, or even took towels home from hotels. If Munro's theory about Shaw's adulterous relationship with Trina Walsh was true, then not one of those things would be his worst indiscretion.

Shaw's attention came to rest upon Eden Harrington. "Eden? Take it from here please."

Eden looked uncomfortable and shifted in her seat. "I'm sorry, sir, but I don't know what you mean?"

Her response deflated the Superintendent's bluster; it was an anti-climax for Shaw who cleared his throat and mumbled a name to Eden as if secretly prompting a bad actor with a missed line during a live show. When Eden looked all the more nonplussed at his utterance, Shaw's face took on an exophthalmic expression, his eyes bulging with suppressed frustration.

"But, sir, he…" Eden said.

"What?" said Shaw and, without allowing time for Eden to explain, he turned to Ali and Cuzzocrea to elaborate. "There's a guy here, Greg Ballantine, amazing techie – nothing he can't do with a computer – he's a master at virtual surveillance and online deep cover work."

"But, sir, Greg Ballantine – " Eden stopped mid-sentence, snared in Shaw's protuberant stare.

Munro saved her, seeming impervious to Shaw's intimidating manner. "He's on the National Sex Offender Registry, sir."

"What?" Shaw's head snapped around to Munro, his glare as dramatic as his earlier diatribe had been. "What?"

"Don't you know?" said Munro, draining his cup of cocoa and stuffing a cookie in his mouth.

"No, Munro, please, enlighten me."

Munro spoke whilst chewing like a clod, "He was nabbed by a team of Special I techs as part of a province-wide sting back in '09. Worst part was that he was in the chat rooms and on the sites because he was working for us, not us as in VIIMIS but us, as in law enforcement. He's freelance so he works out of his own office and uses his own IP address. He was scooped up and prosecuted along with the very guys he'd been asked to infiltrate for us."

"Jesus Christ Almighty." Shaw held his head in his hands and rubbed the top of his scalp. Ali worried he might dislodge more of his already thinning hair as a result.

"Couldn't his lawyer prove his involvement in the case? That he was working undercover?" asked Cuzzocrea.

"Apparently he was left high and dry because his methods, though highly effective, could be seen as entrapment in the eyes of the law and so everybody denied working with him for fear that his involvement would bring the whole case to its knees," Eden explained.

"Wow. The fuck-ups just keep coming," said Ali. "I take it this Ballantine guy would be reluctant to work alongside us again."

Shaw looked up at her. "You think?"

Cuzzocrea made a suggestion to Ali: "Can't hurt to speak with him."

"I'm up for it if you are?" Ali agreed.

Cuzzocrea looked to Shaw. Shaw spent a few brief moments deep in thought before replying to the idea: "Okay. Worth a shot. We have nothing to lose." He seemed to regain a semblance of his earlier enthusiasm. "Okay. Okay," said Shaw, soothing himself with his own reassurance, "So, Ali, Rey, you're the analysts. Thoughts? Any insights? What are we going to be faced with here? I'm sure, like with everything else, Ali, you've probably been there, done that and got the t-shirt."

CHAPTER 19 - CRIMSON TARNISH

As *Serenade No.7 in D Major* became *Violin Concerto No.3 in G*, James Bartholomew conducted an imaginary orchestra pit with his copper ViRTU cheese knife. The music was set at the ideal volume for him to experience the inevitable thrall of Mozart's brilliance and yet it was quiet enough so as not to disturb the opiated skull upstairs.

He'd carefully laid out the delightful birthday fare he'd purchased at Cheese Heaven – for a few dollars shy of ninety bucks – on a wooden board. He placed a sprig of thyme between the new cheese he had yet to sample and his favourite blue. In the gaps between cheeses and his selection of cured meats, James placed miniature white ramekins of pickles and various relishes. The final touch, and the perfect aesthetic addition to any good cheeseboard, was a snipped bunch of organic black grapes, a delicate shade of powder blue in their gentle, waxen coats.

As he levered his Trudeau corkscrew he heard and simultaneously felt the tight squeak of cork birthing free of bottle. Although reasonably priced, the Seven Poplars 2009 was, in his opinion, BC's finest Pinotage. Admiring his creation, James carefully aerated the fine wine, expertly allowing the fluid to fall from the bottle in fat, hiccupping glugs rather than forcibly pouring it into the decanter. Yet resentment bit at him. Must he be raped of even this simple pleasure?

His enjoyment of this exquisite charcuterie had been

tainted. Was it not enough that he should be doomed to spend his birthday worse than alone – for absolute solitude would be preferable to celebrating his advancing years in a home shared with a thing half dead, a wife on the fringe of her mortality – but he'd also received disturbing news from a friend on Hollyrood Estates who had informed him that Danny Gilbert, Peter's simple son, had been murdered. Stabbed to death. And more worrying was that the idiot boy had allowed that final indignity to happen in the playroom.

First Tristan. Now Danny.

Despite his hubris earlier that evening in Cheese Heaven, James had to admit now that he hadn't been entirely impervious to panic even then, before he'd received news of Danny Gilbert. Two murders in just a few days. Two of the group had been killed. He would be remiss to discount that as inconsequential or coincidental.

After exhausting the regular channels, he'd used his role as Editor-in-Chief of *The Echo* to acquire the cell number of one of the officers assigned to the investigation but had gotten nowhere. No statements were being made at this time. The RCMP station, it seemed, had decided to close for the night, although he doubted that was actually the case. A recorded message advising him to dial 911 in the event of an emergency was all that greeted him when he'd called the station and although there had been the option to leave a voice message after the tone, James instead decided to delegate the task – better his lead reporter's name appeared in official documents than his. Besides, Tanya had been thrilled with the request as it came as a welcome departure from reporting upon the latest desecration of Big Rock or late-night drug busts on Pine Nut Circle.

James settled himself in his chair in the den with his cheeseboard and his wine. He swished the wine in his mouth and pulled back on the air through pursed lips, just like he'd been taught during his tour of the Okanagan vineyards last summer. He thought he detected oak.

Quispe and Cápac. Both murdered.

Perhaps his pleb of a brother had been right. Perhaps it was time to contact Apu.

James was a man intimidated by little and very few individuals managed to make him feel subservient to them. But subservient to Apu, James Bartholomew – *Sapa* – would always be.

While moments earlier his stomach had growled at the promise of his edible delights, now it growled again with the dread he felt in anticipation of his forthcoming interaction with Apu.

He studied his private phone – a phone his wife had never known he possessed during all the years of their tiresome marriage. This was a new one, the latest model. James was most pleased by the purchase because it was secure – only he could access it with his unique fingerprint. Pressing his thumb on the button, James was hit with the suddenly cloying tang of the Roquefort sweating on the board beside him. Within seconds he was rushing to the lavatory where he splattered the toilet bowl with what appeared to be as much Pinotage as he'd earlier decanted rather than the solitary oaky sip he'd briefly enjoyed.

CHAPTER 20 - GOT THE T-SHIRT

"Not quite got the t-shirt but studying deviancy is at the heart of what Cuzzocrea and I do," said Ali.

"It's the fundamental difference between criminal analysis and regular psychology," Cuzzocrea added.

"But if what you expect here is for us to outline a perfect, I don't know, A to Z of sexual deviancy and in particular, paedophilia, then that's a big ask. Deviancy is a huge discussion and very difficult to compress or simplify."

Shaw nodded and gulped down the last of his hot chocolate. "Yeah, yeah. I get that."

Ali frowned, knowing Shaw was ignorant of how far away from 'getting' the concept of deviance he was. "So what is it that you wish to learn from us? Are we talking about paedophilia or – "

Shaw cut her off mid-sentence, "Yeah, whatever." He beckoned impatiently with his hand and sat back. "The way I see it, our only clear lead here is your theory that both of our victims are linked. What links them? Their deviancy, right?"

Ali and Cuzzocrea both nodded.

"So, go on, explain. Give us something," said Shaw.

Cuzzocrea looked at Ali and shrugged. "Deviance?"

Ali took a breath, then began, "In a nutshell…hmm, where to begin…"

"Okay. So, control systems?" Cuzzocrea suggested. Ali agreed it was as good a place as any to start. Cuzzocrea continued: "Sociologist Walter Reckless developed the control theory to explain how some people, people like you, like Ali, regular people resist the pressure to become deviant. First, there's inner control – internalized thought processes such as our sense of morality, conscience. Fear of punishment or even just a fear of how guilty we'd feel if we did act outside of society's accepted norms."

Shaw narrowed his eyes. "By that, are you suggesting that we are all deviant by nature but it's our inner morality that stops us from acting upon it?"

"Absolutely. It's likely, unless you've had to study and analyse it for a specific reason, that you're in denial about your own basic instincts and desires, your dark potential. Human nature is naturally deviant," Cuzzocrea replied.

"Hmm," said Shaw, crossing his arms, "go on."

Cuzzocrea continued, "Now, *outer* controls consist of the people in our lives. Our families, partners, kids, parents, friends. They all encourage us, indirectly, not to stray. Also, on a wider scale, so does the existence of law enforcement and justice systems, religious leaders and teachers, our communities as a whole."

"In what way?" asked Shaw.

"Because in the moment of temptation we either consciously or subconsciously evaluate how those people will react to our behaviour. Most of us want to conform to society's expectations," said Cuzzocrea.

"Travis Hirschi developed the control theory further," Ali explained. "He identified four elements that would render an individual more or less likely to commit deviance," she held up four fingers and dropped one for each element, "Attachment. Commitment. Involvement. Belief."

Cuzzocrea picked up Ali's line of explanation. "Attachment: People who are strongly attached to others are less likely to be deviant. Yet someone who has weak personal relationships would feel less pressure to conform and would therefore be more likely to commit a deviant act."

Ali continued, "Commitment refers to people committed to legitimate goals. They tend to conform. So someone committed to their career, education, financial stability and long-term relationships is unlikely to become deviant. People who lack confidence in the future struggle with commitment are hopeless and more likely to engage in deviance.

"Then there's involvement. Activities, clubs, organizations. Belonging in some way and contributing makes one less likely to commit acts of deviance. For two reasons: no time because you're too busy being involved and also because you have a lot more to lose if you do."

"Belief is obvious," said Cuzzocrea. "It's all about values. Sharing the values of the dominant society. Such as respect for authority, work ethics, and, of course, religious beliefs, the element of sin. Those conditioned beliefs control us and prevent us from acting in a deviant manner."

"Simple enough," said Shaw.

"Not quite," said Ali. "Howard Becker proposed the labelling theory, which posits that deviance is that which is so labelled."

"Exactly," agreed Cuzzocrea. "Who decides what should be classified as deviance? Society does. No act is inherently deviant until other people judge it so."

"Woah," said Shaw. "Murder is wrong whichever way you look at it. Rape? Theft? All those things are wrong, not because we say so, they just are."

Ali shook her head. "No. They are perceived as wrong because we, as a society, decided we don't like those things. We don't want people just killing other people, or raping or beating and abusing. That's why we have laws to control deviance. Potential punishment and judgement is the deterrent; a system designed to punish deviant acts in the hope it can prevent the recurrence of deviance. However, the deviant enjoys the act; the deviant believes his actions to be justified in the very least."

Shaw sat silently for a moment, deep in thought. "I'm sorry guys, but I'm having a hard time accepting that certain things are only 'bad' because society says so."

Ali smiled. "It's a tricky concept to grasp and one you're

just going to have to trust us on. That's why I tried to explain how difficult it is to condense. Trust me when I tell you that the only decisions you've ever made were ones based on choosing *not* to be deviant. Your moral code is not inherent, it wasn't born with you, it was shaped by your own analysis of consequence. Your moral code is just a good habit you adopted and one that has become so honed and well practiced that it feels real.

"It's conditioning. Conditioning that starts with our parents and siblings, then later through interaction with friends and teachers, then with the people we choose to have in our lives. We learn early on that biting gets us into trouble and being in trouble makes us feel bad. We learn how to control our temper because Mum got very cross with us and said we embarrassed her in the store. We were punished accordingly and that punishment made us feel bad about ourselves; it damaged our self-esteem. As children we're taught to cover up our bodies; we're told that we aren't allowed to touch other people in certain places and that people shouldn't touch us in certain ways. We're taught that fighting is wrong, what good manners are and that we should be kind and share our belongings with others. From the day we are born we are conditioned and taught what is deemed to be appropriate behaviour.

"*Pre*-social conditioning, *prior* to our first taste of what it feels like to disappoint someone we care about, we spat, we bit, we wanted to eat gross things. We touched our intimate places freely because it felt nice and we wanted to explore those places on other people. Children – pure, honest and unconditioned – say and do inappropriate things if not mean and cruel things, naturally; they see a baby and they want to press its eyes just to see what happens; they notice a disabled or deformed individual and they pass comment as loudly as they please. Our morals, our empathy, these are not automatic attributes, they are shaped by our early interactions with our immediate community and later by greater society."

"But society is responsible for causing deviance too," said Cuzzocrea.

"How so?" asked Shaw.

Cuzzocrea explained, "By excluding and judging others. For example: a kid, let's call him Adam, likes to torture cats. For Adam, torturing cats is fun, a hobby, a laugh and it's what he and his brothers and sisters do to strays sometimes around, I don't know, around the farm. One day Adam is at school and there's a cat in the playground. Adam catches it and he tortures it. Instead of joining in and laughing, as his siblings would have, the other kids are shocked. They run to the teacher and they report Adam. Adam is punished, admonished. He is judged. Nobody wants to be Adam's friend anymore because, all of a sudden, he is a social pariah – the weird kid who does things to cats. He's excluded by his peers and he's no longer treated well as a result. So, torturing cats was Adam's *primary* deviance and it had little to no effect on his self-esteem at home because it was acceptable behaviour amongst his siblings. But once he repeated that behaviour in front of another societal group and they excluded him as a result, it causes Adam to commit *secondary* deviance – a kind of 'fuck you' to the latter societal group who judged and bullied him. He accepts his outcast status and engages in other, more serious deviant acts."

Ali leaned forward and elaborated upon Cuzzocrea's point, "So you see, when a community makes someone an outcast, they force that individual into deviance because they have inadvertently stripped them of all control systems. Further, if a societal group has also labelled an individual, that label becomes a self-fulfilling prophecy. So if a child comes from a dysfunctional home, perhaps there's not enough money, they are exposed to drugs, mental health issues abound, etcetera, the rest of society assumes that that kid will follow suit, 'a bad egg', 'the apple doesn't rot far from the tree'. Every interaction with society that that child has, reinforces the label and cements the expectation. The child begins to adopt those ideas since it is as effective a form of social conditioning as any other. It becomes a self-fulfilling prophecy that creates and encourages deviant behaviour."

'In short," said Cuzzocrea, "and stay with me, because this may sound like hyperbole but every act of deviance is of our creating. Every drop of blood or tears shed from the eyes of victims is on our collective hands."

"Well, that's entirely depressing." said Shaw. "Okay, so this case, McMenemy and Gilbert are a team, yes? If not part of a larger group. How does that happen? How do two or three or however many deviants find each other? Do they scan the classifieds? Or is one the leader, the true deviant exerting power over weaker individuals?"

"Subcultures are formed naturally by people excluded from society," said Ali. "They naturally migrate towards each other. They have the same basic needs as non-deviant people: they wish to succeed within a group, they wish to live up to or exceed expectations. Deviants create their own sense of belonging through the creation of their subculture. It's the same psychology behind gang mentality. Their deviance excludes them from society yet it is the very thing that binds them to their subculture."

Cuzzocrea continued: "It's called differential association. Re-socialization. The deviants create a subculture that differs from the dominant culture. It's a formula that works when an individual is accepted by the new group after feeling alienated from the larger one."

Ali nodded in agreement. "Today's world is conducive to deviancy as there is a growing disconnect, a breakdown in our sense of community. It's due in part to advances in technology which allow us to exist without the need for human interaction or physical proximity to each other. Twin that with the systematic disenfranchisement of certain groups; lack of government funding within poorer communities; a lack of care, support, education for youngsters from indigent pockets of society who are largely neglected and ignored by community leaders. Modern society has fashioned itself in such a way that the number of deviant subcultures is growing. Now, once a subculture is created, it sanctions and even encourages further acts of deviance and recidivism."

Munro regarded Ali and Cuzzocrea. "Do you two rehearse this shit? I bet you just sit around discussing random sicko stuff constantly, huh?"

Ali smiled at Munro before turning once more to Superintendent Shaw. "The symbols present at the crime scene tonight are a common feature of any coterie, any subculture. It's the equivalent of gang colours. Symbolization is important to them and creates meaning and a sense of group identity. Just as a Christian proudly wears a crucifix about his or her throat, so would a paedophile sport similar symbolization to demonstrate their passion and commitment to their group. They advertise their deviance to each other through arcane symbols so that they can communicate with each other in both the virtual and the real world."

"These symbols are how each subculture covertly builds into a network," explained Cuzzocrea. "So if I was a pervert, say I'm into little girls, I would wear symbols to advertise that fact. For instance, I might wear a pink shirt or tie. I might wear a ring with a heart engraved on it or a pendant of the same, even cufflinks or a tie pin. My clues would be subtle enough so that a non-paedophile wouldn't even notice but if a colleague of mine was also into little girls, he'd notice immediately and a dialogue could begin. The symbols used by paedophiles – by all subcultures – are relatively innocuous and so they can be believably explained away so that if my boss were to confront me and ask me why I always wear something pink, I could say that my niece bought my tie for me or that it just happens to be my favourite colour."

"Go to any city on April the twenty-fifth and you can see it for yourselves," suggested Ali.

"April twenty-fifth," said Eden, "Alice Day, right?"

"Alice Day?" asked Munro.

Ali nodded. "It's a day marked on any paedo's calendar.

Alice Day is their day of celebration, when they are all duty bound to display the symbols of their deviance for and to each other."

"Why Alice?" asked Shaw.

"It's a nod to *Alice in Wonderland*, specifically to the author, Lewis Carroll – the paedophile community have him as their exalted idol, he's their Jesus. I'll let you all guess why," said Ali.

"Paedophiles are bold. They act unapologetically. They even petition governments to change the laws regarding age of consent. They believe that 'child love' is a natural, beautiful thing that should be decriminalized and they talk openly on websites and in chatrooms about what they will be doing on Alice Day, using their various acronyms to describe in detail how they will be marking the day and with whom," Cuzzocrea said.

"There's Boy Love Day too – June twenty-third, I think," said Ali. "Listen, if we can't use the registry to look up and interview sex offenders in Cedar River then our best bet is to go undercover with a tech expert and look at websites and chatrooms. It wouldn't take long to find and infiltrate the group McMenemy and Gilbert belonged to but the next twenty-four to forty-eight hours would be crucial because it's more likely that the murders would be talked about amongst the group within that time.

"Let's face it, someone else is clearly familiar with the group and I'm willing to bet that our perp isn't going to stop at two kills. I'm sure you understand by now that deviant subcultures are networks; there will be more members and those members are potential victims. Two murders in one week, that's extreme escalation. Assuming our link theory is correct, our killer has very little down time between kills."

"I agree with Ali," said Cuzzocrea. He turned to her. "Could be someone in the grip of brief psychotic disorder."

Ali was impressed by Cuzzocrea's theory. "Yeah, reactive psychosis, with an obvious stressor, perhaps?" She turned to Shaw. "If that's the case, then we're already losing. He or she has a major head-start on us."

Shaw pondered the idea. "I'm wondering if I should approach the Chief Super. See if we have a chance at getting a Feeney warrant for the Gilbert house. For the computers, devices, phones and such."

"Sir, it might be our only hope of catching a lead. Obviously, Ali and I can still take a run at this Ballantine guy but if he refuses to cooperate – and who can blame him – we're screwed and we'll need that warrant," said Cuzzocrea.

Shaw chewed on his bottom lip before replying, "Okay. Eden, you get Ballantine's details together and a summary of everything that has occurred and send it to Rey and Ali. Rey and Ali, you get yourselves over to him in the a.m. Munro, I want you following up on Gilbert, the father, gather statements and canvass the area, see if you can find any link between him and McMenemy besides the tattoos. Paul, you're going to focus on finding the estranged mother. Eden, speak to your counterparts here, see what information regarding paedophilia in the region anyone has, you never know what you can find out. But be careful of breaching the legislation – I don't want to see your name on a complaint. I'll communicate our theory upstairs and see where we stand with the Chief. I'll check on Trina and see if she has anything new for us. Briefing back at the station at eleven a.m. tomorrow, by then we might have something to go on."

Once the team had left, Cuzzocrea and Ali relaxed back into the sofa together. Eventually Cuzzocrea spoke. "What deviant acts does your moral conditioning prevent you from committing?"

"Honestly? Murder. Battery. Vehicular manslaughter every time I go grocery shopping. Threesomes. Orgies. General cruelty. Actually, my moral conditioning must have been weak as shit because I can't say it's prevented me entirely."

Cuzzocrea looked at Ali. "Sometimes I have no idea when you're being serious or just kidding in your own twisted way."

Ali remained silent.

"You think it's a kid?" asked Cuzzocrea.

"Yes." Ali replied.

"You really think a kid is capable of that?"

"Unfortunately, because of past cases I've worked, I know all too well what kids are capable of. If it is, this won't be the first child murderer I've brought down."

"Jesus. Well, it will be my first."

"You know what I'm beginning to hate about this one?" Ali said, turning to look at Cuzzocrea. "That our victims are the bad guys and our bad guy is a victim."

"If, that is, any of our theories are right. I hope we're not making the mistake of tunnel vision here, of working to give a theory legs."

Ali shook her head. "You know him better than I do but I get the feeling that Shaw's strongest characteristic is his cynicism. I don't think he'd ever become so invested in one idea as to allow his team to run with something plucked from nowhere. I think he'd have fucked us off already if he didn't see the link himself. Besides, he's got the team working other angles too."

"Just saying, I hope our theories are right because if they are wrong, we'll look like a pair of idiots and Shaw'll never listen to us again," said Cuzzocrea.

"And Strap-a-dick-to-me Walsh will have a field day."

"Okay, now you've made it so I'm crossing my fingers in the hope that this *is* a case involving a child perpetrator." Cuzzocrea stood and gathered his belongings. "And so, on that sweet note, I bid you a fond farewell."

"You picking me up in the morning?" asked Ali as they stepped through the lobby.

"How about seven? Give us a chance to get ready for Ballantine."

"Sounds good, what d'you think our chances of getting him to work for us are?"

Cuzzocrea shrugged. "Slim to none. You?"

"I'd tell us to go and get fucked."

Cuzzocrea shook his head. "Well, if he does, at least we'll have something to do until the briefing with Shaw. Goodnight."

"Night."

Ali watched him leave through the sliding glass doors of the hotel foyer and, as they allowed a blast of the snowy night beyond to chill the air inside, she decided to forgo her usual pre-bedtime smoke.

If she hadn't been so tired, Ali might have allowed herself to ponder Cuzzocrea's parting statement further but she was barely able to keep her eyes open in the elevator and awoke the next morning to the sound of her annoyingly chirpy alarm, fully clothed and sprawled on top of the queen bed closest to the door.

PART TWO
THURSDAY 30th NOVEMBER

CHAPTER 21 - BACK TO SCHOOL

Too many noises. High-pitched cackling, shouts and exclamations. The piercing squeak of rubber soles changing direction on the polished gym floor to the left of her, penetrates the air and the sound startles Maiden.

At the bank of brightly coloured lockers, Maiden has to squeeze through a group of eleventh grade girls. They all look at her and she thinks that they know because they're staring at her jeans and her sweatshirt in such a way that Maiden glances down expecting to find she'd only imagined washing Danny Gilbert's blood away last night.

There's no blood but there is a long necklace, one she'd made out of pasta in kindergarten. Maiden doesn't remember putting it on or where it even lives in her room. She rushes to hide the necklace inside the neck of her Coca-Cola hoodie.

Behind her, the girls are speaking in whispered voices. One of them covers a giggle and Maiden feels the thumping of bloody anger behind her eyes.

She turns to her locker, still aware of the girls' sibilant susurrations. As she turns the dial of her lock, sure of the number but somehow unable to click it open, she hears them uttering a name, over and over again: Sinchi Roca…Sinchi Roca…Sssssinchi…Sssssinchi…Sinchisinchisinchisinchi.

Maiden looks at the girls but they have gone. The corridor is almost quiet now, as if the dissipating crowd of high schoolers is under a muffling enchantment which will lead them to a fiery pit somewhere secret in the school where they will all tumble to their deaths.

The blood pounds now in her ears, battering behind her eardrums and the new noise makes her squish her eyes tightly shut.

The combination to her lock, focussing on that now…4, 9, 6, 2, 3… No…3, 4, 9, 2, 6…5 maybe, there's a 5 and an 8…8…8… Eight. Tommy's age.

Is Tommy still eight?

Maiden's eyes widen as an elusive yet terrible thought pokes at her; her nose tingles and a lump forms in her throat.

"Kristen? Honey?"

Maiden snatches herself back to the real world. Her hands are trembling. They are in mid-air, reaching for a locker that she now realizes isn't even hers.

"Kristen?"

Maiden turns to see Mrs. Mooney, the school counsellor (or Colleen, as she prefers to be called) looking at her. Mooney's brows are close to meeting above the rim of her glasses and Maiden wonders what she knows. "I'm just…" she sees that the buzzer must have sounded already, the corridor is empty but for the two of them, "I'm late. I'm sorry."

Mrs. Mooney frowns and bends down so that she is nearer to Maiden's eyes, "No, Kristen, it's okay."

Mooney reaches a hand out, she's going to touch Maiden's shoulder. Maiden pulls back, she hears herself hitting against the lockers, the tinny bang echoes through the hallway all the way up to the skylights where she sees a raven picking at the glass.

"It's okay, Kristen. Why don't you come with me? We'll have a little talk. Okay?"

Maiden doesn't want Mooney to touch her. Sometimes when Mooney touches her, she sees into Maiden and if she did, then there'd be trouble.

Mooney takes the hint and leads the way to her office, checking behind her every few steps to see that Maiden is obediently following behind.

Maiden likes the posters in Mooney's office. There's one of a man on top of a big mountain, he seems really happy to be there. Her favourite is the one of a puppy with floppy ears, it seems to be pointing its little paw at Maiden and under it is the question: WHO'S AWESOME? And then there's the DESTINY poster, it's dumb, a quay, a wooden pier jutting out into an ocean of a colour not from here and at the end of it is a little hut with a pointy roof. Maiden thinks that's stupid, that's not destiny. Maiden thinks she knows a better destiny than a crappy old hut.

"So, Kristen," Mooney gives Maiden a paper cup filled with water and then perches on the corner of her desk, "it's always nice to see you of course but, I have to say, Mr. Trumbleau and I are concerned that you came to school today."

Maiden wonders why Mr. Trumbleau is concerned. Bad. Bad if the principle is involved; he didn't even get involved the time that Child Protective Services met with Mooney about stuff.

"Do you remember we talked about how you might need some time away? Kristen?"

"Yeah," Maiden lies.

"Did your mum say it was okay for you to come to school today?"

Maiden thinks for a while then shakes her head.

"Is your mum at home? Maybe I could give her a call?"

"No," *don't call home*, "she's not home. I…I just…" Maiden feels the poke of the terrible thought again, except now she knows it's not a terrible thought – it's a memory and one she ponders through the water in the paper cup. "I was just coming to pick up my social studies book. I wanted to do some work at home."

Mooney seems relieved. She steps around her desk to her chair. She sits and turns over a frame filled with colourful sand and blue liquid sandwiched between two squares of glass. She smiles at Maiden. The sand and fluid gently swap places, a line of silvery bubbles pop away at the top of what now looks like a blue sky above a sloping alien beach.

"That's good. That's good, Kristen, but now isn't the time for you to be worrying about schoolwork. It's very soon. You need time now, honey. It's important that you take a break so you and your mum can work through all of the feelings you might be having, just like they taught you both in the counselling sessions."

Maiden nods and sips her water.

"So your mum's out is she?" says Mooney, cocking her head to the left. Mooney is always cocking her head this way and that, sometimes she looks like a demented parrot.

Maiden looks at the puppy again and it's just as cute as before but now it isn't asking Maiden WHO'S AWESOME? Instead, it's telling her something.

Mooney's standing up. "Kristen? I'm just going to pop to Mr. Trumbleau's office. I'll be right back. You sit tight."

Mooney's gone. And now Maiden has to leave too because it's clear again.

Her destiny.

The puppy knows too because now the white words under it read: SINCHI ROCA.

CHAPTER 22 - THE PARANOID GEEK

Ali often judged on appearance. She could tell a lot about people by how they presented themselves to the world and Greg Ballantine's shell satisfied the preconceived clichés Ali had arrived at the techie's house with.

Not only was she now viewing him through a sleek, high-tech monitor to the right of his front door, but he was bespectacled and sported a shock of wild hair that seemed to hint that the skull beneath it contained a highly complex and superior brain. She also noticed the rim of what had to be a turtleneck sweater at the bottom of the frame under his weak jaw.

Cuzzocrea had already introduced himself and, at Ballantine's request, was holding his identification up to the small camera. The IT geek was studying the ID carefully from somewhere inside the neat townhouse.

"What's this about? Are you here with a warrant? If not, you need to...*fuck off,* man."

Greg Ballantine used the word 'fuck' with all of the confidence of a child trying the curse out for the first time.

Neither Cuzzocrea nor Ali had expected to be welcomed with open arms by Ballantine considering what had happened to him as a result of his work alongside other ID-touting officers of the law in the past.

Numb with cold, Ali's toes were a catalyst to her impatience. She pushed Cuzzocrea aside and leaned towards the camera. "Greg? My name is Ali. I'm not a cop and believe me, if I were you, I'd be telling us to fuck off too but we need your help as part of a major, time-sensitive investigation. Please let us in to talk to you. Just for five minutes. Then, if you still don't want to help, we'll leave you alone, no problem at all. Greg, we're in serious need of a brain here and the stuff I need to tell you isn't the kind of information I want to be shouting out to you within earshot of your neighbours."

There followed such a long silence that Ali had almost lost hope and was just turning to face Cuzzocrea when she heard a click followed by Ballantine's voice through the speaker.

"Five minutes."

Ali and Cuzzocrea heard a series of beeps from the other side of the door. Ali assumed it to be the sound of a sophisticated security system being deactivated in readiness for their entrance. The front door sprung open a few inches and by the time Ali and Cuzzocrea were closing the door behind them, Greg Ballantine was standing at the end of the long hallway. Ali liked how his roll-neck sweater, a curious shade of mustard, also sported an essential element of any garment nerds and intellectuals favour: deep pockets.

Ali approached him and held her hand out. "Greg? I'm Ali Dalglish."

Ballantine reluctantly shook her hand but turned quickly away to avoid doing the same to Cuzzocrea.

Ali and Cuzzocrea followed Ballantine into his living room, which was set up less as a place to relax and watch TV than where the man made his living. In the room's centre was a desk, above which were numerous flat-screen monitors. A vermicular screen saver, a colour-shifting worm, moved across all of the monitors. Although the monitors were separate, it was clear the system they were linked to was connected. The worm danced an undulating routine of dips and curls smoothly and seamlessly across all the screens and, to the left of the desk on a separate workstation, a pair of smaller monitors displayed CCTV footage featuring the exterior and interior of Ballantine's house. She could even see a live shot of the three of them standing in the living room together.

Cuzzocrea pointed to the monitors. "Quite the system you've got. I'm impressed."

Ballantine shook his head. "You guys have some balls showing up here for my help."

Ali took a step closer to him. "Well, Greg, granted, my nether regions haven't seen much action over the past couple of years, but I'm pretty sure I haven't sprouted any testicles yet." She noticed that he blushed. It was what she wanted, to disarm him. "However, if you're referring to finding yourself on the Sex Offender – "

"I didn't find myself there. I didn't wander onto it! You guys put me there," Ballantine said.

Cuzzocrea spoke: "We're aware of what happened to you, Greg, and I assure you that we are in no way linked to the team responsible. We are from the Vancouver Island Integrated Major Incident Squad. We are a specialized unit and we are called in to investigate – "

"I don't care!"

Ballantine's stress carried in his voice and reminded Ali of how her son used to sound a few years ago when his voice was breaking.

"Do you know why I have a camera on my doorbell?" asked Ballantine. "Who else do you know that is so scared they have to monitor visitors and passersby?"

"We're very sorry, Greg. Truly," said Ali.

"Sorry? Not all of you, take my word for that."

Ballantine seemed to be losing whatever patience he may have mustered to open the door to them. Ali decided not to waste time. "Allow me to make the most of the five minutes you've given us. Someone in town is killing what we suspect to be members of a local paedophile ring. We've had two murders this week alone. We know you're the best techie there is and that you've managed to infiltrate local networks before so we're asking for your help again. We need a list of potential targets. We want you to tell us where the killer might be headed next."

"You already have the list. The National Sex Offender Registry. Work your way down it and go door to door."

"Problem there," said Ali, "and I only found out about this last night, is that nobody, not even cops, have access to that list. It's sealed. We're not even allowed to know who's on it or use it to investigate anything. If we don't get outside help on this one – help from you, Greg – then we'll just be sitting and waiting for the next homicide to happen."

Ballantine shook his head. "So your system's screwed and you want me to swoop in and save the day? To be a sitting duck and help the very people who fucked my life up? You want me to help catch a guy that's killing perverts, right? Am I right? That's what you want from me? For me to get on my system and pollute it with that shit? To play pervert for you? Then what? I go down? End up in prison? Or maybe worse, maybe dead this time?"

"Nothing would happen to you," Ali said. "We wouldn't let anything happen to you."

"That's what the last guys said."

"You wouldn't even be part of the official investigation and we'd make sure you worked from our squad room this time – not from your own system," said Cuzzocrea.

Ballantine looked at Ali and she wondered if she only imagined a glimmer of potential trust in his eyes. Whether real or imaginary, she had nothing to lose by taking advantage of the moment. "Look, you never know who'll be watching. Do this for us and the right people, people who might have sway and can influence things like a wrongful conviction appeal, might hear about it."

Ballantine stared incredulously at her. "You're really that naïve?"

"What do you mean?" Ali asked in all honesty.

"You're an inspector, right?" Ballantine said, turning to Cuzzocrea. "Are you RCMP? Yeah, I know you're on that island squad but, you're RCMP, correct?"

"Yes. But I'm no – "

"Forget it. Get out." Ballantine pushed himself between Ali and Cuzzocrea and headed out of the living room, towards the front door. "You know, for a second I was hoping that you were onto something big, something big enough to change things for me. I should have known better."

"Two murders in one week isn't big enough for you, Greg?" Ali said, feeling confused as she followed Cuzzocrea down the narrow hallway to where Ballantine had reached the front door.

"You two know nothing about what's really going on here. But I will tell you this, you want me to come into your RCMP station and work on finding local perverts? Been there. I found them all and guess what? Someone didn't like what I found. It landed me on the NSOR but that isn't the worst thing that they could do to me."

"Who, Greg?" said Cuzzocrea. "What are you talking about?"

Ballantine held open his front door and beckoned them to leave, "I'm saying nothing. Now please leave and don't come back here."

Cuzzocrea paused in the doorway, "Are you really comfortable with whatever happens to someone if you don't help us? Like it or not, that would be on your conscience."

Ballantine laughed but it was a false laugh. His hands were shaking as he shoved them back into his deep pockets. Ali could see they would make no further progress with him. She took out her notepad and pen and scribbled on a blank page as she listened to Ballantine's response:

"You want whatever happens to me if I do on your conscience, Inspector? Please leave now or I'll call my lawyer. This is harassment."

Cuzzocrea stepped out onto the snow-laden path. His and Ali's tracks were the only ones leading to Ballantine's doorway.

Ali spoke to Ballantine on her way out, "If *we* can't access the registry, if it's sealed? Then who is it that you're scared of, Greg?"

"What?" Ballantine said. This time Ali could see he appeared to be on the edge of tears and she felt sad for him.

"The camera. Your security system. The list is sealed, why would you think you're in danger? Who are you scared of? It isn't about the NSOR is it?"

"Tell me this, are you good at what you do?" Ballantine asked her.

"Yes. I am. Very good at it."

"And you're not one of them? You said you're not a cop."

"No." Ali leaned to him. "Between you and me, I'm not too keen on coppers either. I just help them out, I'm a consultant."

Ballantine nodded. Ali was sure he wanted to tell her something, but she was equally sure he wouldn't in Cuzzocrea's presence.

"Here." Ali ripped the page she had filled from her notebook and handed it to Ballantine. "My info and a couple of names you may or may not have come across before. If either of those mean anything to you, I'd really appreciate it if you could let me know – remember, I'm not one of them, I'm independent."

"Sometimes it's hard to tell the good guys from the bad guys, Mrs. Dalglish," said Ballantine.

"*Ms.*," Ali corrected him, "like I said before, a long time since I've seen any action." Ali smiled at him and Ballantine almost joined her. He threw a furtive glance towards Cuzzocrea before speaking directly to Ali once more, "Watch your back."

Ballantine closed his door. Ali heard him bolt it shut and activate his alarm system.

Inside the Prius, Cuzzocrea spoke as he pulled away from the curb, "That's one paranoid dweeb."

"He's scared of something," said Ali.

"We expected that. Once bitten, twice shy, I suppose."

"No. More than that. He wasn't scared of you. The fact that you're RCMP pissed him off for sure but he was scared of something else, as if…I don't know…"

"As if by talking to us, he was putting himself in danger?"

Ali thought, running portions of the conversation through her mind. "He said something back there, something that made me wonder. It struck a note with me but I can't remember what he said, exactly…something about the last time he was tasked with finding local perverts."

"Let me pull into Timmy's next to Quality Foods and we'll have another listen."

"What?" Ali looked at Cuzzocrea. "You recorded it? That's illegal."

Cuzzocrea shrugged. "You know what these smart phones are like, they have a mind of their own. How many times have you been butt dialled?"

"You are a dirty cop, Rey Cuzzocrea." Ali looked at him, surprised. "But I kinda like that dirty side of you."

"What did you give him?"

"My contact details – phone, email, where I'm staying. The usual. You know, thinking about it now, maybe I should get some cards printed up."

"What else?" Cuzzocrea said with a smirk.

"Huh?"

"Oh please, Ali. I may be a little dirty, but compared to you, I'm a saint. What did you give him?"

Ali relented. "The names. The Latin or French or whatever they are – from the tattoos."

"You thinking they could be pseudonyms? Online handles?"

Ali shrugged. "Worth a try. Could be something there."

Cuzzocrea pulled his Prius into the drive-thru lane outside Tim Horton's.

"And you think he'd come to you if he did know

anything?"

Cuzzocrea pulled up to a metal tower from which a voice emanated, welcomed him and then asked for his order. Cuzzocrea ordered an extra-large decaf Double-Double for himself and a medium Single-Single for Ali.

"More likely that he'd come to me than you *and* he also knows I'm starved of sex – that's a big incentive right there."

Cuzzocrea looked at her.

Ali explained, "Never underestimate the horny nerd, Cuzzocrea, they're predatory, hungry beasts. Believe me, I went to Cambridge."

"Are you serious?" Cuzzocrea followed the line of traffic around the outside of the building but seemed to be paying more attention to Ali than the road ahead.

"Watch you don't hit the curb," said Ali, keeping her face straight and enjoying how wound up Cuzzocrea was by her comment.

"Ali, I'm serious. You wouldn't. Him?"

As they pulled up to the window and Cuzzocrea handed a ten-dollar bill to the cashier, Ali put him out of his misery.

"Cuzzocrea, I may get my leg over less than a frigging Jain nun but no, I'm not going to be jumping Ballantine's bones anytime soon."

"Good," said Cuzzocrea, as he handed Ali the coffee cups and took his change.

"Why? You jealous?" Ali teased as Cuzzocrea headed out of the carpark, onto Dogwood.

"No." Cuzzocrea snatched his Double-Double from Ali.

"You are! Admit it, go on, you're jealous."

"Shut up, Dalglish. You are a nightmare. I should never have agreed to be your partner." Cuzzocrea scowled at her, "Get your leg over…what?"

"Less than a Jain nun? They're the ones who pull out their own hair and brush the ground before they step on it so they don't harm ants."

"Where do you get that shit from?"

Ali tapped the side of her skull. "All here, my friend. My

mind is a swirling mass of useless trivia and witty bon mots."

Cuzzocrea's phone chirped from its place on the dash. Ali's phone signalled receipt of a message a split second later.

"What is it?" asked Cuzzocrea as Ali looked at her phone. He was already speeding up.

"We're needed back at the squad room."

"What do we know?"

"Fuck." said Ali.

"What?"

"Trina. She found something new. Shit. I hate that stuck up cow."

"Now who's jealous?" Cuzzocrea said with a smile.

"Oh fuck off, Cuzzocrea."

"Trina's going to be teacher's pet now."

"Whatever. It's probably fuck all anyway *and* she'll have to send it off to Regina for analysis. Stupid turd face." Ali looked at Cuzzocrea who was still managing to smile smugly despite his new elevated speed. "Wipe that grin off your face."

"You know what they say, karma's a bitch, Ali."

CHAPTER 23 - BARTHOLOMEW'S MONSTER

Last night his wife's cancer had taken physical form and manifested itself into a gnarled and twisted hulk of bones beneath a hunchbacked carapace of sharp, warty calcifications which had insidiously bypassed the doors between rooms and found its way into the gloom of the spare bedroom where James chose to sleep.

He'd awoken from a dreamless yet febrile slumber with a feeling of ineffable menace looming above him and in the darkness the weight of the abomination had perched with cloven feet upon his chest. He had felt trapped beneath its ominous presence and could still recall the vile stench, the effluvium of putrefaction that seeped from the thing and densely coloured the darkness the hues of human decomposition. It was, he knew with uncanny certitude, the odour of his wife's rot soon to come, and he'd somehow sensed in that moment that the ethereal demon was a messenger of hell, bringing him the news that Ellen's final transition was nigh.

With the coming of that knowledge the creature had evanesced. Not just the pressure of the crouching dark ambassador atop his chest, but the vile heft of the endurance required to quietly witness the foul demise of a wife in the master bedroom, a wife clinging selfishly to a life that had already forsaken her, content to rot within her own raddled carcass.

Once roused fully from sleep, James's step had been

lighter and he felt that on this, the first real day of his new year, he would be buoyed by his fresh understanding and able to gracefully transcend all of the petty hurdles in his path –the midnight stalker's revelation had been sent to him so it might succour him during the day ahead.

The respite was welcome and came on the heels of heightened stress. Last night he had been forced to reach out to Apu with the grim news that another of their flock, Danny Gilbert, had been murdered. Apu had reacted angrily and hit James with a barrage of cruel admonishments and bitter criticisms. It had made James quite ill, feverish even, and had called an abrupt and premature end to his evening.

Still, Apu had agreed to meet. That much was reassuring. Perhaps Apu's initial reaction had been purely instinctual – born of habit, a knee-jerk response to his strict rules being broken – just as James himself had reacted to his brother Steven not twenty-four hours earlier when he'd contacted James to inform him of Tristan McMenemy's similar fate.

James respected Apu's boundaries. As first in line to succession, it was James's responsibility to ensure that all protocols were strictly adhered to on behalf of Apu. For James, he saw his duties as less a burden than an honour. However, surely in the light of such drastic, unforeseen circumstances, even Apu would have to agree that face-to-face contact was unavoidable.

James adjusted his tie and lifted his chin, checking carefully to ensure he hadn't skipped over any morning stubble. He wanted to be as dapper as possible for the meeting. Satisfied by the distinguished reflection before him, James whistled *The Marriage of Figaro* but stopped abruptly when there came a timid knock on the bathroom door.

"James? James, are you in there?"

James gritted his teeth, *of course I'm in here.* Donning his expected mask of jollity, James opened the door to find Ellen's nurse, Lana, looking disturbingly apologetic.

"Lana. How's our girl?"

Lana's expression informed James of the prognosis to

come even before her lips gave passage to it.

"James, I've called the team. It's time."

James was struck immediately by the timing of the news. Ellen couldn't die just an hour from now? Even ten minutes from now would have been enough for him to be believably unreachable. Lana's expression took on a queer sentiment, one that baffled James until he realized he was still smiling down at her.

James remedied his faux pas by pursing his lips and taking a deep breath. His mind was in a dualistic whir – on one hand, he knew to be mindful of an appropriate reaction to the news, but on the other, he was compelled by his concern about punctuality and the words he spoke betrayed the fact.

"Oh, dear, Lana. Now, I'm afraid I have to be somewhere. How soon will it be, do you think?"

"Soon, James. Now, I'm afraid."

Lana placed her pudgy hand on the arm of James's freshly laundered suit. He looked down at the nurse's hand and detected the scent of her vocation. Must he carry the smell of disinfectant upon him today of all days? James wiped at his eyebrow, panic mounting within him.

"Oh dear, dear. I have a very important meeting, you see…"

James felt Lana's hand rubbing at his upper arm and pressing the stench of ethanol deeper into the wool.

"James, why don't we take a seat?"

James wanted to protest but Lana's desire to care for him was insurmountable as she led him to the wingback reading chair on the landing.

"It's okay, James. It's the shock. It's quite normal."

"Ah, but you see, I have to go, Lana. Very, very important that I…"

The cartilage in Lana's knees cracked loudly three times as she knelt before him. "It's time. There's no need to worry about anything else today. It's time to be with Ellen. It's time for her to say goodbye, James."

James was no longer aware of his facial expression; he was only aware of the dishonour he would display when he didn't show for his assignation with Apu. Unfortunately, he was also sickeningly aware that somehow his wife had schemed to choose the very worst moment imaginable to finally die and, were he to leave now, James Bartholomew would surely garner the deserved and unshakable reputation of being a heartless monster. And a reputation like that would spread faster than cancer in a place like Cedar River.

CHAPTER 24 - MAJOR DEVELOPMENTS

It wasn't unusual, Ali had observed, for VIIMIS to have to make themselves at home in makeshift places. In essence, the team was a peripatetic troupe of nomadic investigators called together in response to major incidents in locales governed by the decisions of a killer and regardless of convenience, available space or the readiness of the destination. As such, Ali had witnessed the team 'set-up shop' in a community centre and once in an RV on the cordoned-off carpark of a popular ski resort. This time they were actually housed in a legitimate RCMP station yet, as Ali watched her breath condense as she exhaled, she found herself wishing for the RV on Mount Washington once more.

While the squad room was large and reasonably well equipped, it seemed to be located in a long-forgotten annexe of the larger, newer main building. Ali rubbed her hands together as she waited for the last spitting dregs of percolated coffee to drip into the pot at the bottom of the machine. Detective Munro, no doubt sensing the near readiness of the brew, appeared beside her.

"Freezing in here, huh?" he said.

Ali nodded. "You'd think they'd do something about it or are they trying to freeze us out?"

"VIIMIS aren't always the most popular kids in the playground. Actually we're usually treated like crap everywhere we go. At least here they give us refreshments," said Munro, as he reached for the coffee pot.

"We could do with space heaters at least. I can't think straight when I'm cold."

"Shaw's getting some." Munro held the coffee pot out to Ali. She grabbed two mugs for him to fill. "He sent a uni out to Home Depot for them."

"Good," said Ali, placing the mugs on the table and adding cream to each. "Why?"

Munro looked confused. Ali explained, "Why are we unpopular?"

"We're the scavengers, we swoop in on their fresh kills…" He noticed Ali searching through a small basket of sachets. "No sugar left, just sweetener."

"Gives you cancer. We're scavengers?"

"Yup. They get this great kill and we take over until we've picked the bones bare and then fly off again."

"It's a stolen glory thing, huh?" Ali was no stranger to animosity brought about by her success.

"Especially in tight little places like this one," Munro added.

"Where they like to keep themselves to themselves and everyone else out." Ali began to cross the room.

Munro caught up to her. "Hey, Ali?"

She stopped to listen. "What?"

Munro twitched his nose, it was his tell; the mannerism he used when he was about to cross a line. "You and Rey? You two…" Munro raised his eyebrows and thrust his pelvis back and forth towards her in lieu of completing the sentence.

Ali pretended to be seriously considering divulging a secret to him and watched Munro almost slaver in response. She spoke quietly to him, "Munro?"

Munro leaned in eagerly to hear. "Yes?"

"Get a life, you sad twat."

Ali smiled sweetly at him, leaving him speechless. She took her seat next to Cuzzocrea and handed him the coffee she had prepared for him. "No sugar."

"Is that your way of telling me I have to lose weight?" said Cuzzocrea without looking up from his notebook.

"No. They ran out." Ali felt Munro watching her from his chair across the room. She leaned into Cuzzocrea and he, though still focused on his notes, automatically leaned towards her, proffering his ear to her. Ali whispered as close to him as she could, "Do you know what I miss most about home? Proper fish and chips." Cuzzocrea looked at her. Ali signalled for his ear again, "You Canadians couldn't do fish and chips right to save your lives."

Ali left Cuzzocrea looking bemused and sat upright. She turned to Munro who made no secret of the fact that he was watching them. Ali threw him a cheeky wink.

"What the hell are you talking about?" said Cuzzocrea.

"Never mind. I'm just winding Munro up. He's convinced that we're bumping uglies."

"Bumping uglies? Really, Ali?"

Ali shrugged. "Also, you really can't get good fish and chips here."

Cuzzocrea returned to writing in his book. "If that guy put as much energy into his job as he does working the rumour mill, we'd solve cases way faster."

"Okay everyone!" Shaw began before he was immediately distracted by something on his phone.

Ali watched Cuzzocrea writing busily. She heard him mumble something under his breath, he was shaking his head. It took her a moment to realize what he had said: *bumping uglies.*

Ali smiled. Her phone chirped and she retrieved it from her pocket. She saw that she had received three text messages, two from her ex-husband – one from his private phone and one from his work phone. There was also a message from Marlene. She clicked on David's first message:

Taking kids to movie tonight

Ali replied:

Okay. Everything good there? Tell them I miss them and give them massive cuddles from me. Kenny at dentist tomorrow afternoon, don't forget. On calendar.

Next, Ali clicked on the message from Marlene:

HI HON!!! ANYT'G 4 ME 2 DO 2DAY? IF X, G'ING 4 LNCH WITH COLLEEN +

WAYNE.

Ali smiled. It was cute how Marlene thought she was doing as 'the young ones' do by condensing the words in her text messages yet she was still a stickler for punctuation and by capitalizing all of her words, evoked the impression of shouting. Ali replied:

Nope, busy. Have fun. Hopefully see you later. xxx

Ali opened the second of David's messages. Her heart felt like it became suddenly heavier as she read it:

I miss you x

That fucker. Ali fumed. David was supposed to be focused on the kids, not texting his slut girlfriend. He should be loving his time with Kenny and Sandy, not missing *her.* She shot a reply to him:

You sent this to me by mistake, David! Concentrate on the kids not slut-bag!!!!!!!!!!!

Ali's phone chirped even as the message to David's work phone was still whooshing from hers. It was Marlene's reply:

KK. <3 :-))))))) XXX

Ali set her phone to silent and shoved it back in her pocket.

Cuzzocrea spoke to her without looking at her, perhaps able to sense her annoyance, "Everything okay?"

"Fine."

"You get the voice memo I sent you? The Ballantine recording?" he asked.

"Yeah but I didn't want to access it here, bit risky with Shaw nearby. What you working on?"

"I'm trying to frame out an analysis."

"How's it looking?"

"All guess work and assumptions."

"Isn't it always?" said Ali.

"I'm working it around the brief psychotic disorder element," said Cuzzocrea.

"Need my input?"

"Depending on what this briefing's about, how about straight after?"

Ali nodded her agreement as Shaw called for attention.

"Okay, guys. Let's get rolling here." Shaw took his place at the front of the room. Trina Walsh had taken her place, sitting atop a desk, close to his left. Eden was in a chair between Trina's desk and Munro. On the opposite side of the room, Abbott was leaning against the window ledge to Cuzzocrea's left, his open laptop balanced in one hand, busily scrolling with the other.

"I'm sorry about the temperature in here. Apparently this block is what remains of the original station and the heating system no longer works in here. I've sent a kid out to get some heaters for us. Right, first things first, Rey and Ali? Any luck with the tech guy?"

Cuzzocrea shook his head. "He was uncooperative. We tried everything from flattery to soft intimidation and then full on promises but he wasn't biting. We're waiting to see if he reaches out to Ali, he seemed to warm more to her since she's not on the force but I wouldn't put bets on it, sir."

Shaw shrugged. "No surprises there then. Paul? You made it sound like you might have something?"

Abbott slapped his laptop shut and straightened, answering with his usual air of nervousness. "Yes, sir. I managed to track down Danny Gilbert's mother, sir. Sarah Gilbert. She lives up-island, in Pearson Creek? She works for a small whale watching tour company up there."

"And?" Shaw pressed.

"I spoke with her, sir."

Shaw looked impatient. "Like blood from a stone. Go on, Paul."

Munro snorted his amusement.

Abbott continued, "She was unaware of what had happened to Gilbert and so I had to inform her of it myself.

I kept the details vague and she's agreed to head down here this morning. She's going to come in and speak with me."

Shaw seemed taken aback. "Good work, Paul. Very good work."

Ali saw that Munro no longer seemed so amused.

"Sir?" Abbott's cheeks reddened and Ali knew it had to be in response to Shaw being pleased with his work. "When I told her that we were investigating her son's death, that it was being treated as suspicious, she went on a rant about her ex, Peter Gilbert? I explained he was not a suspect, that we had verified his alibi but she said – and I'm paraphrasing here – she said that it would be his fault anyway. I think she was implying that Peter Gilbert must somehow have been responsible for their son's death regardless of his alibi for the time of the murder."

Shaw moved his head from side to side, stretching his neck out – something Ali had noticed him do when he was thinking.

"Well, I've yet to meet an ex-wife with anything nice to say about her former husband. And after major incidents, even otherwise happy couples fall into the trap of the blame game." Shaw stretched his neck again before continuing. "Talk to her. Try and see if it's just good old resentment talking or whether there might be more there. Find out her reasons for leaving all those years ago too if you can."

"Yes, sir," said Abbott, opening his laptop again.

"Munro?" Shaw turned his attention to Munro who snapped himself out of a daydream.

"Yep, sir, nothing new from Peter Gilbert. Eden sorted out a liaison officer for him. I canvassed the area again last night and early this morning. Nothing's standing out, it's a quiet street and the only comings and goings during the period we're interested in were school kids. The school bus stops at the bottom of the estate and from there they all head up and split off onto the various streets. I'm still on it and I'm going to cross-reference them all to see if anything stands out. After that I'm heading to the Sunshine Valley

Centre. It's where Danny Gilbert spent most of his time when he wasn't at his dad's store."

"That's the learning disability place, right?" asked Shaw.

"Yeah. It's attached to the Baptist church on Glen Forest Road," replied Munro, folding his arms.

"So basically nothing of any use whatsoever, am I right?"

Munro frowned. "I'm still looking into it. Working leads."

Shaw huffed and looked at Eden with a question. Eden spoke: "Last night I put together everything regarding Ballantine, sir. I sent it over to Cuzzocrea and Ali, as per your instructions, and then I contacted a local family liaison officer I know. I've worked with her before and I trust her. I briefed her on the case and I sent her over to the Gilbert residence first thing this morning. I instructed her to keep her eyes and ears open for us.

"I tried to fish for info regarding local sex offenders but the team here are pretty shut down and I don't know whether that's just towards me specifically or generally. Maybe I'm being paranoid but I get the feeling that I'm not welcome and neither are my questions. I'm not holding out hope for a magic bullet."

"Keep at it, Eden. I know how good you are at putting people at ease. Charm them, Sergeant. Good effort though."

Munro shifted in his chair and sulked like a moody teenager, clearly miffed by Shaw's satisfaction with Eden's work.

Shaw clapped his hands together. "So, Trina, I hope I'm in for a treat. Take it away." He retreated a few steps back allowing Trina to take her place, centre stage.

Ali tutted. Cuzzocrea nudged her side.

"Before I get to the really important stuff, I want to update you all on the forensic evidence gathered at the scene yesterday and this morning. All of the prints, hair, blood and fibre samples have been sent to Regina for analysis…"

"There's a fucking shock," Ali muttered to Cuzzocrea.

Trina Walsh continued, "I analysed the wounds to the

torso of our first vic, McMenemy, and compared the measurements to those of the wounds on the torso of victim number two, Gilbert. The wounds appear to be consistent with each other, leading me to believe that both McMenemy and Gilbert were killed by the same perpetrator using the same knife for both attacks. My initial investigations show the wounds were made with a serrated blade. I'll be able to give you approximate measurements after the autopsy. Multiple small, superficial parallel-incised wounds extending from the stab wound margins indicate that the serrations of the blade are gently undulating, not sharply pointed, which would correspond with the type of serration one finds on a bread knife, for instance, rather than those commonly found on the blades of specialist hunting knifes. However, I'll know more when I open him up and I examine the underlying bony structures. I've been granted authorization to perform a full autopsy on McMenemy and I'm awaiting the same for Gilbert. Sir, I'd like to request that Dalglish assist?"

Shaw appeared to be as taken aback by Trina's request as Ali had felt. Shaw looked at Ali. Ali nodded and Trina looked satisfied.

"I removed several patches of the carpeted flooring from the SOC; they too are over in Regina but I did have a guy I sometimes work with in Nanoose come up to work on a two-foot square section first. It was one patch of the carpet I was most interested in, between the entrance to the room and the bed. The patch of carpet there had indentations consistent with feet. Someone had been standing there.

"The guy I use is Jerry Vincent, a former ME from Vancouver who retired out here and developed his own patented software designed to analyse, amongst other things, surface indentations and blunt force impact.

"Jerry got back to me a little over an hour ago and let me know the size, make and style of the shoe worn by the person who was standing in that spot. Not only did he indicate they were most probably the footprints of a child he also told me that this child tends to over-pronate and he assured me that within the next few hours he could tell me the child's approximate height and weight. He forwarded the details of the specific sneakers the unique markings on the sole belong to. They are the Champion Girls' Gusto Runner. They are exclusive to Payless Shoe Source stores and retail for $26.99. They come in a variety of colours. Our markings were made by someone wearing a pair in a size five and a half, although he said the shoes were at least a half size too big and the measurement of the child's foot is actually closer to a five."

"So we know someone, probably a child, was in that room at some point," said Cuzzocrea.

"Actually, we now know that the child was present in the room at some point during or soon after the attack."

"What? How?" Cuzzocrea asked.

"Because blood, human, most probably Gilbert's – but I'm waiting for the results from Regina to confirm it – was on one of the shoes. Blood splatter from the inner rise of the sole of the left sneaker had transferred onto the carpet fibres directly next to and jutting up against the indentation site made by that shoe. It is possible the transference happened the other way around, of course, from the carpet onto the shoe. I'm working on it."

"Shit. That's huge," Cuzzocrea said to Ali.

"Don't you just hate being right?" Ali replied.

"Hold on, guys. Let's not get ahead of ourselves," said Shaw. "All we know for sure is that a kid was there, not that a kid killed him. We still need the DNA back to make sure it was Gilbert's blood."

"Two more things," said Trina. "Firstly, I think you might have grounds for a Feeney warrant for the computers in the house, sir."

"Oh? Details," said Shaw, looking eager.

"I returned to the scene this morning once I finished in the morgue. I had to double check the HD camera. I wasn't sure whether my team had checked the inner monitor for prints, the flip-out screen built into it. Well I don't know what happened, maybe it turns on automatically when you flip the screen open but anyway, when I flipped the screen open, the camera began to play…"

Ali smiled; she knew what Trina was doing. She had pressed play but also knew that Shaw hadn't yet gotten a judge to sign off on the warrant to access the camera's contents. Trina Walsh had pulled a 'plead ignorance' move. It was a move worthy of Ali herself and she couldn't help but like the woman a little for it.

"I only caught a brief second or two of footage before I realized what had happened and found the stop button but what I did see was troubling. The footage featured Danny Gilbert and an unknown male minor and it was clear that Peter Gilbert, Danny's father, was the one filming."

Shaw pursed his lips. "Those were a few highly informative seconds, Trina."

Ali got the feeling that Shaw also knew what Trina was up to. Trina shrugged, feigning innocence and Ali found herself smiling again.

"Well, we'll get on that straight away, Munro?" Shaw began.

"Wait, there's something more important, sir," said Trina.

Everyone in the room was equally impressed with the amount of discoveries Trina had made alone overnight. Shaw raised his eyebrows and motioned for her to continue.

"There were markings present on Gilbert's…"

Ali jumped as she heard a sharp knock on the glass of the squad room door. Shaw also startled at the noise. A dark figure was on the other side of the door.

"Hold it there, Trina. Yes?" Shaw called out to the visitor. "Probably those heaters," he added.

The door opened and a tall, uniformed officer entered the room. As everyone present began to stand, Cuzzocrea whispered to Ali, "Chief Superintendent McLaughlin."

The man had a commanding presence and even if Cuzzocrea hadn't informed her of his rank, Ali would have guessed at his elevated status because of the air of superiority he had about him.

Chief Superintendent McLaughlin smiled at the team. "Please, please, no need. I just wanted to check in with you, ensure you have everything you need."

Ali was aware of a unique tension in the air even though McLaughlin seemed pleasant and surprisingly charming.

Shaw rushed to the doorway. "Take five." He threw the words back at them as he stepped into the outer corridor with McLaughlin.

Almost immediately the tension dissipated. Munro stood and stretched out his back. Ali heard it crack as he did so. She watched what she could see of Shaw through the small pane of glass in the door. She could tell by Shaw's body language, particularly in comparison to that of his more composed superior, that Shaw was overplaying his propitiatory, ass-kissy role. It reminded Ali of how David used to behave whenever she had seen him interact with those he wished to please; like a desperate puppy.

"So, Trina threw you a bone there. Maybe she wants you two to be buddies," Cuzzocrea said to Ali.

"I doubt it, but I was surprised, I'll give her that."

Ali stood and crossed to Trina, who was busy sorting through stapled sheets of paper.

"Hey," said Ali.

Trina looked back at Ali. "Hey," then continued with her work.

"So, the autopsy?" said Ali.

"What about it?" Trina said, still focused on the paperwork.

"What time shall we do it?"

"I've arranged for us to use one of the operating theatres at the hospital – they have so much space up there that they said one of the two smaller ORs is never used. I'm having some equipment transported up from the lab in Nanoose. The techs are going to set everything up for me. It's not ideal but I can't do an autopsy in a morgue, too much risk of cross-contamination."

"Wow. You've been busy, Trina. Did you even go to bed last night?"

"It won't be ready until tomorrow afternoon. Maybe we'll have been signed off on Gilbert by then too."

"Sounds good."

Ali wondered why Trina still hadn't turned to speak to her. Why would she still be playing childish games? But Trina had requested Ali's assistance. *Assistance*. Now that Ali thought about it, it was actually an insult. Ali chided herself for being so cynical, it was obvious Trina was attempting to bridge the gap between them; she'd extended the olive branch and it was up to Ali to accept it.

"Listen," Ali said, "I just want to say, the thing you pulled with the camera…"

Now Trina looked at Ali. "I didn't *pull* anything…"

"For God's sake, will you just let me say something nice? It doesn't happen often, Trina, you should take it and run." Trina folded her arms across her chest and nodded for Ali to continue. "I'd have done the same thing. Sometimes stepping into the grey areas is the only way to move things along. So, yeah, well done. I respect you for it."

Trina smiled. "You are unbelievably arrogant, Ali. It's sickening. You realize that you just complimented me – for the first time ever since you joined the team, incidentally – because I briefly reminded you of *you*."

Ali was lost for words.

"And, as if that wasn't insulting enough, you also accused me of being deceitful – if not a law breaker? So I'm a liar and a criminal?" Trina's voice was loud enough to have caught the attention of gossip-hungry Munro.

"You're twisting what I said," Ali said.

Trina turned her back to Ali, shaking her head. Ali had to fight the temptation to slap the back of Trina's skull but restrained herself. "You know what, Walsh? Why don't you shove your autopsy up your arse?"

"Excuse me?" said Trina, turning once more to face Ali.

Munro was now hovering nearby.

"Do it yourself, I'm sure you're more than capable of fucking it up on your own."

Trina put her hands on her hips. "Are you refusing my invitation to assist?"

Ali took a steadying breath. "Yes, but if you ever want to invite me in to give you some pointers, maybe pass on some of my superior knowledge, I'd be more than happy to help you out." As Ali walked away from Trina Walsh, she passed an excited looking Munro. "Sit down, Munro, before you shit yourself."

Ali returned to her chair next to Cuzzocrea and stared at Walsh's back.

"Looks like you two won't be shopping together any time soon," said Cuzzocrea.

"I tell you, if you lot weren't coppers, I'd ram her fucking jaw up that interactive whiteboard."

Cuzzocrea made a poor attempt at concealing his amusement.

"It's exactly what she wanted. The manipulative cow just played me."

"I doubt that."

"She did. Now she can tell Shaw that she tried but it's me with the problem."

"Forget it, Ali. She's like that with everyone. We've all been through it with her."

Ali growled in an attempt to rid herself of her aggression. It didn't work. She took a deep breath. "I am a kind, intelligent woman and all good things come to me. I am a kind, intelligent woman and all good things come to me."

"What the hell?" Cuzzocrea said as he listened to her chanting.

Ali closed her eyes. "It's a mantra…I'm trying to refocus my negativity."

"Wow." Cuzzocrea watched Ali silently muttering the mantra.

Ali opened one eye and peered at him. "I need alcohol.

Have a drink with me tonight. Munro says that Shaw's giving us the night off."

"Are you asking me out on a date, Dalglish?" said Cuzzocrea.

"Might be."

"In that case, yes." He smiled at her. "And I'll try to ignore that you're just using me to take your mind off Trina Walsh."

Shaw reentered the room looking as flustered and sweaty as he did whenever he turned up to early briefings immediately after his morning run.

"For those of you who don't know – and by that, I mean Ali – that was Chief Superintendent McLaughlin. I was just briefing him on what we have so far and he's going to do what he can to have a Feeney warrant for the Gilbert house rushed through. Good work, Trina. You have something else?"

"Yes, sir. I came across two markings on Gilbert's back, near his kidney area on the left side."

"I'm listening," said Shaw.

"The marks were consistent with a CEW."

Ali leaned into Cuzzocrea, Trina spotted the move and spoke directly to Ali, "CEW stands for conducted energy weapon, a taser."

Ali was furious with Trina's condescending manner.

"Upon discovery of the markings on Gilbert, I checked to see if there were similar injuries on McMenemy's body. There were."

"Where? I examined McMenemy and there were no taser burns or bruises," Ali said.

"Actually, there were," said Trina with a hint of a smile, "on his scrotum. Quite obvious when you know what to look for."

Ali's fists clenched. Trina was taking every opportunity she could to make Ali look like a fool.

"So the killer takes control of his or her victim, overpowers them, with the use of a taser," Shaw suggested.

Trina nodded.

Shaw turned to Ali and Cuzzocrea. "This, along with the footprints? It's all supporting your theory, guys."

Cuzzocrea nodded. "Sir."

"There's bad news," Trina continued. "The markings were consistent with one particular model. The 44000."

Complete silence befell the officers in the room.

"You're sure?" said Shaw.

Trina was.

Ali scanned the room, she was glad to see she wasn't the only one looking dumb. Abbott and Eden also appeared to have missed the significance of the taser's model number.

"Shit," Shaw mumbled.

"What's the 44000, sir?" asked Eden.

Shaw rubbed his head and stretched his neck. "Law enforcement issue. The 44000 was phased out to make way for the X26E model 26012 – the taser you all carry. The 44000 was the one RCMP officers carried from the early 2000s until 2010."

"We have to contact NCROPS," said Cuzzocrea who then turned to Ali and Eden to explain further, "NCROPS is National Criminal Operations; they maintain records of all CEWs in the division – the serial numbers of each, maintenance logs and any findings resulting from actions taken following the use of the weapon. Most importantly, they monitor the location of each CEW and its operational status."

"If an officer's CEW is lost or stolen? What then?" Ali asked.

"It'd be documented as such by NCROPS," said Cuzzocrea.

"And when they were phased out?" asked Eden.

"They were all recalled and destroyed," said Shaw. "Rey, I want you to liaise with NCROPS and then I want you working on a profile. Eden, keep fishing. Paul, you're meeting with the Gilbert mother. Ali and Trina, you're on autopsy."

"Actually, sir…" Trina began.

Ali decided to rob Trina of the opportunity to defame her further and interrupted, "Trina and I agreed it's probably best if she handles the autopsy and I follow up on some stuff I'm working on with Cuzzocrea regarding the profile. It's more pertinent that I focus on that, sir. The evidence on the DBs isn't going anywhere, but we may only have a short window of opportunity before our perp starts planning or executing another attack."

Shaw nodded. "Good with me, if that's what you've all decided?"

Ali smiled at Trina, forcing her into the same as Shaw studied them both.

"Give us the files you've prepared before you head over to the hospital, Trina. Munro, you and I need to hustle. I want a warrant for Peter Gilbert's arrest. The Chief said Trina's witness testimony should be enough. Trina? Hang back for five so; Munro can take an official statement. The Chief said it's imperative that we dot all the i's and cross the t's before we apply for the warrant. Okay, anything big, let me know. Let's hit the ground running, guys. Stay available until eight tonight for any further briefings at which time I'm taking you all off the clock until eight a.m. tomorrow morning – that is, if nothing major happens in the meantime. Good work, all of you. Stay safe."

"Wow," said Cuzzocrea, turning to Ali. "That was insane."

"What are your thoughts on the taser?" Ali asked him as they packed their belongings up.

"Same as Shaw's, probably. Not good."

"A cop's kid?"

Cuzzocrea stilled momentarily and looked at her. "I hope not."

Ali flipped the mute switch, her phone chirped almost immediately.

"I've got five to nip for a smoke if you're interested?" Munro asked Ali.

“Sure, I’ll see you out there.” She saw she had received another text from David.

“You want a coffee before we take a run at the analysis?” Cuzzocrea asked as he passed her.

“Yep, please.”

Ali unlocked her phone and read David’s message:

Not a mistake. I miss you, Ali.

Ali wasn’t sure what she was feeling but she knew it was similar to dread. She locked her phone, put it in her pocket and headed downstairs for a cigarette – one she now needed more than ever.

CHAPTER 25 - 712

The Geese are unfazed as Tommy giggles between them, arms flapping wildly, hoping to inspire the gaggle to scatter into flight.

Tommy loves geese.

Today the little park is just a gloomy and forgotten patch of melting snow speckled with the watery dark greens and yellows of goose droppings, but during the summer months it's a busy picnic spot boasting unobstructed views of the harbour and one of Cedar River City Council's obligatory totem poles.

Deserted are the slanted parking spots outside the shops. Two of them are always empty though, even in summer, because they're reserved for those new plug-in cars that nobody drives. An artsy café, a tacky tourist shop (full of Canuck shirts, maple-leaf-shaped bottles of syrup and fake native carvings that only a tourist would be dumb enough to buy), and the only A&W franchise in town are bereft of customers and sit just across the street from the park, taking up most of the ground floor of Cedar River's newest apartment building, Harbour Haven.

But Maiden isn't here for the geese or a picnic or even A&Ws yummy chicken because she is busy watching the windows of Harbour Haven. It is nine floors of gleaming glass and steel which come to a point at the front making the apartment block look like a futuristic ocean liner anchored between voyages, questioning whether it possesses courage enough to set sail once more.

Because of its architectural triangulation, each apartment on the front of the tower has a living room window that juts out to a point overlooking the marina where the commercial fishing boats unload their catch of the day. Most of the nooks are furnished with similar looking bistro style tables and chairs and Maiden imagines how nice it would be to sit there in the mornings, watching the sun rise over Quadra Island. She decides then that would be a very nice thing to do; that seems like a worthy destiny indeed.

One of the apartments is unlike most of the others because the owner of apartment 712 has furnished the angled space with a blue beanbag chair instead of a bistro set. Maiden knows the beanbag chair well and has sunken herself into it many times before. She remembers how squishy it feels and how it makes a loud rustling noise before it finally hugs you just right so you're as comfortable and warm as you can possibly be. There's a tiny hole in the stitching along one of the seams and there's always a cluster of styrofoam balls making good their escape. The polystyrene balls are sticky, statically charged, and so, no matter how careful Maiden is not to step on them, she always brings home a few with her by accident, stuck to the bottom of her socks.

Harbour Haven is one of those ultra-secure buildings where, unless the person you're visiting buzzes you in, you need a little black fob to access the door to the residential part of the foyer. Once you reach the apartment you don't even need a key, all you need is a secret number for the little metal keypad above the handle. Maiden knows all of this because she's special – she is *Maiden*, after all – and she watched the owner of apartment 712 (the one with the blue beanbag chair in the pointy window) put in his number and make the red light turn green to open his front door.

Maiden puts her hand under her. The damp wood of the picnic table makes her jeans feel wet and cold. She wonders if being out here is such a good idea; it might make Tommy even more sick. Maiden looks at him. At that moment it's hard to believe there's anything wrong with Tommy as he leaps from a picnic table, his unzipped jacket waving a happy goodbye as he lands and rolls on the snow without a care. Maiden will have to check his clothes for goose shit when they get home.

An old couple appears, seemingly out of nowhere. They pass her and the old lady says hello. They're walking a funny little dog with long white fur. The dog's pulling on its leash, desperate to set off and feast on a Canada goose. Maiden watches Tommy get up and brush himself off, half his hair is unnaturally dark and wet now. He's smiling at the dog.

Tommy loves dogs.

Maiden looks back at the building. A light's now on in 712. Steven Bartholomew – Sinchi Roca – is a late riser. Although it's probably lunch time by now, she wants to wait. To watch him for a little longer. Tommy seems content enough to watch the little fat dog do an inordinately huge dump.

Maiden waits until she sees Sinchi. He stands at the apex of his living room window drinking from a mug. He's wearing those Bud Light pants you get from the liquor store when you buy two boxes of fifteen. Sinchi likes those pants. He's wearing no shirt. She can see the twinkle of the pink heart pendant he wears against his bare chest. He's beginning to gain the thick weight of his big brother, James. It makes Maiden happy to know that Sinchi's little paunch has gotten as fat as it's ever going to get.

"Come on, Tommy. Let's go home now," Maiden calls to her little brother.

Tommy runs to her, flapping his arms and barking like the geese do in flight. It makes Maiden laugh and when she does, the old couple looks at her. Maiden smiles at them as she takes Tommy's cold little hand in hers. The old man shakes his head, nudges his wife, then minds his own business. He makes a clicking noise to his dog and walks towards the harbour with it, but the old lady, she keeps staring at Maiden and Tommy until they've made it almost all the way to the other side of the street.

CHAPTER 26 - THE PROFILE

Ali wondered if the profile was brief because she'd nailed it or because her head wasn't quite in the game. Was she so distracted that she'd been overly succinct in her analysis of the unknown subject? It was turning out to be a shit of a day – one of those days when everything is just a little out of kilter. She'd already had a heated tête-à-tête with Trina Walsh and, Ali was loathe to admit, Trina had not only outplayed her but had also outshone her.

Ali Dalglish was brought in by VIIMIS to be the expert consultant who could analyse and interpret evidence, clues and behaviours to piece things together objectively, bringing her unique dual areas of expertise in forensic pathology and criminal psychology to help the team mount their hunt for a killer, encircled in a bullseye by Ali's unerring focus and attention to detail.

As egotistical as it was, Ali was depressed by the nagging notion that her usual light was dimming in comparison to Walsh's sudden illumination. However, Trina Walsh was merely the waves atop Ali's ocean of discontent. The dangerous riptide below was far more worrying and made her professional dilemma pale in comparison. Having battled to unburden herself of the malcontentedness she had struggled with in her role as an unemployed wife and mother, she now found herself battling against being sucked into its whirl once more. It was typical of David to dip himself selfishly back into her life at the very worst time possible – a time when Ali was on the cusp of defining herself once more in the professional field and of reacquainting herself with the woman she once was.

Ali closed her eyes. Mantras weren't working and she could feel her brain swelling in response to her inner turmoil. She placed her thumbs over her eyelids and exerted pressure. She found the technique sometimes helped to alleviate the pressure which was often a precursor to one of her brain maelstroms. She blinked open her eyes and watched as the blackness blotted and seeped away, leaving the lingering ghosts of demonic moths, a Rorschach test of her own making, seared upon her retinas.

"Ali? You okay?" Cuzzocrea said from across the squad room.

Ali wondered what it would be like to say no. To admit a weakness to him. She wondered if that would make her feel better, if that by asking for his help or even just his counsel, her stress would diminish in the same way as the blackness forced upon her vision had.

"I'm good. NCROPS get back to you?"

"Not yet," Cuzzocrea said, with the same look of concern. "Were you crying?"

Ali thought the idea appeared to repulse him and there was no longer a question in her mind. "Fuck off. I haven't cried since the eighties. You want to compare notes? I've been working a profile based on your theory. It's not brilliant though."

Cuzzocrea carried his notebook and laptop and took the seat across the desk from her. "By theory, you're referring to brief psychotic disorder?"

"Well, I call it brief *reactive* disorder but let's stick to your terminology – when in Rome, and all that."

"Fair enough. It usually affects men between the ages of fifteen and thirty, it's later in women – eighteen to thirty-five – and it affects five out of every one hundred people on average."

"And considering Trina's new evidence regarding the

shoes, I think it's safe to assume we're building our profile around a female?" Ali suggested.

"Yes, Ali, when brief psychotic disorder strikes outside of the average high-risk age bracket, it's usually as a result of a significant stressor. Now, with the height you suggested during the trajectory rod examination and the size of footprint in Gilbert's room, our suspect is small – a size five. So maybe she's a lot younger than eighteen and has suffered a recent highly stressful, traumatic event."

"Thinking out loud," said Ali, "size isn't necessarily an accurate indicator of age. I'm a size five and have been since I was thirteen – well, it's a size three in Britain – anyway, if you factor in genetics and other considerations such as early childhood stress, malnutrition, premature birth, etcetera, then it's a bit of a leap to assume someone's age based on their shoe size or height alone. But I looked up those Gusto sneakers, or whatever she said they were, and they're girly – it's clear that they're designed with younger girls in mind. So those *three* factors – the shoe size, the estimated height of the perp and the design of the shoe – do combine together to give us a strong indication of age."

"So by that do you mean it's safe to assume that we are looking at a young girl? Early to mid-teens, for instance?"

Ali nodded. "Who has, according to our theory, suffered a recent traumatic event. One resulting in significant stress, a major accident or a bereavement."

"If our perpetrator is a victim of abuse," said Cuzzocrea, "that in itself could have triggered an episode."

"If she was raped, yes. Attacked."

"Perhaps by our victims."

Ali thought for a moment. "All we know for sure is that if she is suffering from BPD, then it is a reaction to an extremely disturbing event. So any of the above events are feasible. But there is an undeniable sexual element involved either with regards to the stressor event itself or to her relationships with the men; why else remove their genitals?"

"*Or*...she has a pre-existing brain abnormality,"

Cuzzocrea suggested.

"Yes. Schizophrenia? Although that's more common in teenage boys, not so much in girls," said Ali.

"Bipolar, maybe? We can we rule out dementia and Alzheimer's because of her age but what about stroke or a brain tumour?" Cuzzocrea asked, relying upon Ali's extensive medical knowledge to bring about some clarity.

"The possibilities are endless unless we narrow our focus and make assumptions. Let's frame out an analysis based on a specific theory – BPD.

"Our killer is disorganized, McMenemy was probably our killer's first victim, it was a passionate attack that began tentatively and progressed quickly. Then we need to apply what we actually know to the BPD theory: McMenemy was stabbed by someone significantly shorter than him; there were small footprints at the Gilbert SOC made by shoes typically worn by young girls, genital mutilation, trophy taking, both victims had similar tattoos and taser markings. The symbols, contents of the fridge and the closet in Gilbert's room, as well as Trina's witness statement, indicate Danny Gilbert was a paedophile and his father may also have been involved in the same."

"McMenemy and Gilbert were killed by the same perpetrator, using the same weapon," said Cuzzocrea, "so their common enemy as well as their tattoos are thus far the only link between them. But are we to assume, for the purposes of our analysis, that paedophilia is not only a further link between them but also our killer's motive?"

"Yes," said Ali. "Our unknown subject is a minor who is seeking vigilante justice in response to being victimized by McMenemy and Gilbert."

"Either in one solitary incident where both of them were present or systematically, perhaps, she interacted with each of them on separate occasions. If McMenemy and Gilbert attacked her together then it is likely that they will be her only two victims and that their attack upon her was the stressor that triggered the killer's BPD, forcing her vengeful wrath upon them, exclusively. However, if she was groomed, if she was used by them and passed around within their larger network, then it's likely that a separate, perhaps unrelated stressor occurred and triggered the psychosis and, if so, then the killings will continue."

Ali looked at her notes, "MO?"

"Multiple stabbings," said Cuzzocrea.

"And the removal of the penis is the signature."

Cuzzocrea nodded. "And the taser? Not part of the MO."

"No, it's a means to an end. She's smaller than her attackers so she arrives with the ability to overpower them. She knows her victims, she's targeting them, and she plans her attacks."

"Good. Our killer will be suffering from symptoms arising as a result of her psychosis and they would be clear to anyone interacting with her."

Ali agreed, "Yes. Everything about her would have changed following the stressor event: eating habits, sleep patterns, mood, loss of energy. But all of those things are common amongst teenagers anyway, especially girls, believe me."

Cuzzocrea shook his head. "But those early symptoms would have progressed significantly running up to the kills and likely for a period of seven to ten days after the major traumatic event she suffered or witnessed. Significant symptoms such as isolation; hallucinations; bizarre and new, unjustified beliefs; delusions, usually of persecution; a perception that other people can read one's mind is common. Those close to the child – parents, teachers, friends – would have noticed this and may well have brought it to the attention of the authorities or Child Protective Services. Sufferers also speak in ways that are confusing – disorganized thinking – they appear to be suddenly mad. The symptoms are not subtle."

"No, and they come with outer signs: bizarre clothing choices, hair, adornments and such. There are memory problems too, affecting both the long- and short-term memory, and it's common for sufferers to have no recollection of the stressor event itself during their psychosis," said Ali.

"So how do we find her?" Cuzzocrea asked.

"Reports of assaults within a three-week period, specifically violent, sexual assaults."

"Obviously, if one involving a minor crops up, then we jump on it."

"But she may have merely witnessed an assault taking place. She, or the people closest to her, may not have reported it to the authorities."

"Let's look into any incidents involving a minor," said Cuzzocrea. "Let's open it up to include other major events – motor vehicle incidents, house fires. Domestic disturbances, specifically ones where Child Protective Services have been called in."

Ali rubbed her eyes. "It's fucking hard to come up with a nice, tight profile because BPD can affect anyone so it renders all of our usual rules moot. With other cases, I can predict things like our perp's job, whether he's married or what kind of vehicle he drives, previous convictions, even what he might wear."

"Everything's out with temporary psychosis," Cuzzocrea agreed. "Never mind that we're dealing with a kid. But, on the bright side, what we have here is about as good as it gets working within our parameters."

"That's not a bright side. Are you typing it up or shall I? You know, I think I'm getting a touch of arthritis." Ali smiled at him.

"I will. You summarize it for me now, I'll input it, then I'll get it ready later, tidy it up for Shaw," said Cuzzocrea as he created a new document.

Ali took a breath, closed her eyes and began, "Female. Most likely caucasian," she opened one eye and justified the conclusion, "given the general demographic of Cedar River." Ali closed her eye again and continued, "Aged between thirteen and sixteen. She lives and attends school in the area and is familiar with the region as well as the home of Danny Gilbert. She has no use of a vehicle. She is of average to above average intelligence. She is likely to have a history of emotional problems and even mental health issues and is therefore likely to be known to local counsellors, medical professionals and regional child protection agencies as a result.

"She is motivated by vengeance. She is likely to have been victimized by McMenemy and Gilbert and possibly others. She comes from a dysfunctional home, probably a single-parent family with an absent father and a non-professional mother.

"She will not return to the scene of the crime and it is possible that she will have little to no recollection of the events leading up to her psychosis or of the crimes she committed whilst suffering from it. A full recovery is likely following a period of therapy and medication, at which point she will become fully aware of her actions and is likely at that time to feel remorse and make a full confession. Officers are advised against the application of any pressure – especially emotional. Interrogation of the subject by law enforcement officers should be avoided following the detention of the subject as this will most likely induce a psychotic relapse. In the event of her capture, immediate assistance should be sought by experts in the field of psychiatry, specifically those specializing in child psychology.

"Her modus operandi is murder by stabbing. Her signature is mutilation and removal of the victim's penis. It is likely that she keeps the severed genitals in a separate location. She hunts and stalks her prey from a discernible group – specifically thought to be local men who interact with each other within their own subculture and who are part of a network driven by acts of paedophilia. She overpowers her prey with the use of a RCMP-issue CEW. Once she overpowers her victim, she proceeds to murder them at the site by stabbing them multiple times with a common household serrated knife.

"Her criminal cycle most likely depends upon the peak points of her psychosis but can be predicted to be within a forty-eight-to-fifty-six-hour period. She is therefore likely to kill again within the next twenty-four to forty-eight hours. She will already have begun to plan her next kill and will have a target in mind.

"At present she will be displaying symptoms of brief psychotic disorder and will have made significant changes to her routine which include changes to sleep and eating habits, dress and her style and content of speech. She will unselfconsciously express delusions, particularly those of a persecutory nature, and she will be experiencing visual and auditory hallucinations. As such there will recently have been a disruption in her ability to partake in her usual childhood activities such as school, sports or social interactions. There will also have been marked changes in her appearance with regards to weight loss and personal hygiene." Ali paused. She opened her eyes and looked at Cuzzocrea. "Anything I'm missing?"

Cuzzocrea hummed to himself as he scanned through the document. "Left or right handed? Do we know that yet?"

"No. There's no way to know that for sure, except maybe in shitty TV shows. I don't think the over-pronation of her feet is significant, that was just Strap-a-dick-to-me showing off."

Cuzzocrea began to type. His phone vibrated with an incoming call. He looked at the screen and then answered it, "Sir?"

Ali watched Cuzzocrea as he listened to the voice on the other end of the call. He looked at her, stood and nodded to her. Ali hurried to gather their belongings and readied herself for news.

Cuzzocrea ended the call and grabbed the bag containing his laptop. "It was Shaw. He's about as mad as I've ever known him to be."

Ali followed Cuzzocrea out of the squad room. "What

happened? Another victim?"

"Looks like Trina's dance in the spotlight is over."

Ali felt inappropriately yet undeniably cheered by the news as she caught up to Cuzzocrea at the elevator doors. He pressed the button impatiently.

"Did he say why?" Ali asked.

"The footage on the camera."

"I knew it!" Ali said. "Stupid bitch isn't clever enough to bend the rules right. I knew she'd fucked up on that – she must have watched a lot more than an accidental couple of seconds to have gleaned the info she gave us from it this morning."

"No," said Cuzzocrea, pressing the button again, "there is no footage. The camera's blank."

The elevator arrived and Ali followed Cuzzocrea into it. Suddenly, she found she wasn't feeling quite so cheerful.

CHAPTER 27 - SHITTING AND PISSING AWAY

The ability to mask one's base nature, to don a cloak of expected empathy to obscure from view the antipathy thereunder, was a force of habit for James Bartholomew. As if he was the reluctant hero in a grand opera, he felt bathed in the limelight cast upon him by the collective glare of the medical team surrounding his dying wife and had almost exhausted his repertoire of improvised reactions by the time they'd lubed and extubated her scaly orifices.

He felt the oppressive, searching eyes of those rousted from sleep to assist in Ellen's overdue departure. Their expectations, as dense as the beast in the darkness of the spare room had been, forced him to acquiesce to the pressure of their appetite for the pantomime of suffering and so James reluctantly took her tremulous forearm between his palms. The feel of the tepid, clammy skin which draped the disaster of bones beneath it filled him with a desire to expel the acids of his empty stomach over his freshly polished brogues, which he tried in vain to focus solely upon.

The hospice team members were as duplicitous as he yet they lacked his velveteen mastery because beneath their vague air of professionally pious respect, he sensed in them an overarching excitement for the final moment to come. They were hyenas circling the feast and James was the lion, Ellen's odious carcass for now was his exclusive territorial right.

His wife's jaundiced, swarthy pallor communicated the

condition of her obsolete liver. Ellen's suppurating lips lay sufficiently agape, a proscenium arch to her long-defunct tongue lolling beyond like that of a drunken harlot, hungry for a kiss.

Lana's substantial shadow temporarily snuffed the lambent glow of the bedside lamp as she leaned over her patient and swabbed inside Ellen's mouth with a giant Q-tip. So transparent was the skin – stretched thin over the cancerous excrescences – that James could see the whiteness of the swab's bulbous tip as it was thrust inside Ellen's cheek. And, as if the swab had been dipped in an elixir of death rather than a glass of lemony water, Ellen's languid, milky eyes widened and her body stiffened, her hideously friable skeleton became rigid, the elephantesque skull took on a comical rictus and James suppressed a cruel chortle in response to the ridiculous grimace before him.

Hideous jaws snapped shut and James heard the sound of teeth as they fractured beneath the weight of diseased bone. He noticed a tiny chunk of the once lolling tongue – bloody like a slither of raw kidney – hanging between a canine and an incisor. His nearly dead wife convulsed frantically, bouncing and banging on the mattress. James smelled the stench of incontinence as Ellen shat and pissed her way to the afterlife.

Every sinew and vein, muscles long since depleted, pulsed and viciously contracted in the throes of a passion he had thus far never witnessed his wife capable of and for an instant, her unprepossessing face was unfathomably spirited and suffused with a most ironic juvenescence.

Then the stillness of mortality blanketed itself down and placed a sudden and determined full stop on the life of Ellen Bartholomew.

From behind him, satisfied lips quietly announced the time of death and the relieved widower wondered if it was now too late to meet with Apu.

CHAPTER 28 - COMPROMISED

On Hollyrood Estates, Ali and Cuzzocrea passed the SOC van. Its rear doors were open and two scene of crime officers in full Tyvek gear were perched inside. Cuzzocrea nodded to them both,

"Shaw inside?"

One of the officers shook his head, the other spoke: "He's with Walsh, in his SUV."

Cuzzocrea paused and looked around the van to Shaw's black SUV. Turning back to the coveralled officers, he asked, "Give us a heads up, how bad?"

The SOCOs shared a look and the previously silent officer pulled down his surgical mask to speak, "Ever seen Trina Walsh cry before?"

Cuzzocrea looked at Ali. "It's bad." He thanked the officers and headed towards the cordoned off home where he and Ali both signed the log and headed through the front door to the spacious foyer at the foot of the staircase. Munro was studying his phone with a concerned look on his face.

"Hey Neil," said Ali. "What's going on?"

"Huh?" Munro looked up from the screen. "Oh, nothing." He held the phone up. "Words With Friends."

"Like you have friends," snorted Cuzzocrea.

"The shit hit the fan big time here. Shaw's giving it to Trina." Munro pocketed his phone. "And not the way she likes him to, either," he added with a chuckle.

Two uniformed police officers appeared from an area

beyond the entrance hall; Ali assumed this to be the main living area of the ground floor. The RCMP officers were in the process of 'escorting' an un-handcuffed man (therefore, one not officially under arrest) from the home. The man was of average height, thin, with a white head of hair and a beard. Ali assumed him to be Peter Gilbert – Danny Gilbert's father and the house's owner.

As Gilbert passed her, Ali took note of the photochromic lenses of his glasses as they darkened on his approach to the front door. She'd found the eyewear to be a common choice of deviants who often attempted to shield their eyes from others for the same reason that those who wish to mask their truth from the world about them often sport facial hair – their reasons are usually entirely sub-conscious, and the deviants themselves are largely unaware of the steps they have taken to disguise their duplicitous nature. However, nowadays with the emergence of the hipster beards and Duck Dynasty chic, facial hair was no longer a discernible feature of deviants alone. Another thing Ali noticed about Gilbert as he passed her – aside from his sheepishly avoiding eye contact with her – was the presence of a silver wedding band on his left hand. Peter Gilbert's wife was long-since estranged from him, and so far there had been no reports of another significant other in his life.

Ali took careful notice of the ring as Gilbert stepped out into the cold afternoon, flanked by the two cops. She would have to take a closer look at it to be sure but she recognized it to be one of the special heart collection – designed by some gravity-defying actress from the sixties – and, although the collection had probably been designed with the purest sentimentality in mind, Ali knew from experience that this item epitomized the message of 'child love' and was often the jewellery of choice for paedophiles.

Ali nudged Munro. "Gilbert?" she asked him.

Munro nodded.

"Assisting us with enquiries?" Ali added.

"Not yet. Shaw will probably want to question him but

for now he's being taken to a local hotel. The SOC team came armed with the photographs taken last night – it's procedure to photograph the whole house, as you know, not just the scene of the crime itself. Shaw had briefed them on the location of all the items to be recovered as evidence under the terms of the Feeney warrant, so they had an inventory of the digital devices and the locations of each in the house. But when we got here, it was like Gilbert had been prepped. As soon as Shaw handed him the warrant, without even reading it, Gilbert says the magic words – 'I'm a business owner, blah blah blah, corruption of data could result in significant financial loss…'. So Shaw called in a Special I guy; he tried to run a live acquire programme but that couldn't happen because, guess what? The hard drives are missing."

"The hard drives?" Cuzzocrea asked.

Munro nodded. "From both of the desktops in the home. An iPad, a laptop and a Samsung tablet, all inventoried last night, were also missing from the house today."

"But this is an active crime scene so surely we've had officers here all night and all day," said Ali.

"And so was Gilbert. But we had a liaison officer with him from the early hours of this morning."

"How was he allowed to stay here? Why would he want to?" Ali asked.

"Because we were able to close off and seal the murder room itself. Once all the relevant evidence had been collected from the rest of the property, there was no justifiable reason for us to deny the owner access to the remainder of the house. He insisted. He didn't leave the premises though, that was the compromise. Shaw's just waiting for a full search and seizure warrant then he's sending a team in and they're going to turn the place upside down, find the missing hard drives and the other stuff."

Cuzzocrea asked about the camera and Munro told him that he and Shaw had found its SD slot empty. A radio crackled and Shaw spoke: "Detective Munro from

Superintendent Shaw."

Munro spoke into his radio, "Detective Munro. Go ahead."

"Clear the scene. We are a go for search and seizure. Search Team 4 are 10-17."

Munro replied, "Copy that, sir. On our way out to you now."

"10-4," said Shaw. "Dispatch from Superintendent Shaw."

Ali, Cuzzocrea and Munro all listened to the communication between Shaw and Dispatch.

"Dispatch. Go ahead Superintendent Shaw."

"Requesting an ETA on Team Sierra 4?"

"Copy that. Team Sierra 4 are 10-17. ETA three minutes."

Shaw finished with a frustrated tone, "10-4 Dispatch."

Munro stepped through to the rest of the ground floor, via the archway under which the two RCMP officers had earlier led Peter Gilbert, Ali heard him whistle sharply and call out to someone: "Thompson? Stand down, we're clearing the scene." He returned to Ali and Cuzzocrea, "I'll catch you two outside. I'm just gonna sweep for anyone upstairs."

As Munro heaved himself up the stairs, two at a time, a man appeared through the arch. It was clear that he must be the Thompson Munro had called to.

Cuzzocrea held his hand out to the man. "Inspector Cuzzocrea with VIIMIS. You're our Special I tech?"

Thompson shook Cuzzocrea's hand. "That's me."

Ali and Cuzzocrea followed Thompson out of the house and once all three of them had logged out of the scene, Cuzzocrea spoke to Thompson as they walked, "This is Ali Dalglish, she's an expert consultant and she has full clearance."

Thompson nodded his acknowledgement to Ali.

"Say, Thompson," Cuzzocrea continued, "you ever known anyone remove the hard drives before?"

Thompson's voice was thick with phlegm and Ali found herself swallowing hard as she listened to him in an effort to clear his throat by proxy. "Most people think that by deleting files they'll be okay but anyone with half a braincell knows that deleting files doesn't actually delete them from the hard drive – nothing does. Anyone with a little more sense usually takes a hammer to the computer or throws it in a fire. I know one guy who threw his equipment out of a fourth-floor rear window as we were gaining entry through the front door. Of course, none of that shit does any good. Hard disks are pretty much indestructible and most people don't even know what one looks like. Even if they did, they'd need to know their shit to corrupt the data one hundred percent and render it irretrievable."

"Okay, didn't really answer my question though, Bud," said Cuzzocrea.

Thompson stopped next to what Ali assumed to be his vehicle, a small van with a built-in cargo space. "Whoever took the hard drives knew what they were doing. They opened the casing, located it and took the whole thing out, then put everything back together again, screws and all. Honestly, there's only one sure way of stopping a guy like me from seeing what you don't want me to see on your hard drive and that's to ensure I never get my hands on it, period."

"You know a guy called Ballantine?" Ali asked Thompson.

"Greg Ballantine? Yeah. What about him?" Thompson opened the cargo space at the back of his van as Ali continued.

"Well, you're what? RCMP?"

"Special I division. We're part of the CEU – Combined Enforcement Unit," said Thompson.

"I'm assuming you're the guys called in for all things technical, right? To retrieve digital evidence?"

Thompson put his hands on his hips and looked at Ali. Clearly he found her questions to be a waste of his time.

"That's right. And surveillance."

"Okay, so why would someone like Ballantine ever be used? Perhaps if your team, or teams, or whatever are already tied up on other cases?"

Thompson rolled his eyes. "No. Because we're ethical and bound by strict guidelines. Guys like Ballantine can do what the fuck they like – except sometimes it backfires. I'm sure you know how Ballantine's story ends."

"Yes, I do. So in a nutshell, someone like Ballantine would be brought in to skirt legislation and circumvent ethical restrictions?" Ali asked.

"And they get the big bucks for it too – I know what I'll be doing when I retire. If you don't mind, I'm going home." He looked at Cuzzocrea. "Let me know if anything turns up but we both know that ain't happening."

"You're confident of that?" said Cuzzocrea.

Thompson blew out his cheeks. "Look, the reason someone only took the hard drives from…you'd call them the towers…of the desktops was to get them out of the house along with the other items without anyone – and by anyone I mean the uni's on duty – noticing."

Cuzzocrea thanked Thompson and he and Ali headed over to Shaw's SUV. Shaw was leaning on the side of it, talking to Munro. Trina Walsh was standing nearby, arms folded, and even in profile Ali could see that her eyes sported the puffiness that came as a result of an abundance of tears. Any compassion Ali was capable of towards the woman was quickly diluted by her lack of tolerance for women who cry in the workplace: it does all professional females untold damage in how their male coworkers and superiors perceive them.

Shaw spoke: "As soon as the search team arrive on site, I'll hand the scene over to them. Gilbert didn't leave the residence and so the digital evidence we need is either in that house or it was taken from the house by someone other than Gilbert."

"Most probably taken, sir," said Cuzzocrea. "All of the

items missing were small enough to be secreted in an average-sized bag. Did you look at the log?"

Shaw nodded. "Nothing seems out of place." Shaw took a deep breath, he looked at Trina and then the rest of the team. "This search is merely to confirm that the items inventoried and present last night have since been unlawfully removed from the premises."

"Can we narrow down the time window? Trina? When was it that you saw the footage on the camera?" Cuzzocrea asked her.

"She doesn't remember, exactly," said Shaw, raising his eyebrows at Cuzzocrea.

Trina looked up at the roof of the Gilbert home. "It's not that I don't remember, Doug. I'd just rather stick to that facts so I don't make myself even more of a target." She spoke to Cuzzocrea, "My time of arrival is in the log, as is my time of departure. I looked at the footage at some point shortly before I departed the residence, around eight this morning. I called Shaw from my car on my way to the squad room. And before anyone asks, that footage was there. I didn't make it up or imagine it and I wasn't trying to *pull* anything."

Ali sighed in place of a response to Trina's obvious attack aimed at her.

"Nobody's saying that, Trina," said Shaw impatiently, "but right now it looks like you provided a witness statement alluding to evidence that simply doesn't exist. Now, a judge could look at that as us – *you* – fabricating a witness statement to procure an illegal warrant. It's paramount that we find out who tampered with the camera and removed the digital evidence from the home and why. And you better hope that we do before any of the evidence is lost or destroyed." Shaw turned his back to Trina whose eyes had begun to glisten once more.

"So what now?" Cuzzocrea asked.

"Not much we can do until the search is complete," Munro said.

"Let me think," said Shaw. "Where are we with the profile?"

"We're on it," Cuzzocrea replied.

"Good. Paul's meeting with the mother and Eden…what's Eden on, remind me?" Shaw clicked his fingers impatiently.

"You had her fishing for information but I texted her earlier and asked her to look into any recent incidents involving a minor," Cuzzocrea said.

"Really? And why did you do that?" Shaw stared at him.

"Something that came up with the profile. It's our only chance of a lead on our killer, sir," said Ali, deflecting Shaw's attention from her partner.

"I see. Good." Shaw looked at his team. "I was going to suggest all of us get back to the squad room, study the log and interview everyone who came and went between us leaving and Trina making her discovery, but looking at you all now and considering the insurmountable delay we're faced with, I suppose it can all wait until first thing. What do you say we all head for Ali's hotel and knock our heads together there over a drink?"

"I'm happy with that," Munro said.

"Guys?" Shaw looked at Ali and Cuzzocrea who nodded in unison. "Trina?"

"I have two autopsies to prepare for," she sniffed.

"Fair enough," said Shaw dismissively. "Munro, call Eden and Paul, tell them to get their asses over there as soon as they're done."

Shaw stepped through the snow which covered the grass of the verge alongside his car and crossed to what Ali assumed was the officer in charge of the search team who was waiting at the yellow police tape on the outskirt of the property. Munro pulled a cigarette from his pack and crossed the street to his car to make his phone calls.

"I'll catch up to you," Ali said to Cuzzocrea. Cuzzocrea glanced at Trina before nodding to Ali and stepping away, leaving the two women alone.

Trina rolled her eyes, "Don't start, Dalglish. What I do not need right now is you gloating." She passed Ali and allowed her shoulder to collide with Ali's as she did.

"Fuck me, Walsh. You are an acidic bitch. I was going to say that I've got your back, that I'm not going to stand by and watch them land this shit on you, but, whatever."

Trina stopped and turned to look at Ali, studying her face, assessing whether Ali was being genuine. Finally she spoke: "I'm sorry, okay?"

Ali stepped up to her. "I'm not going to pretend that I like you 'cause, frankly, I'd debate pissing on you if you were on fire *but* I think whoever's behind this doesn't give a flying fuck about you, me or anybody else. They're covering their own tracks. Tampering with that evidence was a clumsy move and a risk, so they must have a lot to hide. They're scared our investigation will lead us to them. That's good. It means we're onto something and maybe we're onto something big."

"That footage was there."

"I know that," said Ali. "Why would you lie? You're a forensics geek. You love evidence, clues through science. You're not about to make shit up, to conjure imaginary evidence – you don't need to, look what you came up with last night, fuck, Trina, the work you put in was remarkable."

Trina nodded, her chin crumpled with suppressed emotion. "I appreciate that, Ali. Thank you."

Ali stepped closer to her. "But you might want to get a grip of this girly crying shit. It makes you look like an idiot and doesn't strengthen your case. Also, men hate it – chemically, I mean."

Trina threw her hands up. "What the hell? Just when I think you're…"

"I'm serious, Walsh. It triggers a neurobiological chemosignal in them; it makes them fucking hate you. It's proven, scientifically. If you want a man to take you seriously, don't ever cry in front of him. And don't cry in front of your male boss, especially if he's also your lover."

Trina's mouth opened to respond but she was clearly lost for words. Suddenly she began to laugh. Trina Walsh laughed so hard that it spurred a fresh batch of tears. Ali noticed that Shaw and the search team officer were looking over at them. "See, woman? You're doing it again. Crying all over the fucking place."

Trina wiped her eyes and sniffed. She looked at Ali. "I hate you."

"What's new? I hate you too," said Ali, "but if someone thinks they can screw with the only other woman I've met who shares my passion for poking around in dead bodies, then they're going to have to get past me first."

Trina nodded. "Thank you."

Ali smiled. "I'd hug you but men hate that shit too…unless we did it in a quasi-lesbian manner after several shots of tequila. Which reminds me, get your arse over to the Artisan Lodge, have a few drinks and find your feet again. You'll regret it if you don't and your DBs aren't going anywhere." She shrugged at Trina. "Up to you, I'm not going to beg you but just know, I've got your back."

Ali left her and joined Cuzzocrea in his Prius. He pressed the ignition starter button as Ali buckled her seatbelt.

"When you guys have an active crime scene, it's totally secure, right?" Ali asked. "Not like somebody could break in, gain access undetected?"

"No."

"So then, Cuzzocrea, something very suspect has happened and I hate to tell you this, one or more of your guys knows about it too."

Cuzzocrea nodded his reluctant acknowledgement and pulled away from the curb.

CHAPTER 29 - EMAIL

The Devereux mum is sweeping the walkway outside all of the apartment doors of the third floor. Why is she doing that? Who does that? Maiden can't remember anyone ever sweeping the front before. Next she'll be scraping up the little grey discs that are decades worth of spat-out gum. Then what? A block party? No wonder people like her don't last long around here. Maiden thinks maybe Mum was right about Mrs. Devereux – about the granola getting to her brain.

It's too late for Maiden to step back around the corner and hide in the stairwell because Devereux's looking at her. She isn't sweeping now; her broom is up straight and her yellow washing-up-gloved hands are crossed over the top of the handle. She smiles at Maiden, sort of. She's out of breath from all the sweeping, like it's wearing her out. She's a pretty lady, Maiden decides. Her hair is pulled into a high ponytail at the back of her neat head and her teeth are a straight row of perfect white, like in some toothpaste ad on TV.

"Hi," Devereux says.

Maiden steps over to the railing where a hump of untouched snow runs along the top of the green metal. Tommy would definitely like to scoop it all off and throw snowballs over the edge. Maiden walks along; she'll have to pass the woman to get to her door. Her hand is like a snow plough and the cold piles up against her palm.

"No school for you today?"

Maiden's heart thumps hard, her cheeks burn, and she feels like they're probably as red as her Coca-Cola hoodie.

The snow tips from the railing and splats onto Devereux's freshly swept concrete. Maiden looks at the mess and then at her neighbour. "Sorry."

Devereux smiles nicely and shrugs. "That's okay, it doesn't matter."

But Maiden thinks maybe it really does matter because Devereux is still looking at the snow as Maiden passes her and then, when Maiden is searching for her key, she can hear the stiff brush pushing the wet snow over the edge of the walkway.

Maiden hears the tight squeak of sneakers on concrete and as she rummages in her backpack for her stupid key, she knows that Devereux is approaching. Maiden's fingers find the cold of the brass and she fumbles it out as quickly as she can. Devereux's right there now. Shit. Shit. Shit.

"Is your mum around?"

Maiden turns. She doesn't want to say anything. Devereux's eyes are the lightest of blues, like a summer sky or tissue paper on a little boy's present.

Devereux smiles big at Maiden. "No?"

Maiden shakes her head and looks out at the cul-de-sac. "She's at work all day."

"Oh," says Devereux. She stamps her broom three times and it makes Maiden's heart thump again. "Okay, well, I just wanted to speak to her about something."

Maiden finds the lock. Her key turns; it only needs one last shove to make it click open but Maiden doesn't want to click the door open with Devereux just behind her – now she's in a pickle (as Mrs. Mooney would say) and her eyes tickle as she waits, like her eyelids are full of little spiders.

"It's just that…I think maybe your mum forgot to take the trash out. That maybe she left it in the kitchen. Do you know?"

Maiden looks over her shoulder at Devereux. Devereux's smile is going away and now she's the one with hot cheeks. She stands straighter and pulls at one of her plastic gloves.

"We can smell it. Not just us but the lady in the

apartment on the other side too."

Devereux tries a different sort of smile but Maiden watches her all the way back until she disappears through the front door to her apartment with its little Christmas lights in the window and its baseboard heaters. Maiden doesn't make the door click open until she hears Devereux's vacuum scream into action and hum its growling monotone back and forth.

Once inside, Maiden waits at the front door. She can feel the cold of the day whistling against her hip through the letterbox. She can still hear the muffled moaning of the vacuum next door. The woman must be one of those neat freaks with OCD. Maybe her teeth are only white because of the fumes from all of the bleach she probably uses. Granola brain.

Maiden sniffs the air. She can't smell trash.

In the living room, Maiden is relieved to see that Mum hasn't moved from the couch. Devereux's lucky that Mum didn't hear her. Mum'd have ripped Devereux a new asshole for saying that about the smell. Maiden pulls the blanket up higher. The belt pulled tight on Mum's arm is making her fingers blue so Maiden flicks it free and lets it drop to the carpet – next to the needle and the spoon and the open cookie tin. She pushes Mum's arm up but it keeps flopping out again so she finally tucks it in with the blanket and then it stays put.

The computer is on a little table under the window, next to the old TV which hasn't worked for a long time. The curtains are still closed. That's how Mum likes it when she's getting high. The curtains are orange but they're thin and so the light from outside makes the room feel warmer somehow, like there's a fire glowing somewhere.

Maiden shuffles the mouse next to the keyboard and the screen goes from black to a blue just like Granola-Brain's eyes. Maiden drops her bag and pulls the stool under her as she navigates her way to the email stream she wants. She feels for her macaroni necklace and pulls it free; she picks at the glittery polish stuck along a section of the pink woollen string.

Maiden sends a short message; it's the same as all of the messages in the stream; the ones that Mum sends out when it's her time of the month and she stays in and lays on the couch:

Maiden is ready

As James Bartholomew lowered himself onto the edge of the neatly made bed in his spare room, it creaked loudly in response to his weight. The creaking was the reason he and Ellen had resigned it to the guest room a little under three years ago; its cheap base had finally relented under the pressure of James's weight at its peak – just before she'd made him go on a crash diet of pulses and white fish, of points and calorie counting. She'd said then he was eating his way to an early grave. Ha!

They'd opted for the Chiropedic adjustable sleeper with a wireless remote control, and it had proven itself a welcome addition to the master suite, a true delight to sleep in. James thought about the bed now and wondered how long it would take them to clear the room so he could have the thing back again and see the end of that wretched hospice bed and all of the paraphernalia and appurtenances that had accompanied its arrival some months ago.

James unlocked his secret phone – although, it occurred to him suddenly, that it was unnecessary to think of it as a secret phone anymore. With Ellen dead, his home was a place free of secrets; he could finally be himself here. James tingled with excitement and decided upon the best course of action. Would it be entirely too bold to call Apu? Or perhaps an email would be prudent.

James typed:

I trust this message finds you well. I myself cannot claim the same as it is with great sadness that I must inform you that Ellen passed away just moments before I was due to leave for our meeting earlier today and despite my greatest efforts, it has proven impossible for me to leave the house. I am, however, now at your disposal should you wish to rearrange. At your earliest convenience, of course.

Thanking you kindly.

Yours, ever faithfully,

Sapa.

Greg Ballantine had spent most of the day pacing his living room. He wanted nothing more than to erase the memory of the morning's unwelcome visitors from his mind and continue with his work but somehow the names scrawled in her hand on the ball of notepaper in his pocket kept scratching at his conscience.

He'd recognized the names immediately; they were indelibly seared upon his memory and synonymous with the contract that had culminated in the besmirching of his reputation, branding him henceforth as a pervert. His tattered reputation aside (and even if that regrettable twist of fate had not occurred) the same names would still have piqued Ballantine's interest since all things relating to the study of ancient civilizations had been seared upon his memory since he was a boy.

It wasn't that he was compelled to help in the way that the inspector had implied he should be through flaccid and clumsy threats, but more because he could not deny his unquenchable desire for retribution. Ballantine knew that the names – provided that they found their way into the right hands, *the right brain* – would ultimately lead to another name, the name of the man responsible for his disgraceful demise. The man responsible for his deeply fractured relationship with his elderly parents. Parents who, Ballantine knew, were of the belief that smoke is driven by fire, despite their protestations to the contrary.

The inspector mattered not to Ballantine, an archetypal gumshoe, a clock-in, clock-out cop. But the woman? She was a different matter indeed and the real reason he had trudged his rug for hours. Ali Dalglish.

He'd accessed all the files relating to her, both here and in her country of origin. He'd delved through information relating to her profession and also files relating to other, more private matters. His exhaustive search had been enlightening. Much of what he'd gleaned was impressive, even by his standards. Some of it was tragic. And it was the combination of both – the tragic and the impressive in near equal measure – that was the elixir of his itching temptation now.

Ballantine made it his purpose to uncover a person's hidden truths before placing his trust in them for he found that a person's essence lies in what they choose to hide from common view. For that reason, Greg Ballantine resolved upon a compromise with regards to Ali Dalglish, a compromise that would put her on her mettle without leaving him vulnerable. He would not risk his own safety by handing her the entire loaf; he would merely provide her with flour and perhaps yeast. If her past was anything to rely upon, and if the scars of her youth seeped bloody beneath her confident shell, then she would follow the recipe he wrote.

If Ali Dalglish had half the mental capacity he believed of her, then she too, as he once had, would happen upon a discovery that would potentially – provided she was as brave and steadfast as her younger self – bring about the downfall of a truly evil being.

Ballantine pulled the crumpled notepaper from his pocket and unfurled it. He began to type:

Ms. Dalglish.

Quispe.

Cápac.

More besides. (Re: Hurin moiety)

Another name for you: Yupanqui/Glen Christie – Vancouver Island Correctional Centre, Saanich.

Mere seconds after sending the email, Ballantine felt his marrow chill, as if by sending it he had inadvertently opened a door to a dangerous world he had hitherto denied entry, a world in which lurked evil charlatans whose metier was to mete out swift, cruel justice upon those who dared to expose them, men with everything to lose, men whose truth was the absolute antithesis of their respective public persona.

Ballantine plunged his hands into the deep woolly pockets of his sweater and swivelled in his chair away from his monitors. He was still, barely a breath. The house was empty save for himself, yet it somehow felt full – full of his own paranoia, perhaps, but brimming with danger nonetheless.

Observing intently what had only moments before been his haven, his sanctuary and the only place where he felt safe, Ballantine slowly stood. He could hear the gentle burp of the air pump bubbling in his fish tank. The sound of a jackhammer upon concrete was far enough away to render its idiosyncratic intrusion strangely calming. Yet intruded upon he certainly did feel and, as the hair on the back of his neck curled tighter, he broke through a line of dust motes, jewelled in a slither of sunshine spilling itself between the curtains closed over his front window. Ballantine tentatively stepped up to the gap. Remaining inches back from it, he realized it was big enough for him to scan his street in both directions without exposing himself to prying eyes.

The street was still and quiet save for the trickle and drip of the thaw. Although it wasn't unusual to see cars parked along the curb of his road, Ballantine's eyes were drawn to a dark SUV parked across the street and several doors down to the left of his own home. Due to the vehicle's darkly tinted windows, it was impossible to discern without doubt whether someone was watching him from the car, yet he was somehow uncannily sure he *was* being watched.

Ballantine stepped closer to the gap, his paranoia igniting a reckless determination to satisfy his curiosity. He pulled open the curtains enough to allow him a clear view whilst shielding his eyes from the sun with his hand. The red light atop the rear window of the black SUV illuminated immediately and he saw a puff of exhaust fumes condense in the cold air before it pulled smoothly from the side of the road and disappeared from sight.

Cedar River's at its shittiest just after a snowfall. Cedar River snow isn't fluffy or even white; it's icy, grey with pollutants and within hours of falling, the council has it ploughed into impacted, dirty heaps at the side of major roads or at the empty corners of large car parks where it sits for weeks, months sometimes, before reluctantly shrinking into a dirty puddle, repentant in the face of spring.

The house Bryce had been watching was still, the curtains drawn. Bryce deduced that the two sets of tracks in the snow on the path to Ballantine's front door belonged to the pair of detectives that had paid him a visit first thing that morning. The deduction had been simple since Bryce knew Ballantine to be a hermit, a loner, an outcast. It was safe to assume that somewhere beyond the drawn curtains, Ballantine was alone.

Bryce had been careful to park a distance from the house, not because he feared for his safety or even that Ballantine would call the cops if he saw him – why would he? it wouldn't do him any good – but because he knew Ballantine had his house kitted out with surveillance equipment and a security system. While Bryce didn't want footage of himself or of his number plate finding its way into a file on Ballantine's computer, he wasn't concerned in the least by what Ballantine clearly trusted to be an impenetrable security system. It wasn't.

Bryce was yet to be thwarted by any attempts to occlude him, ever. He'd made short work of the Gilbert house only half an hour ago to clean up Gilbert's – and his dead son's – clumsy mess. As far as Bryce was concerned, he had an access-all-areas pass in Cedar River; it was his town, and they were all his minions. He wasn't about to let anyone fuck with his freedom, his power – not Peter Gilbert, not a Crime Scene Entry Log, not snivelling Shaw and certainly not Greg Ballantine, the mousey fucking freak show.

There was movement in the Ballantine house, a shadow between the drawn curtains. Bryce's phone chimed. An email. *Fuck.* James Bartholomew, prattling on in his artsy-fartsy way, making excuses about today – dead wife or not, Bryce'd have to give him a reminder about respect and etiquette, teach the cunt a lesson or two.

Pulling from the side of the road, checking his blindspot as he did, Bryce saw Ballantine in the window of his house. Ballantine had made him. The twat was watching him pull away, shielding his eyes from the sun like a troglodyte emerging from a cave. Maybe James wasn't the only one who needed reminding of a few things. Maybe, Bryce thought, there were a few people who needed little reminders about how things work in Cedar River.

CHAPTER 30 - THE TÊTE-À-TÊTE

With Cuzzocrea's laptop balancing on her thighs, Ali was busy reviewing the profile as they drove to the Artisan Lodge. Cuzzocrea had assured her that, regardless of Shaw's choice of venue for the upcoming team meeting, their boss would nonetheless be cracking the proverbial whip, so Ali mumbled her way through edits and amendments, ignoring her growing nausea, a result of focussing on the bright screen as opposed to the passing landscape.

"Shouldn't I be approving changes?" Cuzzocrea said.

"Yeah," Ali replied, absently.

"Hello, Dalglish, I believe we're both credited on that document."

Ali huffed and looked at him. "What?"

"We're partners, remember? I know it's an alien concept for you but…"

"Keep your knickers on, Cuzzocrea. I'll let you at it before I give it to Shaw."

Cuzzocrea shook his head and drove past a Quonset hut, home to a company that claimed to be the world leaders of something. "I bet you didn't share your toys as a kid either, did you?"

Ali's attention remained on the screen as she answered, "By that you're assuming my childhood was one filled with toys and friends."

Cuzzocrea couldn't read her face; he was unsure whether her statement had been flippant or depressingly truthful. He let it pass as he made the turn into the hotel's driveway. Ali's phone signalled for her attention. She looked at the screen, tutted and pocketed the device.

"Fuck off!"

"David?" Cuzzocrea asked.

"No. Spam email, some sender I don't know, probably telling me that I 'very very need please to collect sizeable inheritance from sad loss of a distant relative'. If only they knew that all I'll be inheriting is gambling debts." Ali saved the document and closed the laptop. "I blame the president."

"Of the United States?"

"No, of Superstore, you know, the 'President's Choice'? Ever since I signed up for their points card I get all sorts of shit in my inbox and if there's one thing I hate, it's shit in my box...what the fuck?" said Ali as Cuzzocrea pulled to a stop in the carpark alongside an oversized pickup with wheels taller than Cuzzocrea's Prius and with the garish decals of a local a hire company emblazoned along the bodywork. "Do not even shit with me."

Cuzzocrea nodded and laughed.

"That's what Marlene picked out for us?"

"I'm afraid so," he said as he circled around to park in a stall near the front of the hotel. Ali sat in stunned silence. "Well, well, well, that's a first: Ali Dalglish, lost for words."

Ali narrowed her eyes at him. "Oh, I have words. I have some very, very bad words in my head right now. She's absolutely bonkers; I should be worried."

Shaw and Munro were already seated in the lounge area and had arranged enough seats to accommodate the team around a central coffee table.

"I'm going to stick some jeans on and check on Marlene, can you take my stuff?" Ali handed her bags to Cuzzocrea.

"Sure. Shall I get a drink for you?" said Cuzzocrea.

Ali looked past him, into the lounge. "Is this a drinking

thing or do we have to have hot chocolate and cookies like teenagers?"

"You can have a drink. I'm guessing that's the thinking behind meeting here rather than the squad room."

"So long as I'm not the only one drinking, I'll have the biggest glass of house red that they do, please." Ali headed for the elevators.

Ali kicked her boots off and threw them into the closet. She opened the top of her trousers and sighed with relief as she let her stomach relax. She dialled Marlene's room number from the phone between the two beds and enjoyed a pleasurable scratch along the lengths of both caesarean scars.

"Hey, hon," said Marlene, answering the phone.

"How'd you know it was me?"

"Peter won't phone the hotel – he's convinced I'll be charged for it if he does. Men. You all done? It's early."

"Actually, no. Come through to my room, will you?"

"I'll be as quick as a…"

The line went dead before Marlene finished her sentence. Ali stepped her trousers down to a crumpled heap on the floor and heard Marlene hammering on the door. She snatched it open. "Okay, okay. I was expecting you Marlene, one knock would suffice."

"Oh, hon, I missed you." Marlene hugged Ali tightly around her neck.

"Missed you too." Ali managed in spite of Marlene's vice-like choke hold.

Marlene followed Ali into the room. Ali had taken her trousers off and Marlene spanked her friend's butt as she headed over to the nearest bed. "It won't look like that for long. Take my word for it. My ass looked like that in my forties too and now look." Marlene pulled her pink shirt up and jiggled her rear at Ali. "Now look at it, like two ten-pound bags of PEI potatoes."

"Shut up."

Marlene flopped herself onto the bed, Ali followed her, crawling the length of the bed and huffing heavily onto the pillow.

"Peter says he likes me with more meat on my bones but that's just bs because I tell him that his stomach is fine too and, Ali, it's not – he looks like he's about to birth a litter *and* we have to push it up to find his tinkle."

Ali laughed. "Marlene!"

"It's true. That's whenever he invests in a packet of those little blue pills he still thinks I don't know about."

"You're outrageous."

"Oh yes – the outrageous Marlene McKean – that's my name. Hey, I learned a bunch of new stuff today, like FOMO."

Ali nodded for more.

"It stands for 'fear of missing out'."

"Marlene, I hate to break this to you but that is so last year."

"It's not, all the kids are saying it. Colleen's been teaching me all the hip lingo like OMG, obviously, and FYI?"

"Uhuh."

"It means for your information. And then there's West Side." Marlene rearranged her slightly arthritic fingers into something not even close to a W and hissed the words again.

Ali laughed. "What else did Colleen teach you, dare I ask?"

"NSFW, it means: not safe for work, so if you see a Tumblr blog that's NSFW you should know it's probably pornographic – not that I know what Tumblr is, but I didn't tell Colleen that because she'd already spent half an hour explaining what a meme is. Okay, what about 'turnt'?"

"Turnt? I have no idea what that is," said Ali.

"I think it means when someone's been smoking marijuana. And fleek means that your eyebrows are nice."

"No it doesn't!" Ali laughed.

"And 'bae'? So, you would think that Rey Cuzzocrea is sooo baeeeee. Or 'hella'."

Ali frowned.

Marlene sat up and faced her, "You hella fine girl – I'm telling you, you're attractive – oh, and don't me giving me no shade, sista."

Ali scooted off the bed, "Oh my God, that's it, I can't take anymore. It's bad, Marlene. How old is Colleen?"

"She only knows this stuff 'cause she works for the school district."

Ali looked at Marlene, an idea sprouting in her mind. "Yeah, now I remember. What's her job?"

"She's a child psychologist so she's a floating counsellor for school district seventy-three."

"You know, there's a kid at the centre of this case," said Ali.

"Oh no, was a child murdered? No wonder you're looking saggy."

"Hey!" Ali exclaimed.

"Just a touch, hon, under your eyes."

"Thanks, *hon.*"

"And a bit along your jowls."

"Marlene! I don't have jowls…do I?" Ali went to the mirror and studied her reflection.

"Course not, sweetie. So go on, fill me in."

"You know the rules?" Ali watched Marlene as she mimed locking her lips shut and throwing away the key. Satisfied, Ali began, undressing as she spoke, "Okay, unfortunately it's looking like our perp is a kid. A victim of abuse, a child who we theorize has been groomed as a sex slave for a group of men – our victims were, we think, members of a paedophile ring here in Cedar River." Ali rubbed deodorant under her arms. Marlene looked shocked. "I don't know any of this for sure. We don't know if we're looking for a boy or a girl yet but you know me, Marlene, *I* know. It's a girl and she's probably one of many victims who has suffered at the hands of those bastards."

"Yes, sick bastards. Ali, this is not very nice at all."

"I know. Anyway, right now all we have to go on is

victimology. We're nowhere near finding the kid and I can't see it happening easily. It's not like we can just swan into schools in the area and pull out suspicious kids and detain them for questioning. The thing that's worrying me is that Cuzzocrea and I predict she'll kill again, and soon."

"Oh no."

"Obviously we have to prevent that from happening but I want to find her because she's in her own private hell right now, not to mention, danger. I don't give a shit if someone kills every kiddie fiddler in town but this girl is in trouble. Psychologically, she's spiralling out of control and I'm scared for her." Ali dressed in jeans and a sweatshirt. "Our theory is that she's suffering from brief psychotic disorder brought on by an extremely traumatic stressor but if she comes out of that state, which she will – that's why it's called brief psychosis – reality is going to hit her hard and she'll be irreparably damaged. In fact, I think her awakening could push her to suicide."

"How can I help?"

"Well, that's where I think your sister in law can help us out. This kid most likely suffers from emotional problems anyway, even mental health issues and certainly she comes from a dysfunctional home so someone like Colleen would certainly have encountered her already. But this girl must have suffered a recent trauma, a bereavement or violence, something significant enough to have triggered her present state of mind; it was the straw that broke the camel's back."

"You know, Ali, I don't know for sure, but won't Colleen be restricted by patient confidentiality?" Marlene asked.

"Certainly. That's why this is perfect for you. I know you, Marlene, you can get blood from a stone. You just have to be clever about it…you never know, it's worth a shot." Ali sat and pulled on her socks and sneakers.

"They're having perogies tonight if you want to come with me?" Marlene suggested.

"I can't. We're having a tête-à-tête downstairs, going over the case."

"All of you? The whole VIIMIS team?"

"Yeah, they're in the lounge now. It's been a shit of a day and our hands are tied right now."

"Is Shaw down there?" Marlene grimaced as if being in close proximity of the Superintendent sickened her.

"Yes, I need to get down there." Ali checked her appearance in the mirror.

"That settles it then, even if I wasn't entering the world of espionage for you, I'd definitely get my big ass over to Wayne and Colleen's place just to avoid Cesspit Shaw."

"I've got go." Ali held her arms open for a hug, Marlene cuddled her tightly. "By the way, Marlene, could you have picked a more ridiculous ride for us?"

Marlene smiled. "Don't you just love it? I tell ya, you haven't lived till you've driven that big sucker."

Ali held the door open for Marlene to step out ahead of her. "I'll need a ladder to get into the bloody thing or I'll break my neck getting out of it."

"Say, I'm right in thinking I can't actually tell Colleen anything about your case, right?"

"Not a sausage," said Ali, closing the door to her room behind her. "But you can maybe talk about a similar case, make one up. Flatter her, like you want her expert advice."

"Flattery does get you places, like when I tell Peter that his gut is sexy." Marlene winked.

"See you later." Ali headed for the elevators.

Marlene called after her: "Ali, hon, if you speak to Kenny tonight, wish him luck at the dentist tomorrow."

"How do you…?"

Marlene held up her West Side fingers. "Social media, beotch, get with the programme…oh no she didn't…shade!"

Marlene dropped an invisible mic. Ali watched her disappear into her room, loving every ten-pound bag of her.

The entire team had gathered in the lounge including, Ali was pleased to see, Trina Walsh. Cuzzocrea angled a chair out for Ali. Sitting, she ensured that everyone was partaking in an alcoholic drinking before happily sucking back a mouthful of the not-so-bad house red waiting for her. Shaw acknowledged Ali, then turned to Abbott.

"Go on, Paul."

"She didn't exactly spell it out…Sarah Gilbert, Danny Gilbert's mother," Abbott added for Ali's benefit, "but she alluded to suspecting that her ex, Peter Gilbert, was a sexual deviant. Obviously, she didn't use those words, she's limited in terms of vocabulary, and she didn't say that he was into kids, specifically…"

"Good because she left her son with him, that would make her a heartless monster," said Trina.

Abbott continued: "He did though, according to her, have an addiction to porn. She said she'd find all sorts of magazines and videos hidden around the house and pictures. She also implied that their sex life was almost non-existent, that over the years, he grew increasingly disinterested in her, sexually. It's why she left, apparently."

"So this pornography addiction? Did she elaborate on the content of the stuff he was into?" Cuzzocrea asked.

"Yeah, she said it was nothing *gay* – her terminology – but it was girls. I asked her if by girls, she meant young girls, possibly children and she said that they all look young in those magazines but she had seen some Polaroids once that had upset her. She can remember thinking it wasn't right and she'd badgered him about who had given him the pictures."

"Anything else?" Shaw said.

Abbott paged through his notepad. "Nothing that helps us. Sir, she's not what I'd describe as a credible witness. I could smell the booze on her breath. I couldn't get much more out of her because then she started on asking where Danny's body was, that she wanted to see him and why were we keeping him from her."

Shaw nodded and sat back with his drink. Ali guessed it was a double Jack Daniels. He rubbed his forehead. "This case is driving me nuts. I hate Cedar River. I've got the Chief

Superintendent breathing down my neck and now, with this warrant being called into question…"

"Doug…" Trina began.

Shaw interrupted her before she could finish, "I'm not doubting you, Trina, you should know that, but the locals in a place like this? McLaughlin and the others, they'd love to run us out of town with our heads hanging in shame. They fucking hate VIIMIS anyway."

Eden handed a file to Shaw. "It's all of the RCMP call outs involving minors from October thirty-one through to November twenty-seven." She looked at Cuzzocrea. "That's recent enough, right? Or should I go back further?"

"No, that's great," said Ali. "If our theory is correct, then our unsub suffered a trauma within the past fortnight."

Eden looked a question.

"The past two weeks?" Ali explained, then leaned into Cuzzocrea. "You don't say fortnight here?" He shook his head.

Shaw opened the file and distributed copies of the printed list of incidents amongst the team. "How many do we have here?"

"Only twenty-nine," said Eden.

"Only twenty-nine?" Shaw repeated sarcastically.

"I included all the incidents involving children – domestic disturbances, motor vehicle incidents, all of them."

"Okay." Shaw ran his finger down the list as the rest of the team scanned the document.

Ali heard the distant ping of the elevator and kept her eyes on the reception area. Marlene appeared in her red North Face parka with a vibrantly-coloured pashmina wrapped around her neck. Ali smiled over at her but Marlene stiffened and hurried out of the hotel.

Cuzzocrea, having witnessed Marlene's swift departure, whispered to Ali: "What's going on with her?"

"That's what it looks like when Marlene McKean is working undercover." Ali leaned into him and whispered in his ear, his intoxicating scent wasn't lost on her, "She's working something for us; her sister-in-law works with troubled kids for the school district. Don't worry, she'll be far more discreet than she just led you to believe."

Cuzzocrea appeared to be doubtful but nevertheless amused.

"There's an incident here that caught my eye, Rey," Eden spoke. "November seven, MVI, a fatal collision. Family of four: Mum, Dad, fourteen-year-old boy and a ten-year-old girl. The youngest died at the scene, the others walked."

Ali marked the incident and read from her sheet. "Here, November twelfth, a domestic disturbance, both parents were inebriated, the father was arrested on a 10-83?"

"Weapons," Munro grunted.

"The mother is listed as a 10-30 dash M?" said Ali.

"She would have been taken for a psych-eval. It says here that the child, a twelve-year-old girl, was taken into the care of Child Protective Services," Eden read.

"There's a kid here who was killed in a hit and run, a boy, eight. Looks like his mum is a known prostitute in the area. CPS were called in on this one too. There's a sister listed here, a fifteen-year-old," said Cuzzocrea.

"What about this house fire?" suggested Munro. "Five kids left alone at home when the place went up, rescued by firefighters but one of the kids was med-evaced to the critical care unit in Vancouver, oh, and the family dog died. Would that fit?"

"Rey, Ali?" Shaw turned to them. "Narrow this down and give me a list of names that fit into the analysis, yes?"

They both nodded and the printouts were discarded. Shaw raised his glass.

"A toast – not that we have much to celebrate yet – but our morale's taken an ass kicking. I want you all to know that I see the work. I see my team working hard and I know we'll get this one just like we get *most* of the others."

Everyone chinked glasses but nobody smiled.

"Trina?" Shaw held his glass up to her. "I know it's been a shit of a day for you but, and I think I speak for the whole team on this, what you brought to the table this morning was remarkable and we shouldn't let the unfortunate events of the afternoon overshadow that."

Everyone agreed and Ali caught Trina's eye, threatening her against daring to cry. Shaw knocked back the remainder of his drink and stood. "Guys, we're all running on empty. You're off the clock but I want you all on your game first thing. Goodnight." Shaw gathered his things and touched Trina's shoulder as he passed her. "Walsh? A word in private, please?"

Trina nodded and collected her belongings, avoiding Ali's eyes even when she nodded a goodnight to the team. Ali wondered if Shaw and Walsh were both delusional enough to believe that the team we're naïve to their affair.

"Sir," Cuzzocrea said to Shaw, "the profile?"

Shaw grunted wearily. "Sorry, guys. Send it to me, will you, Rey? No disrespect intended but I'm bushed."

"Sir." Cuzzocrea nodded.

They all watched Shaw and Walsh leave, confident they'd seen the last of them both for the night.

Munro let out a loud groan. "Thank fuck for that. Maybe he'll screw the tension out of her and do us all a favour."

Eden slapped Munro's arm. Munro shook his empty beer bottle at a member of staff at the reception desk. "Don't know about you guys but I need one for the road."

Abbott was already zipping up his windcheater. "Not for me, bud, I'm off. Night all."

Eden slipped her shoes from her feet and wiggled her stockinged toes. "Ah, you know what I want? A bath. A tub full of lavender bath foam."

"So go have one," said Ali with a smile.

"I can't. They only have shower cubicles in The Ocean Lookout – it's not like the Artisan Lodge."

"Sucks." Ali sympathized.

Eden leaned forward and put her shoes back on. "Say, Ali? How'd you get Shaw to put you up here?"

Ali snorted. "You're kidding, Eden. I upgraded myself.

My rule is that if a hotel isn't fancier and cleaner than your own house, don't stay there."

Munro took a fresh bottle of beer from the waiter and placed his credit card on the empty tray. "Where'd you get all your money from, Dalglish?"

"Shut up, Munro," Cuzzocrea warned.

Munro continued regardless, "Seriously, you live on the ocean, you drive a Porsche and you stay in five-star hotels. What gives?"

Cuzzocrea placed his hand across Ali's, his pinkie finger briefly wrapping around hers before he took his hand away. "Don't answer that, Ali. Munro, you should make your move before I help you on your way, get what I mean, buddy?"

Ali fished her cigarettes out of her bag and shook the packet at Munro. "If I tell you something, you promise to keep it to yourself?"

Munro shook his head as the waiter handed the card machine to him. "No, you're not getting me with that. You are so full of shit, Dalglish."

Cuzzocrea sat forward. "Hey, Neil?"

Ali stood. "I swear, I'm not shitting you – there's a story there…I'll walk you out."

Munro put his credit card in his wallet and looked at Cuzzocrea past his bottle as he drained it. He slammed the empty on the table and belched loudly. "You know, Cuzzocrea, maybe you need the tension screwing out of you too. Think about it, bud."

Munro grabbed his things and met Ali in the foyer where she linked his arm and led him out. Ali looked back at Cuzzocrea and shot him a reassuring wink.

"Another fine night with the VIIMIS team," said Eden, slipping into her jacket.

Cuzzocrea exhaled. "Munro's a menace. I don't know why Shaw keeps him around."

"Because he makes the rest of us look competent?" Eden suggested.

"He does that, for sure."

Eden followed Cuzzocrea's gaze to the doors, "I think she can look after herself, Rey."

"Huh? Oh, Ali? Yeah, I know that."

"Sure you do. You and the rest of them, you're cuckoo around her. She knows exactly what she's doing to each and every one of you."

Cuzzocrea frowned at Eden. "Meaning?"

"Oh please. I mean, you all run round her like she's this delicate little princess when she's a total ball buster. Sometimes I wonder what it is about her, maybe because she's small? I don't know, but I can see what she's doing. She plays all of you for chumps and you all fall for it."

"By 'all', you mean men?"

Eden hugged her paperwork to her chest and checked her phone. "Not just men, she does it to everyone. She tries to do it with me. As for Shaw, God, you know it's lost on him that she's totally surplus to requirements; she doesn't do anything you can't do but she causes all this tension between you and Munro and Trina. Between you and me, Rey, I wouldn't underestimate her for a second – if you do, she'll chew you up and spit you out and probably take your job once she's done with you."

Cuzzocrea watched Eden start to leave before asking her a question. "That family liaison officer at the Gilbert house, a friend of yours, right?"

Eden nodded. "I recommended her, why?"

"Have you asked her about today?"

"Unofficially?"

"Of course."

"Yes, she said nobody came or went but us cops. Night, Rey."

Ali met Eden on her way out of the hotel, "Hey, you leaving?"

Eden smiled. "Yeah, I'm going to dive into that nice cold shower I was telling you about. See you tomorrow."

In the lounge, Ali allowed herself to drop into the chair next to Cuzzocrea. "I told Munro that my dad is the Viscount of Burton." Ali nudged him. "There's no such thing, by the way. It's a biscuit, a chocolate cookie in Britain – the Viscount, made by the Burton company. Great to dunk in tea."

Cuzzocrea gave her a half-hearted smile and gathered his things.

"You're going?" Cuzzocrea didn't respond. "Did I do something?" Ali asked him.

"No. I'm tired."

"Fuck off, Cuzzocrea, what's up?" Ali sipped her wine, watching him. "Go on, what did she say about me?"

"Who?" he said.

"Come off it. One minute I have to save Munro from you punching him in my defence and by the time I come back I'm enemy number one. What happened in the meantime? A complete personality transplant or did Eden say something about me?"

Cuzzocrea sat back in the chair and looked at Ali. "Do you ever just switch off or are you always watching us, analysing everyone and everything?"

"Will you just tell me what she said? I have a right to know, to defend myself. I have to say, I'm surprised at her. I thought Eden was a nice kid but she's obviously a wolf in sheep's clothing." Cuzzocrea scratched his head and remained silent. "You know, I just wanted to have some nice time with you, Rey, some one-on-one but if you want to go, then just go, piss off."

"That. She said you do that."

"What?"

"She said you play us all, manipulate us and get us to pander to you."

"What? What's *that*, by the way?"

"How you used my name, I think it's the only time that you've ever called me by my first name. Funny you should do it now, when you're being challenged."

"This is silly. I'm not even going to waste my time with this bullshit. I'm not playing you or anybody else because, frankly, I'm not capable of it. If I was playing you all, I'd have to be coming from a very sorted, centred place and you know as well as anyone, I'm about as far from centred and sorted as you can get." Ali put her glass on the table and grabbed her things. "Now it's my turn to leave and not because I'm tired but because I don't want to become angry and defensive. I've been that way my whole life and I don't want to be that person with you. Anyway, it's Eden I should be angry with, not you, you only listened, but that, Rey – *oh my God, I said your name again, what kind of an evil bitch am I?* – the fact that you did listen is just as disappointing."

Ali crossed the foyer and rounded the corner to the elevators with as much dignity and poise as she could fake.

Cuddled into the fleecy white Artisan Lodge robe, Ali wound the hairdryer's cable around its handle and returned it to its drawer. She swiped a clear arc across the steamed mirror, looking for saggy jowls and adding a second layer of anti-aging serum, just for luck.

There was a knock upon her door. It wasn't Marlene's signature seven knocks and so Ali felt her stomach tighten. She tiptoed to the peephole and saw Cuzzocrea standing on the other side of the door. He ran his fingers through his hair and knocked again before taking a step back.

Ali's decision to open the door came not because she pitied him but in response to Cuzzocrea's obvious discomfort. Observing her own hand on the door handle, Ali had to fight her instinctual desire to shut him out, to barricade any feelings for him behind an internal fortress. She looked once more through the peephole. He looked to be as unsure as she was, despite all that was between them, and it occurred to Ali that it's only when one is faced with something profoundly important and potentially life-changing that one feels doubtful enough to almost deny oneself the pleasure of it.

Ali pulled the door open and met Cuzzocrea's gaze. He stood a polite distance from her and seemed unsure of his next move and Ali suspected that he hadn't thought that far ahead, that he'd assumed she wouldn't answer the door.

"I'm sorry. I'm a jerk," he said.

"Come in." said Ali, stepping aside to allow him entry.

As the door closed, Ali felt a beat of hellish regret pass between them, an air of insecurity and awkwardness. The dynamic of their relationship had been irreparably altered, not only by Eden's ungracious words and Cuzzocrea's reaction to them, but more because they now stood before each other in Ali's hotel room.

Cuzzocrea gave Ali no more time to indulge her doubt. He lowered his face and his lips touched hers, his fingers found the nape of her neck. He kissed her gently in a predictably tender way; the way she had always imagined he would kiss her. But then Cuzzocrea's grip tightened in an entirely unexpected way, his fingers were in her hair, clutching, tugging. She felt the confident fingers of his other hand as they found her beneath the robe.

Ali realized then that there was a game afoot in the Artisan Lodge Hotel – one she was more than willing to play.

PART THREE

FRIDAY 1st DECEMBER

CHAPTER 31 - NOT A WASTED WANK

"He just lied," Ali said from her place against the rear wall in the shadows of the darkened observation room.

Cuzzocrea crossed his arms and stepped up to the window, the other side of which masqueraded as a mirror in the insipidly lit interview room next door.

"Rey?" Superintendent Shaw said as he stood alongside the inspector. "Did he lie?"

Cuzzocrea clenched his jaw and turned to Shaw. "He's being deceitful, for sure."

Inside the interview room, Munro looked especially tired and Ali couldn't decide whether the fluorescent rods caged to the ceiling above him were to blame or the fact that the detective was questioning his ninth of ten log officers in succession, Sergeant Terry Collins.

"I have an idea," said Ali.

Shaw turned to her. "Go on."

"It's a technique I've used back in the UK on occasion. It might get the truth out of him." Cuzzocrea turned to listen as Shaw nodded for Ali to continue. "Send Cuzzocrea in there. Send him in with an internal file, one with Sergeant Collins's name on the front – it doesn't need to be an actual file on him, just random paperwork, even blank sheets of paper. Put an iPad and a laptop in evidence bags." Ali looked at Cuzzocrea. "You should go in there, put the file on the table and the evidence bags off to the side. Don't refer to them, just put them there and then fuck with him."

"Fuck with him how?" Shaw asked.

Cuzzocrea was smiling at Ali as he picked up on her plan,

he explained it to Shaw: "John Douglas referred to it as the 'ass pucker factor'. It's one of the many techniques he developed during his time with the FBI's Behavioural Science Unit. He would turn the lighting down low, making it feel late at night then he'd go into the interview room carrying mysterious files on the suspect and evidence from the crime scene which he'd place at a forty-five-degree angle from the suspect. To see the contents of the evidence bags, the suspect has to turn; if he makes the effort to turn, then he's paranoid about the importance of the evidence against him. The longer you don't mention the evidence or the file, the more paranoid he gets."

"Then you give him a face-saving scenario," said Ali. "That's how you fuck with him. Cuzzocrea should give him a way of explaining his actions – suggest to him there's a way out of the mess, he can avoid disciplinary action, even criminal charges. Cuzzocrea should come from a place of understanding; he should make Collins feel like he already knows what happened and that he has the evidence to prove it but that he understands how much stress Collins was under at the time; that it was an impossible situation for him." Ali's phone trilled, signalling the arrival of an email in her inbox. She stepped away to read it.

Cuzzocrea spoke to Shaw: "We know he's lying, we just don't know what he's lying about. We do know someone removed items from that house – the search came up empty – so it's reasonable to deduce that Collins, since he's the only log officer we've interviewed who has displayed deceit, along with his partner – Constable Smith? – allowed someone to leave that house with vital evidence. I'll go through the log book, I'll exhaust him with questions, I'll boondoggle the guy. He'll crack and if he doesn't, then we move on to Smith. Douglas – the FBI profiler – always made sure, when he was using the 'ass-pucker' method, that there was another officer present, an authoritative figure from the local PD. Someone intimidating who should remain silent throughout the process."

Shaw thought for a moment. "Get Munro out of there. Let's let Collins sweat on it for a while. We'll get the items we need and I'll see if the Chief Superintendent would be willing to step in with you."

"McLaughlin?" Cuzzocrea said. "The Chief being there'd definitely increase the ass-pucker factor, sir."

"I'll see if he's free." Shaw made to leave, but Ali stopped him.

"Sir, I might have something."

"What?"

"I just got an email, just crap…but then I looked again at an email I received last night, on the way to our meeting at the hotel. I thought it was spam at the time so I didn't open it, but it was actually from Greg Ballantine – the tech guy we interviewed yesterday." Ali noticed Cuzzocrea's eyebrows raise in surprise. "I think he knows what the names mean."

"What names?" Shaw asked.

"The tattoos on Gilbert and McMenemy…Cápac and…"

"Quispe," Cuzzocrea added.

"Yeah. And he gave me another one too." Ali read from the email, "Yupanqui, Glen Christie – apparently serving time at Vancouver Island Correctional Centre."

"The VICC in Saanich?" Shaw said.

Ali nodded. Shaw looked at Cuzzocrea. "Pull this Christie guy's file then the two of you head down there and interview him. I'll handle the ass-pucker thing with Collins. I'll get Munro out of there and see if he knows how to dim those damn lights."

Shaw slammed the door behind him as he left. Cuzzocrea smiled at Ali. "Well, Dalglish, it seems Ballantine wasn't impervious to your devious charms."

Ali shrugged. "What can I say? I'm irresistible."

"Let's check out this Glen Christie," said Cuzzocrea as he held the door open for Ali to pass through it before remembering her vehement aversion to all things gentlemanly or remotely chivalrous and stepped ahead of her instead.

"How much you wanna bet Christie's doing time for sex offences?" said Ali. "Ten bucks?"

"I'm not taking that bet, Ali."

"Come on, Cuzzocrea, YOLO." She held her hand out for him to shake. "A tenner, put it there."

Munro called after them as they passed him in the corridor. "You're going to Saanich? Hey, Rey? Guys?"

Although they didn't stop, Ali and Cuzzocrea both looked back at Munro.

"Get me a Romeo's meat feast pizza on your way back, will you? Signature crust with extra cheese." Munro held his hands out, exasperated. "What kind of town doesn't have a Romeo's?"

"Cedar River, that's where," said Ali with a wave to Munro. She caught up with Cuzzocrea. "Hey, if we're stopping at Romeo's on the way back, can we take another detour, just five minutes out?"

"Where to?" asked Cuzzocrea before turning back to Munro. "Munro? I'll get that pizza for you if you liaise with NCROPS about the taser for me."

"I'm grilling the log officers."

"Not anymore," said Cuzzocrea. "Where d'you need to stop?" he asked, turning to Ali.

"My house? Kenny was at the dentist for an extraction today. I'd love to drop by and check on him – David's a wasted wank with painkillers and fevers."

"A wasted wank?"

"You don't know what a wank is? It's jerking off, masturbation? Don't pretend you're not familiar with the act, Cuzzocrea. So, if it's not too late by then? Just five minutes in and out? About as long as the average wank, come to think of it."

"Sure," Cuzzocrea said pushing open the door to a busy incident room. He approached the nearest desk and spoke to a uniformed female. "I need a 10-29 on a Glen Christie."

Ali watched as the officer accessed the PRIME database.

"He's a 10-89. He's serving a two-year sentence at the

Correctional Centre," said the officer, reading from the file on screen.

"Print that for my colleague and send it to me." Cuzzocrea scribbled his information on a post-it as the officer pulled the file from the printer tray and stapled the sheets together. "I need you to send me everything on him and all the files relating to his record, I need known associates and defining characteristics, identifying features, specifically tattoos."

"It'll all be in the file I send you but…" the officer began.

"It's for Superintendent Shaw, VIIMIS. Any questions, you'll need to approach him directly. I'll need that stuff ASAP. Thanks."

Ali followed Cuzzocrea into a waiting elevator as he pressed the button for the staff parking level of the building. "What's a 10-89?"

"You should have those ten codes down by now." He smiled. "He's a sex offender."

Ali slapped Cuzzocrea's arm. "That's ten dollars you owe me."

"I didn't take the bet, Ali."

"Bollocks! Don't be a bad loser, Cuzzocrea." Ali opened the browser on her phone. "In his email, Ballantine said I should look into the Hurin Moiety, whatever that is."

The elevator arrived in the parking lot. Ali, lost in her perusal of her phone screen, stepped past him through the elevator door which he was holding open for her and into the passenger seat of his car as he held that door open for her too. Cuzzocrea smiled and decided he liked her more when she let the feminist chip on her shoulder slip.

As he buckled his seatbelt, Ali read to him: "Apu – meaning the divine one…bladeblabla… Sapa – meaning the only Inca…emperor of the Inca Empire…holy shit, Cuzzocrea…they're all here, in the list of the emperors of the Inca First Dynasty: Cápac, the name on Danny Gilbert's back; Quispe, tattooed on Tristan McMenemy's back; and Yupanqui too. I'd take another one of those bets on Glen

Christie having that name tattooed on his shoulder."

Cuzzocrea consulted Glen Christie's file and nodded. "Yep. Yupanqui, same font, same location. What other names are on there?"

"Let's see. First dynasty? Sinchi Roca, Mayta, and, of course, Sapa and Apu. That's just the first dynasty though."

"How many dynasties were there?"

"I'm assuming two," said Ali, her brow creasing as she scrolled through her phone. "Yes, then it appears there was the Inca Civil War which led to them being conquered by the Spanish, then there were the post-conquest Incas."

"Both of our victims, as well as Glen Christie, are linked to that list of the first dynasty Incas. How many names are there besides those?"

"Thirteen, no fourteen. Although some of the names are repeated in later dynasties as if they are perhaps familial names or even indicators of rank or affiliation but we're potentially looking at as many as fourteen."

Cuzzocrea drummed his fingers on the steering wheel. "These adopted pseudonyms – if that's what they are – are arcane and presumably known by few, as is the wont of clandestine subcultures, then why the Incas? Why would a paedophile ring, if that's what we're onto here, choose to honour or emulate the Incas specifically? Just to mimic the hierarchy? Or is there something significant about that particular civilization with regards to children?"

Ali didn't need to consult the web further for the answer to Cuzzocrea's question. "Fuck a duck, Cuzzocrea! Glen Christie is not a wasted wank. *The Incan Child Mummies*?"

Cuzzocrea shook his head to indicate his lack of knowledge on the subject and started the car. He pulled out of the stall to begin their two-hour journey south to Saanich and listened contentedly to Ali's mellifluous voice as she told him all that she knew of the mummies unearthed in a tomb on the summit of a volcano in Argentina in 1999. Discovered therein were the expertly mummified and therefore beautifully preserved remains of two children:

Lightning Boy and Maiden.

CHAPTER 32 - THE RUINED CARPET

He's still wearing the Bud Light pants from yesterday and he smells; it's a mushroomy odour of stale saliva and dissipating fart that makes Maiden feel sick. His short hair juts out at one side of his head but is flattened above the side of his face, which is crumpled and rubescent with afternoon sleep.

He gives her a puffy-faced 'hey' and tells her to come in as he absently slips his hand beneath the elastic waistband of his pilled pants and scratches at his bits. He sniffs and yawns out to the side and she can smell his rotten, white tongue. As nerves bite at her bowels, Maiden shrugs and smiles sweetly.

"Drink?" He says, poking at his hairy belly button.

Maiden nods and watches him smell his bellybutton finger as he moves past the kitchen island to the fridge. Suddenly she's aware of her backpack and its contents. She can't help feeling like Steven Bartholomew – *Sinchi Roca* – must know what she has in it. She crosses to the beanbag chair, desperately grasping at her courage but her mind seems to be forgetting why she's even here, why she sent an email and waited all night and all morning, eager for his reply.

Beyond the pointed window the sky over Quadra Island is fat with the promise of a storm. The blanket of ominous grey is sliced open by a flash of silver which Maiden takes to be lightening before realizing it's actually a reflection, the refrigerator's internal light as it opens in the kitchen behind her.

In the harbour, fishermen unload their catch with hoods pulled tight around faces pink with the sting of the Pacific. Tommy is nearby. He's dangling from the lowest branch of an Arbutus tree. She watches her little brother drop from it and land squarely onto his gum-booted feet. She so wants him to look up at her. She wants to reassure him, for him to know everything is okay.

Bottles chink together as the fridge door sucks itself shut and Quadra is shrouded in dank bleakness once more. From the kitchen he whistles through his teeth and tells her to go right through, he'll be in in a minute. A bottle top hiss-pops free and tinkles into the sink.

"Hey? Maiden?"

Maiden turns and looks at him, his shoulders are freckled ginger. He tips his head towards the door to his right, the door to his bedroom.

"Go on through, babe."

Maiden pulls her backpack higher up on her shoulder. She glances out at Tommy but he doesn't see her; he isn't looking for her because he's busy chasing geese again. She crosses to the bedroom but Sinchi Roca stops her with three clicks of his fingers as he swigs from a bottle of beer. Maiden takes a breath and dares to look at him, feeling sure now that he must know – about the things she brought with her in the bag – but Sinchi just points at her shoes with his pinkie finger. Sinchi Roca's particular about his bedroom rug. Maiden kicks her shoes off, keeping her eyes on him. Sinchi's eyeing her but it isn't with suspicion; it's the look he always gets when he's ready. Maiden slides her sneakers across the laminate floor to rest against the front door.

Sinchi nods his approval at her naked feet before belching like a pig. He gets busy on the rest of his beer. Maiden smiles and heads for the bedroom, noticing he's opened a vodka cooler for her, a purple one. Maiden hates the grape-flavoured ones because they never taste like grapes.

Inside the bedroom the comforter is crumpled in a pile

upon the mattress. His bedroom is carpeted white and suddenly she's really looking forward to ruining it. Maiden moves swiftly. Normally she would be in a rush to hide her nakedness beneath the sheets but today her rush is to quietly unzip the backpack and retrieve her taser then slip into the space behind the open door where she waits, trying to ignore that she needs a pee. It'll be better this time – this time she won't have to put him in her mouth like with McMenemy or get undressed like with fat Danny Gilbert.

Her legs goose-bump with the anticipation of his arrival as she flicks the on switch and waits for the taser's signature buzzing noise as it heats up for drive-stun mode. But the taser doesn't make that noise; it stays quiet and the little dome that is a bulb next to the switch which usually flashes yellow then goes green, stays black.

Movement beyond the door, through the gap between hinges, catches her eye. Maiden flicks the switch again but the bulb remains dark. She slaps the taser and shakes it, flicking the switch over and over. Maiden feels the heat of panic blotting her cheeks as Sinchi's shadow is a slab of grey on the white carpet past the open door and Maiden feels like time slowed down. She feels the switch beneath her thumb and watches as he steps into the room, an open bottle in each hand. As she expected, he's naked now and she notices a vague fuzz of red hair on his bare butt.

The sight of him from this refreshing vantage point – making her the predator and he the prey – renews her confidence and makes the back of her tongue throb and her eyes quiver in their sockets. She hates him so much, she hates him and she can't wait to kill the fucking asshole, to stick the knife as far as it will go into him, all over, back and front till blood bubbles out between his dirty lips and coughs up into his eyes.

She sees him, first in profile as he turns to see her, then as his eyes widen when he notices that she's fully clothed behind the door, a taser in her hand. Thin wisps of hair tickle against her forehead, mimicking the beating of her heart as she flicks the switch once more and hears the crackling buzz of the copper nipples coming to life.

Then time catches up with her. The pink pendant around Sinchi's neck slaps itself onto his shoulder as he lurches forward. The bottles drop from his hands and he is almost upon her, his eyes wild and nasty. But Maiden is ready for him. All Maiden has to do is lift the taser and squeeze and his own momentum does the rest.

Maiden's grip is true as she squeezes along with the rapid jolting of the taser buried deep into the jelly of his vile paunch and she watches with delighted excitement as Sinchi Roca's eyes roll back in his skull and he gives in to the stunned agony, grimacing his way to a crumpled heap on the white carpet below.

Maiden takes the knife from her bag and stands over him. He's no longer Sinchi Roca; now he's merely Steven Bartholomew and Maiden vibrates with a rush of adrenaline when a stream of gold piss trickles from his little pink dick, flaccid against his twitching thigh.

CHAPTER 33 - THE OATH OF SECRECY

Sergeant Terry Collins narrowed his eyes and weighed his options. He could barely keep a smirk to himself. He was being tested and he had a feeling that if he passed the test, he was going to be propelled a few rungs higher on the ladder. The only problem facing him was figuring out what was being tested – was it his honesty or his loyalty under the microscope?

He ran confidently through the events of the morning for the fourth time at the bequest of Superintendent Shaw, ensuring every word matched all his previous accounts detailing his morning shift as log officer at the Gilbert SOC. But while he was mindful of his words he took time to simultaneously read the room.

Shaw was transparent and doing a shitty job of the good cop act, empathizing and nodding but unable to hide the judgement and suspicion thick in his eyes. Chief Superintendent McLaughlin, however, was his usual self – bad cop came naturally to him and Collins wondered if he'd ever seen the man smile – he was leaning against the wall behind Shaw, arms crossed. When Shaw and the Chief had arrived in the room (the dimming of the overhead lights had signalled the commencement of the game), Shaw had placed a thick file with Collins's name on it on the desk between them and two pieces of fake evidence in bags beside him, an iPad Pro and a black Dell laptop. Collins was grateful as always for his keen observation skills for they were the reason he was able to determine that the two items of 'evidence' were merely props. Collins felt a slight surge of excitement as he watched Shaw tap the cover of the file with his name on it – no doubt another prop.

Collins had put requests into Shaw on a number of occasions in the past but he hadn't, until today, received a response to a single one. Ever since he'd been a young peace officer back in the early 2000s his ultimate ambition had been to catch the eye of the head of the VIIMIS team and to be recruited. He'd watched the team swoop in and take command back when a number of dismembered feet had washed up along the Black Creek shore. At the time, Collins had secretly prayed for the remains to be the work of a deranged and prolific serial killer. The case remained open/unsolved. A group of scientists brought in from a leading research facility had theorized that the feet were merely the remains of suicides from the Thomason Suspension Bridge somewhere on the northwestern edge of Washington State (apparently it's common for tightly shoed or booted feet to become detached from the rest of a corpse in the water) and the scientists had confirmed that for a matter of weeks during the months, prior to the dismembered body parts washing ashore on the east coast of Vancouver Island, unusual riptides had been recorded through the Juan De Fuca straight and carried the detached feet up through the Inside Passage from the American coast. Regardless of the scientific theory, Sergeant Terry Collins had since retained the hope that new evidence would one day emerge and set the VIIMIS team on a history-making hunt for a serial killer, and if that ever did happen, Collins wanted to be part of it.

Collins felt sure now that the hostile interview was all a ruse devised to allow Shaw, under the watchful eye of Chief Superintendent McLaughlin, to analyse him and assess him with a view to recruiting him.

Collins looked at the Chief and saw in his look something that brought to mind one of the three oaths he had taken as a naïve rookie – the Oath of Secrecy: *"Do you solemnly swear that you will keep absolutely secret all knowledge and information of which you may become possessed through your position with the Royal Canadian Mounted Police; that you will not, without due authority in that behalf, discuss with members of the Force, or any other person, either by word or by letter, any matter which may come to your notice through your employment with the Royal Canadian Mounted Police, so help you God?"*

And then Collins was sure of the purpose of the test; it wasn't just a test of loyalty, or of something as irrelevant as honesty – they were testing his dependability; could he keep the secrets? Yes. When he was finally permitted to leave the room, Collins was confident he had played the game well when Chief Superintendent McLaughlin winked at him and almost smiled.

Collins passed his partner, Smith, in the corridor as she was being escorted to the interview room. He already saw panic in her demeanour and knew then she'd probably fuck it up and crumble under the pressure, needlessly too because, after all, it was him they had their eyes on for VIIMIS, not some stupid bitch like Joanne. Collins sniffed at her and headed for the cafeteria; he was jonesing for a coffee.

As she glanced sidelong at the evidence bags, silver rain drizzled her vision and she knew a mammoth migraine was about to besiege her brain. Constable Joanne Smith pressed her back against the chair hoping to stanch the journey of a bead of sweat between her shoulder blades before it reached her belted waist.

She cursed Sergeant Collins under her breath. It was no secret that he hated women and he'd treated her badly since day one as her training officer some eight months ago. He was a selfish prick and everybody knew it; Collins looks after Collins. Whatever was about to happen to her here in the depressing interview room with two of the scariest top dogs she could imagine being faced with, Collins was to blame, but Joanne was willing to bet that Collins was out there somewhere probably drinking a fresh coffee, migraine free and with no sweat trickling down his back.

"You're second generation, Smith. I know your father, in fact. I came up with him." Superintendent Shaw sat back and patted a fat file with her name on it as if expecting an answer but Joanne wondered where the question had been.

"Sir." Joanne acknowledged.

Shaw pursed his lips. He shook his head as if exasperated by her somehow. "I'm going to be straight with you, you fucked up. I know what happened today."

Shaw stared at her; his face reminded her of her father's and she was already dreading him finding out that she'd been hauled before the Superintendent in charge of VIIMIS and the Chief Superintendent of Cedar River RCMP. She shifted in her chair; her trousers were stuck to the back of her thighs. She looked at the evidence bags again. There was something off about them but she was too panicked to know exactly what.

"Here's the thing, Joanne: I know what happened but I also know that you found yourself in an impossible situation. One where, perhaps, you felt an overwhelming pressure – unimaginable pressure…"

Joanne swallowed but remained silent.

"I get it. I do. Been there myself. Multiple times. We all have. But let me give you a little piece of advice: now is the only chance you are going to get to rectify this mess. That's why you're in here with us and we haven't called in Internal Affairs. You want to continue in your father's footsteps, right? To honour his name?"

Fresh sweat pooled on her back. Joanne looked at the laptop and the iPad in the bags to her left and suddenly it struck her: they weren't the items she'd seen placed in a briefcase earlier in the day. The laptop taken from the Gilbert house wasn't a Dell and the iPad Pro in the evidence bag was the latest model she herself had been saving for since last June, not the iPad Mini she'd watched being removed from the house.

Joanne peered through the zig-zag of buzzing silver across her vision at Chief Superintendent McLaughlin and he confirmed her suspicions; this was a setup and Shaw had nothing. In fact Joanne decided then that maybe Superintendent Shaw was way out of his depth.

Constable Joanne Smith stuck to the events of the duty shift yesterday as they had been given to her by Sergeant Collins just after he'd persuaded her to omit a particular name from the Crime Scene Entry Log.

CHAPTER 34 - YUPANQUI

It had looked like a storybook castle – not a vomitus Disneyesque, princessy one, but a solidly dark, intimidating structure worthy of the Brothers Grimm – and had promised Ali much with its embattled parapets, all machicolations, crenels and merlons. Ali had been intrigued to experience the undoubtedly haunted atmosphere of a maximum-security prison more than a century old. However, the frontage of the Vancouver Island Correctional Centre – or 'Old Wilkie' as it was nicknamed due to its location on Wilkinson Road – was a mere façade of character and the only remaining portion of the original prison-farm erected in the early 1900s.

Alas, the interior of the building was a huge disappointment. Low ceilings sat atop white-washed cinderblock walls adorned with amateurish abstract art. The modern interior was a graceless contradiction of its daunting exterior. But it wasn't just the awkward juxtaposition of the atmospheric old and the sanitized new that grated on Ali – it was the stench of safety, functionality and security. The up-to-date systems and protocols had robbed her of an element of danger that the building's façade had teased her with.

The visitor's lounge felt like an urban youth centre sans youths or the teen section at a library sans books.

Ali and Cuzzocrea were directed to one of the many clusters of seating dotted around the room like giant plastic flowers. The seats were red plastic discs, the petals to an octagonal yellow central table, all of which were mounted on a spider-like heavy metal sepal bolted to the floor.

Ali watched Cuzzocrea feel for his gun; his fingers brushed over his empty holster. It was the third time she'd seen him check it since they'd arrived. He'd been required to relinquish his sidearm by security and he was clearly missing it. Ali could understand that – she was beginning to take for granted the feeling of absolute safety that Cuzzocrea and his gun brought her.

Ali had managed thus far to secrete her memories of the previous night from the forefront of her mind, but now, bored and utterly disappointed by her bland surroundings, their encounter was seeping forth and demanding her attention. Ali's eyes were drawn to Cuzzocrea's wide shoulders, the swell of his bicep against the fabric of his shirt, his strong hands. She remembered them on her but not in a gentle, kind way – gripping her tight and digging into the flesh of her tits. Around her neck. She thought about his dick – big, thick – bulging for her, filling her, stretching her tight, almost too big to take.

Almost.

As she felt herself blush, Ali pretended to study a painting on the wall behind her – a ghastly attempt at an English pastoral scene in cheap, unmixed acrylic – and struggled against a feeling of near-virginal gratitude that licked inside her. Ali's sexuality had never been feminine in nature; she'd always been hungry for sex, predatory even, never romantic or soft or remotely lovey-dovey – she'd left that crap to David. Ali wondered if love even mattered to her anymore. After last night it struck her as a silly, childish notion. The truth was that for much of her marriage, Ali had found herself fantasizing about being taken by a man, taken and used, fucked hard – really, really hard. The level of arousal she'd experienced with Cuzzocrea in the Artisan Lodge last night had exceeded her expectations and although initially surprised by the brutality of his seduction, she'd succumbed to it and had, for perhaps the first time in her life, found herself perfectly comfortable to bestow absolute control upon a lover. Now, frowning at the blobs of white on green where some incarcerated artist had presumably attempted to depict a flock of sheep in a meadow, Ali felt herself whetting up for him once more.

She closed her eyes and inhaled. She had to calm down. These were ridiculously unprofessional thoughts. She tried to remember the last time she'd felt even close to this level of arousal which led her to another thought… Ali tried to remember the last time, before last night, that she'd had sex.

Fuck.

"Huh?" said Cuzzocrea.

Ali opened her eyes, realizing she had spoken the word aloud. She looked at Cuzzocrea and made a poor attempt to expel thoughts of his huge dick from her mind.

"Two fucking years," she said out loud again and chided her lack of self-control.

"What?"

Ali scrambled for a believable justification for her outburst. "The…maximum sentence here. Murderers and rapists – all serving two years or less. It's a fucking disgrace."

Cuzzocrea frowned at her, then smiled. Ali's cheeks reddened and she saw Cuzzocrea's eyes glisten with knowledge. He could see all of her truths; he had found his way into her somehow and she was powerless against him.

The door at the farthest end of the visitor's area opened and in stepped Glen Christie, escorted at the elbow by a corrections officer. He was dressed in a red sweatsuit with large black letters on his chest: VICC. He was wearing white socks under velcroed flip-flops. Ali was struck by how small his feet were.

To the untrained, uncynical eye, Glen Christie would pass as a harmless, invisible a-sexual. Dark rimmed glasses, too large for his small round face, had slipped themselves down to the bulbous tip of his stubby nose. The lenses were as thick as bottle bottoms, giving him a comical, cartoonish look, his eyes disproportionately huge and bug-like. Christie was stout but short, a blockish, sturdy-looking man with a bald head over which he'd plastered a few long, greasy strands from the otherwise short black hair above his ears.

He sat on the red disc opposite Cuzzocrea and brought his cuffed wrists up to his face, pushing his glasses up his nose. Ali saw one of his tattoos, one she'd been sickened by whilst reading his file – a smiling Mickey Mouse on the inside of his left wrist. Another distinguishing feature she was keen to observe was the missing digits on his right hand. He was missing his ring and pinkie fingers above the proximal phalanx, at the second knuckle, but Christie placed his hands in his lap before she was able to see them.

The sight of Christie and the knowledge of the crime he was serving a sentence for was almost enough to purify Ali of all of her distractions. She managed to engage herself enough to listen to Cuzzocrea with at least an outward appearance of professional objectivity.

"Glen, I'm Inspector Cuzzocrea and this is Ali Dalglish."

"Okay." Christie nodded.

"We've just driven down from Cedar River. We want to ask you a few questions in connection with a case we're currently investigating. We think two of the men involved may be friends of yours."

Christie shrugged. "I don't see my lawyer here?"

Cuzzocrea shook his head. "You don't have a lawyer, Glen. That being said, the questions we'll be asking you aren't in relation to your conviction. We're here requesting your cooperation. You're not under investigation or arrest. But, if it did appear that you were likely to incriminate yourself in any way, I would be duty bound to advise you of your rights at that time. Do you understand that, Glen?"

Christie shrugged again. "I guess so." He tilted his head back and eyed them both through the thicker, semi-circular bottom of his bi-focal lenses. "Who are these friends of mine?"

Cuzzocrea sat up straighter than before and began, "Tell me how you know Tristan McMenemy?"

Christie's mouth opened slightly, he glanced at Ali. "Who?"

"Tristan McMenemy?" Cuzzocrea repeated.

Christie made an act of thinking before he replied: "No. Never heard of him."

"Danny Gilbert, then. You know him," Cuzzocrea said.

Christie pursed his lips then spoke: "Can't say I do."

"Can't?" Cuzzocrea asked.

"Nope." Christie clapped the palms of his hands together beneath the table. "Never heard of him neither."

Ali tried: "Mind if I give you another couple of names, Glen?"

Christie looked at Ali as if she'd said something highly offensive. "Wait! Say that again."

"I have two other names for you. I wonder if you're familiar with them?" Ali clarified.

"*I wonder if you're familiar with them*?" Christie made a poor attempt of mimicking Ali's accent. "What's that? Irish?"

"Scottish, actually," Ali said, unfazed.

"You're Scotch?" Christie laughed. "You shouldn't have come here, girl, you know what they to do the Scotch here?"

Ali and Cuzzocrea shared a look, communicating their mutual boredom for the benefit of Christie.

"They hanged a Scotch man here once, back in the day, for being a drunk. You lot like a bit of that," Christie mimed drinking, "don't you? You people. You like a *wee dram*."

Ali waited until Christie's child-like giggle dissipated. "Quispe. Glen, does that name mean anything to you?"

Christie pushed his glasses up his nose again.

"Or Cápac? Quispe. Cápac." Ali took her time with the names. Christie was silent. "How about Yupanqui? Surely that one rings a bell?" Ali raised her finger before he replied. "Don't lie to me, Glen."

Christie placed his cuffed wrists on the yellow table and surrendered his palms towards her. Ali saw the grotesque little stumps on his right hand. "You know I know that one."

"Tell us about it, Glen," said Cuzzocrea.

"Nothing to know, it's just a tattoo. You know, you get them, you regret them. What's this about, eh? What's with all the questions?"

"We're investigating a series of murders up in Cedar River," said Cuzzocrea.

"But you didn't recognize the names, so…you don't need to know about them," added Ali, making to leave.

"I might know them." Christie's curiosity was piqued. "Cedar River's a small place. Who was murdered?"

"We told you," said Ali, "Tristan McMenemy and Danny Gilbert." Ali watched Glen Christie's face pale. "I shouldn't really be telling you this, but…" Ali made a pretence of getting Cuzzocrea's permission to divulge details, he responded with a reluctant nod. Ali leaned in to Christie. "The murders were pretty gruesome actually. McMenemy and Gilbert weren't just killed, their you-know-whats were cut off first."

Ali gave Christie a moment to process the information. She watched as he smoothed his combed-over strands against his domed head.

"We think someone hunted them both down, that they weren't random victims," Ali continued. "Thing is, the only link we can find between them is that tattoo, same as the one on your shoulder. That's why Inspector Cuzzocrea thought we should come and see you. He thinks that whoever targeted them might be coming after you or other men in your group. But then, you're safe. You're in here. How long is it that you have left on your sentence?"

"Two months."

Cuzzocrea blew his cheeks out; he and Ali shared a look. "That should be fine. We'll get a lead before then, probably," he said with deliberately thin confidence.

Christie blinked in rapid succession. Ali noticed his neck reddening. "You know, if I were you, Glen, I'd help Cuzzocrea here as much as I could. Let's be honest – you and the victims were friends, a little club. A ring, I think we can call it. A group of guys with something in common, a shared interest. You all like kids." Ali held her hands up. "There, it's out now, nothing to hide."

Christie stared at her wide eyed. "Now hold on right there…I don't know who you think you…coming here and saying those things about me…"

Ali tutted, "Come off it, Glen. You're dumb – *Scotch is a drink, not a person* – but you're not that dumb. You guys are into kids. We know it, you know it. It's why you're in here in the first place. What? You think we didn't look at your file?"

Christie shook his head and banged his cuffed hands on the table. "No! That was a lie. He was lying because he was jealous that me and his mother were such good friends, so he…he said things…terrible things about me."

"Oh God, Glen, please, save it for someone who gives a flying fuck. We're not a jury, you don't have to plead your innocence to us. We know what you did, we know that Matthew Sutter wasn't lying. You like little boys. We don't give a shit about that. As far as we're concerned, it's none of our business, we don't even work sex cases. We're here because you might be the only one who can help us to stop this killer, to prevent you or anyone else in your little 'child love' ring from getting their dick sawed off."

"Hold on a minute. I know what this is, right here…you're not here about a murder…you're here for us…you're after us and this bullshit is just a trick to get me to talk, huh?" Christie's neck was almost as red as his sweatsuit.

"Us? Who is *us*, Glen?" Cuzzocrea asked. "If there is a list, if the killer is targeting guys in your group – guys with those tattoos – we'd need to track them all down. To protect them. To get to them before the killer does."

Christie grinned. "Very stupid, Inspector, very, very stupid. This…this is…entrapment." Christie clapped his hands together and laughed, he pointed at Cuzzocrea. "You'll be…there'll be charges for this. I bet Danny ain't even dead, or Tristan."

"Now it sounds like you do know them, Glen,"

Cuzzocrea replied.

"I didn't say that. You told me their names. You're not getting me that easy, no way. I'm done." Christie turned to his escorting officer. "Take me back to my cell."

The corrections officer looked at Cuzzocrea who shook his head and retrieved two photographs from his laptop bag. He placed them on the table and slid them over to Christie. One was of Danny Gilbert, one of Tristan McMenemy, both taken post-mortem and both displaying the genital mutilation sustained by each during the attacks.

Christie leaned close to the photos and peered through his thick glasses then baulked and recoiled from the images.

"We're not lying to you, Glen," said Cuzzocrea. "Your friends were killed, just like we said. We're here because we think you and others you may be associated with are in danger. That's all. No hidden agenda, no ulterior motive. We're just doing our job."

Christie pushed the photographs away. His breath caught in shallow gasps and his lips trembled. A tear dripped from behind his glasses, and he quickly wiped it away, "I'm very upset…I don't feel well…I think I might be sick."

Christie turned in his seat and bent over as if to vomit. The corrections officer stepped up to him, grabbed him by the elbow and helped him to his feet. He spoke to Cuzzocrea: "I'm going to have to call it a day there, buddy."

Cuzzocrea nodded. They watched as Christie, sobbing a pathetic whimper, was helped to the door. Ali called to him:

"Maybe you'll be safe in here, Glen, maybe not. But what about Sapa? What about Apu?"

Christie stopped walking and turned to look at her.

"They're next and you know it. Are you going to sit back and just let this happen to them?" Ali tapped her finger on the photograph of Danny Gilbert's body.

Christie pushed his glasses up his nose and allowed himself to be led from the visitor's room, keeping his eyes on Ali until he disappeared from view.

Ali turned to Cuzzocrea. "What do you think?"

“I think we nailed it.” He smiled.

“He’ll make the call?”

Cuzzocrea held his hand out to her. “I’ll bet you ten bucks he’ll make the call.”

CHAPTER 35 - JUST ONE STAB

His thick phlegm gargles in his throat and Maiden lowers herself onto him, straddling him across his hips. His still warm urine saturates the knee of her jeans as she grips the handle of the knife in both of her hands as tight as she can to stop it from shaking. The knife trembles with potential energy and her mind is already predicting the upcoming assault, the satisfaction she will feel as the blade bursts through the first layer of belly and easily, slickly onwards. Then, as if afraid that her courage may forsake her, Maiden's mind replays memories – a theatre screen of images, images of other things bursting through and moving onward despite a little boy's muted cries.

Maiden grips tighter still, her anger grunts from her as she plunges the blade as far as it will go, twisting it in his stomach between his belly button and his ribs. Bartholomew lets out a wail and Maiden pulls the knife back up, thrilled by the spray of blood. She's going to slam it back into him but Bartholomew's left arm windmills its way up to her and his flaccid hand belts her across the side of her head. Sparkles flash in her eyes and somewhere there's a popping sound and the world's volume is turned down. Maiden feels her cheek bounce onto his chest and she slides up into the crook of his neck. The knife lands beyond her; she reaches for it but pain clenches at her upper arm. Bartholomew is biting her, his teeth grind into the flesh. She pulls away, tearing the skin from his jaws, but still he holds fast to the red fabric of her hoodie. His heavy, almost lifeless arm drops heavily against her back as she scrambles from him towards the knife, but she watches her hand become a starfish as her spine curves from the ground and agony jolts through her from the copper nipples that bite into her thigh.

Maiden's stomach is clenched tight somewhere deep inside and it feels like she is having the breath squeezed from her by an invisible giant. Her limbs are useless, jelly-like, and her mouth tastes like metal. From her immobile state, spit dribbling out onto her cheek, Maiden watches Bartholomew grasp at the bedclothes. He wants to pull himself up but the sheets give way and puddle next to his head. He pulls the sheets, an inch at a time, down to his stomach. He presses the fabric against his belly, the deep claret of his blood saturates the cloth. He looks at it, then at her. She watches as he deliberately slows his breathing and reaches out for the wooden base of the bed, finally pushing and pulling himself up so he's sitting with his back against the bed.

Maiden can't breathe slowly – she is desperate to fill her tight chest with air. Her lungs feel crumpled inside her and she wants them to pop open again like a life raft. She knows now that she's in a race, a race between her and Bartholomew and whoever regains the power to move first will win. Her thigh is a useless hard lump of meat and the toes beyond look skewed and dead. She presses her arms into the carpet below her which looked soft but feels like it's made of a thousand glass splinters as her weight presses upon her elbows. She pulls with all of her might until her arms bend and her torso lifts so she can bring her good leg under her and almost sit.

Bartholomew is reaching with a foot; his toes curl around the knife's handle and he winces as he inches it closer to him, finally close enough for him to have it right next to him. She scans the carpet for the taser but can't see it anywhere. The patch of blood is bigger where he's pressing the sheet against his stomach and she can see that it hurts him to do it. His face looks grey and Maiden hopes he bleeds to death, that maybe she got him with just one stab.

His lips move and he looks like he's going to speak to her but it's just because of the effort he's now exerting as he walks his fingers up the front of the little chest of drawers, the cabinet that sits next to his bed. He rests his fingers on the small nob of each drawer as he goes, but he is nonetheless determined to reach its surface. Maiden stretches up as best she can to see what it is that his fingers are in pursuit of.

There's a cell phone on the top. Bartholomew's eyes are focused on her but his hand is focused on the phone. Maiden's fingers and toes buzz like seeds are sprouting from them or like the blood inside is bubbly and sharp. She wiggles her fingers and she can nearly make a fist. She's dribbling and her eyelids are twitching and now she can feel snot running from her nose and she can feel where Bartholomew bit her arm.

Soon she'll be able to move but she knows there's only one sensible direction to go in: she has to get out.

Bartholomew's fingers find the phone and at first they just nudge it enough to make it spin a half circle but then he flicks it off the cabinet. Somehow Maiden knows Bartholomew won't be calling the police and so she uses what little strength she has regained to pull away from him. She reaches first with her hands then pulls her butt along the carpet. It's exhausting but by the time she's near the door, one of her legs is alive again and she can push herself onto the wooden floor beyond the bedroom where it's easier to slide along. Maiden is tired and shivery and cold and she rests by her sneakers at the front door. Maiden is so drained and when she hears Bartholomew's gargling, garbled telephone call to Apu, she's almost too tired to be scared.

CHAPTER 36 - LIMITED HOSPITALITY

Doug Shaw ended his call and his stomach growled loud enough for Chief Superintendent McLaughlin to hear it all the way across the squad room.

"My apologies, sir," said Shaw to McLaughlin. "Where were we?"

"As far as I can tell, the Crime Scene Entry Log is in order. The log officers corroborate its accuracy. I don't know where you go from here except to acknowledge the possibility that Sergeant Walsh conducted herself in a highly questionable manner and I hope for your sake, Doug, that she wasn't acting under your instructions because if I find that VIIMIS tried to cut corners and obtain an illegal warrant…"

"Sir, I assure you that the members of my team adhere to guidelines and procedure without question. I would go as far as to say that – "

McLaughlin held his hand up to quiet Shaw. "Doug, Doug, I've no time for your defensiveness. I want answers and I want heads to roll. Either the log officers – members of my force assigned to assist you – have all made false statements or Trina Walsh is lying. Which is it?"

Shaw nodded grimly. "I've yet to interview the family liaison officer. Perhaps we'll get something from her?"

McLaughlin fingered through the documents and files on Shaw's desk. "Where are you going with this, Doug? Are you anywhere yet? I see very little progress here, minimal evidence and zero suspects."

"Actually, sir, we have several lines of enquiry...multiple leads."

"Oh? Please delight me with tales of your ongoing progress," said McLaughlin, his voice thick with sarcasm as he folded his arms and leaned against Shaw's desk.

"Our focus is on victimology right now. In the absence of a viable suspect, it's our best bet. We are progressing with two theories in conjunction: one, McMenemy and Gilbert were members of a larger group of men being targeted by a vigilante; and two, our killer is a child, a child who was victimized or was a witness to victimization at the hands of the aforementioned group."

McLaughlin snorted. "Theories? Plucked from thin air? Where did you get this stuff? Is any of this based on actual evidence?"

"Cuzzocrea's on his way back from Saanich right now. He was following up on a tip-off regarding the group I mentioned. We're hopeful that it'll lead somewhere. We're going to be monitoring the calls of a known associate of the deceased men to see if he reaches out to other members."

"Monitoring calls? Doug, you can't be serious. After this morning's disaster, you expect me to believe that a judge granted you a warrant to monitor a citizen's private telephone calls?"

"No, sir, the guy's in Old Wilkie." McLaughlin raised his eyebrows. Shaw took the reaction to be a positive sign and continued: "Munro's following up with NCROPS regarding the CEW."

"The CEW?"

"There's evidence a taser was used on both victims, presumably prior to the knife attack in an effort to overpower them and render them helpless. The markings on the bodies are consistent with the RCMP issue 44000, so we're liaising with NCROPS to track down any CEWs unaccounted for since the recall."

McLaughlin tipped his head to the side and considered

Shaw's account of the investigation thus far. "So now our prime suspect is what? A minor? An RCMP officer? Which is it? Jesus, Doug, this would be laughable if there was anything remotely funny about it. It's farcical, and it's all beginning to sound a little desperate. You're grasping at straws."

Shaw clenched his jaw. "I don't think so, sir. With all due respect, Chief, every investigation feels a little like grasping at straws until we grasp the right one – the magic bullet, so to speak."

"Where'd you get the tip about Glen Christie?"

"The former techie here in town, the guy Cuzzocrea and Dalglish interviewed yesterday, he was reluctant at first but then he just dropped the tip in Dalglish's lap." Shaw attempted to reassure an increasingly impatient looking McLaughlin. "We are going to get there, sir. I have full confidence in the team and I'm standing by Trina Walsh, somebody removed the evidence from the Gilbert house and I'll find out who that was."

McLaughlin stepped up to Shaw. A full head and shoulders taller than him, McLaughlin towered over his subordinate. "Missing RCMP-issued CEWs and the possible alteration of a Crime Scene Entry Log? A crime scene secured by my officers. Maybe you do have a list of suspects, after all. Maybe you're investigating members of my force?"

Shaw frowned and stretched out his neck, considering his response carefully before it left his lips. Thankfully, much to Shaw's relief, McLaughlin's phone rang. He took it from his pocket and clicked what Shaw assumed to be the ignore button.

"I have no suspects, as yet. But my team and I are working on one singular profile, a profile of a vengeful victim, a child," said Shaw.

McLaughlin's eyes narrowed. His phone bleeped; he tutted as he looked at the screen. "One moment, I need to check this voicemail."

Shaw watched Chief Superintendent McLaughlin as he

stepped away and listened silently to his voicemail. Shaw quickly wiped his brow and adjusted the waistband of his trousers, determined not to allow himself to be intimidated further by his superior.

McLaughlin ended the call and turned to Shaw. Shaw spoke first: "Sir, I'm about to speak to the liaison officer who was also present this morning, would you like to step in with me? She could clear this whole thing up for us."

"I can't. I have a more pressing matter. I suggest you stop flogging that particular horse and focus on the evidence we have, not the mythical evidence of your Sergeant Walsh and her outlandish claims that only serve to cast doubt upon my officers. Oh, and let Peter Gilbert go home to grieve the passing of his only son before we get sued." McLaughlin turned in the doorway and glared at Doug Shaw. "I shouldn't have to remind you that this is my town, Doug, and these are my people. You're here to find a killer, do it, do it quickly and then get out. Do not test the limits of my hospitality."

Shaw watched as McLaughlin let the door slam shut behind him. As he found himself alone in the squad room, a thought struck Shaw and it was a thought that kicked aside any feelings of intimidation and replaced them with an overwhelming sense of doubt. Shaw reacted to his gut feeling and sat at his desk. He placed a call requesting the video footage of the interviews he had conducted earlier that afternoon, which had been supervised by Chief Superintendent Bryce McLaughlin, and as he replaced the receiver and waited, Doug Shaw turned one question over in his mind: how had McLaughlin known the identity of the Old Wilkie prisoner?

CHAPTER 37 - DAVID'S MESS

In her kitchen, Ali was greeted by the inimitable odour of damp dog. As the reluctant owner of several pets, it was a smell Ali hated and had become adept at battling – actually, not so much battling, but masking with a variety of scented oils, carpet powders and perfumed candles.

Ali kicked her way through an array of shoes discarded against the back door. She was immediately depressed by the sight of the kitchen sink filled with dirty dishes, as was the countertop surrounding it. Every preparation surface in the kitchen was littered with empty takeout containers, dried food and a rainbow of crusted spills.

The floor was an embarrassment alone. The white tiles lay somewhere beneath the dried muddy paw prints and thereabout was enough moulted fur to make a king-sized blanket. Ali imagined the fur being sent airborne by the heat pumped through the vents in the floor, tainting an entire winter of food.

Ali was relieved that she'd asked Cuzzocrea to wait for her in the car while she checked on her son. Avoiding the sticky, ketchupy surfaces, Ali put her bag and keys on a nearby stool. She muttered as she picked up and tipped a wine glass containing something stiff and creamy-yellow in colour, "Fuck sake, David, you douche-bag mother-fucker." Was it fat? Judging by the clusters of black that had presumably once floated in the now semi-solid lard, she guessed the substance had been poured from a frying pan between batches of bacon.

Through the housewife's hatch cut into the wall between the kitchen and the rest of the living area, Ali could hear the TV was on at a low volume and she could see the blue light from it flashing across the walls of the adjoining room. The dining room table was home to three drying plates of spaghetti, a pile of unopened bills and the latest edition of the *Mochetsin Mews*, featuring a cover photograph of this year's Polar Bear Swim.

Kenny was snuggled beneath his comforter on one of the two couches. David, with his mouth agape and one leg slung over the back cushions, snored from his place on the other. Between them the wooden coffee table was another disaster zone and Ali fumed at the sight of six empty beer bottles. She was, however, heartened by the sight of as many bottles of Gatorade amongst the empty beer bottles – five empty, one half full – and a tub of Advil. It seemed that, despite being a drunken slob, David had managed to remain marginally mindful of their son's health.

Ali placed the back of her hand against Kenny's forehead; he was hot but not feverish. His left cheek was only slightly swollen, his lips were cracked and crusted at the corners of his mouth. Ali detected the faint scent of dried blood on his breath as she knelt to him. Kenny sensed Ali's presence and opened his eyes. "Hey, how you feeling, bud?" Ali smiled at him. Kenny winced at the taste in his mouth and nodded. He tongued the new hole in his gum and winced again. Ali handed the remainder of the blue Gatorade to him. "You'll feel better in the morning, baby." Ali kissed him on his head. "I promise."

"Hey."

Ali chose to ignore David's sleep-croaked welcome and adjusted the Liverpool FC pillow beneath Kenny's already snoozing head.

"You're back."

Ali heard the couch creak as David sat up followed by the sound of Shadow, the Cocker Spaniel who had been asleep on his chest, jump to the floor and flap his ears loudly.

Ali stood and spoke with her back to her ex-husband, "Has he had all his meds for today?"

"He can have another two at eight and then midnight."

Kenny was already asleep. Ali placed his drink within reach of him and turned to look at David who was yawning and scratching his head. He looked at her and blinked.

"What?"

"What the fuck, David?" Ali whispered. "Where's Sandy?"

"How should I know? In her room probably."

David attempted to reach for Ali's hand as she passed him on her way to find Sandy, and Ali pulled from his reach. "Really? How drunk are you? It's not even five o'clock."

"And it's my day off," said David in a loud whisper. "Ali! Ali!"

Ali didn't respond, she headed downstairs and along the hallway to Sandy's room with both the Cocker Spaniel and her chocolate Labrador at her heels. Even before she'd fully turned the handle of Sandy's door, Ali heard the wild yapping of her daughter's Chihuahua from inside, which sparked the same from the two larger dogs as she kicked them back and closed the door behind her. "Shut up, Spock!" Ali said. The Chihuahua growled before disappearing under the comforter from whence it came.

"Mum? How come you're home?" Sandy asked, pausing her movie.

Sandy's room was neat and tidy – the absolute antithesis of the rest of the house. Ali breathed in the ambiguous yet very pleasant odour of a scented candle which she could only think to describe as pink.

"It's like a bomb went off up there," said Ali.

"Tell me about it. Dad's a pig."

"Nothing's been done since I left, Sandy. It's not fair."

"OMG, Mum. So, I should clean up after them because…why? because I'm a girl? No way!"

"No, not because you're a girl, Sandy. You are going to

get your arse out of that bed and clean up – *with* your father – and you're going to do that out of respect for me because I'm telling you this, *Lady Muck*, if you think for one second I'm going to come back to this shit hole when I'm done and do it all for you with a brainless, mumsy smile on my face, you're sadly mistaken."

"But I've been at work all day, why should I – "

"Tough shit, Sandy, how do you think the rest of the world does it? Come on, get a move on. Bloody life of Riley." Ali heard Spock yapping again as she slammed Sandy's door behind her and trotted back upstairs where she checked on sleeping Kenny once more.

She found David in the kitchen, retrieving a teaspoon from the over-filled dishwasher. The kettle rattled noisily on its base.

"Hi. So? You're all done with the case?" David asked, wiping the spoon on his tea shirt and reaching for the tea bags. "You want a brew? I'm making one." He pushed a carton of dried egg noodles to one side and put two mugs in the space he had made by doing so.

"Really?"

David looked at her. "The mess?" He shrugged. "Yeah, sorry. I was just about to blast it."

"Yes, you're going to blast it, with a litre of frigging bleach. You and Sandy, tonight. And no, I'm not done with the case, I'm on the clock right now. Jesus, David, look at this place, look at you. You've been drinking. You're supposed to be looking after Kenny."

David shook his head and leaned against the countertop. "Chill out, Ali. He's sixteen, he's not going to die because he got a tooth taken out. Yes, I had a few beers. It's been a hard week and I'm chilling at home with my kids. So, we didn't clean up after supper, so what?"

Ali smiled and shook her head. "Nope, I'm not doing it, I am not being drawn into a screaming match with you. I came back to check on Kenny, that's all…"

There was a soft knock on the back door.

"Who's with you?" David asked.

"It's Cuzzocrea," said Ali absently as she crossed to the door and marvelled at how exhausting her five minutes at home had been. Ali opened the door to an apologetic Cuzzocrea. "Come in, excuse the e-coli and the stench of decay…it's okay though, David was just about to blast it."

Cuzzocrea nodded a hello to David.

"You want a cup of tea, I'm making one," said David.

"Nobody wants a fucking tea, David!" Ali snapped at him.

"No thanks, David. Ali?" Cuzzocrea beckoned her to him and then spoke into her ear.

"Okay, I'll be right out," said Ali.

Cuzzocrea left the house and Ali grabbed her bag and keys from the stool. "I have to go."

"Working are you, you and him? Yeah, it really looks like it." David tossed the teaspoon in amongst the dirty dishes in the sink. "You must think I'm an idiot."

"Oh, God, David, yes we are working." Ali suddenly remembered that she didn't have to explain herself to him. "But even if we weren't, even if I was wrapping my legs around him and letting the fucker have his wicked way with me, it'd be none of your business, not since you put your dick in other vaginas. Now, please try and just do your job as a father, for once. You never know, you might find that you actually like your children."

"You know what, Ali? Go fuck yourself."

Ali waved to David and smiled sweetly. "I might, or I might get someone else to do it for me." She stepped out of the back door and started down the stairs where Cuzzocrea was waiting for her.

"You fucking bitch!" David called after her, "Fuck you, Ali."

"Come on, ignore him, he's been drinking," Ali said as Cuzzocrea moved out of her way.

"You know, I take it back! I don't fucking miss you, you uptight…crazy…"

Cuzzocrea ascended the steps, bringing himself face to face with David.

"What are you looking at?" David said to him. "This is between my wife and I."

"Ex-wife and you need to calm down, David."

"Fuck you," said David.

"Can we go please?" Ali called from the foot of the stairs, "David, go inside, you're making a fool of yourself and you're going to scare the kids."

Cuzzocrea held eye contact with David for a little longer before descending the stairs. He heard David call out: "You're welcome to her mate, she's a crazy bitch."

Ali glared at David as he returned to the house. Cuzzocrea looked at her over the roof of his car. Ali avoided his eyes and got into the car.

"You okay?" Cuzzocrea asked as they pulled away from the house.

"Fine. Whatever," said Ali with her face turned away from him.

CHAPTER 38 - ALI'S GUILT

They were almost in Cedar River and Ali had barely spoken to Cuzzocrea. She was embarrassed by what had happened and hoped her silence might somehow erase David's cruel outburst from Cuzzocrea's memory.

But even if Ali had wanted to speak, she wasn't sure she could. Her throat was barbed with the sting of swallowed tears and silent truths, with all of the intolerable injustices her life had forced her to consume, with the acidic spew of vicious resentment thick in her oesophagus.

David was a prick, a pathetic cretin, a shallow-minded, soulless specimen somehow forsaken by evolution. Fighting with him had been a mistake because it was always a mistake. It was futile, after all, to reason with a pig-headed, egomaniacal bullying bigot, especially if that same bigot is uneducated and misogynistic.

Ali often tried to recall her past reasoning, to remember why she'd married the self-righteous twat in the first place but she remained bereft of a reasonable justification every time and so she tended to blame nature – it must have been an animalistic attraction, something base and uncivilized. Yet that pull hadn't been exciting or particularly sexual – if it had been she would've had no need to sneak off and masturbate after sex to allay the feelings of empty disappointment, of feeling like a faceless slab of meat with two breasts and a vagina, or wondering when exactly she had allowed her sex life to become nothing more than a series of passive-aggressive rapes.

Perhaps the presence of an invisible, undetectable pheromone had been between she and David when they met? Maybe hormones were to blame for their union and nature had decided the combination of their respective genes would combine to result in a minutely improved strand of DNA, ensuring the survival of the species in just as minute a way.

Ali wasn't just angry with David or even herself; she was frustrated by the inequality of the sexes and the conditioning we all fall prey to – both men and women. She switched places with David and imagined it had been him returning from working a brutal murder case up-island to find Ali asleep with empty beer bottles around her, the filthy detritus of the week strewn about and a sick child asleep on the couch. David would have written her off – as he had once before – perhaps had her confined to a psychiatric institution – as he'd also done before. She'd have been branded the worst of the worst – *a bad mother.* An irresponsible wreck who cared more about alcohol than her own ailing child. But what truly pissed Ali off was that, had it been her lying there instead of him, she'd have labelled herself the same because what comes hand in hand with motherhood? Guilt.

The moment a child leaves the womb – even before that, when the white stick is first pissed upon – a woman is suddenly held to a higher standard by everyone around her and what's worse is that women hold themselves to that same standard. When a woman gives birth she no longer has the luxury of a life, of being an individual, a developing human being. She is expected to cease changing, to stop learning. She must not adapt, neither improve nor decline. She is no longer present within her own life; she merely exists to serve others as they navigate theirs. She cannot think or develop new opinions; she cannot possess a unique perspective. Why listen to her? She has nothing to say. She is capable of neither invention nor creation beyond the boundaries of the home – of how best to poach an egg or remove a stain.

Why is it that because one chooses to reproduce one must also discard the essence of one's individuality, to stymie progress, sacrifice ambition and shrink every drop of one's potential to become what society expects a mother to be? But it is only women who have to stop, to pull the brakes on brilliance simply because they reproduce, because it is only women who are expected to devote themselves entirely and selflessly, like robots, to their offspring. Ali had never regretted having children, even in her darkest days when she would reflect upon all she had sacrificed for them, but she did regret the guilt that came with them and the feeling of being a lesser being somehow because of them.

Sandy and Kenny had been born to two people, a man and a woman, Ali and David, yet as Ali watched the silhouetted pines flitting by on the highway, she questioned whether their births, their existence, had had a single negative effect upon David's life. Had his choice to reproduce resulted in any repercussions whatsoever? Did fatherhood prompt change in him? Did society expect anything more or less of him as an individual? Was he held to a higher standard as a result of his offspring?

No. David had had two children yet he had continued in his career uninterrupted and had been allowed to progress and earn at the same rate as his childless peers. He had remained 'David' in essence – he was a father but free of imposed expectations. Nobody would judge him for behaving in a particular way and his behaviour would never affect society's perception of him as a father. David could drink, swear, fight, wear whatever he wanted, skip a shower and go out looking however dishevelled. When David had an affair, he wasn't seen to be less of a father because of it and neither had fatherhood rendered him sexless in the eyes of women. He'd had no trouble finding women who wanted to have sex with him; he wasn't deemed aged, used, baggy or saggy. And, as a single father, he didn't come with baggage, he was simply a man who had had children.

No, David wasn't expected – regardless of how unfathomably ludicrous and insulting the idea might be – to take on the sole responsibility of cleaning the house, the laundry, cooking, shopping, clothing, health checks and immunizations, bedtime stories, library visits, potty training, teething, breast feeding, introducing solid foods, school, socializing, parents' evenings, boyfriends/girlfriends, gardening, plumbing, general labouring, eye tests, hearing tests, ER visits, allergies, vitamin supplements, birthday shopping, the buying *and* wrapping of Christmas presents, painting and decorating, clearing hair from plug holes, scrubbing toilet bowls, swilling away vomit, and taking care of the dogs and the family budget.

David had two children and yet nothing was expected of him as a result. No sacrifice needed to be made, ambitions needn't be thwarted. And then, at the end of it all, who should be celebrated and consoled? Fast-forward a few years and David will walk Sandy down an aisle and when someone asks, "Who gives this woman?" David will say, "I do." Ali, the unpaid livery maid slash nanny, will watch from her rightful place – sitting silently in the background, observing.

David doesn't feel new pinches and pains from the scars of childbirth as they thicken and harden with age. David doesn't even know how it feels to have blood dripping from him every three weeks for five days never mind how that blood congeals with the approach of menopause so that you suffer mild contractions as you pass golf-ball sized clots which drop down the leg of your jeans or onto the floor you just mopped when you were too slow to get your soaked tampon into a dog-poo bag because God forbid, you flushed the sucker and brought about the ruin of an otherwise perfectly efficient (man-made) septic system.

With all her inner bitching spent, Ali was still filled with guilt. It was Ali herself – not David or society – that was forcing her to bite back tears every time she thought about her little boy on the couch in need of tender care and comfort, a boy who Ali had selfishly left in the care of a useless father. Ali had chosen herself over her own child, to selfishly fulfil her own needs. And even though her needs involved gruesome work investigating the vicious murder of two men, Ali still felt self-indulgent.

Her maternal guilt drew Ali's thoughts back to the case. Instinctively, she knew that at the heart of this case was a child. Her gut told her it was a girl, a girl in turmoil who, as an act of revenge upon the sick fucks who had sexually abused her, was hunting them down and killing them. A girl who needed help and who had become her own terror made manifest. Somewhere out there a child was drowning in a murky pool of madness and Ali knew how it felt to be her.

CHAPTER 39 - THE STAIRWELL

She keeps herself small, near the ground with her shoulder pushing against the heavy stairwell door so there's enough of a gap for her to see apartment 712 at the end of the short hallway. Maiden isn't sure what is scaring her more – the thought of Bartholomew wrapped in a bloody sheet coming after her or that Apu might have listened to his message by now. But then she thinks about the key fob for the front door to the building and feels better.

Her leg's a bit better too but it feels like she got punched a lot and when she rubs her thigh she feels a lump as big as a satsuma. She's pretty sure the stairwell is heated – she can feel a warm tickle of air on her neck coming from a vent somewhere nearby – but she feels colder than she's ever felt before. It's a cold that isn't just on her skin; it's a cold that makes her bones sore. It's a cold that makes her think about Tommy. Tommy must be cold because Mum didn't sign the papers yet so he has to just stay there, alone.

Something dings somewhere. An elevator? Maiden scrambles to her knees and crouches closer to the gap she's made. Now she's not imagining the door to 712 opening; she's remembering something she was too dumb to think of before. Some people have special ways of getting past security measures like little black boxes on doors – the kind of people who have to get into secure buildings in emergencies. Cops.

Maiden listens and hears a heavy swoosh then a solid

cathunk; the elevator's opening on the seventh floor. Maiden hopes she's going to hear the soft *beep-beep-beep* of someone pressing the buttons on another apartment door, a door far away from number 712. *Please please please.* She presses her eyes tight shut and prays to Jesus because mad Amber from next door told her that Jesus saves people even if they're bad. But it must be Jesus's night off or maybe Maiden's just too bad to be saved because as soon as she's done praying, she sees Apu step up to the door of Bartholomew's apartment.

Crouched down low, the sight of him reminds her of when she was little and all the times he would bash his way in and shout at Mum and pull all the drawers out and kick bottles out of cupboards and grab Maiden and check her all over. Mum would say he was just protecting her, protecting his investment, but sometimes it left bruises and it always scared Maiden.

Apu towers as big and thick and dark as always. He is carrying a bag. He presses his ear against the door to listen but doesn't knock. He's at the other end of the short hallway – too close for Maiden to feel safe and she feels tears hot in her eyes. She knows it would only take three or four of his giant strides to get to her if he sees her, and if he does, then she's sure he'd snap her neck like he said he'd do to Mum once, snap her neck with one hand and that nasty look in his eyes.

Apu puts his bag down and opens it. It's the kind of bag she'd seen a cloaked figure carrying in a graphic novel at the library about Jack the something-or-other from the olden days in London. He shakes out something purple from the bag, a pair of doctor's gloves, and he seems annoyed with them as he stretches them on. He keeps checking over his shoulder, over where the elevator and the other apartments are. Then he puts two things over his shoes that look like the old lady shower hats you can get in the More For Your Dollar store. Then Apu picks up his bag again and stands. He checks over his shoulder except this time he checks the other way too, down the little hallway to the stairwell where Maiden is hiding. She clenches her lips tightly shut and tries Jesus again.

Maybe Apu is just playing with her and he's seen her but is just acting like he hadn't because he starts pressing the little number buttons and the red light goes green. He pushes the door open a tiny bit and looks in. He pushes his head further in for a better look before stepping all the way inside and quietly closing the door behind him.

Maiden isn't cold anymore because now she's sweating under her bangs and she pulls up all of the fight she still has in her and takes the stairs two at a time, sometimes three, until she's at the bottom where she bursts through to the fancy foyer and out into the night.

CHAPTER 40 - THE TUNNEL

Eden Harrington had the audacity to smile at Ali as she and Cuzzocrea entered the squad room. Munro sniffed the air and turned to grin at the pizza box in Cuzzocrea's hand. Ali was reminded of an old television advert from her childhood where two kids were enticed to the dining table by the visual vapours emanating from a gravy boat full of instant Bisto. Munro kissed the Romeo's pizza box as he took it to his desk.

"Did Christie make the call yet?" Cuzzocrea asked Abbott, referring to the prisoner he and Ali had earlier baited.

"His pod get phone privileges at eight on Friday nights. The warden assured me that any change to the routine might cause suspicion," said Abbott.

Cuzzocrea checked his watch, seven forty-three. He crossed to the pair of desks Ali and he had claimed as their own in the squad room. As Ali followed Cuzzocrea she noticed Shaw at his desk. He was looking tired and frustrated, hunched over a laptop, staring at the screen.

"Quite the atmosphere in here," she said.

Cuzzocrea threw his windcheater over the back of his chair. "Yeah." He looked at Ali. "You okay?"

Ali considered her response. "I want to find this kid. I don't buy into the criminal cycle thing. I mean it's not like you look at the clock to see if you're hungry and so a killer doesn't necessarily leave an exact time between kills but, despite that, I do think we're running out of time."

"I actually meant…never mind." Cuzzocrea refocused. "I do work on the criminal cycle theory so I think we may already be out of time, particularly with the perp's brief psychotic disorder in mind."

Ali signalled for Abbott to join them. She was annoyed when Eden followed him to their desk. Ali spoke to Abbott: "What's going on here? What's Shaw looking at?"

Abbott shrugged. "Your guess is as good as mine but he's barely looked up from whatever it is for hours now and, heads up, he's in a bitch of a mood, even for him."

Ali scanned the room. "Where's Trina?"

"She got a call from the lab," Eden said.

Ali spoke to Abbott again: "So no new leads all day?"

"Not so far," said Eden. "He's had Steph waiting in an interview room all afternoon."

"Who's Steph?" Cuzzocrea asked.

"Stephanie Bridgestone? The Gilbert family liaison officer?" Eden clarified.

"The log officers gave us nothing then," Ali said to Cuzzocrea.

"Nope. Sticking to their statements," Eden chirped again.

Ali looked at her. "What the fuck is this? The Eden Harrington show?"

Eden looked shocked. "Excuse me?"

Ali stared at her. "You just have so much to say, Eden, don't you?"

Ali couldn't deny the pleasure she felt watching Eden's cheeks blush as she flicked a look at Cuzzocrea and realization apparently dawned upon her that Cuzzocrea had shared with Ali Eden's comments about her.

Eden began to step away, then seemed to change her mind. She turned to Ali. "I didn't realize this was a private conversation. I thought it was a team thing."

"Don't play the naïve innocent, Eden, it's unbecoming." Ali took her seat. She heard Eden mutter 'wow' as she moved away to sit at her own desk. Cuzzocrea and Abbott were trying not to appear uncomfortable in light of the exchange between the women but were doing a bad job of it. Ali broke the tension. "Be honest, Paul." She pulled a section of her hair towards him. "Do I smell of meat feast pizza? The car was stinking of it all the way back."

Abbott sniffed Ali's hair and reluctantly smiled. "A bit, yeah."

Cuzzocrea smelled his own shirt. "Shit. Me too."

They laughed and Ali seized the opportunity to glance at Eden who was watching them sulkily from her desk. Ali's glance communicated a very clear, 'don't fuck with me'.

Shaw cleared his throat and stood as Trina Walsh entered the squad room. He addressed the VIIMIS team. "Guys? We're all here now, let's get to it. Rey, hook this thing up to the board, will you?"

Cuzzocrea connected the cables for the interactive whiteboard into the back and sides of Shaw's laptop.

"While he's doing that, Trina? What did the lab have for us?"

"The blood transferred from the girl's sneaker to the carpet – or vice versa – was a match for Gilbert's. Numerous strands of hair – caucasian, mid-brown, long – present not only at the Gilbert scene of crime but also retrieved by crime scene techs from McMenemy's bedroom – his pillows and sheets and also in the kitchen of his home – the hair is virgin."

"What does that tell us?" Shaw asked.

"Virgin hair, never coloured, never bleached. Most likely a child's hair, sir. It's extremely rare to find a grown woman who hasn't been to the hairdresser or even bought an in-home kit. It's not impossible but I'd be surprised."

"What else?" he asked Trina.

"The knife, it's red."

"The handle?"

"No. The blade. Handle too, probably, but the evidence I have is from the blade itself. I brought McMenemy's autopsy forward to today and I was able to confirm the cause of death. The sharp force injury which led to death was a perpendicular piercing, a stab wound – obviously we know he was stabbed multiple times – but the actual wound that caused death was one in the cluster of slit-like wounds to the posterior medial section of his rib cage, his upper back, just left of central. The knife penetrated between two of his ribs and pierced his heart resulting in hemopericardium and a massive mediastinal haemorrhage which resulted in death. The longitudinal axis are squared off on the left angle, the right angle, not so. It's a red knife with one blunt edge and one sharp edge – serrated, as evidenced by the multiple incised wounds along the right-angle longitudinal axis – contusions and abrasions adjacent to the injuries give us an indication of the shape and dimensions of the base of the hilt but, due to elasticity in the skin, subcutaneous tissues and internal tissues, I can't determine the exact length of the blade since a three-inch blade can produce a wound that is many inches deeper than that."

Shaw shook his head. "But you do know it's red?"

Trina nodded. "Yes, thanks to the fatal wound. As the knife journeyed through the victim's body, on its way to the thoracic cavity, it hit the fifth rib to the left of the thoracic vertebrae. It moved through the fourth rib interspace and as it did so, it left behind trace evidence – a polyepoxide, specifically EP42HHT-2FD, a non-stick bonding and food-safe resin coating commonly used on stainless steel blades, kitchen knives. The resin itself is transparent, however, many manufacturers add pigment to it to colour the blade – it's a gimmicky thing but it's popular – go to any housewares franchise and you'll see the packs of multi-coloured knives. I'm looking into various brands but I'm inclined towards this particular bread knife." Trina held up a photograph of a long knife with a red handle and a matching blade, serrated. "It's part of a seven-piece Tomodachi set by a company called Hamilton Anvil. Mass produced, available everywhere."

"Okay, good," Shaw said. "Anything else?"

Trina paged through her file. "Sticking with the red

theme, red fibres were collected – cotton and polyester mix – from the carpeted area inside the doorway to the bedroom where Gilbert was killed. Additionally, blue fibres – ninety percent cotton, seven elastomultiester, three percent elastane – consistent with denim jeans, skinny jeans to be exact, cheap ones."

"And?"

"These fibres were concentrated in the area where there was a cluster of indentations made by the girl's Gusto Runners. So, the girl in the room…can I assume it's a girl, girl's sneakers, skinny jeans, the hair?" Shaw nodded an affirmation. "She took her clothes off there; they were discarded in a heap around her runners which leads me to deduce that she was naked. Or at least undressed down to her undergarments."

Shaw took a beat before responding. "Thank you, Trina."

"You're welcome. I have the go ahead for the Gilbert autopsy. I've scheduled it for the time I'd originally planned to do the McMenemy post-mortem."

"Red fibres?" Munro pulled a triangle wedge from the semi-circle of pizza remaining in the box.

"That's right," Trina replied.

Munro took a bite and spoke. "Fits with a witness statement I took canvassing Hollyrood Estates."

"Go on," said Shaw, making little effort to hide his disdain for Munro.

"It was school bus drop-off time, right? Well, one witness, a neighbour who lives kitty-corner from the Gilbert house, she said she remembers one kid out of all of the others because this one – a girl – was walking against the crowd. You see, the school bus drops kids off at the highway/Hollyrood junction, this kid was walking towards the highway." Munro swallowed and immediately filled his mouth with a fresh bite. "Anyway, this kid? She was wearing a red hooded sweatshirt and jeans."

"Hair colour?" Trina asked.

Munro shook his head. "Hood was pulled up, I believe

there was mention of a backpack. I'll double check my notes."

"Sounds promising." Shaw turned to face his team. "Now, I want you guys to take a look at this for me. I've been studying the tapes of the interviews I conducted with the two log officers present when we believe the evidence was removed from the Gilbert house. I need your collective objectivity, I may have tunnel vision on this and I don't want to find indicators just in a subconscious effort to confirm a theory of mine. Regardless, take a look and tell me what you see. Ali? Rey? I need your eyes especially on this one."

Ali and Cuzzocrea pulled chairs out from under nearby desks and sat together in front of the interactive whiteboard. The rest of the team gathered behind them. Shaw asked Munro to dim the lights and pressed play on the footage recorded inside the interview room.

Ali watched Sergeant Terry Collins as he sat alone in the room. He appeared confident if not bold; he wasn't an easily intimidated subject. His arms were folded across his chest and he was blowing short, rhythmic puffs of air out between his lips, tapping a matching beat with his index finger on bicep.

At the top of the screen were the words: INTERVIEW ROOM 3, and below those was the date and time stamp, the seconds counting up. The lights above Terry Collins dimmed – it was step number one of the ass-pucker technique Ali and Cuzzocrea had briefed Superintendent Shaw on before they'd left for Saanich. Collins's reaction to the lights dimming struck Ali as curious; he simply raised his eyebrows and continued his rhythmic tattoo.

Less than a minute later the door to the interview room opened and Ali watched two men enter the room – Superintendent Shaw followed by his superior, Chief Superintendent McLaughlin. Shaw placed a thick manila file on the desk between himself and Collins. Ali watched Sergeant Collins's reaction to the file – his lips tightened and he uncrossed his arms and, although his oral rhythm ceased, he took up the same percussion upon his thighs under the table, out of view of Shaw and McLaughlin. Ali wondered whether the action could be construed as nervousness but then postponed judgement since the action could equally be because the man was entirely confident. If so, was he confident because he was honest or was it just bravado? Beside her, Cuzzocrea shifted in his seat and Ali guessed he too was debating Collins's ambiguous body language.

Ali watched the footage as Shaw placed two evidence bags, containing what Ali could see contained the kind of equipment that had been reported missing from the Gilbert house. Shaw placed the items on a table to the left of Terry Collins, out of reach and at a forty-five-degree angle from him. Collins was almost nonchalant in his observation of the evidence and he seemed to smile before turning and looking directly at Chief Superintendent McLaughlin who was leaning, arms crossed, against the wall next to the door. The Chief looked bored and communicated what Ali read to be resentment. Perhaps McLaughlin felt his time was being wasted; maybe he felt it was beneath him to attend interviews or maybe he didn't approve of Shaw conducting interviews with members of his police force.

Shaw had taken the seat facing Sergeant Collins, placing himself between the subject and the Chief Superintendent. Shaw tapped the file with Collins's name on it and Ali watched as Collins became instantaneously engaged, sitting higher in his seat and rubbing his hands together under the desk.

"He's excited?" Cuzzocrea muttered.

"I think so, yes." Ali whispered back to him.

Shaw asked Collins to recount his statement with regards to the events occurring during his duty shift as log officer at the Gilbert scene of crime. Once Collins had obliged, Shaw made him run through it all again, and then again. Meanwhile, Shaw was also referring to the actual Crime Scene Entry Log.

Shaw asked questions, probing Collins, suggesting that

he'd forgotten something, that the interview was off the record and that this was the time to come clean. Shaw assured Collins that he, as well as Chief Superintendent McLaughlin, were already aware of what had happened, but they just needed Collins to confirm their suspicions.

At that, Sergeant Collins had taken pause, he seemed to be reflecting upon Shaw's words, considering them carefully. Ali noticed he was doing so with suspicion, mistrust, he was eyeing both of his superiors and their respective poker faces. Collins then placed both of his hands on the table, smiled and repeated, word-for-word, his account of the previous day's events.

Finally Shaw permitted Collins to leave the room. Collins smiled and stood. Ali watched him as he crossed to the door and she saw something peculiar take place, something that might justify why Terry Collins's ass hadn't puckered once throughout the interrogation: Chief Superintendent McLaughlin winked at him.

Ali turned to Cuzzocrea. "Did you see that?"

"Fuck," said Cuzzocrea.

"Wait! Wait!" Shaw said from behind them as he clicked on another video file. "Watch the next interview first, this is Constable Joanne Smith, Collins's partner, his trainee."

Ali and Cuzzocrea focussed once more on the whiteboard as the seconds counted up on the second interview. Shaw was already seated at the table, the Chief was standing in the same place behind him, alongside the door as it opened, and a young female officer entered the interview room.

Ali could see immediately that Joanne Smith was the antithesis of her partner. Everything about her was tense, her shoulders were stiff and high, and Ali assumed she would cave under the pressure and confess any misconduct. A deep frown furrowed her brow as she nodded to Shaw and noticed the file in front of him with her name on it. The young officer visibly tightened at the sight of the two evidence bags to her left when she sat opposite Shaw. Smith seemed to be pressing herself into the chair, perhaps she hoped to slide the chair further from her interlocutors.

Shaw opened by talking about Smith's father, an RCMP officer, no doubt high-ranking since Shaw mentioned they had completed basic training together. It was a clever move on Shaw's part. By mentioning Smith's father and alluding to his reputation as well Shaw's personal relationship with the man, Shaw was smearing on a thick layer of threats of potential disgrace and dishonour.

Ali saw Joanne Smith squeeze her eyes tightly shut for a second; she was scared, rattled, intimidated. Ali took her body language to be a clear confirmation that the log book had been altered, and Constable Smith was aware that evidence had been removed from the scene during her watch.

Ali smiled as she watched Shaw act like a skilled psychologist and not just someone who had been given a handful of pointers by herself and Cuzzocrea less than an hour before the interviews had taken place. He was laying it on a bit thick, lecturing rather than interrogating, giving Smith no opportunity to respond but he was, after all, Doug Shaw and Ali was no stranger to his overactive zeal.

But even if Constable Smith had had a chance to respond, it was likely her words would have betrayed her. Ali watched the woman blink in rapid succession, her brow furrowing further. She flicked a glance at McLaughlin, back at Shaw, McLaughlin again and then at the evidence bags. She was feeling trapped, weighing up her options, unsure of whether to come clean and what the repercussions might be if she did.

She was still looking at the evidence bags. Ali knew this was a clear sign that someone, someone guilty, was trying to determine the weight of evidence against them. Ali sat forward – this was the moment that all would be revealed. But then something happened: a jolt. Joanne Smith jolted. It wasn't a dramatic start; it was a tiny, almost imperceptible shift, but it was definite and it made nerves flutter in Ali's stomach. Joanne Smith's head tilted a little to the right and her once tense shoulders simultaneously relaxed. Then Constable Joanne Smith turned once more from the evidence bags – her brow now free of the merest frown – she blatantly ignored Shaw's diatribe. She looked directly at CS McLaughlin and without apology recounted Collins's statement of events verbatim.

Cuzzocrea looked at Ali. "Holy shit."

Cuzzocrea and Ali turned to Shaw who was leaning against a desk, arms folded, looking grim.

Munro spoke through pizza. "What did I miss? What's with the holy shit?" Munro looked at Trina Walsh, Paul Abbott and Eden Harrington. Each of them shrugged vacantly back at him, unaware as he was as to what Ali, Cuzzocrea and Shaw had gleaned from the footage.

Shaw stood. "Not tunnel vision then?"

"Far from it, sir. It's clear," Cuzzocrea confirmed.

Shaw stepped to the front of the squad room – the paused image on the interactive whiteboard behind him was frozen on Joanne Smith as she exited the interview room. Shaw cleared his throat and spoke, "Eden, get your colleague, Miss Bridgestone, from the interview room and bring her here, please. Don't speak with her."

Ali interrupted, "Sir, I think that's a job better suited to Trina." Shaw looked a question. Ali explained, "Eden is this family liaison's friend. The Bridgestone woman is bound to want to have a conversation with her, only natural. Better if Trina fetches her, transports her here and blocks any conversation or questions."

Trina nodded that she was willing to do so and Shaw asked her to be as fast as possible.

"Rey, Ali, a quick word?" Shaw said as he led them to the rear of the room, out of earshot of the remainder of the team. He rubbed at the top of his head and spoke: "During a conversation earlier today – actually it was more of a dressing down – with Chief Superintendent McLaughlin I mentioned that you guys had gotten a tip-off about a possible associate of our suspected paedophile ring, an inmate at the VICC. I did not refer to said inmate by name. I know I didn't because, frankly, at that time, I couldn't even remember his name – I'd only heard it once, in the observation room when you read Ballantine's email, Ali. Anyway, McLaughlin did – he said Glen Christie, mentioned him by his name. McLaughlin knew which inmate at the VICC we suspected might be linked to McMenemy and Gilbert."

Cuzzocrea shared a look with Ali and turned to listen to Shaw as he continued.

"Further to that…NCROPS got back to us."

"The taser?" Cuzzocrea asked.

Shaw nodded. "Three Cedar River RCMP tasers were missing during the recall and they're unaccounted for to this day."

"Let me guess," said Cuzzocrea, "one of them was registered to Chief Superintendent McLaughlin?"

"Well, he was just Inspector Bryce McLaughlin back then. Mislaid following a training exercise."

There followed a silence, pregnant with the magnitude of the daunting task that potentially lay ahead for the VIIMIS team. Cuzzocrea was the first to speak, "Are you going to declare Chief Superintendent McLaughlin an official person of interest, sir?"

"Let's speak to this liaison officer first. If someone could acknowledge that McLaughlin was present at Gilbert's home yesterday then at least I know his name was deliberately omitted from the log book."

"And if she implicates the Chief? If she tells us that he removed the evidence. We have to go on the record, we have to include him in the investigation, he might be our only way of finding this kid, our perp," said Ali.

"One step at a time. If McLaughlin is involved – and I really hope he isn't – then he's involved in paedophilia. Our task is to solve the two murders and apprehend the killer. Any case sparked by our enquiry regarding the paedophile ring will go to sex crimes and if I hang Cedar River's Chief Super out on that one, then it has to be with a weight of evidence behind it, nothing circumstantial, nothing open to debate and nothing that could be inadmissible later on."

"Well, just so you're forewarned, McLaughlin's never going to spout the Confiteor, there'll be no mea culpa. It's just not in his psychological make up," Ali warned.

Shaw nodded. A telephone rang. Abbott answered it and called out to Shaw and Cuzzocrea, "Glen Christie made the call."

CHAPTER 41 - SINCHI'S SACRIFICE

The open concept living area which incorporated the kitchen, was clear. Bryce stepped sidelong through the door, into the apartment. He supported the weight of the door as it closed, ensuring that it did so as silently as possible.

Bryce placed his bag on the floor and flicked his coat open, resting his hand on the butt of his holstered RCMP service pistol. He stepped quietly along the wall towards an open door, a door he knew led to the only bedroom in the apartment. As he neared the room he could hear the rasp of fast but shallow breaths inside.

He stilled and watched the patch of soft light emanating from the room onto the wood-laminate flooring of the main living area. The light was suffused and honeyed, cast through an un-curtained window, probably from a streetlamp. The light remained undisturbed, whoever was breathing in the bedroom wasn't moving. Bryce sidled up to the doorway, flicking up the strap of his holster as he did. He unsheathed his Smith & Wesson and slid the safety off in one movement. With the gun in both hands, pointing to the floor, Bryce first looked around the jamb, dipping his head swiftly in and back out again only long enough to take note of Steven Bartholomew's presence and placement. Bryce moved quickly into the room. Steven was seated on the floor, leaning against the bed. Bryce cleared the left side of the room. He raised his gun to shoulder height, aiming it at the open door which he pushed closed with his foot to reveal the emptiness it had obscured form sight. Next, Bryce opened the door to the closet; he scanned it then searched it, moving aside hangers of clothes until he was confident that the room was empty save for Steven who was pressing a bloodied sheet against his abdomen.

"Apu…help me…"

Bryce ignored Steven's croaked plea and left the bedroom to ensure the coat closet and the guest bathroom, both situated at the other side of the kitchen, were also empty. Satisfied the apartment was free of danger, Bryce secured his sidearm in its holster and returned to Steven.

Despite the gloom, Bryce could see that Steven was ashen and his lips were blue at the corners of his mouth. He looked up at Bryce, focus wavering.

"It was the kid…Maiden…she…fucking…"

Steven's shallow breath hiccupped, his eyes widened. Bryce crouched over him, placing two gloved fingers on his neck to find Bartholomew's pulse. The sheet was saturated with blood, the edges of the stain dark, oxidizing. Steven's pulse was weak but rapid, beads of sweat had formed on his brow yet he was shivering with cold. Bryce spoke to him:

"How long since she left?"

Steven winced. "When I called you. Fuck, Apu…am I going to die?"

Bryce analysed the scene. A cell phone and a red knife lay next to Steven's thigh. A taser was discarded against the skirting board nearest the back of the door. Bryce recognized it immediately. He hadn't seen it for fifteen years but he knew it was his old 44000 – the one he'd given to Josie Devlin, the one he'd taught the dirty gash how to use in drive-stun mode. He smirked at the irony; he'd given the taser to Devlin when she was pregnant with the very kid that had just used the weapon on Steven Bartholomew.

"Maiden tasered you?"

Steven nodded. "Bitch tased me…then stabbed me, look."

Steven pulled the sheet down. His skin was reluctant to

kiss itself free of the sticky blood. Fresh blood oozed from the knife wound followed by the putrid ejaculation of a darker, thicker substance that made Steven pale further and instinctively bundle the sheet back against the wound. His voice was wet and gurgling,

"Fuck…I need an ambulance, Apu."

Bryce reached for Steven's phone. "Did you call anyone else?"

Steven's bottom lip trembled. He shook his head.

"What's your passcode, buddy?"

Even in his state of near-death, Steven appeared flattered by Bryce's endearment. "Five…two…" Steven had to think hard for the remainder of his passcode, "seven…zero."

Bryce spoke as he scrolled through Steven's call log, "When did you arrange the date with Maiden?"

Steven shook his head, confused now, his lips bluer than before. Bryce knew enough to know that Steven was going into hypovolemic shock, time was running out. Bryce slapped Steven's cheek. "Stay with me, bud. When and how did you arrange the date?"

"Josie…she emailed last night…I got it this morning."

"The email account on this phone?"

Steven shook his head. "On the computer…laptop."

"Where's your laptop, buddy?"

Steven coughed and winced. "I need a fucking ambulance, Apu…I'm fucking dying here." He coughed again and the grimace that followed displayed his blood-stained teeth.

Bryce held Steven's phone up to him. "I'm calling them, buddy. I'm calling them but I need to take care of anything that could land you in jail first. Where's your laptop?"

"Living room…or kitchen…through there."

"And that's the only one you use? That and the phone, yes?"

Steven nodded.

"No burners, no pay-as-you go?"

"No! Fuck!" Steven gargled through the blood in his

throat.

Bryce pocketed Steven's phone.

Steven frowned and looked at Bryce's gloved hands, the blue covers over his shoes. "What're you doing?"

Bryce held Steven's wrists and began to pull them gently away from the sheet. "It's okay. Trust me, you're going to be just fine."

Steven's eyes widened with panic. "No…keep pressure…"

In his weakened state, Steven was no match for Bryce's strength as Bryce pulled his hands free and held them palm down at either side of Steven. Bryce nodded and smiled at him. "You know, Sinchi, I want to thank you. Your sacrifice will save us all. They were getting close, so fucking close, and if you hadn't called me, if *they'd* have found you, well, it would have made their case – the email, the taser. And just when it looked like it might start to point to me, you saved the day, Sinchi. Now, all I have to do is make this look like…"

Bryce left his sentence unfinished. Steven was gone. Bryce lifted his hands from Bartholomew's, careful not to leave evidence of the pressure upon them at the time of death – Bryce was aware of how quickly ante-mortem markings become indelibly preserved upon a body as soon as the heart stops pumping and the blood stops moving.

Bryce stood and took Steven's phone out of his pocket; he opened it and scrolled through the contacts. He found the number he needed and called it. As the call was answered and he spoke, Bryce retrieved his taser and placed it in his bag along with Steven's laptop and its cables.

Bryce ended the call and looked at his watch. He estimated he'd be busy for the next forty minutes or so, depending on how long it would take for James Bartholomew to arrive. With time to kill, Bryce took his untraceable burner phone from his inside jacket pocket and called Josie Devlin's number. Bryce listened to the landline as it trilled, unanswered. Either Josie wasn't home or she wasn't answering. If Maiden had headed there as soon as she'd left Steven to bleed to death – and he had every reason to assume she would since he knew she had nowhere else to go – then she should get home within the next ten or fifteen minutes. He closed the phone and decided he'd try again later. Regardless of whether anyone answered, as soon as he was done here, he'd drop by and pay the little fuckers a visit.

Bryce had a few loose ends to tie up – loose ends that could prove the crime scene he was about to manufacture was in fact staged, loose ends that could all lead back to him. He'd do the rounds: first stop would have to be Josie Devlin and her kids, then he'd pay a little visit to Greg Ballantine, the computer geek who, it seemed, couldn't take a cunting hint.

CHAPTER 42 - HOME

Lungs feel like they're fizzing. Maiden catches the bus, the number nineteen that goes from the falls all the way through town to White Creek. It's uphill all the way from the bus stop on Ash Street to home but she can't slow because the drone of the traffic carries with it a chant: Apu's voice grunting a promise to snap her neck like a dry branch.

Breath condensing and wetting her cheeks and nose. The cold wind dries her nostrils prickly. It's not just the incline or the cold air that's hurting her chest though – it's the aching, the grief and the horrible, horrible sadness in her heart.

Tommy.

Maiden steps from the curb but decides she can't make it across in time because there's a big truck, its tyres thundering against the street. It's going way too fast. Her hesitation mid-step makes her foot slam into the gutter; her ankle twists under her weight and vicious pain shoots up her leg.

Pain pulses hot and sharp, sharp enough so that she almost doesn't notice where Sinchi has bitten her arm. Every step, all the way up to Pine Nut Circle, feels worse than the last and finally she has to rest a moment against the metal pole that is home to the white 'NO THRU ROAD' sign which was replaced last month by Cedar River City Council only to be tagged the same day with an ejaculating neon cock.

Maiden scans the cul-de-sac which is home to her building, Mamisîw House. The usual cars, usual kids, usual lights on. There is something new, a once-white mattress, stained with piss and period, has been added to the trash yard since this morning.

Maiden limps towards the apartment block. She looks up at her floor. Amber, her neighbour from apartment 3A, is having another one of her 'bad days'. Amber says she's a princess and some sort of witch doctor. She says Mamisîw House was built on an Indian burial ground and that the dead – or undead, as she calls them, but not in a zombie way – wander the floors of the block looking for weak souls to take.

Maiden's ankle stings when she has to put her full weight on it as she climbs the stairs. She thinks it must be really swollen now because, despite the frigid temperature, it's really hot. On the landing, Amber's chanting in what Maiden suspects must be a made-up language. She has a bowl of the stuff she burns when she says that the spirits are hunting and she's pounding on a drum too, but very softly because sometimes the neighbours call the cops when she gets too loud. Sometimes Amber gets so crazy that they come and take her away and when she comes back, she's all quiet and she doesn't have feathers in her hair anymore and she stops talking about the spirits of dead Indians for months.

Maiden stays close to the wall. She doesn't want Amber Princess to talk to her but Amber sees her almost immediately and picks up the bowl and wafts the smoke out towards Maiden with an eagle feather. The smoke smells like turkey stuffing. Amber's talking about bad energy and dark entities for the whole time it takes Maiden to get inside the front door.

She can still smell the smoke through the letter box but there's another smell too. It's the smell that Devereux from 3C had said was old trash left out in the kitchen.

It wasn't old trash.

Maiden ventures along the dark hallway to the living room where she flicks the switch for the ugly Re-Store ceiling light and wonders whether it is really possible for the ghosts of the dead to wander and watch.

Mum hasn't moved – for some strange reason, Maiden has been hoping all the way from Ash Street that she'll get home to find Mum gone. The blue arm has worked its way loose again. Now it is more purple than blue, at least the fingers are.

Maiden limps to her mother's side and picks up the edge of the blanket because she has to see – doesn't want to but *has* to. Peeling back the fleecy cover – the smell is way worse when she does and makes her vomit without vomiting – she sees two dull eyes pushing against their lids. Mum's eyes have gotten fat, in fact, everything about Mum has gotten fat, like she's eaten a thousand Big Macs as she's lain dead on the couch.

Maiden nearly screams when her Mum begins to wail. But it isn't Mum – it is the phone ringing louder and angrier than it has ever rung before. The phone used to be mounted on the wall but it had gotten knocked off during one of Mum's binges and the plastic frame is split, half of it gone, half of it still screwed to the wall.

Maiden wonders who is phoning? Probably one of Mum's johns. Maiden used to think it was funny how all of Mum's boyfriends were called John, until she was old enough to get it, that was – if it was a john then they'd keep calling till they got what they wanted, keep calling and maybe even come round. If someone did come round, then they'd probably smell Mum through the letter box, even with Amber's turkey stuffing smoke outside.

The phone is next to the TV. Maiden decides she'll have to answer it. She'll tell whoever it is that Mum is at karaoke or that she is sick, or something. She swallows, trying to lubricate her dry throat and wonders when she last spoke. It feels like a long time since she heard her own voice because there isn't anybody to speak to anymore. Maiden's fingers touch the phone just as it stops ringing.

The quiet is thick. The quiet hums too. Maiden feels fat emptiness pushing down and into her. She tries to shut the quiet out, covering her ears with her hood and holding her hands tight on top of that but the thick, humming quiet gets louder and louder.

The light on the ceiling is brighter too, even though one of the three bulbs is dusty and dark; it glows hotter and makes Mum's fingers look like black sausages. Maiden feels sick, sick and dizzy and shaky behind her eyes. She follows the wallpaper out of the living room and down the hall, tracing the edge of each oversized maple leaf in faded oranges and browns.

Into Tommy's room because it smells of him. She presses play on Tommy's little TV with the built in VHS slot and hears the tape buzz up to speed and then Rafiki is shouting about Simba being alive.

Maiden curls herself up on the red mattress, pulling Tommy's Sonic the Hedgehog comforter over her head and she tries to remember Tommy. Tommy happy, Tommy chasing geese, Tommy on his skateboard…Tommy's head like it was on the wrong way, Tommy's tooth cracked off and stuck in his tongue, Tommy's brains on a tyre and his hair black with blood.

Maiden's heart hurts again because it should have been nicer. Everything should have been nicer for Tommy.

CHAPTER 43 - VINDICATION

"He called the offices of *The North-Island Echo* newspaper here in town," said Abbott regarding Glen Christie's outgoing call from prison.

"What's he trying?" Munro punched a crease in his empty pizza box, folded it and pressed it into the small wastepaper basket next to the refreshment table. "To sell his story? 'Reaching for the soap and other true stories of the VICC'." Munro laughed at himself.

Abbott continued, "He called the Editor's direct line and left a message, seems he knows the guy. He told him he has to visit and that he'd heard about Tristan and Danny. I have the transcription."

"Do we know who this Editor is?" Shaw asked.

Eden spoke from her desk, "I looked him up: James Bartholomew, fifty-seven, caucasian, six feet two, two hundred and seventy-five pounds, married, lives on Thurber Road. He's been the Editor-in-Chief of *The North-Island Echo* since ninety-four, prior to that he was a teacher at a local elementary school. He's been voted Cedar River Citizen of the Year three times."

Shaw nodded. "We'll look into this Bartholomew." He acknowledged Trina's return. She was accompanied by the family liaison officer.

Trina led her to a chair in the centre of the room and asked her to take a seat. Shaw sat across from the woman and began:

"Thank you for your patience Bridgestone, take a seat. I have a few questions for you and depending on the information you provide us with, you may be required to make an additional, official statement following this meeting."

Stephanie Bridgestone dropped her bag beside her, crossed her legs and nodded her agreement.

"You arrived at the Gilbert residence at…?" Shaw already knew the answer since he had the Crime Scene Entry Log in front of him, however, the purpose of the interview was to determine how accurate the log was.

Corporal Stephanie Bridgestone was sitting in the centre of the room; Shaw was facing her, he too was seated. Ali and Cuzzocrea were standing, watching Bridgestone carefully from behind Shaw. Trina was standing near the front of the room biting her nails, something Ali had never witnessed her do before but something she understood her resorting to under the circumstances. Paul Abbott and Eden Harrington were seated together at a desk behind Stephanie Bridgestone. Munro was pacing near the back of the room – Ali suspected he was pacing less because he was eager to discover the truth about the log book and more because he was struggling to digest the entire meat feast pizza he'd scarfed without offering even a single slice to his team mates.

Stephanie Bridgestone replied: "I signed in at 6:01, sir."

"You were assigned family liaison duties by Eden Harrington, correct?" Shaw asked.

"That's correct."

"Charged with the direct supervision of Peter Gilbert, the victim's father?"

"Yes, sir. Peter Gilbert had insisted on remaining in his house and refused to be temporarily relocated. Eden called me in because of my liaison training. Eden and I used to work together in Special Victims and I have bereavement counselling training, however, she indicated she was bringing me on board to monitor Gilbert within the home since there was a possibility he could have been involved in illegal behaviour which may or may not be connected to his son's murder."

Shaw nodded. "Do you recall who the log officers were at the time of your arrival?"

"No, but it's my practice to keep my own log, sir. If I may consult my notes?"

"Please do." Shaw and Trina exchanged hopeful glances at each other as Bridgestone retrieved her notebook from her bag.

Bridgestone paged through her notes and then spoke: "Sergeant Brian Fawkes was the duty officer who signed me in. He directed me inside where I encountered a Corporal Chris Hoyne. Corporal Hoyne had, prior to my arrival, been tasked with guarding the victim's father throughout the night since the commencement of his duty at three a.m. He introduced me to Peter Gilbert. At that time, Constable Julia Trent was also on scene. She was on sentry duty at the entrance to the crime scene proper."

"By that you're referring to the room in which Danny Gilbert's body was discovered?" Shaw asked.

"That's correct, sir."

"Who else was present in the home at that time?"

Bridgestone consulted her notes. "Sergeant Trina Walsh," Bridgestone nodded at Trina and continued, "Sergeant Walsh was inside the murder room with another man who I assumed to be a forensic tech but who I didn't recognize and was not introduced to. The man, Walsh's colleague, left the residence a little over half an hour after my arrival – actually, it was 6:39, to be precise."

"Vincent, Jerry, my guy from Nanoose," said Trina Walsh.

Shaw acknowledged Trina and turned once more to Stephanie Bridgestone. "Now, looking at this log I see that the next entry is for Sergeant Walsh's departure at 8:08. Could you take a look at your notes and tell me if that is accurate?"

"That's correct. Then there was a shift change at nine

o'clock. Fawkes, Hoyne and Trent were replaced by..." Bridgestone read from her notes, "...Sergeant Collins, Terry Collins, and Constable Joanne Smith, sir. The then off-duty officers had all left the premises by 9:05. At that time the Gilbert residence was free of any additional personnel – it was just me, Peter Gilbert as well as Sergeant Collins and Constable Smith."

"Good," Shaw said. "Now, as far as I can see, nobody came or went until my arrival along with Detective Munro at 11:19 a.m. Could you confirm that this information is accurate?"

The VIIMIS team collectively held their breath, even Munro stopped pacing. All eyes were on Stephanie Bridgestone as she took an inordinately long time to respond to Shaw's question. Her answer would either vindicate or vilify Trina Walsh.

"That is not accurate, sir."

Ali heard Trina Walsh exhale.

"Explain, please."

"Chief Superintendent Bryce McLaughlin arrived at 10:52, sir. He cleared the scene," Bridgestone said matter-of-factly, ignorant to the gravity of her statement.

"He cleared the scene?" Shaw asked.

"It was apparent from the moment of his arrival that C.S. McLaughlin and Peter Gilbert are friends. The Chief Superintendent insisted on having a private conversation with Gilbert, sir."

"Insisted?"

"He ordered myself, Sergeant Collins and Constable Smith to remain outside the house during his visit."

"For the entirety of his visit?" Shaw asked.

"I remained outside the residence, yes. Sergeant Collins and Corporal Smith were called in briefly by the Chief before he left."

"Was the Chief carrying anything when he left?"

"He had arrived with a briefcase and he left carrying what appeared to be the same briefcase, sir," Bridgestone replied.

"What happened after Chief Superintendent McLaughlin left?"

"Collins and Smith were talking when I entered the foyer of the home. They stopped upon my arrival and returned to their posts. I found Peter Gilbert in the kitchen where he remained until you and Detective Munro arrived at 11:19."

Shaw paused. He nodded at Stephanie Bridgestone. "Corporal Bridgestone, Detective Munro is going to take you along to the interview room where he's going to take an official statement regarding your account of yesterday's events. After he's taken that statement, your notebook will be held as evidence."

Bridgestone nodded, picked up her bag and followed Munro out of the squad room.

Shaw called to Abbott, "I want Collins and Smith brought in and get IA on the phone." Shaw watched Abbott commence his calls. He put his hands on his hips and turned to Ali and Cuzzocrea. "Remember to stay focused on our case, don't let this distract you."

"Yes, sir," said Cuzzocrea as Shaw crossed to Trina Walsh.

"McLaughlin took the hard drives and the camera footage and anything else that could have given us a lead and proof that Gilbert was a paedophile," Ali said.

"And he had two of his officers cover it up for him, coerced them into falsifying the log," Cuzzocrea added.

"So, Collins and Smith both lied," said Ali.

"Followed orders, orders given directly to them by their Chief Superintendent."

"Bullshit, procedure is procedure," said Ali. "They knew what they were doing was wrong."

Cuzzocrea nodded. "And they're going to pay for it. What I want to know is how involved McLaughlin is, was he just covering for Danny?"

"Danny, the paedophile…"

"Right, so was McLaughlin aware of the ring? Was Peter, his buddy, part of the ring and, more importantly…"

"Is Bryce McLaughlin part of that same paedophile ring?" Ali finished.

Abbott spoke to Superintendent Shaw, "Sir, I have the Internal Affairs Division on line three for you."

"Thank you, Paul." He crossed to Abbott's desk and picked up the phone, his finger hovering over a flashing red button as he asked Abbott a question, "Collins and Smith?"

"Units are en route, sir."

"And get someone out to pick up the newspaper guy," Shaw said and then took the call.

"Oh, before I forget, Ali?" Abbott said. "The front desk called, there's someone in reception looking for you, a Mrs. McKean?"

Ali looked at Cuzzocrea. "Marlene, she must have something on our perp."

"What?" said Cuzzocrea, confused. "How?"

Ali was out the door before Cuzzocrea could get an answer.

CHAPTER 44 - MAKING A SCENE

He'd ridden the elevator to the seventh floor but James Bartholomew was still out of breath. Mind you, he had been ever since Apu's call – in person, not an email, not a text, an actual call. It was a rare occurrence indeed to be summoned, let alone be summoned directly by the man himself.

It had been a disorientating day. From dawn onwards James had been on tenterhooks. Apu's silence in response to James's email yesterday was enough to quiver even the strongest constitution but add to that the farce of arranging for the removal of Ellen's body and all of the paraphernalia that accompanies in-home palliative care.

James had vacuumed out the indentations made in the carpet by the hospital bed and that, in and of itself, had been exhausting. In the end he'd called a local firm called Two Brawny Guys With A Van (a duo of former loggers he was well acquainted with since they ran weekly ads for their business in *The Echo*). They had fetched his precious Chiropedic adjustable sleeper from its place in an air-conditioned storage unit downtown. When James had mentioned in passing the death of his wife, the fellows had been kind enough to set up the complicated gubbins of the thing for him at no extra charge, for which James had thanked them kindly.

Their kindness hadn't, however, extended as far as wrestling with the king-size bedding, which included a particularly stubborn duvet cover, the opening in which was frustratingly small in relation to the goose-down quilt that belonged within its heavy thread count. By the time James had returned the master suite to its former (pre-cancerous) glory, he had been soaked through with vinegary sweat and so had taken an afternoon shower.

Clean and dressed, James was just about to unwrap his preserved birthday cheeseboard and enjoy a glass of Seven Poplars when, with fantastical thoughts of slipping his feet between the fresh bedding and finding his perfect angle of elevation in his bed, he'd received a call from Apu, summoning him to meet with him at Steven's apartment, *asap*.

James held a breath as the elevator doors opened on Steven's floor. It was curious that Apu had called a meeting at Steven's apartment. Steven wasn't even third echelon. Why would Apu wish to associate with him at all? Unless…Steven had contacted Apu. Had he gotten so agitated by the recent murders of two fellow members that he had finally lost his mind and reached out to their leader directly? If so, Steven's actions were a transgression of Apu's strict rules with regards to etiquette.

James's finger hovered over the entry keypad of his brother's door. James had nominated Steven, had been his sponsor and so the responsibility for such a transgression would tarnish his reputation as much as it would his younger brother's. James keyed in the code and heard the locking mechanism of the door unlatch itself and, not for the first time, he regretted having ever thought it wise to vouch for Steven's discretion.

The lights were off in the still apartment but James was able to orient himself by the ambient glow cast from the street lamps beyond the room's garish feature window.

"Hello?"

James managed a sing-song cheer to his voice despite his growing sense of unease. He stepped to the centre of the living area and waited for a response. Had he misheard Apu? No, no, that wasn't possible, surely. Besides, he'd been buzzed into the building by one of them.

"Hello? Steven? Apu?"

Nothing.

Something – a dark imagining – prodded at James's conscience, poking at him with warty fingers. It reminded him of the gnarled and calcified abomination that had entered his dozing mind as a prequel to Ellen's death.

James saw that the door to Steven's bedroom was ajar and although the sight of it made him feel like a fly inescapably bound for the centre of a sticky web, James mustered his courage and told himself not to be ridiculous; he had nothing to fear. After all, he would never trespass upon Apu's principles or policies.

Still, as he pushed open the door, his instincts were overwhelmed with a sudden need to flee as if that crusty demon of death was stalking him, watching him from shadowed corners and through the cracks of doors. His hand trembled as the door opened; James blamed it on not having eaten enough since breakfast – he was a type-2 diabetic and he'd been saving himself for a platter of fine cheeses and charcuterie capable of inducing an instantaneous bout of gout all day – but once the door opened fully and bounced silently at the extent of its opened hinges, it was obvious that his instincts had been right and his trembling was in reaction to the grim scene before him and nothing remotely connected to blood sugar levels.

James knew it had been futile even as he had gasped his brother's name but it seemed appropriate somehow to acknowledge him even though Steven was very clearly, very obviously dead.

Murdered?

James's mind ran through the past minutes. What had he touched? The entrance to the building – not just handle but the pane of glass in the door. The buttons for the elevator on the ground floor and inside the elevator too, and number seven would surely be dusted for prints. The entry keypad, the handle, the door itself, the bedroom door.

Obviously, James hadn't murdered his brother but something was niggling again – an instinct – he was the fly again and he couldn't quite reason why he was so keen to negate his presence in the apartment…because he'd been summoned here. Summoned here by Apu.

James stepped deeper into the room. He studied his dead brother and wondered what he – James Bartholomew, brother to the body before him – was feeling. He analysed his own feelings, hoping to find some emotion because surely *something* was warranted. But James felt nothing. Not a shred of sadness, no despair. With Ellen, he had been relieved that his suffering was over and that he was finally free of the interfering shrew but Steven was his brother, his blood. He'd known him as an infant, watched him grow. They'd lived together and faced things together yet the only thing he was overwhelmed by at the sight of his sibling's exsanguinated corpse was validation: he'd warned Steven time and time again that his actions would get him in trouble, such was his brother's stupidity and blatant disregard for consequences. James felt something now…James felt smug. It served Steven…

James gasped as he was pulled backwards, just managing to keep his feet under him but aware that something – *someone* – was choking him. James felt at his neck. Something was around it, tight, cutting into his flesh. Damn, the thing was garrotting him. He fingered it, trying desperately to get between it and his throat to no avail. He tried to turn, to see who was doing this but the thing wound tighter still and blood pulsed in his head and air moved neither in nor out.

James screamed a mute scream. He tried to fight, to reach back and to lash out at his assailant. Two arms, two arms hard to find with useless, backward punches. His chest heaved a pantomime of aspiration and utter, desperate panic shuddered through him. His heart raced as if it were banging on his ribs to alert him that he was suffocating, like he didn't know or he'd just forgotten to breathe.

James's knees gave way beneath him and his thighs

crumpled too. He kicked out, hoping to gain traction with his feet and push back. He scratched viciously at the flesh enveloping the cord around his throat. The darkness blotched purple and orange. Silver bursts of light came from within him and peppered his vision. He grinned, clenching his teeth together hoping to expand the sinews in his neck, to make space to breath from within but it was futile and he was blind to the pain there must have been as he felt himself chomp down hard on his own tongue.

And it was then, in his final moments, that James's vanity rattled him enough to succumb to his demise. He remembered Ellen in the throes of her final mortal battle and how she had bit free a sliver of her tongue and how pathetic and undignified he had thought the act to be. How pointless and tiresome and embarrassing a show it was to piss and shit yourself away, to chew off your own damned tongue fighting the fight we are all destined to lose.

Instead of fighting, James accepted his inevitable fate and relaxed; his own substantial weight against the tourniquet garrotte would have been enough to snuff him but still, his determined attacker facilitated the end with a firm knee pressed against his back.

It was always simpler and more effective to hide in plain sight. Bryce had managed to do so, perfecting the practice, for the entirety of his career. And so Bryce made little effort to conceal himself, the gloom was enough along with the bloodied body of Steven, of course – the illusionist's staple: misdirection.

Bryce concealed himself not because he feared a confrontation – why would he fear a confrontation with a fat fuck like James Bartholomew? – he had only stepped into the shadows of the closet because it was imperative he leave no evidence of a struggle; there must be no marks left upon James's body other than the ones that would make sense to a forensic pathologist. It was vital that when Bryce chose to strike, it was from behind and with as little movement around the room as possible.

Bryce heard the release of the locking gear for the front door to Steven's apartment. He took a step back and slipped between two hanging shirts. He heard James's voice from the living room. He must have been standing there in the gloom, just talking to himself. He always did like the sound of his own voice.

Bryce fumed with impatience. He had a long night ahead of him and he had to remain alert with every step, ever mindful of trace evidence and witness statements. How long was James going to stand there, wasting precious minutes? Bryce twisted the electrical cord around his fist once more and pulled the remaining length taught between his hands.

At last, Bryce watched James push open the door to Steven's bedroom and gawp uselessly at his brother.

Fuck!

He was a slow motherfucker, looking like a slack-armed fucking orangutan in the doorway.

Finally!

Bryce had to keep from saying it aloud as James stepped into the room to take a closer look.

Well? Step over to him, you cunt! Check for a fucking pulse or something, you dumb twat!

Ideally, he would have liked James's footprints in the blood immediately surrounding Steven's body but he could easily remedy that later. James – *the most unpredictable witness to a violent death ever* – was displaying an unnatural capacity towards detachment under the circumstances and so Bryce made his move.

Taking three silent steps out from the closet, Bryce wrapped the coaxial cable he'd earlier disconnected from Steven's flat screen TV around James's chubby neck. He crossed his fists and pulled tighter, tighter. His force was unrelenting – this had to be quick.

James was a big guy but he was weak; his size was just fat – he'd probably never even looked at a gym – whereas Bryce matched him in height and breadth of shoulders but had trained his body, worked it hard throughout middle age. Bryce's size consisted of muscle and strength, not flab. James clawed at the cord, even at his own skin. Bryce liked that; it would fit nicely. Bryce had been to enough suicides during his years on the force to know that, regardless of how determined a suicide was entering into the action, they were never fully impervious to the will of their own survival instinct at the very end. The bodies of people who have hanged themselves often bear the scars of their own desperate attempt to live once it's too late, then there're the ones who overdose on prescription meds, usually chicks, who phone an ex five minutes later.

Pussies, every one of them.

James's pudgy fists beat out at Bryce's arms but his blows were puny. He began to weaken nicely which was good because it would take some effort to right the pile of the carpet as it was. James dropped to his knees and then to his butt, he kicked out and Bryce had to pull him further back so he didn't kick the body because that would make no sense to the crime scene unit. The pull did the trick – James flopped forward and seemed to give up – so Bryce helped him along by pressing his shin into the fat man's spine, not too hard, though, couldn't bruise him. Bryce twisted the cord and the man's substantial weight did the rest. James succumbed.

Bryce checked James's dead face to see that he hadn't puked. No puke but some blood in his mouth and so Bryce had to struggle to tie the knot at the back of his neck without lying Bartholomew down and risking spilling his blood on the white carpet.

Once the first knot was secure, Bryce tied the free ends of the coaxial together over and over so that a rigid, bulbous knot was formed at the end of its length. The knot had to be strong enough to have taken James's weight mid-struggle.

Moving James was more of a struggle than Bryce had anticipated – death seemed to have doubled his weight. He pulled him from the centre of the bedroom to the far left side of the closet. Lifting the body had been almost impossible, and it took Bryce three tries, grasping under both arms and over James's chest with just one arm, leaving Bryce's other arm free to flick the knotted end of the cord through the gap between the closet's sliding door and the wooden frame, to rest atop the highest hinge.

Once the knotted end was through, Bryce carefully supported James's weight as he lowered him down. Bryce grinned, not only had he made the knots strong enough, he'd judged the length perfectly – James's ass was a good ten inches from the floor at the fullest stretch of the cable.

It was time to dress the scene. Bryce had six items on his mental check list.

First: the marks made by James struggling against Bryce's assault upon him. Bryce carefully brushed what felt like every individual strand of carpet pile back and forth until the patch of carpet where Bartholomew had actually died looked pristine.

Second: Bryce removed James's shoes and placed them on his gloved hands, hating the sweaty heat at the toes. He pressed them into the carpet which had been saturated with Steven's blood. Bryce held them in the blood for long enough to give him transferability. He then walked them around the centre of the room, in circles, back and forth in the formerly pristine spot of his own making. Bryce wanted the prints to communicate James's panic, the pacing of a man who'd murdered his friends then murdered his own brother, a man who was so shocked by his actions that he could no longer live with himself.

Third: at the cost of two snagged lumbar discs, Bryce hand-walked the shoes through the living room, spread-eagled, careful not to step the same path with his own Tyvek-bootee covered shoes. He walked the shoes to the flat-screen TV and stepped a cluster of invisible markings around where the coaxial had originally been. Although the blood had been almost entirely transferred to carpet already, Bryce knew that under the scrutiny, sprays, and special lights of the VIIMIS forensic team, the footprints would become luminous. Satisfied that he'd portrayed the footsteps of a man planning his suicide, Bryce walked his shod hands back to the bedroom and over to James's hanging body.

Fourth: he pressed the soles into the area directly under James's butt before returning them to the man's already swelling feet. He took a thick ankle in each hand and pulled at Bartholomew's legs roughly, digging the heels of his shoes back and forth in the carpet, replicating marks similar to the ones he'd brushed away just minutes before – marks denoting desperation, struggle, pain and then regret and cowardice.

Fifth: Bryce retrieved the red knife from Steven Bartholomew's side. He wiped the handle clean of prints and carefully pressed it into James's palm before letting it drop to the ground. Bryce renewed his surgical gloves, just to be extra careful, and found James's phone inside his pocket, the one that he had been so excited to buy because of its advanced security feature: fingerprint identification. Bryce smiled as he pressed James's thumb onto the button of the iPhone 6 and the screen brightened for him.

The sixth and final step: Bryce composed an email. An email from James in which he confesses to the murders of Tristan McMenemy, Danny Gilbert and his brother, Steven Bartholomew. In the email James prattles on in his usual way, apologizing for his failings, for not living up to his stellar reputation and for letting everyone down. He alludes to having reasons, good reasons for the murders but he is too loathed to actually put down in words exactly what depravity forced him into it. He assures all Cedar Riverites that they can sleep safer at night knowing that he, their Editor-in-Chief, rid their unblemished landscape of the troubled blots that were these men and, he was saddened to admit, himself. He apologizes for killing himself but, knowing his nature and now with Ellen already gone, it was the only decent thing left to do.

Bryce scrolled through James's contacts, looking for a

recipient who would waste no time in alerting the authorities and spreading the word throughout the community. Ha! Bryce found the perfect woman – James's gossipy, know-it-all, do-gooding secretary, the pregnant one. Bryce pasted Fern Clarke's address onto the email and hit send before dropping the phone next to James's corpse.

Bryce analysed the scene with pride and through his professional eyes, the eyes of a Chief Superintendent with five murder-suicide cases under his belt, it looked good. James's eyes were protuberant in his skull which made him look like he too was impressed with Bryce. Bryce couldn't help but laugh. He wondered if the pressure of the strangulation had also forced James's rectum to protrude – he guessed yes, it wasn't unusual for the hanged to shit themselves empty.

As he exited the apartment, Bryce heard James's phone ring – a predictably pompous ringtone, Beethoven or Handel – James's secretary was prompt and efficient as always. Bryce took the stairwell and the rear exit out, slipping his double-layered gloves and his bootees into his bag as he went.

It was time to get to Pine Nut Circle and drop by on smack-head Devlin and her little shit of a daughter.

CHAPTER 45 - A SOLID LEAD

In reception, Ali hugged Marlene and led her outside. The timing of Marlene's visit gave Ali an opportunity to have a much-needed smoke. Ali inhaled deeply and held the smoke in her lungs until it forced its way free with a cough.

"Fuck," said Ali, "I've only had about ten fags since I got here. If this case lasts much longer I'll need patches before I get maudlin."

"You should quit anyway," said Marlene, rummaging in her coat pockets. "You're entering the danger years."

Ali looked at her friend. "You should loan yourself out to hospices, cheer up the patients. Anyway, there's no cancer in my family." Ali felt lightheaded as the nicotine entered her bloodstream.

"Doesn't mean you won't be sucking on canisters of oxygen at the end, drowning in your own lung stew."

"Okay! Enough!" Ali snapped. "Anything for me?"

"As you know from my text, I couldn't get anything from Colleen last night, the flattery backfired and she got all uppity about confidentiality. She has a tendency to rise above her station, by the way. Buuuut…" Marlene looked pleased with herself.

"You did get something for me?"

"I did indeed." Marlene handed Ali the piece of paper she had been looking for amongst the old tissues and candy wrappers.

Ali looked at the paper and at Marlene's neat cursive.

"What do we know?"

"One of Colleen's students, or patients, whatever she calls them. Anyway, very troubled, mum's a junkie and a hooker, no dad to speak of and there have been a lot of problems in the past. However, something big happened recently, so big that Colleen was called out in the night which is a first, apparently. Seems she was called in to assist Child Protective Services and this all happened a couple of weeks ago and so I thought it might fit nicely with your profile, hon."

"Excellent. What was it that happened? This 'big' thing?" Ali asked.

"He doesn't know, like I said, she's uppity, but she did mention the kid's name because Colleen's had previous run-ins with her and the mother."

"He? He, who?"

"Wayne."

"Your brother?"

"Obviously. Pillow talk, Ali, it won the war," said Marlene. "Wayne had been eavesdropping last night – he does that – when I was picking Colleen's brains and well, he called me today and gave me this name. He said Colleen's been worrying about it all, that it's been keeping her up at nights. Wayne said Colleen's having to liaise with the family therapist because Child Protective Services are going to pull the kid out of the home and put her into the system. She might not be the one you're looking for, but hey, it's worth a try."

Ali slipped the paper into her trouser pocket. "Thanks, Marlene. Listen, I have to get back up there."

"You'll be at it all night then?" Marlene asked.

"Probably. It's looking that way." Ali crushed her cigarette butt beneath her foot and hugged Marlene. "What will you be doing?"

"I might have a dip in that jacuzzi again but if you need me, just call."

"I will. Thanks again."

Ali parted ways with Marlene and heard the engine of her monster truck grumble to life in the carpark as she waited for the elevator. She looked at the name on the sheet of paper again and wondered what Kristen Milligan's story might be.

Back in the squad room, Ali handed the name to Cuzzocrea.

"What's this?" He asked.

"Let's cross reference this name with the names on that incident list of ours."

Cuzzocrea brought up the list he'd condensed to include incidents involving children from October thirty-first until November twenty-seventh, incidents where Child Protective Services had been called in. He scanned the document. "What was the family name again? Milligan?"

"That's right," said Ali, reading over his shoulder, "Kristen Milligan."

Cuzzocrea highlighted a hit-and-run fatal dated November seventeenth. "Yes. Thomas Milligan, eight years old, killed as a result of a hit and run, the case is still under investigation. He was struck by a red pickup truck whilst riding his skateboard. Pronounced dead at the scene. His sister was there and witnessed the whole thing – Kristen Milligan, fifteen." Cuzzocrea turned to look at Ali. "How'd you get this name? Please don't say Marlene."

"Marlene's sister-in-law is a school counsellor, I told you," Ali said.

"Shit, Ali. This kid…this is a solid lead but we can't use it. We have no way of explaining how we came about the knowledge. We can't cover this up; Internal Affairs Division are already all over this case because of McLaughlin."

Ali shrugged. "Ballantine? He gave us the Glen Christie tip."

"Only because you gave him the names from the tattoos; there's no way he'd know that we'd profiled a minor."

Ali held her hands up. "Well we have to think of

something. I don't fucking know, do I? This girl could be our perp, Cuzzocrea. Does it really matter how we came about the lead?"

"Of course it really matters." Cuzzocrea turned to see that his raised voice hadn't drawn attention. The rest of the team, including Shaw, were busy elsewhere in the room. Cuzzocrea tapped his desk, thinking. Eventually, he whispered to Ali. "Disappear."

"What?"

"Go out. Find a payphone and call it in, get switch to put you through to me, here. Anonymous tip."

"Don't they record incoming calls?"

"So?" He frowned.

"Duh! My accent, I'm fucking Scottish. You think IAD won't put two and two together if it comes under scrutiny?"

Cuzzocrea smiled. "Then, it's time for you to get your Canuck on…you've been here what? nearly a decade? Be Canadian."

Ali huffed and reluctantly acquiesced. "Fine. But I warn you, I'm not much of an actress, and if you take the piss…"

"What will you do? I look forward to it, whatever it is."

Cuzzocrea had a mischievous look in his eye that made Ali's stomach flutter. "In the meantime, you get an address and anything else on this girl." Ali grabbed her windcheater and her bag.

"Can't," said Cuzzocrea, "Can't have a search on record until you've made the call so vamoose."

Ali shook her head. "Jesus you guys are anal. Vamoose? Who says vamoose?"

"I do, now go! Scoot!" He waved her off.

Ali called back to him as she crossed to the door, "Scoot? That's what dogs do on the carpet when they've got clinkers of shit on their arse."

Ali's nose was pink with cold by the time she got back to the VIIMIS squad room and she could hear Shaw barking orders even as she stepped out of the elevator. The squad room was buzzing with activity; the team was getting ready to leave. Ali found Cuzzocrea. "What the fuck? I didn't expect this reaction."

"It's not about the kid."

Shaw whistled for attention. "Okay, guys? Just to clarify, we have a report of two DBs – apartment seven-twelve in the Harbour Haven Building on Wharf Street. Male one: looks like homicide, single stab wound to the stomach, suspected murder weapon was found at the scene, a long, serrated-edged knife, red. Victim is thought to be the owner of the apartment, Steven Bartholomew."

Ali whispered to Cuzzocrea, "I know that name, why do I know that name?"

Cuzzocrea whispered back, "Christie, remember?"

Ali didn't understand the link but Shaw was talking again.

"Officers were responding to a call for an emergency welfare check, suspected suicide. A Fern Clarke called 911 when she received an email from her boss and couldn't reach him via telephone. Her boss is James Bartholomew, Editor-in-Chief of *The North-Island Echo*."

Ali understood the connection, Glen Christie had called James Bartholomew regarding the murders of McMenemy and Gilbert.

"As I said: two DBs, looking like a murder-suicide, James Bartholomew is thought to be the second male and appears to have hanged himself at the scene after sending a suicide note via email to his secretary, Ms. Clarke, in which he confesses to the murders of Tristan McMenemy, Danny Gilbert and his brother, Steven Bartholomew. Let's get over there and investigate this for ourselves because we are taking nothing for granted at this stage. Trina, Munro, Eden and Paul, you guys are with me. Rey and Ali, grab a squad team for back-up and get your asses over to follow up on that tip."

"Sir," Cuzzocrea said, pulling on his windcheater.

"What the hell?" Ali said as the bulk of the VIIMIS team

hurried out of the room.

"Seconds after you called, just as I was telling Shaw about the Milligan girl, he got a call about these DBs."

"This guy confessed to the murders?"

"Seems that way."

"By email? To his secretary?"

"I know what you're thinking."

"That it's fucking bull," said Ali, following Cuzzocrea out of the squad room. "It's too tidy and it doesn't fit the profile or the evidence." Ali kept up with Cuzzocrea's pace as they headed down the stairs and into a busy RCMP squad room where he requested a team of uni's to accompany them.

"I don't disagree but whatever's going on, we'll get to the bottom of it. All we can do is follow up on the Milligan lead and hope it's good. Stick to our profile," Cuzzocrea said.

Ali pulled Cuzzocrea out of the squad room to continue the conversation in the relative privacy of the corridor. "And what about McLaughlin? We can't just let that go."

"Shaw won't let that go. Problem is, like you say, it's tidy – Glen Christie called James Bartholomew which made him a person of interest even before his confession. It looks like the knife is the one used during the previous two murders. If it is a cover-up, then it's a good one."

"Yeah," said Ali, "by someone who knows just how to wrap a case up and put it to bed – a case that might just be getting too close for comfort – someone with insider knowledge, a high-ranking cop, for instance?"

CHAPTER 46 - THE BALL-PEEN HAMMER

As if the place wasn't enough of a god-forsaken shit hole already, Bryce saw that someone had added to Mamisîw House's exterior ambience with a piss-and-blood-stained mattress. Having parked safely just outside the horseshoe loop of Pine Nut Circle, Bryce had taken from his trunk a pair of disposable gloves and his trusty ball-peen hammer, discreetly secreted in the deep pockets of his overcoat.

It was Friday night and the addled denizens of the cul-de-sac were embarking upon the start of their usual alcohol- and narcotic-fuelled weekend pursuits. He could feel as much as hear the thumping bass emanating from one of the row homes across the street from Mamisîw House as he passed by. Between the beat of the music, a dog's incessant and gruff bark – no doubt that of a pit bull or a Rottweiler – was the treble accompaniment.

The rusty gate heralded Bryce's arrival with a lazy whinge in keeping with the work-shy idleness abundant amongst the residents. Bryce let the gate separating the abject poverty of Mamisîw House from the relative civilization of the rest of the street bang behind him and heard the beginnings of a violent domestic disturbance underway in one of the ground-floor apartments.

It wasn't unusual for the smell of pot to overpower the stench of piss in the dank stairwell of the place, but as he mounted the penultimate flight of chipped concrete steps, Bryce recognized a cleaner, more herbal undertone beneath the pungent scent. It wasn't any strain of weed he was familiar with.

On the third-floor landing, the crazy from apartment 3A was wafting a smouldering bowl of something potent but it wasn't cannabis. This one – he'd forgotten her name – was a frequent flyer at the island's mental hospital and yo-yoed back and forth between the inadequate care of her elderly mother to St. Fillan's at least twice a year. She was a total nut job and so Bryce fixed her with a cold stare.

Witnessing the effect of his power never failed to buoy Bryce. Criminals, the mentally unstable, scumbags and kids alike all cowed and cowered before him, scuttling back to whatever rathole they'd come from. Bryce was like Moses parting a sea of human detritus whenever he graced Pine Nut Circle with his presence, and he smiled as he watched the lunatic of 3A shuffle her psoriasis-mottled canckles back into her apartment, leaving a trail of green-grey smoke in her wake.

At Josie's door – the kitchen window alongside it was dark – Bryce gave the cul-de-sac one last cursory glance, cursory because no resident would ever dare rat him out. The bass was still booming but the pit bull was quiet. Bryce was reasonably confident that the domestic two floors down would ultimately result in a late-night arrest, if not a visit to the ER by one or both of the participants, but that would be after several more hours of imbibition of illegal substances.

Snapping his surgical gloves on, Bryce turned his key in the lock and pushed open the door. He rushed to close it behind him. To a man in his line of work, the odour of human decomposition is as distinct as a wife's favourite perfume might be to a regular civilian. So strong was the stench that Bryce guessed, had it not been for the flabby crazy next door wafting her stuff, he'd probably have smelled it all the way from the stairwell.

Something was ripe. It couldn't be the girl, Maiden – or Kristen as other people, people not of his ilk, might know her – because whoever it was had been dead a while.

Bryce took a handkerchief out of his inside coat pocket and covered his nose and mouth so as not to inhale microscopic particles of rotting flesh. In the living room, the cause was clear. Josie. Dead on the couch. She was beyond stiff and Bryce judged that she had moved on to internal putrefaction, her flesh swollen and blueing and in the cold room she was a subtle yet undeniable source of warmth. Bryce supposed her innards were probably mush and teeming with larvae.

The cause of death was obvious. She'd OD'd – her tin of shit was open on the floor beside her. It was no shock to Bryce. In fact, the sight of Josie Devlin alive and well year after year had always baffled him. Bryce wondered briefly if the overdose had been deliberate. It would be plausible, understandable even, for any other mother to have wanted to die after her eight-year-old son's skull was flattened beneath the tyres of an unidentified Ram 3500 but Josie wasn't any normal sort of mother. She was a mother only too happy to pimp out her own kids and take it up the shitter in exchange for a speedball, so it followed that she was undoubtedly incapable of such a noble act. It was more likely that she'd accidentally taken too much for even her hard-earned tolerance or maybe she'd gotten her hands on some of the new, questionable gear that had recently infiltrated the local drug trade in Cedar River thanks to Nanoose's very own Demon's Fang Outlaw Motorcycle Gang. Bryce smirked: how fitting that the scumbag biker who'd knocked Josie up twice might be responsible, however indirectly, for her death.

Dirty fucking abortion that she was.

Clearing rooms becomes second nature for a cop on or off the job, and Bryce had already checked the kitchen on his way to the living room. The windowless bathroom of the apartment was clad in a sickly pink tile, the grout black with the mildew that had spread over most of the ceiling and was creeping like pointillistic stalactites down the corners of the room. The bathroom was also empty as was the orange-tinged pink tub behind a shower curtain stiff with soap scum.

A quick glance was enough to confirm that the boy's room was empty too, as he'd expected it would be. Josie's room (he supposed a realtor would class it as the master) was as much of a dump as he remembered it to be; a yellowed Axl Rose poster, ripped at one corner, hung loosely from thumbtacks on the wall above the bed. The room and its closet were both empty. The only room left to check was Maiden's bedroom.

The kid wasn't in there. She hadn't come home as he'd expected she would. Nevertheless, Bryce was confident she'd have hidden something else he needed in there, so he set about finding the severed penises.

Her sleep is deep. Deep and more peaceful than it has been in so long. In her dream it is summertime, sunny and warm and she can feel the kiss of a tepid breeze as it brushes the fine hairs on her arms.

In the dream, Maiden is happy and it is a happiness more profound than anything she's ever felt, a carefree joy that tickles inside her. She is smiling and then laughing at the sound of Tommy's giggle, his hiccupping laugh. A ticklish scream, a squeal of delight, then a playful growl and a chase.

The sunlight dapples his hair with flecks of gold. Narrow shoulders, barely wide enough to support the neck of his white t-shirt above a tummy still baby-plump. He's on the sand, on a beach like the ones depicted on big canvases in the window of the travel shop in the mall. His jeans edge down his funny little butt as he runs and that makes them both laugh more. Tommy pulls the waistband up but too far and she can see his pale, skinny ankles.

He flaps his arms and runs in the surf where the ocean licks the land. The saltwater kicks up behind him and splashes his jeans dark. Tommy looks at his big sister with that open-faced trust of his and he grins a toothy grin and beckons her to him. She wants to go, she wants to run to him, down the sloping dunes, faster than her legs can go but it's a dream and so she feels herself gliding down, feeling the sun-dried grass tickling her legs. Effortless and smooth, all the way to the tidal flats where her feet touch down on sand deeply ridged by the ocean's retreat.

So close now she can see the halo of blue that rings black pupils stubbornly defiant of the bright sun. Tommy reaches his hand out to her, his grin wider and kinder than ever but then there's a thud. A bang. Scraping.

Maiden looks to the sky and it is portentous, ominously mottled. The sun blinks out and a frosty chill envelopes the beach. The waves build and frothy flotsam spits up in the wind.

Bang.

Crash.

Scrape.

An angry tempest looms behind an unsmiling Tommy and forewarns of danger. His eyes are dull and his hair no longer glistens with dappled sunlight but instead with oozing claret. Blood spews from his cracked skull, a skull unable to hold its shape as an eye socket skews and the blue recedes into a pool of black. The blood from his head is now speckled with globules of porridgy pink and Maiden remembers what the globules are: lumps of Tommy's smashed brain.

The ocean bulges angry and noisy, banging its wrath loud about him and it rises up, a towering torrent of evil above the tiny, broken boy, then slams down upon him, breaking him fully at last and ripping him and all of the joy and light from the world.

Maiden opens her eyes. She's in Tommy's bed; his smell is all about her and makes her heart heavy. She presses her face into the mattress, knowing she will never touch him again, never see his smile or hear him giggle.

Bang.

Crash.

Scrape.

The sounds she's heard in her dream remain and they're

coming from somewhere real, somewhere in the apartment. Maiden pulls the comforter down from over her head and listens in the dark.

It always struck Bryce as ironic that the poorer a person is, the more shit they have. It seems that perhaps lack results in the hoarding of pointless junk. Maybe it is borne of desperation, a futile attempt to allay future neediness.

Had Bryce been unfamiliar with the owner of the room, had he been part of a search team tasked with determining who might have inhabited it based on the contents within it, he would probably have gotten it wrong. It seemed that every toy the kid had ever owned had been kept. Every piece of clothing and scrap of paper, shoes and even baby onesies had been retained.

One drawer in the packed closet was filled with empty bottles of shampoo and tubs of cream, cheap dollar-store perfumes and old lipsticks. Broken remotes, disk and even cassette players, the batteries long since removed, filled another drawer and the last one was brimming with curled and crumpled fashion magazines pilfered – according to the stickers on the front of most of them – from various places including a doctor's waiting room, the library and even the therapist's office above HSBC. The kid was a collector of all sorts of shit: belts and scarves, hats and bangles, all hanging from nails rammed into the drywall and working themselves free of their crumbling holes under the weight of their tacky displays.

Bryce had been hopeful about a shoebox on the top shelf, hidden behind some pilled sweaters, but it had contained only a collection of kiddy drawings and paintings, birthday cards and Christmas cards. Bryce had snorted when he'd seen a homemade Mother's Day card signed by both of the kids, their names scrawled inside their respective handprints, splurged on the paper in thick and cracking paint.

He'd almost cleared the whole closet before he finally

tipped out a box of neatly balled socks and underwear and he'd heard the dull thud of his quarry on the carpeted floor. Sealed in two separate zip-lock bags were the severed cocks he'd been searching for, the previous owner's name written neatly in Sharpie along the opaque central strip of each: Cápac and Quispe – pseudonyms he himself had assigned to the deceased – and neutered – men.

Bryce held the bags at arm's length. Loathe to put them in his pocket as they were, he pulled a stained t-shirt from the floor and wrapped the severed genitals in it before shoving them deep inside his pocket, alongside his hammer.

Bryce kicked his way back through the mess of his search. Besides the girl, he still had to find one more thing that could, theoretically, link him to the victims: the charging base for the taser. He had put it in the kitchen more than a decade and a half ago, he guessed it might still be there, next to a stove he knew Josie Devlin had never cooked a meal on.

Maiden pulls her feet out from under Tommy's comforter and slowly kicks it down the bed. Sitting up, she listens. She can feel heat emanating from the apartment next door but the banging is coming from the other side of the wall on the opposite side of the room, the wall that separates Tommy's bedroom from hers. The banging and rummaging has to be coming from inside her closet.

Someone is in there and they are pulling all of her stuff from the shelves, not just the clothes but she hears the scrape of her boxes too. She hears the familiar sound of her bottle collection being searched, the plastic and glass vessels chinking against each other and against the wooden base of the drawer in which she keeps them.

Maiden's heart beats hard in her chest. Who is in the house? They haven't put lights on and so they are searching in near darkness. Is it one of Mum's lot? Junkies, all of them, so maybe one of them is ransacking the place looking for Mum's stash – but Mum's stash is right next to her, out there for anyone who walks in to see. Perhaps someone she owed money to, then? A dealer? But all of the dealers know Mum enough to get cash up front; everybody in Cedar River knows not to do Josie Devlin a favour.

Maiden stands. The door is open enough so she can slip through it undetected if she is careful – the hinges on Tommy's door are noisy and there is a sunken piece under the linoleum in the hallway that creaks and clicks if you step on it. She takes three steps closer to the door. The hallway beyond is way brighter than the bedroom thanks to the yellow coming from the light screwed to the ceiling on the walkway outside the kitchen window.

The intruder in the next room goes quiet. Maiden slips between the door and the doorframe, through the gap, without a sound and tiptoes carefully towards the front door.

She is almost there, her fingertips upon the brushed steel of the handle when she hears his voice.

A shaft of dirty yellow light spilled through the open door of the kid's bedroom as he made his way to it and it momentarily darkened. Somebody cut through the light, someone was in the apartment.

Bryce stepped around the door and looked down the hallway. Maiden was there. Creeping along the wall. She must have been hiding the whole time, in one of the other bedrooms. She was heading for the front door, ballsy bitch.

"Maiden. I've been looking for you," he said.

Bryce started down the hall, finding the handle of his ball-peen hammer as he went, pulling its length from his pocket.

The kid was still, her red hood up over her hair. He understood this type of body language; he was trained to understand it and react to it: it was the freeze; the moment a person takes to debate whether to fight or to flee.

Bryce made the decision for her.

Maiden knows the voice. She's been familiar with it ever since she can remember. Apu. She doesn't have to turn around to see the mean in him; the mean is what Apu is all about and it spills from him, the air is thick with it.

Maiden takes a breath and closes her fingers around the door handle.

It is too late. Her face smashes into the door and the pain of it is matched instantaneously by something sharp and cold at the back of her head. Her lip catches on the frame of the letterbox as her face skids down the wood of the door, her balance lost, she drops onto her knees.

Something clatters after her. A hammer, its metal head glinting with light that belies the gloom of the hall. The cold air from outside slinks across her fingers through the gap at the bottom of the door.

Then he is on her, she sees one of his booted feet before her head snaps back, her hair tight in his grasp. In one fast blur, the air is squeezed from her as Apu grabs her around her waist, still holding her hair, and hauls her up.

But Maiden knows something Apu doesn't.

As he'd grabbed her up, her fingers had clutched the handle of the hammer.

Bullseye!

He'd been aiming for her back but his ball-peen had cartwheeled itself high and smacked her dead-on at the back of the skull. She face-planted up the door and before she'd even known what had hit her, he'd grabbed a chunk of hood and the hair below it and then swept her up from the floor.

The little shit was as light as a feather and she wasn't going anywhere. He pulled her hair tighter and whispered into the ear beneath the hood.

"Listen, you little cunt, calm the fuck down. You understand me?"

Bryce felt her nod. At least she knew enough to be quiet

and compliant – years of training'll do that.

He stepped back with her tight against him and looked into the kitchen. He could see the cube-like charger base for the taser, still plugged into the same socket he'd put it in all those years before. Josie Devlin really was a scruffy bitch and had probably never even wiped the surfaces of the kitchen.

Bryce tightened his grip around the girl and gave her a quick, firm shake.

"You going to be good for Apu? Huh?"

He felt her nod again just before he felt metal on bone – his bone, his skull, just above his ear. It was a nausea-inducing thwack that stung like a motherfucker, enough to make him cry out in temper as much as in pain.

The silence squealed but the noise was from inside his head as it snapped sharply to the right in response to the blow. His grip on the girl loosened beyond his control and he felt her slide from his grasp and saw her slip out through the front door. He reached for her but only managed to brush the denim of her jeans.

The hammer she'd used to strike him – *his hammer* – clattered on the concrete beyond the threshold and Bryce scrambled against the wall of the hallway and pulled himself past the loose jamb. He stooped and grabbed his ball-peen, his brain whooshed inside his skull and made him stumble to the ground. He fingered the site of the blow, no blood but a lump as hard as the bone beneath it.

He spied a flash of her red hoodie, almost brown beneath the sickening yellow of the caged lights above him, as Maiden disappeared around the corner and down the stairs. Despite his dizziness, Bryce pulled himself to his feet, vertigo forcing him dangerously close to the railing against which he propelled himself away with a push, slamming into the door of apartment 3A and onwards, around the corner where he reached out and managed to grasp the metal of the handrail.

He took the first flight fast but careful, one step at a time, his head still smarting. His brain seemed to swim itself back to a semblance of equilibrium but it was enough for him to gain steady momentum. He had to get to the little shit before anybody saw them.

Maiden's twisted ankle gives way on the last set of steps, her left foot stuck where it is while the rest of her body continues downwards. She grips the railing hard as she falls, the skin of her palm ripping against the spikes of painted rust; she feels her left kneecap pop away from the joint and slip all the way around to the side of her leg. The pain is incredible and so intense she can't scream. Her lungs seemed to clamp shut until she instinctively punches the side of her dislocated patella. She feels the circle of bone snap back to the front of her leg, then suck itself back into place.

She has no time to assess her injuries, Apu's boots are hard and heavy on the flight above her, vibrating through the metal railing she is still gripping tightly. Despite her stinging palm, Maiden uses the handrail to pull herself to her feet and haul herself onward, her left knee boiling in angry protest with every step.

Along the path, through the gate, hearing it screech, then bang shut. Seconds later it screeches open and bangs shut again.

Apu.

The lights are on in one of the townhouses across the street, and she can hear loud music pounding from it. Silhouetted figures pass behind the thin drapes. A party. People. Lots of people. People who will help her.

Maiden shouts but her breath, what little there is, is snared by her dry throat. Somewhere nearby a dog barks. It has heard her. The house is close. Maiden steps into the street and her knee, the stupid knee that has twisted, buckles beneath her and she falls onto the concrete, her hands splaying out to break her fall. Little sharp stones dig up into the raw flesh freshly grated on rust, stabbing fresh pain through her.

Tears – or sweat, she doesn't care which – hot on her cheeks and Maiden swallows the agony; it will keep; she'll feel it later when the nightmare is over. She catapults herself up and across to the other curb, just feet from the path to the party house now.

But as she leaps onto the sidewalk she is snatched back again, same as before, by her hair, but this time there are no whispered threats. This time she just gets the hammer, the silver ball of it twinkling a shiny wink at her as it passes her nose and smashes into her face with an ugly crunch.

He could have taken her just out of the rusty gate. She'd been close enough then for him to catch her. But Bryce wanted to enjoy the moment. Savour it. He refreshed his grip on the ball-peen first, setting it up just right.

Striding now, no need to run, analysing his trajectory. She shouted out feebly to a house where people neither heard nor cared. She stumbled and spilled into the road. She pulled herself up and maybe she thought she was nearly safe, heading for the house that's pumping out the intrusive bass.

She got up, limping badly. He let her make it all the way to the curb and then all he had to do was reach out and take a fist full of her hair, free of hood now, flying out behind her.

Bryce yanked that little fucker's head back and arched the blow around, hitting her square in the middle of her face, just where lips stretched to nose and he heard the satisfying crunch of splintering teeth.

Lights out, you little gash.

And so conveniently close to where he'd parked his car, too.

CHAPTER 47 - MAMISÎW HOUSE

Ali rolled a used hypodermic syringe under her foot. "Nice place," she said to Cuzzocrea and kicked the needle to the concrete edge of the area reserved for the shabby apartment block's overflowing trash cans and barren recycling bins.

Cuzzocrea turned to her as he headed towards a set of steps leading to the upper floors of the building. "You know the residents protested against refugees being housed here after the Syrian influx in 2016? I guess they thought it'd cheapen the area."

Cuzzocrea's radio crackled. "Inspector Cuzzocrea from Sergeant Tremblay."

Cuzzocrea spoke into his radio as he and Ali ascended the urine-stained stairs – the smell of urine on concrete always took Ali back to the old red public telephones in Britain which had been phased out in the early nineties; it had been impossible to find one that hadn't been pissed in. "Go ahead, Sergeant," said Cuzzocrea.

"Sir, the front door to apartment 3B is open and…we're going to need you up here, sir."

"Copy that."

Cuzzocrea looked back at Ali as they both instinctively picked up their pace. Turning right out of the stairwell on the third-floor landing, Cuzzocrea led the way to the two uniformed RCMP officers. Ali was a short distance behind him when she detected a distinctive odour in the air.

"Cuzzocrea?" He looked back at her and she added:

"Decomp."

Cuzzocrea acknowledged her warning, released his 9mm and unclipped a Maglite torch from the other side of his belt.

"Wait there," he said to Ali as he simultaneously released the safety and clicked on the flashlight, crossing his hands and pointing both to the floor. "I'll clear," he spoke to the two officers, "secure this floor, no-one in or out, residents of these apartments need to stay indoors. Call it in, 10-18, units needed."

"Sir." The uniformed officers responded in unison.

Cuzzocrea stepped alongside the open door to apartment 3B. He pushed the door wide with his foot and looked in before proceeding, the gun and flashlight now raised to shoulder height. Ali heard him identify himself as a police officer and shouted a warning to anyone who may be inside. The two police officers split off, their hands covering their sidearms as they monitored the stillness of the walkway. The officer farthest from Ali began to speak into his radio.

Guns made Ali nervous. She wasn't green to police procedure but she hadn't quite gotten used to firearms. In the UK, on the few occasions she had been involved in cases where the services of SCO19 were called upon (the Specialist Firearm Command of the Metropolitan Police Service), everyone else, including regular officers of the law, were held back behind a cordon about half a mile from the scene and even then the AFOs (authorised firearms officers) would need authorization directly from the Home Office before they could even deploy a 'ferret' canister and gas a potential threat out – never mind release the safety switches along the barrel of their rifles.

"This country's fucking bonkers," Ali muttered to herself.

Not content to hang around doing nothing, Ali dialled Shaw. He answered immediately.

"Sir, we're at the Milligan girl's address. Cuzzocrea's inside, front door was open when we arrived. I don't know the ten-code for this but, if my olfactory receptors are anything to go by, we've got at least one dead body here."

"Shit," said Shaw. "Trina's working the Harbour Haven scene…look, I'm going to get a SOCO team over there and I'll instruct the commanding officer to liaise with you."

"Right," Ali said, feeling her stomach lurch with excitement.

"You good with that, Dalglish?"

"Of course."

"What do you know? Is it the kid?" Shaw asked.

"Don't know yet, sir. Cuzzocrea's clearing the place. There are two uni's here and I think they called in support units."

"Good. Tell Rey to call me, *asap*."

"Will do, sir," Ali ended the call as Cuzzocrea stepped out of the apartment.

He spoke to the officers: "Cordon it off. Give the immediate neighbours the option of leaving but let them know, if they do decide to stay, they have to remain indoors."

"Is it the kid?" Ali asked, crossing to him.

"No. Looks like it might be the mother…what was her name? Devlin? Something Devlin. We need to process the scene. We need SOCO."

"Shaw's sending a team over for us. You have Tyvek gear in your car?" Ali said, already walking back to the stairs.

"Yes. In the trunk." Cuzzocrea tossed his keys to Ali. "I'll meet you down there, I just want to check that these guys are on it."

Ali trotted to the stairs, adrenaline a catalyst to her haste. She stopped and called to Cuzzocrea, "We need to find that kid, and now."

"I'll put out a BOLO."

Ali decided the acronym had to stand for be-on-the-look-out, similar to Britain's all points bulletins. She wondered if Canada partook in the AMBER alert system. "Do you guys do AMBER alerts?"

Cuzzocrea shrugged. "I can get information out through Translink so that it loops on screens at train stations and on buses but, honestly, not much use here, no railroad on the island. I'll check with Shaw first."

Ali started for the stairs and clicked her fingers, remembering Shaw's instructions for Cuzzocrea. "Shaw wants you to call him asap."

At the bottom of the stairs, Ali stopped and backtracked half way up the first flight. She peered at the handrail, her nose inches from it. "Cuzzocrea?" she called, her voice echoing off the concrete walls. She saw Cuzzocrea's head appear, looking down at her from the third floor. "I've got blood here, might be unrelated but it's fresh. We need to tape off these stairs too."

Ali heard Cuzzocrea talking into his radio as she headed out of the building and through a rusty gate, which she pushed carefully and propped open with a large rock she'd found in the smattering of grass alongside it.

The bleep of Cuzzocrea's car unlocking was lost amongst the growing wail of sirens on their approach. Red and blue reflected light sluiced the curtained windows of a row of terraced houses across the street. Ali wondered if the partygoers in one particular house would hear the approach of the RCMP squad cars in the din of their music and, if they did, would they even give a shit?

CHAPTER 48 - A MANUFACTURED SUICIDE

"Tread carefully," said Trina as she led Superintendent Shaw through the apartment. He heeded her warning and stuck to the edges of the natural path one would take through a room; the central, 'beaten path', which had been covered with thick heavy paper rolled from a bolt and taped to the floor at regular intervals to secure it in place. Shaw shuffled carefully along the edge of the paper and slipped through the bedroom's doorway. Trina's scene of crime officers had illuminated the entire apartment with floodlights and the bedroom was especially stark as the cold white light bounced off the surface of the nearly white carpet within.

"Talk to me," Shaw said to Trina.

Trina pointed to a deceased male slumped in a seated position against the unmade bed, a bloody sheet pooled atop his naked thighs. "DB1: Steven Bartholomew. Forty-three. Single sharp force trauma wound to the abdomen. Rectal temperature is four degrees lower than normal and rigor has begun in the eyelids, neck and jaw only so time of death is between two-and-a-half to three hours ago. He has a tattoo, same as McMenemy's and Gilbert's, same font, same location. His says Sinchi Roca." Trina momentarily focussed her attention on the clipboard in her hand; she scribbled her signature on a form and absently jabbed her thumb over her shoulder to indicate the second dead male in the room. "DB2: James Bartholomew, fifty-seven. We're assuming they're brothers but an official ID has yet to be conducted.

Cause of death: strangulation by ligature. Please know that all of my findings are only confirmed once I have performed a complete post-mortem examination. The ligature used was a coaxial cord, approximately six feet in length, tied once at the back of the victim's neck and three times using reef knots at the ends."

"Victim's neck? Not a suicide?" Shaw inquired.

"No. I don't believe so." Trina looked at Shaw who was frowning, confused, as he looked at James Bartholomew's body on the floor. "We took him down after initial photography and examination, and we removed his undershirt, shirt, bowtie and jacket as well as his overcoat. He has a tattoo, same location, same font, but his reads Sapa. He had been hanging from here." Trina pointed to the hinges securing the closet door to its frame. "The reef knots were slipped through the gap here and the knots caught at the rear of the door so it would look like he had committed self-strangulation – similar to hanging except that the suicide's feet are in contact with the floor. Instances of self-strangulation are very rare because one has to be determined to strangle oneself even though escape is possible. It's most common in prisons, places where there are no means to hang oneself in the traditional sense. Notably, this is the way that Robin Williams was rumoured to have killed himself."

"And you're sure this isn't one of those cases?"

"I'm not signing off on COD until I get that post-mortem done but, no, no I don't." Trina crouched next to James Bartholomew. Shaw joined her and listened as she explained her findings: "There are several ligature marks on his neck, crisscrossing here and here, see? Ligature marks like this are consistent with a victim struggling against an attacker who is strangling them from behind.

"Now, in cases of genuine self-strangulation, there is only one deeply bruised ligature mark. Also, if this had been a suicidal strangulation, I'd have expected to see venous congestion prominent at the root of the tongue and above the ligature due to the slow tightening of it as he allowed his own body weight to do the work but there is very little venous congestion present.

"Additionally, James Bartholomew keeps his nails neat and trimmed and he trimmed his fingernails as recently as this morning and, as you can see here, here and here, he scratched his own neck in what looks like a desperate attempt to release the ligature when all he had to do – if he was committing suicide by self-strangulation – was stand up. I'm guessing the skin we scraped from under his nails is his own.

"Now, take a look at this particular ligature mark; it's a grooved impression, free of ecchymoses – this kind of mark is made after death, and this is the ligature mark left by the coaxial cable around his neck when he was in the 'hanged' position we found him in upon our arrival.

"Doug, it's procedure to treat all strangulations as homicidal until the contrary is proven. Nevertheless, I'm confident that this was not suicide."

"Time of death?" Shaw asked.

"Within the past ninety minutes, two hours at a maximum push."

"So he wasn't killed by our DB1, Steven Bartholomew."

"No."

"I know you still have to do the PM but, Trina, are you sure about this?" Shaw asked quietly.

Trina huffed. "Of course I'm sure…"

Shaw held his hands up in surrender. "Just asking…"

"Jesus, Doug, a little trust would go a long way…"

"I apologize."

"…and he didn't kill his brother, either," said Trina, sulkily.

"Who?"

"James Bartholomew. In his 'suicide email', he confessed to killing our vics and his brother, Steven, over there. He didn't stab him – no trace of blood on his clothing, his prints are on the knife but it's one full, neat hand print, no smears, no double prints and no other latents on the handle. It was wiped clean and then placed in his hand, probably post-mortem. This whole scene is manufactured."

"Explain," Shaw demanded, standing up to allow the circulation in his legs to return.

Trina stood and pointed to Steven Bartholomew. "Two perfectly planted footprints in DB1's blood at either side of his body."

"I'm assuming those prints are James Bartholomew's?"

"Yes. The footprints then cluster here," said Trina, pointing to the centre of the room, "and then off through the living area where we have the paper down, they cluster again around the TV where the coaxial cable used as a ligature was taken. Then the footprints return to where we were supposed to believe he died."

"So, whoever set it up knew what you'd be looking for?" Shaw suggested.

"Exactly. Put it this way, if I were to manufacture a scene like this, I would do it better but not by very much. Whoever did this has more than a basic knowledge of crime scene procedure and evidence retrieval."

Shaw nodded. "I take it they weren't moved? Or were they?"

"DB2 was moved but only from somewhere else in this apartment, probably this room. I put his weight under three hundred pounds but over two-fifty. He wasn't moved far and certainly not by a child. The necrosis in the tissue margins above the ligature marks caused ante-mortem are pinched by the grooved ligature mark produced post-mortem so he was strung up, suspended from the closet minutes after he had been strangled to death. DB1 was stabbed close to where he is. Over there by the spilled drinks." Trina pointed to the area between the doorway and the bottom of the bed. "His assailant ambushed him from his or her hiding place behind the open door. Steven Bartholomew ended up on the floor, on his back. He was then stabbed in that section of the floor as evidenced by the fine blood spray and spatter – not necessarily visible to the naked eye – on the edge of the door and the bottom right corner of the mattress."

"On the floor? How'd he get there…you know what I'm asking here, Trina," Shaw said.

Trina stepped carefully over Steven Bartholomew, her feet planted in an isosceles stance at either side of his body. She crouched over him and stretched open a deep crease in his stomach, "Step around here, Doug. Stay close to the little cabinet there so you don't disturb anything. Look here."

"Taser marks."

Trina carefully stepped back. "Same as on McMenemy and Gilbert. However…"

Shaw finished her sentence, "No taser."

"No taser."

"Any evidence that puts the same girl in the room?"

"Yet to be analysed but I found hair consistent with the other two sites and trace fibres in the carpet – red cotton and blue denim. Also, a perfect imprint of two very small, bare feet over there on a part of the carpet which is practically virgin, behind the door, against the kick board – it's where she waited to strike. I'm going to get Jerry Vincent back in with his indentation technology."

"Okay," said Shaw. "Now. The bloody sheet on DB1?"

"The blood is from the knife wound to his abdomen near the umbilicus. His penis is in situ."

"That's a change in MO."

"No, I think it's evidence of a struggle," Trina explained. "She comes at him from behind the door, tasers him, he falls, she stabs him but he fights back. I found the same red fibres in his teeth; he probably bit her through her red sweatshirt. She falls, as evidenced by the fibres collected from the carpet."

"So Steven, DB1, fights back. The girl either watches him die, in which case she would have cut off his penis then, once he was dead…or…she was overpowered?"

"Can't say. Maybe, after the struggle, as he was dying, she left. The clothing fibres indicate she pulled herself along the carpet from close to the centre of the room and out through the bedroom door."

"How can you tell?"

"In layman's terms: think of the window as north, the door as south, the closet west and so on. The fibres are predominantly attached to the northern exposure of the pile, indicating that the material from which they were deposited moved along the carpet heading in a southerly direction, towards the door."

"Okay," said Shaw. "So what brought James Bartholomew here? Was he already here?"

"Can't say," said Trina.

"Well someone killed him here, got his sizeable weight up high enough to slip the knotted end of the cord around his neck through the top hinge of that closet door."

"You can rule out the girl," Trina said. "If those are her footprints, she's tiny. No way she'd even be able to drag him over there, certainly couldn't have lifted him."

"Someone did and that same someone then manufactured an almost credible murder-suicide."

"Any witnesses? Neighbours?" Trina suggested.

Shaw shook his head. "Half of these apartments are empty, especially during the winter. The average Cedar Riverite can't afford to live in a building like this. They're mostly vacation rentals or second homes for rich mainlanders."

"You heading over to the other crime scene?" Trina asked, flicking through pages on her clipboard again.

"Yes."

"Remember, you can't go in. Your name can't show up on both logs. Cross-contamination. If our perp is the Milligan girl then any hair or fibre evidence matched to her will be inadmissible if either of us were present in this room and her apartment on the same night."

"I know that. Keep me posted on any new developments."

Shaw followed the same awkward route out of the

apartment as he'd taken going in. He slipped under the tape across the front door and took the stairs down to the entrance of the building where he called his team over to him.

The cold wind whipped viciously at the top of his head and depleted the volume of his voice as he addressed them: "Okay guys, listen up. Eden, I want you to find this kid. A BOLO's been issued but I want you to follow up on that, get in touch with teachers, doctors, anyone who can give you some insight and I need a recent picture of her. Exhaust your Special Victims contacts. We can assume she's wearing a red sweatshirt or jacket of some sort and blue jeans – see if you can get a photo of those sneakers Trina IDed for us. We have officers canvassing here and tracing James Bartholomew's movements over the past week. I need CCTV pulling from around the city – everything in the past twenty-four hours. Paul, you get on that." Shaw beckoned his team a few steps further away from the police cordon and the log officer securing it. He continued: "What I'm about to say is strictly off the record and will not appear in any statement until I make the order official, do you understand? I want you looking for McLaughlin's SUV in the CCTV footage, Paul. Munro, I want you to locate Chief Superintendent Bryce McLaughlin."

"And arrest him?" Munro asked.

"No, you donut! I said it's unofficial. Just find him and get eyes on him – *your eyes, Munro* – when you do, let me know and I'll give you further instructions."

"Yes, sir," said Munro.

"I'm going over to Rey at the other apartment block."

Shaw zipped up his windcheater and pulled it tight around his face as the icy wind bit at his face. He crossed the street to the stall he'd parked in earlier, near the greensward where a herd of Canada Geese were barking louder than the wind.

CHAPTER 49 - MEAT AND METAL

Meat and metal when she swallows. Are her eyes closed? She can't tell and so she has to find her eyebrows and feel down to her eyelids. A tickle of lashes and, yes, her eyes are open – so, she's somewhere very, very dark.

It smells leathery and she's lying down. Her body is swaying gently onto her shoulder and back off it again and with that swaying comes a nice hum, soothing despite her dire dread. And then she's shaken, shoved hard almost onto her back but back up again and there's a noisy clatter of things mechanical.

She knows, just knows then that she's in the trunk of a car. Apu's car. And something else she just seems to know is that nothing can matter anymore because if he has her, he'll finish her.

The meat and the metal is the taste of drying, chewy blood on her tongue. It's filled her mouth and throat and swallowing it back makes her feel sick because it's like jelly but hot and cold at the same time.

She tentatively reaches for the front of her face where she remembers a glint of metal before the hammer had struck. She moans before her fingertips touch flesh, as if the heat of her hand is tangible enough to hurt.

Where once there had been one upper lip, there are two. Split and swollen out like a fortune cookie on her face. A sob escapes her as her tongue reaches from inside to explore further. Gingerly poking with her tongue she passes things sharp that may have been her teeth once, then she's finally licking her own quivering fingers.

She slurps back her blood-salty spit and pants, open-mouthed, because she cannot do otherwise. Her jaw is shaking and Maiden thinks she must look really silly now and she nearly laughs but the car hits a speed bump because she feels her other shoulder, not the one on the carpet, hit against whatever is above her. She feels in the dark and again she's unable to know for sure whether her eyes are open or closed. There are cold, metal squares and grooves with soft edges. At the edge of her reach a curve of cold metal, rougher at the sides, ridged in the middle like two strips of steel sandwiched together and stuck, bolted, one end to the ridged metal top and one end to another piece of carpet which feels like a stubby wall.

She feels all over the carpet where she can manage to reach but lying back makes her choke on bloody jelly and she has to spit up a lot of the meat-metal crap. Spitting up is hard because she has no top lip anymore and so she just has to gather stuff from her tongue, scraping it against what teeth she has left and 'tut-tutting' it out. Her tongue finds something in her cheek. Careful not to bash the really, really sore front of her face, she slips her finger inside her mouth and persuades the thing out, 'tut-tutting' it into her other hand. It's too dark to know for sure but Maiden thinks it might be half, if not a full, tooth.

Weird that finding her own tooth would be the thing that makes her cry, not finding out that she has a hole in the front of her face or that Apu's driving her to a place where he can finish her off privately. It was a tooth that broke her.

Maiden snorts and sniffs, her chest heaving and gulping as she presses her broken tooth deep into the funny little pocket inside a pocket that jeans always have. She'd always wondered what that silly little pocket was for.

Now she knew.

CHAPTER 50 - FAMILIAR DEMONS

Stepping out onto the walkway awash with light cast by bulbs shining through yellowed plastic domes, Ali unzipped her Tyvek onesie, pulled back the hood and brought her face mask down to her neck. She breathed deeply of the relatively fresh air, even the hint of stale urine in the block was a welcome respite from the smell of the dead junkie on the couch.

Ali rested her elbows on the metal railing and looked down at the crowd of residents who had gathered at the edge of the taped off boundary. Ali could only imagine what stories might be circulating amongst the group – urban legends in the making.

Having fished her cigarette packet out of her inside pocket, Ali sparked up and breathed in her favourite type of air. She closed her eyes and pinched the skin between her brows. Her brain ached as it always did when her two areas of expertise merged, ping-ponging between pathology and criminology.

Eyes still closed she smiled as she felt the firm and muscular weight of Cuzzocrea as he joined her and pressed his arm against hers, as close to her as their professional environment – and the throng of onlookers – would allow.

"Hey there," Cuzzocrea said.

Ali smiled at him, wanting to lose herself in his embrace but resorting instead to a soft bump of her head against his bicep.

"Long day." She exhaled. "Can you believe we were in Saanich this morning?"

"Feels like days ago," he replied.

"And last night? I can barely remember it."

"Ouch," Cuzzocrea said, feigning a bruised ego.

Ali nudged him. "Not like that. You know what I mean. But, I think I'll need a little refresher course when this is all over."

"Refresher courses are too short." He smiled.

"You're right, I need a good three- or four-day course. I'm very rusty."

"Unlike you, I remember last night. Take it from me, you're not rusty." He straightened and took his notebook out of his pocket. "You've handed over to Evidence Collection, what's your take?"

Ali smoked and talked, "OD. The tourniquet was removed recently but long after she died. Someone knew she was dead but didn't report it."

"The kid?"

"I think so. I think the mother's death was the catalyst that triggered Kristen Milligan's psychosis. The mother's been dead for a week."

"So, last Friday? According to my timeline, that was the one-week anniversary of Thomas Milligan's hit and run."

"Run me through the calendar of events," said Ali, pinching the skin between her eyebrows again.

"Friday the seventeenth of November, Thomas Milligan is killed – sister witnessed the incident – police are called, they can't track down the mother, Josie Devlin, a known prostitute and addict. Child Protective Services are called in and they intervene. They assign a grief counsellor and Josie agrees to attend therapy sessions with her daughter every day while an assessment is undertaken. I spoke to the social worker assigned to the case and he informed me that arrangements were underway to have the girl placed with a foster family. According to the Family Services guy, there's a history of neglect. The therapist's report was damning and it was her recommendation that Kristen should become a ward of the province, that her brother's death had taken a significant psychological toll upon her and that she was vulnerable."

"So why the fuck was she still here?"

"They were in the process of tracking down the father, some legal loophole, technically, even though he's estranged, he'd have to relinquish custody too but he's somehow off the grid. Last known address was Nanoose."

"What else did you get from the therapist?"

"Eden interviewed her but didn't get much, confidentiality. But she did say that only Kristen appeared for the last session, her mother was AWOL. The session was scheduled for the afternoon of Friday the twenty-fourth. Fits with your estimated time of death."

"Josie Devlin died on the twenty-fourth so when she missed that therapy session she was either dead or she was getting there," Ali said.

"Could Kristen have been responsible for her mother's death?"

Ali shook her head. "No sign of resistance or of a struggle. Devlin was a junkie. It was probably accidental, could have been suicide. Nothing that points to murder though, no."

Cuzzocrea rested his elbows on the railing. "So, Josie's dead, Kristen comes home to find her dead. She doesn't call it in. Why?"

Ali knew the question wasn't because he needed an answer from her; he was thinking out loud, an invitation to a brainstorming session. "She was already having psychological issues as a result of her brother's death. Her junkie mum is dead on the couch. Maybe she doesn't know what to do, maybe she's scared or untrusting of authority. She doesn't know what to do, so she just waits. All weekend she sits in that stinking apartment watching her mother stiffen up, gasses building up and releasing. The smells? The trauma of that? She spirals."

"Into brief psychotic disorder," Cuzzocrea added.

"McMenemy was found on Tuesday morning; he'd been killed the previous day. Gilbert was killed on Wednesday afternoon."

"So on Friday she's a normal kid, grief stricken and vulnerable but otherwise normal, and by Monday she's on a killing spree?"

Ali cringed. "Fuck, it's depressing to think of what that kid's been through. A fucking crack whore for a mum, no dad. Little brother – probably the only thing she lived for anyway – is killed, God knows what seeing that did to her. But with this kid, that's not the worst, her entire life is a fucking nightmare. She's groomed by this group of sickos, passed around since whatever age and systematically raped by them. She won't be the only one; you saw Gilbert's room, blue and pink, and Trina said the footage was of Danny Gilbert with a boy, remember? Maybe Thomas Milligan was a victim of the same group – this Inca-obsessed cabal of dirty twats – maybe Kristen was their Maiden, Thomas was their Lightning Boy? Perhaps, grieving the death of her brother and in lieu of the actual person responsible, she turned that anger and frustration, her need for revenge, outward and chose to punish the men who victimized Thomas in life."

"A type of transference? In her psychotic state, she placed the blame she attributed to her brother's killer onto the men she associated with his suffering," Cuzzocrea suggested.

"Perhaps."

Cuzzocrea nodded at the apartment. "Did you find any physical evidence in there that puts her at either of our scenes of crime?"

"DNA. Hair. A shoebox for the Girls' Gusto Runners. A charging base, I think it could be for the taser."

"Circumstantial. How can we link her to the actual murders?"

"Depends on what Trina found at the other SOC." Ali

dragged deeply and shook her head. "The introduction of a confession, the apparent murder-suicide of the Bartholomew brothers – everything's up in the air. It all pulls focus from the pertinent issues."

"We'll need a confession. From the girl," Cuzzocrea said.

"We'll get one, as soon as she's medicated and calm it'll pour out of her but you and I both know that that isn't going to happen."

"Why?"

"Her room was the only one trashed, right? Why trash your own room looking for something? You know where everything is. Someone, someone other than Kristen, was searching for something in that room. Think about it, what does Kristen have that would prove she killed McMenemy and Gilbert?"

"The dismembered penises."

"Correct."

"Someone could have been helping her. Trying to cover up for her, putting the murders on James Bartholomew instead?" Cuzzocrea tried.

Ali shook her head. "There's blood on the back of the front door, fresh blood. Someone had cut themselves on the edge of the metal frame for the letterbox. There's blood on the handrail downstairs and blood was also transferred to that little gate, there."

"Okay?"

"I'll bet the blood comes back a match for Kristen Milligan. I think she was attacked by and then she was running away from whoever had been searching for something in her room. Someone who desperately needed to find the severed dicks because their presence in her room would prove that James Bartholomew's confession was a fabrication."

Cuzzocrea picked up on Ali's theory. "And whoever fabricated that confession is trying to lead us away from something we were close to being able to prove: that Kristen Milligan targeted members of a paedophile ring."

"So it's someone who has a lot to lose if our investigation takes that focus. It's the same person who owns the taser, the same person who removed the digital evidence from the Gilbert house and the same person who influenced the log officers' statements."

"Chief Superintendent McLaughlin."

Ali nodded and pinched the end of her already burnt-out cigarette. "His worst-case scenario happens if we find the Milligan girl. He knows as well as we do that she'll confess and…"

"Tell us why she targeted men with the tattoos, about their group and all the members of it and how CS McLaughlin is linked to them."

"Yep. So, you see? We won't get a confession, Cuzzocrea, because all we're ever going to get is the dead body of that fifteen-year-old girl. I think McLaughlin was in that apartment, I think he attacked her in there then chased her down the stairs and out of the gate. He either caught her or he's about to and if that is so, then she's dead."

"Shaw's got Munro out looking for him now."

Ali shrugged. "It's too late. We were too late. She's probably already dead and you know what? She's better off dead. Shitty fucking life."

Ali and Cuzzocrea stood in silence together until they noticed an SUV pull to a halt across the street.

Cuzzocrea tapped the railing. "Shaw. We'd better brief him."

Ali huffed and followed Cuzzocrea down the steps and out past the police cordon to Shaw's idling car. Cuzzocrea held the rear door open for Ali. She smirked and slid along the back seat, making room for Cuzzocrea to sit next to her. Ali welcomed the heat from the vents.

Shaw twisted around in the driver's seat to face them both. "Trina suspects foul play at the Harbour Haven location."

Ali could smell Shaw's stale breath in the hot air of the small space. "Cuzzocrea and I expected as much."

Shaw nodded. "Both of the DBs have tattoos similar those on McMenemy and Gilbert. Steven Bartholomew's reads Sinchi Roca, and James Bartholomew's reads Sapa. Both of those names are on the list of the child murdering Incas that Ali supplied me with.

"Trina is of the belief that the Milligan girl stabbed Steven Bartholomew but then he fought back and she escaped before she had an opportunity to complete her task – Steven Bartholomew is in full possession of his manhood."

"James Bartholomew?" Ali asked.

"Strangulation made to look like self-strangulation. A different unknown subject killed him – someone big enough and strong enough to have strangled and lifted James Bartholomew who's a good two hundred and fifty pounds. According to Trina, the Harbour Haven unsub has more than a basic knowledge of crime scene procedure."

"McLaughlin?" Cuzzocrea asked.

Shaw huffed and Ali suppressed a reaction to the smell of his unbrushed teeth. She felt suddenly thirsty and in need of a mint herself.

"I've got Munro out there looking for him. McLaughlin's not at home or in his office, his cell is either off or out of range," said Shaw.

"He's after the girl," said Cuzzocrea.

"If he has her, he'll kill her, sir," Ali added.

"What's your theory, guys?"

Ali shuffled in her seat. "Evidence of a struggle in there, an intruder, specifically in the girl's bedroom closet. There was blood evidence – probably Kristen Milligan's – on the rear of the front door, also on the handrail at the foot of the communal stairs, then again on the gate leading away from the apartment block."

"I see where you're going. McLaughlin sets up the murder-suicide, sends a confession. Comes here to tie up his loose ends. Girl's there or she finds him there, he attacks her, chases her…"

Ali nodded. "Or he overpowered her there and the blood

was transferred from her dead or unconscious body, although the blood on the railing is as a result of a person injuring themselves on it and holding onto the railing as the wound bled; there's tissue on the rusted sharp surface, obviously it still has to go for DNA analysis."

Shaw looked at Cuzzocrea. "Please tell me there are witnesses."

"The neighbour in apartment 3C, Mrs. Devereux, hasn't seen the girl since yesterday afternoon when she'd raised concerns about a smell emanating from apartment 3B. The Devereux woman had thought it might have been some left out trash. We now know what the source of the smell had actually been: Josie Devlin's week-old corpse. The neighbour on the other side…" Cuzzocrea flipped through his notebook. "Apartment 3A. Amber Graminga. She saw the girl return home tonight; she's not sure what time it was but it was dark. She claims that she saw a large man in a long black overcoat approach apartment 3B – she estimated his height to be a little over six feet, large build, salt and pepper hair – approximately two hours after the girl had gone inside. Amber Graminga said the man scared her and so she returned to her mother's apartment but from there she heard him enter the girl's apartment."

Shaw looked shocked. "So we have a neighbour who saw a male matching McLaughlin's description follow our prime suspect into her home?"

Cuzzocrea shook his head dismissively. "It's no good to us, sir. Unreliable witness. History of mental illness – schizophrenia, according to one of the uni's up there – she wouldn't even speak to me unless I addressed her by her preferred name: Princess Amber of Magenta."

Cuzzocrea continued: "As well as claiming to see the girl and a man fitting McLaughlin's description, she also described various other entities she had encountered and 'battled' this evening – a legion of demons, according to her. She also said she thought the RCMP officers were lying about a crime scene next door because they were trying to scare her into going back to the psychiatric hospital she was recently released from, sir."

"Shit. Worthless then," said Shaw.

Ali, as tired as she'd ever felt, was only vaguely aware of Shaw shooing them from his car and ordering them both to meet him back at the squad room.

CHAPTER 51 - KRISTEN

She finds it accidentally as she is feeling along the edge of the carpet. She happens upon what feels like two loops of plastic-like material, flat rope, and when she pulls the loops, the whole carpet pulls up with them. It is awkward to position herself flat against the cold part of the trunk so that she has room enough to pull the flap of carpet back, bending it to get her arm past and feel what is below. It is difficult to hold the stiff material under her chin and twice the carpet pings free and scratches against her sore face sending screaming pain into her that throbs ugly in her head.

But under the carpet her fingers find a wheel, an entire wheel in a basin and around the wheel are various metal things in their own basins. Maiden supposes they must be what mechanics use to swap out the tyres. One of the tools is shaped like a stretched out 'Z' and is stuck tight inside a mould that mimicks its shape. It is straight along its long body with a little cup at the end of both bends. It is hard to snap out of the tight coffin where it belongs and she has to squish her fingers under it and pull it hard to lever it out.

Now Maiden can let the carpet fall back where it wants to be. With the heavy, cold tool in her hands, clutching it tight to her chest, she rests awhile and sways with the movement of the car while she plans her attack on Apu.

The swaying changes. It is bumpier and she finds herself pressing against the draughty edge of the trunk again. Apu is driving uphill.

Way uphill.

He'd passed two logging trucks on the road north towards Gold River. He had Highway 28 to himself all the way to the signs directing him up to the General Hill Trail and closer to his final destination: Cedar River's new jewel in its crown, the Rotary Club's latest addition to the region.

Bryce had always been a champion of the Rotary Club but now he was more grateful than ever for their tireless fundraising and generous donations. He vowed to shake the hand of each and every member at their upcoming Annual General Meeting.

It was a steep drive to the entrance to the trail and the gradient tested the mettle of his more than capable four-by-four. Bryce smiled. Two wonderfully serendipitous coincidences had conspired to facilitate what was to come:

First, the Rotary's new installation had necessitated the introduction of a less taxing and more accessible trail – hence the long uphill drive. The new trail was unlike the trickier predecessors to it, which remained open and led to Dead Man's Plateau via opposite sides of the canyon. The new trail had been designed so that less experienced hikers, the elderly and even the marginally disabled could access it and so, with the quarry he'd be lugging along it, Bryce would manage it easily.

Second, the discovery of Quispe's body on Tuesday last meant that, although it was no longer an active crime scene, the area was still closed to the general public. Bryce was pleased to note that the word had spread and the carpark was conveniently and fittingly as quiet as a morgue.

He cut the engine and sat in the dark peace of the car. He ran through his mental check list once again. Had he overlooked anything? The taser's charging station, yes, but there was nothing unique about it; it could be anyone's, not a problem. Ballantine. It irked Bryce that Ballantine wouldn't get his due for giving VIIMIS the tip about Yupanqui however, upon reflection, it was more prudent to give the geek a wide berth for the time being. Maybe he'd have a freak accident in the new year, once Shaw and his team finally left to investigate other cases.

Bryce engaged the handbrake and resolved to make Ballantine pay later, once fat Sapa's disgraced reputation was cold in the earth next to his rotten wife.

Maiden's face buzzes with pain as she crouches in the darkness. The engine is quiet now. The car is still. She has the tool in her fists and she manages to wriggle herself off her back with her knees underneath her so that she can spring up once Apu opens the trunk.

The downward pressure has forced the blood to the front of her face and now her mouth is bleeding again. Fat, heavy tears of blood are dripping onto the steel of her new weapon making it first slippery then sticky in her hands.

A terrible thought strikes her. What if Apu doesn't open the trunk? What if he is just going to leave her in it, to starve to death? Or what if he intends to set it alight and watch it burn, roasting her alive inside?

Maiden listens. She can hear something, a constant hum. But it is low, powerful, like she can feel the noise too. It isn't the humming a machine makes, not a generator or a vehicle. It's monotone, arrhythmic, persistent yet chaotic. Then, as she strains to hear the hum and to detect its source, it becomes familiar. It is a sound she knows well because it is the sound that was left behind in her ears all the nights she'd lain awake in her bed, after Quispe. Quispe had a thing for the outdoors – at one with nature, he'd say – Quispe only ever brought her to one place to do it: Eden Falls.

What if Apu is planning to push the car with her shut inside it over the edge of the cliffs? But, to the best of Maiden's knowledge, there isn't any way to get a car close to the waterfalls. The closest you can get in a vehicle is to the carpark, the new carpark that leads to the new trail opened last year. The one that leads to the Rotary Club's fancy suspension bridge.

Maiden hears the clunk of one of the car doors as it opens. She tightens her grip on the steel in her hands and shuffles her legs further beneath her hips, ignoring the clenching agony of her still sore knee as she does.

The whole car shakes as the door slams shut. It is a mean slam and her heart thumps and the blood drips hotter and faster.

Footsteps crunch over gravel. A *bleep* and a *chicunk* near her right ear.

This is it.

Blue light and a kiss of pine needle air, cold and clean on her cheek. She is ready. Her thighs quiver with the promise of movement.

The trunk lid opens. Apu. Dark, shapeless, looming. Pine trees skirt a black but bright sky. Stars.

Maiden swipes the tool at him, as hard and fast as she can.

A fucking lug wrench? How'd she get that?

Bryce caught the thing mid-swipe and pulled. Her body, all seventy or so pounds of it, came along for the ride and she flopped over the edge of the open trunk, half in, half out.

She was flailing for a surface with one hand as he twisted the lug wrench out of her other. Bryce stepped back and watched her as she found the bumper and steadied herself then looked up at him.

Fuck. Her face – what was left of it – was a fucking mess.

Bryce paused for thought. Carpet: vacuum? Bleach? Solid surfaces inside the trunk: bleach? Rear bumper: definitely bleach. Lug wrench: has to go with her.

She was still looking at him and it gave him the creeps. Her eyes darted around the carpark and back at him, bloodied hair hung over her face and made her look like something feral or maybe zombie roadkill. She was panting and grimacing at him. Ready for a fight and Bryce was almost impressed by her zeal.

"Give it up, Maiden."

Maiden reacted like he'd slapped her in the face then she spoke but it was hard for him to understand her, not that he cared, because her lips were kind of gone, .the top one had split from the nose down and was splayed open like theatre curtains on an old stage and little nubs of broken teeth blinked white through blood in the moonlight.

"I'm not Maiden. I'm Kristen."

Half of the work was done for him as she lurched forward and met his punch on its way to her jaw. Her head snapped back and ricocheted off the open trunk hood.

"That's better," said Bryce as he scooped her floppy body up and threw her over his shoulder. He pulled the trunk shut with his free hand and kept hold of the lug wrench as he headed along the metal grated trail. Her head bounced rhythmically against the small of his back.

The coat: Burn it?

Kristen. Her name is Kristen.

Hearing the word from his mouth: Maiden. It had done something, changed something. A thing had unravelled inside her when he'd said it.

Whatever it was had sat tight and hard in her brain, had sat there and fumed ever since she'd found herself alone. No Mum. No Tommy. Alone. That's when she'd taken Maiden and let her be something, be that tight angry thing. Like a warrior, someone capable of taking from them the power they had yielded over her and Tommy.

But Maiden's hold has loosened.

She isn't Maiden now. She is just Kristen. Not a warrior. Just a girl. A big sister. Tommy's big sister.

Her face is hot and fat.

But it doesn't matter.

Her face is hot and fat and it's banging into him because he's carrying her somewhere.

But it doesn't matter.

Her stomach tightens and a noise comes from her then her mouth and nose flood with sick. It's stingy and hot, it tastes spicy and metallic. It spews out onto him and some of it puddles in the roof of her mouth.

But it doesn't matter.

His boots clang and bang on the metal underfoot. The silver grid is on top of the dirt and she can see the soil packed flat beneath it. Then the ground drops away and wind blows into her eyes. The thunder of the falls becomes angrier and there's nothing under the metal floor now. Just rocks and trees and the mad white river.

Although she was well under a hundred pounds, she was still a pain to carry and Bryce's shoulder was beginning to tire.

Only three hundred yards to go until the centre of the bridge, to the highest drop. A full sixty metres down to the boulder-covered bottom, battered by the unrelenting torrent of water heading for the drop off and the trio of falls growling beyond.

They'd bragged about the height of the bridge – the Rotary Club Board – when they'd been interviewed at the grand unveiling last year, bragged about how it was over one hundred and ninety feet to the bottom from the centre of the bridge. Why the wire-fenced sides were barely as high as his nipples was beyond Bryce. He decided it must have been designed by some engineer who lived a safe, cosy, insulated life. A life where he'd never imagined what a body flattened by a fall from a third of the height looked like or how sometimes the body bursts right open and some poor fucker has to hose the street down afterwards.

The bridge swayed with the vibration of his steps and for the first time Bryce could understand why his wife and pussy of a son had refused to venture over the bridge with him last summer.

He stopped at the centre and glanced around him. Were there eyes upon him? He didn't think so. But if there were, it was too late. It was the very definition of being caught red-handed to be found with a half-dead fifteen-year-old over your shoulder at the centre of the Eden Falls suspension bridge at night. Hardly two people out for a fucking picnic.

Bryce dropped the wrench over the edge and counted.

1…2…3…4…5…6…7…8…

There was no sound as it disappeared into the steaming white froth and was swallowed out of sight. Bryce wondered if it would be the same for her.

He leaned to the left and she flopped around the side of his arm. He sighed with relief as her weight left his shoulder. Her head lolled back and her eyes stared up at him in that creepy way again. The gaping hole that had been a mouth – fuck!

Puke? On her cheeks and spilling out of the hole.

Fucking cunt had puked on him.

He hoisted her up and over the fence. He watched her go. Faster than he'd imagined, must be a good sixty miles per hour.

1…2…3…4…5…

Silent. Not a scream. Maybe, he thought, she even smiled? Weird.

Coat and trousers, boots too: burn it all.

He drops the silver tool first. It's quiet and she likes that. She slips down his arm and her chest feels dented in. Then there's sky again. It's beautiful and twinkly. Tommy would love the stars tonight.

He's pulling her up. Her body's bent backwards over the railing and the edges poke at the soft bits of her back.

She can see the trees, upside down. He'll push her over now and she'll go the same way as the tool had.

But it doesn't matter.

And then he does it. Her feet pass her head then her head catches up and suddenly she's flat in the wind.

Her hair snaps over her face but she can still see the stars and her tummy tickles inside and she remembers Tommy who loved giggly tickles.

A spray of water like the start of rain falling upwards and she knows it'd be better to close her eyes now.

Because now, nothing matters anymore.

CHAPTER 52 - ALI'S BREAKING POINT

Ali steepled her fingers and looked over the desk at Cuzzocrea who was staring blankly at his laptop. He was difficult to read – the readers of people are often deft at camouflaging their truths – and now she questioned whether or not he was feeling as frustrated as she was. Except *frustrated* was a dilution, a watered-down simplification of her current state. Ali turned her focus inward in an attempt to analyse herself and find a suitable adjective for her inner turmoil. There wasn't one but what she did find inside was a bleak admission tucked away, a realization about herself: she was useless. Inept.

If she could be of no use to a child like Kristen Milligan, then who could she possibly serve? In her line of work, the closest Ali ever got to saving a life was to identify a killer before that killer claimed further victims. In this case Ali had been driven less by a need to protect Kristen's victims and more by her desire to save Kristen herself – save her from further psychological damage and from her ultimate and inevitable escape from it: suicide. Ali had failed to predict that their investigation would endanger the girl – that they would unwittingly put her in a position where she would be hunted down and slaughtered by a ruthless bastard who thought himself above the law, drunk on his own omnipotence.

Ali moaned and thrust her fingertips into her hair, grasping handfuls and squeezing, inflicting pain enough to distract herself from a near insatiable desire to stand up in the middle of the squad room and scream at her fellow investigators.

The VIIMIS team – except for Munro, who was still on the hunt for CS McLaughlin, and Shaw, who had been summoned to the regional court house twenty miles away in the neighbouring city of Courtenay – were scattered about the squad room. While Ali could see that Eden, Abbott, Trina and Cuzzocrea were clearly subdued and exhausted, she wondered if they too felt as *frustrated* as she. Why the hell weren't they out there, doing something about it? They were the cops. Ali was just a private citizen contracted to aid them by focussing their investigation, by calling upon her skills and her previous experience to shed light on their darkness.

Ali saw Abbott yawn and it made her stomach ache. She blinked back tears. It occurred to her then that as much as she was silently blaming the VIIMIS team for the current stalemate and inactivity, they had equal reason to blame her. In fact, if the scales of blame tipped they would tip in her direction. Ali had failed the VIIMIS team. Ali had failed Kristen.

Ali was startled out of her self-loathing as something smashed against the front wall of the squad room. She turned just as Superintendent Shaw slammed the squad room door shut in his wake. Ali didn't know what he had thrown but whatever it was, lay in pieces beneath the whiteboard.

Trina stood and spoke to him, "Doug?"

"Fuck! Fuuuuuck!" Shaw growled and headed first towards the back of the room before abruptly changing his mind and stepping to the front.

"What happened?" Trina asked him.

Doug Shaw put his hands on his hips and glared at his team. "You know what happens when you get called to the judge's chambers this late…or early, rather? You get screwed." Shaw's outward breath trembled. "We've been denied a warrant."

Cuzzocrea looked at Ali, then asked Shaw a question, "McLaughlin?"

"McLaughlin, Milligan. Both. We can't touch him, can't go near him. Insufficient grounds."

"But in the footage of the interviews. You can see – " Trina began.

"Well the judge *didn't* see," said Shaw, cutting her off.

"He was at the Gilbert house. We have a statement to that effect, the family liaison officer – " Ali added before Shaw interrupted her too.

"McLaughlin's two RCMP officers are sticking to their statements. The Crime Scene Entry Log is accurate – they didn't retract, they didn't budge. Internal Affairs Division will be looking into it but as for our investigation, we have no justifiable reason to suspect his involvement."

"Shit," Trina said. Ali suspected she was dismayed less by the effect the decision would have upon the case than the negative effect on her career failing to prove that McLaughlin removed evidence she had claimed existed as grounds for a warrant.

Shaw turned to the board and plucked the cap off a dry-erase marker. "That's not all. The BOLO we issued with regards to the Milligan girl stands but we are not permitted to arrest her. She is to be viewed strictly as a missing person. Once she is found, we have to get permission from Special Victims to interview her as a potential witness to a crime, not a person of interest, so I can't even commandeer RCMP officers to look for her."

"She's in danger, sir. We need everyone out there looking for her, all of you should be out there now," Ali said.

Shaw snorted. "Let me show you how the judge broke it down for me when I protested, okay?" Shaw drew a vertical line down the centre of the whiteboard. He wrote the name Milligan at the top of one column and unsub 2 in the other. "Unsub 2 is McLaughlin. Okay, so, here's what we have on Kristen Milligan." Shaw drew a big circle in the centre of her column. "And here's what we have on unsub 2." He drew a matching circle in the remaining column. "Nothing." Shaw slapped the lid of the pen back in place and turned to the team. "Guess what? He's right. Unless any of you guys have information that changes those zeros into viable leads. If you do, please speak up because I'd be very fucking happy to hear it."

Shaw crossed his arms over his chest and looked at Trina.

"Me?" said Trina.

"As good a place as any to start. It was your information that got us the first illegal warrant and so now the judge thinks all of our evidence is a fiction. Oh, oh, don't tell me, you're waiting for the lab results?"

Trina was rendered temporarily speechless. Shaw made a show of waiting for her response.

"When the DNA of the hair is matched to the blood and tissue samples from the Milligan apartment complex – "

Shaw raised his voice as he interrupted Trina, "All you'll have is evidence that the Milligan girl was in Gilbert's room at some point. In McMenemy's house – *at some point.* And in Steven Bartholomew's apartment. AT SOME POINT!"

Ali watched Trina swallow nervously. "Gilbert's blood was transferred from her shoe to the carpet…or…vice versa. That's not *at some point*, that puts her in the room while Gilbert was bleeding."

"Great then she, at best, witnessed the murder but she more likely turned up at Gilbert's house and found him stabbed to death and didn't call it in, just like she didn't report that her own mother's been lying dead in their living room for a week."

"She didn't turn up and find him dead. She killed him, Doug," Trina replied.

"You're missing the point I'm making, Trina. You see, what we've done is spend the past week building a case for the Milligan girl's alibi. The only thing we're actually close to proving is that McMenemy, Gilbert, Steven Bartholomew and James Bartholomew are all part of a paedophile ring and how do we make that assumption? Because they all have one thing in common: the damn tattoos on their shoulders, same as the tattoo on the shoulder of an incarcerated child sex offender. So, of course, it's feasible that the girl has been in every one of their homes – she'd been there because they were all fucking her, not because she killed them!"

"No, sir," said Cuzzocrea. "She did kill them and it was because they were using her in that way, and probably her little brother too. The victimization fits with the profile. Kristen Milligan fits the profile."

Shaw applauded and turned his focus to Cuzzocrea. "Ahhh, the profile. Your expert criminal analysis. Let's talk about that, shall we? Kristen Milligan fits the profile and so that's it, is it? We're good, are we?"

Ali and Cuzzocrea shared a bemused look.

Shaw slapped the whiteboard and Ali's fists clenched. Her anger was mounting. She silently dared Shaw to venture further down the path he appeared to be taking because she needed nothing more than to let off some steam, having the opportunity to let her temper loose was her version of one of Eden's deep bubble baths except way more cathartic.

Shaw's voice was comically high as he set about berating Cuzzocrea and Ali, "The profile! Let me ask you guys this, you two…"

Shaw pointed his finger at them and approached their desk. Ali could see that, beneath his thinning hair, his scalp had turned a curious shade of purple.

"This theory of yours, the…" Shaw clicked his fingers as a cue to Cuzzocrea.

"Brief psychotic disorder," Cuzzocrea reminded him.

"That's the one! Now, remind me, which one of you came up with that horseshit?"

Ali sensed Cuzzocrea stiffen. He started to answer Shaw's question. Ali stopped him. "Rey, don't go there." Ali looked at Superintendent Shaw. "Doug, you're frustrated. We all are. However, I think you're lashing out at the wrong people and I think it's a mistake to start tearing your team apart one by one." Shaw made to speak and Ali stood, she held a finger up to him. "I especially advise against attempting to hold our analysis responsible for the problems we now, as a team, face. Just to be clear, BPD is a well documented and proven disorder. It's a current diagnosis and you can read all about it in the reference section of your nearest library, so you see, it isn't horseshit. Our profile was built in the very same way all profiles are built – no horseshit involved – Rey and I analysed the evidence and victimology and we debated motives. We stepped into the mind of the killer – as we have been trained to do – and we came out with a sound theory, one that fits plausibly within everything we know. Yes, profiling is largely theory but it's also a proven method, a valuable tool to assist officers of the law in time-sensitive investigations where there is little to no physical evidence or witness statements. It's not and has never been the beginning, middle or end of an investigation; it's a small, often vital and frequently accurate weapon in a team's arsenal and it's therefore unfair to ever make it – or the few intellectuals capable of building it – the scapegoat of a failing case."

Shaw fumed at Ali, his jaw clenched and unclenched repeatedly. "The Chief's right, you just pluck shit right out of the air, don't you? You plucked it out of nowhere that some random kid was our killer and now I look like an idiot."

"Fuck you!" Ali shouted. "We didn't pluck anything out of the air; it's not a leap to conclude that Gilbert was killed by a child or the parent of a child bent upon vengeance because the sick fuck was a paedophile. That's obvious, not because he shares a style of tattoo with a convicted paedo but because he was fucking open about it. You don't just happen upon those symbols and then decorate a whole fucking room in your house with those same symbols all over the fucking walls. You don't fill a closet in that room with pageant-style dresses and quasi-sexual Halloween costumes all in kiddie sizes by accident or stock a refrigerator full of alcoholic drinks designed to appeal to immature palettes and you especially don't do all of those things when you don't even have kids in the family.

"Furthermore, everything we assumed initially was then backed up with the physical evidence gathered by Trina – the footprints, the fibres, the hair. The same hair found in McMenemy's house: it doesn't just put Kristen Milligan in the same room as both victims; it links the two victims better than a fucking tattoo does. Then there was the witness that puts a child wearing clothing consistent with the fibres collected at the scene of the Gilbert murder, walking down Gilbert's street at the time of his death against the flow of all of the other children who had alighted from the school bus minutes earlier. The use of a taser indicates that our perp knew that he or she was smaller than his or her chosen victim. Maybe a child?

"So, the big question Rey and I were left with was, what would make a child go on a murder spree? Thousands, millions of kids are victimized and abused every day but they rarely kill the people who victimize them. So what made our kid kill? BPD, Doug. That's what. So, no, not plucked out of the fucking air."

"Okay, okay," Shaw said.

But Ali wasn't done with him. Ali was just warming up.

"And Chief Superintendent McLaughlin? Let's have a think about why we all thought he might be involved? Huh? First, the taser, remember? Okay, so it didn't single him out but it did cast suspicion in the direction of RCMP involvement. Maybe an officer had gone postal, or whatever you lot call it. Maybe it was an officer's kid? I know that that possibility was going through all of your minds when we found out that the killer used the model 4-what-fucking-ever. Then later, after we already suspected McLaughlin's interference, we found out that his was one of the tasers missing during the recall.

"Second, McLaughlin was at the Gilbert house *after* Trina saw the footage on the camcorder, *after* she told us and shortly after *you* stood outside that very door and told McLaughlin about it. By the time you had your hands on a warrant, the visual evidence in that house was gone. We have an objective witness who, unlike the two cops who blatantly lied, doesn't work at this particular station and who is prepared to testify that CS McLaughlin was in that house before you arrived to seize the digital evidence. Additionally, we have clear fucking evidence – regardless of what your inbred, addled judge might think – of McLaughlin intimidating the officers who he coerced into omitting his name from the Crime Scene Entry Log.

"Third, someone – not a little kid – murdered James Bartholomew and made it look like suicide, someone with 'more than a basic understanding of crime scene procedure' according to Trina. And then that someone sends a very convenient email from a supposed suicidal Bartholomew who takes full responsibility for all the murders for reasons he's too ashamed to state and yet there's absolutely not one shred of evidence at any of the crime scenes linking that man to the murders and, hate to say it, he doesn't fit the horseshit profile.

"Kristen Milligan killed Tristan McMenemy, Danny Gilbert and Steven Bartholomew because she was in the midst of brief psychotic disorder following the death of her little brother and the fatal overdose of her mother a week later. Chief Superintendent McLaughlin is linked to the paedophile ring – he removed evidence from Danny Gilbert's house and he knew Glen Christie's name even though you hadn't given it to him. He knows that if we find Kristen Milligan she will eventually confess and tell us everything and when she does, we will discover the truth about the Chief. So he went after her because, unlike you, he trusted the evidence; he had confidence in the profile, and he deduced that the killer was her, probably because she used a taser he knew she had access to. So he's out there doing something about it – killing a fucking kid, but at least he's doing something – and we're sitting here like a bunch of fucking plums listening to you projecting the shit you took from some fuckwit small town judge onto us."

Ali picked up an empty mug from Cuzzocrea's side of the desk and threw it at the wall.

"There! See? We can all throw shit, Doug, but it doesn't actually fucking help!"

Shaw and Ali stared at each other. Ali was prepared to stand and stare at him all night if she had to; there was no way she would back down now, even if it did put her newly resurrected career in jeopardy. The tension was finally broken by Eden.

"I'm Special Victims."

Shaw looked at Eden impatiently. "What?"

Eden explained: "Everything hinges on a full confession from the girl."

Shaw glanced at Ali. She nodded at him and sat down.

Eden continued: "We're not allowed to arrest her as a suspect or even interview her as a person of interest, right? But you said the BOLO's still in effect. We need to find her because she's a missing person, possibly a witness if she was a victim of the alleged paedophile ring."

"Get to the point, Eden, or are you going to lecture me for ten minutes like she did?" Shaw said, rubbing his thinning hair.

"Sir, I'm Special Victims. Paul works for IDENT, missing persons. Kristen Milligan falls into our respective jurisdictions."

Shaw nodded slowly, then brightened slightly. "Get on it."

"Sir," said Abbott, nervously, "I tracked down Kristen Milligan's father. Andrew Milligan, Nanoose. I couldn't get a physical address for him but he's the president of the Nanoose chapter of the Demon's Fang biker gang."

Shaw considered the information. "She may be there. You have to look into it. There could be other family members we don't know about too. This Milligan, was he the father of the dead boy too?"

"He's listed as the father on both certificates of birth, sir," said Abbott.

"I seem to remember someone telling me that CPS were trying to get in touch with him. He may not yet know about his son's death so tread carefully. Good work, Paul."

Shaw stepped over and spoke quietly with Trina as Eden and Abbott set about their respective tasks.

Ali sat and looked at Cuzzocrea. He raised his eyebrows at her. "I need a list of all the things I should never say to you."

"Don't worry. You're not an egomaniacal prick with a tiny little dick."

Cuzzocrea leaned forward on his elbows. "Just think yourself lucky – you don't actually work for him."

"Yeah, and I probably won't again after that."

"If he stopped working cases with you because you stood up to him then he really is an egomaniacal prick with a micro-penis. You were right, about it all."

Ali shrugged. "No. I was defensive. What Shaw said struck a nerve because it's what I was thinking too."

"That our theory was plucked from the air?"

"No. The profile's accurate and everything we know now shows that. Proving it is the problem and if we can't, what good were we? What good did I do?"

"Ali, you're talking like it's over. We'll get another way in, trust me."

A sharp knock on the door pulled the team's attention to it. Ali recognized the figure beyond it immediately. McLaughlin opened the door and looked in at the team. He smiled.

"Doug. Officers." McLaughlin stepped into the room.

Ali looked at Shaw who stared blankly at Chief Superintendent McLaughlin as he spoke.

"Thought I'd drop by and see what's going on in the VIIMIS squad room. I hear it's been an eventful night. James Bartholomew?"

Ali watched how McLaughlin crossed to the centre of the room. Confident, in command. McLaughlin's confidence worried her and she felt a weight descend inside her chest.

Shaw cleared his throat. "Sir, we were actually, ah, trying to get hold of you…"

McLaughlin frowned and pulled his phone from a velcroed pocket on his upper arm. It was a similar strap to the one Ali had seen Shaw wearing during early briefings after his morning run. Ali took note of McLaughlin's attire: Under Armour leggings and top, Adidas running shoes. McLaughlin apologized as he waited for his phone to power up.

"Right, yeah." He smiled, looking at the screen. "I never have it on when I run."

Shaw nodded. "You were out running?"

McLaughlin patted his flat stomach. "Fighting the mid-life spread, Doug, you know what that's like. So, what can I do for you? Was there something I can help you with?"

Ali saw the Superintent's jaw clench and unclench as it had with her. "Nothing. Just updating you on James Bartholomew."

McLaughlin nodded. "Right you are."

Smiling at the team, McLaughlin nodded an unctuous goodbye, then turned in the doorway, feigning an afterthought. "By the way, that taser you mentioned, I have one. Laura'd packed it away in the basement in a box of medals and awards and such, I thought it might come in use for post-mortem purposes, I don't know. Anyway, I left it at the desk for you, help yourselves. And, Doug? I know you'll need a few days to tidy up so please, use this room, make yourself at home and don't leave without saying bye."

McLaughlin left. Ali watched his figure disappear beyond the glass panel in the door.

She took a deep breath, then stood and gathered her belongings.

"Where are you going?" Cuzzocrea asked her.

"Back to the hotel and then home."

"What? Ali?" Cuzzocrea reached for her.

"It's over, Cuzzocrea. You know it as well as I know it," Ali said and looked at Shaw. "If you find Kristen Milligan's body, call me please."

Ali left the squad room just as blinking away her tears proved to be beyond her. She neither had the desire to wake Marlene in the middle of the night nor the energy to drive back to Mochetsin and so, as she waited for the lift to arrive, Ali decided to pay a visit to a friend who might just make her feel better.

CHAPTER 53 - A NEW TEAM

The rug under her feet felt awesome, awesome, awesome between her toes as Ali held her breath in her lungs and concentrated. Either her lung capacity had diminished (not entirely surprising) or pot had gotten way stronger since 1995. She blew out slowly and marvelled as the smoke dissipated.

"Holy moly. That is good." Ali said as she passed the joint across the rug to Greg Ballantine who had pretzeled his legs with a proficiency unique to yogis. Greg took a series of short puffs and managed to speak to Ali without exhaling a drop, a skill beyond Ali's comprehension.

"You can't drive now." Greg smiled and exhaled. "This bud kinda fucks you up, in a good way."

Ali's laughter farted out between her lips which made them both laugh. Ali shrugged. "If you can't get fucked up, what can you do? I mean it's…it's not like we're elephant handlers or, or surgeons." Ali nodded sincerely to emphasize her insight.

Greg smoked and seemed to consider Ali's words carefully. Finally he appeared to approve of her sentiment and returned a version of her sincere nod. He exhaled and offered the last of his spliff to her; Ali waved it away. Greg lay back on the rug and Ali crawled over to join him. They both stared at the light fixture above them with shared wonderment and although it felt like an hour of silence had passed during their admiration of the light, Ali knew it had more likely been several minutes by the time Greg spoke:

"Are you absolutely sure about this?"

Ali looked at Greg. She really, *really* liked his curly hair. "Yes. I am." She smiled.

"It's dangerous. You'll be in, like, *danger.* Aren't you scared?" said Greg, turning to look back at her.

"If I tell you something, do you promise to keep it to yourself, you can't tell anyone?"

Greg frowned. "Huh?"

"I don't really get scared. Never have except this one time when I was younger." Ali's voice dropped to a whisper, "But that's a secret. Anyway, I don't care how scary this shit might get, it's something I have to do, I'm compelled to do this. Do you get that? I have to, have to, have to do this. For Kristen. For you."

Greg grinned at Ali. "You're a pretty lady."

Ali giggled. "Thanks, Greg." She rolled her eyes. "Pretty," she repeated. "Hey? You know what's not pretty?"

Greg's eyes widened, eager to know what Ali knew.

"Donald Trump," said Ali.

Greg and Ali laughed until they tired themselves out and had forgotten what it was they'd been laughing at.

"Greg? You'll have to watch your back too, you know? You'll also be in danger. You know too much. If this goes tits up and McLaughlin finds out that you helped me, he'll come after you."

"I know but, you see, I do get scared. Because of him, I'm scared all the time. I don't want be scared anymore."

"So we'll fight fire with fire," said Ali.

"*Fire with fire.*" The phrase seemed to carry with it an epiphany for Greg.

Ali sat up and reacted to a pleasant wave of vertigo. "I have to go. Can you call me a cab?"

"You're a cab."

Ali laughed.

"Don't go, let's get the bong out and put on some Bowie and eat pizza," Greg pleaded.

Ali shook her head. “Na, that pot got me horny, I’m going back to the hotel for a wank.”

Greg Ballantine was befuddled by the word and, as he set about looking for his phone, Ali was amused to hear him repeating it over and over again:

“Wank, wank, wank.”

EPILOGUE - LEX TALIONIS

Only a few weeks ago Ali had been ranting about the lingering cold of winter and she'd lamented over why she'd even bothered to move five thousand miles if she was still going to freeze her tits off most of the year.

Now, Ali enjoyed the smell of melanin rising through the upper epidermis of her skin, a nutty aroma that never failed to surprise her Scottish complexion year after year. She watched a rotund bumble bee contort itself and disappear inside a cerise flower with a name she either couldn't recall or had never known, but it was one she'd seen whilst holidaying in the hotter regions of Europe…somethingvillea?

Cuzzocrea's home had become something of a luxurious hideaway for Ali. It was a blocky, many-windowed, contemporary house perched atop a plateau on the eastern edge of Denman Island, overlooking the Georgia Strait.

His house was perfectly inaccessible and remote. A place where they could both escape reality and rid themselves of the pollution they absorbed as a result of their work. Cuzzocrea's glass palace on a cliff was both a physical and a spiritual refuge for Ali, somewhere that she attained stillness and a sense of centredness. The only thing that mattered in the house on Swan Road was what to eat, what to drink and when to make love.

Ali held her hand up, tiptoeing like a giddy girl as she waved back to Cuzzocrea. He was half way back from his paddle-board trip across the strait to Denman's smaller, more bucolic neighbour, Hornby Island.

Even at this distance, Ali could see the strength in his broad shoulders and her body tightened in anticipation of his return. But Ali knew she'd be on the ferry to Vancouver Island by the time Cuzzocrea came back, glistening and sun kissed. Ali wanted to stay but she wanted something else more.

Twenty minutes earlier, Ali had received a text she'd been waiting half a year for. The wait had been torturous but necessary. However, the final three months of that wait had been the worst of all.

Three months ago, human remains had been discovered by the pilot of a floating log raft in Gold River, snared between the downed trunks of two of the hundreds of trees he was transporting. A week later, authorities announced what Ali had known since that night in the squad room last December: the remains were of Kristen Milligan who had been reported missing at the end of the previous year.

Every day that had passed since had brought with it a growing desire in Ali, a desire for retributive justice. Ali's secret role as Kristen Milligan's avenger had become all-consuming and even the monthly stack of open/unsolved cold case files she received from Superintendent Shaw were no longer enough to snare her focus from her primary métier. Ali had conjured patience at odds with her personality awaiting the day that the plan would commence – a less than perfect plan, she knew, but one initially drawn out by two people high on White Rhino weed.

Greg Ballantine's text had simply read:

Demon's Fang MC. We have an in.

Ali admired Cuzzocrea from afar for a few moments longer and breathed in the scent of nature's sunscreen and Denman's burgeoning summer.

"Bougainvillea!" Ali exclaimed, remembering the name of the pink-flowered bush.

Ali finished the note she had been writing for her lover

and secured it beneath a small boulder in the centre of his patio table.

The bottom corner of the note flapped in a breeze and the words 'I love you' flitted in and out of view.

Ali headed down to her Porsche and pushed away the question of whether she should take it as an ominous sign of what lay ahead.

THE END

Ali Dalglish will return very soon in

SILENT SISTERS

Also published by Fahrenheit Press

Acknowledgements

My gratitude begins with an individual who must remain anonymous. This person's input brings a level of realism and believability to the RCMP elements of the Ali Dalglish series. Thank you for your patience, candor and on-going support.

Thank you to Chris McVeigh of Fahrenheit Press for taking a chance on my work, for being an endless source of support and guidance and for all of the brave and inspiring work you do. Being welcomed into the Fahrenheit Press family has made the publishing process a dream come true and I feel blessed to be part of such an exciting team. I also wish to thank the network of bloggers I have connected with who work tirelessly and selflessly to help put books like mine in the hands of readers.

My biggest thanks goes to the three people without whom I am nothing: my husband and two children. Alexandra, your enthusiasm, encouragement and support is vital to me, your memes and inspirational lists and quotes, your smiling face and your own courage keep me going every day. Jamie, you are my constant companion, the little man who listens patiently as I test plot twists, kicks my arse back into my office when I'm mooching in the kitchen for crisps and, most importantly, makes every day a true blessing. And Simon, my one and only, my hero, my best friend. Your unquestioning support and counsel, your pure love and understanding is humbling. Thank you for reading the twisted stuff I write regardless of the fact that it makes you feel sick and a little bit scared of me. Always and forever, Big Man, I adore you.

About the author

Jacqueline Chadwick is probably best known for her roles in the British soap operas *Emmerdale* (1994–96) and *Coronation Street* (1998–2001).

These days she lives happily ever after on a small Canadian island with her husband, two kids and too many dogs, joyously penning her twisted wickedness.

More books from Fahrenheit Press

If you enjoyed Briefly Maiden by Jacqueline Chadwick you may also enjoy these other books published by Fahrenheit Press;

In The Still by Jacqueline Chadwick

A Savage Art by AE Rawson

Hidden Depths by Ally Rose

On A Small Island by Grant Nicol

66621691R00217

Made in the USA
San Bernardino, CA
14 January 2018